THE PUZZLE MASTER

WILLIAM TURNER

©INKSPIREGROUP

PROLOGUE

The weight of its secrets pressed against Detective Alan Hart's tenth-floor office window. Darkness enveloped the city like a mournful cloak. He stood there, a shadow against the city's dim light, his eyes lost in the maze of streets and shadows stretching towards the horizon. He held a crumpled piece of paper in his hand, faded from years of being folded and unfolded. The message remained clear in his mind. For seven long years, he had been grappling with a mystery he couldn't solve—a farewell message from his wife, Rebecca, on the night she passed away.

Around him, the office was a testament to his obsession. Once filled with family photos and honours, the walls now displayed a mosaic of maps, newspaper clippings, and mysterious symbols connected by a web of red rope. On his desk, books on maths, cryptography, and criminal psychology piled haphazardly, their pages covered in Post-it notes and coffee rings. In the corner stood a blackboard loaded with symbols and equations that most people wouldn't be able to decipher. But they spoke to Alan a language he had once shared with Rebecca—one of patterns, logic, and hidden meanings.

He moved away from the window and glanced at the framed

picture on his bookcase. It showed a younger Alan, his face still free from loss, his arm around a happy woman with bright eyes and a mischievous grin. Rebecca had been his friend in every way: a brilliant mathematician who challenged him academically, a loving wife who anchored him emotionally, and a kindred spirit driven by her passion for uncovering the universe's secrets. Two graduate students, drawn together by their love of puzzles and their belief in the power of the mind, had met at university. Together, they had set out to develop a new type of cryptography—a code that couldn't be broken, a language that could convey facts beyond the reach of ordinary words.

Their studies had taken a somewhat ominous turn. Delving deeper into the abstract world of numbers and symbols, they stumbled upon patterns that hinted at something sinister—a hidden message concealed within the very fabric of the city, a conspiracy spanning millennia. Rebecca became convinced that they were on the brink of uncovering a truth that powerful forces desperately wanted to suppress. She spent countless hours in their lab, scribbling mathematics everywhere and muttering about patterns and codes that only she could perceive. Her mental state deteriorated rapidly, becoming increasingly neurotic and compulsive.

She had pushed him away, arguing that he couldn't see the truth because he wasn't looking hard enough. Alan had tried to reason with her, to pull her back from the edge of madness. On the night she vanished, she left him a single piece of paper folded into a perfect square and a riddle penned in her own handwriting.

"In the city of shadows and light, where knowledge is power and ignorance blight, seek the pattern that dances in plain sight.
The key to unlocking the truth might be solving the equation that balances the scales. And find the answer that ends all tales."

Over the past seven years, he had spent his time searching for clues in their old study notes, the pages of obscure mathematical books, and even in the very streets and buildings of the city, trying to decipher her last message. Having abandoned his academic path, he turned his sharp mind towards the field of criminal investigation, determined to solve Rebecca's mystery by unravelling the mysteries of human depravity.

However, the city had kept its secrets until now, and the answer remained elusive.

Alan awoke from his dream by a knock at the door. Turning to find his friend Detective Clara Morgan standing against the doorframe, he saw her hazel eyes filled with concern and understanding as they took in the regulated chaos of his workplace.

"Hey, Alan," Rebecca said, handing him a file. "We've got a new case. It's a homicide in the historic banking district. The victim was found without an ID in an alleyway, and there's no obvious cause of death. But there's more..." She paused, her eyes darting to the document Alan was holding. "There was a note sent. It arrived at the scene, and it directed you here."

Alan shivered down his spine. He felt a familiar rush of excitement, like when he was solving a new mystery. He gently folded Rebecca's puzzle, slipped it into his pocket, and grabbed his coat.

"What did the message say?" he asked, his voice firm despite his racing heart.

Clara's face was grim as she handed him the file. "It said, Professor Hart, welcome to the game. In seven years, let's see if you've learned anything."

Alan's mind raced. He started brainstorming different possibilities and looking for patterns as he followed Clara out of the office. This wasn't your average case; it wasn't a random violent act. This was a challenge, a test by someone who knew his past and spoke riddles and codes.

And as he stepped into the night, the city seemed to change around him. The shadows grew darker, and the buildings stood like silent sentinels. Their secrets pressed against him, and the weight of their hidden truths pulled him forward.

Alan Hart was ready to play the game.

1

SHADOWS OF THE PAST

The alley cupped the darkness like a jealous hand, releasing just enough for Detective Alan Hart to distinguish the body from the shadows. He crouched, careful not to disturb the constellation of evidence surrounding the victim, his grey-blue eyes scanning with the precision of a machine calibrated for death. The city's heartbeat —distant sirens, the hum of traffic—seemed to fade as he entered that familiar mental space where only details existed, where a human tragedy became a puzzle waiting to be solved.

The rain had fallen earlier, leaving the pavement slick and reflective under the occasional splash of streetlights. The victim—male, mid-thirties, well-dressed despite the undignified sprawl of his limbs —lay partially illuminated by the beam of Alan's flashlight. No wallet. No phone. There was no immediately apparent cause of death apart from the strange carving on his exposed chest, visible through the torn fabric of what had once been an expensive shirt.

Alan leaned closer, the scent of iron and alley decay mingling in his nostrils. The symbol carved into the flesh resembled an interlocking sequence of geometric shapes—meticulous, almost academic in its precision—not the work of rage or passion but of calculation.

The skin around the cuts had barely bled, suggesting the marks were made postmortem.

"Just like the Fulton Street case," he murmured to himself, the words barely audible beneath the ambient noise of the city. His finger hovered over the symbol without touching it. "And Morrison before that."

He pulled a small leather-bound notebook from his coat pocket. Its pages are worn with constant reference, and the symbol is sketched with practised strokes. His hand moved automatically, but his mind churned with possibilities and patterns, linking this fresh horror to cold cases that had long haunted the department's archives and his memory.

The crime scene technicians moved around him like respectful ghosts, documenting and collecting. Alan barely registered their presence until a familiar voice cut through his concentration.

"Let me guess—you've been here since they called it in, and you haven't eaten anything but coffee." Detective Clara Morgan stepped under the yellow tape, her practical boots navigating the wet ground with expertise born of similar scenes.

Alan didn't look up from his notebook. "Coffee isn't food."

"Exactly my point." Clara crouched opposite him, her hazel eyes taking in the scene with efficient sweeps. Her presence shifted the air somehow, bringing pragmatism to balance his intensity. "Same signature as the others?"

.   .   .

"Similar, not identical. The precision has improved, as has his technique." Alan traced the air above the symbol. "The elements are consistent—triangular base, bisected circle, these small marks at each vertex—but there's an evolution."

Clara studied the carved pattern and then Alan's face. "Do you think it's connected to Morrison and Fulton?"

"Three victims with precise geometric carvings, all positioned in alleyways facing east, all missing personal identification." His voice carried the quiet certainty that Clara had learned to respect, even when it frustrated her. "Yes, they're connected."

"Do you have any theories on what the symbol means?" she asked, pulling out her digital notebook to contrast with his analogue preference.

Alan's gaze lifted to the narrow strip of night sky visible between buildings. "It has elements of cryptographic notation, but is corrupted. Academic, but twisted." Something flickered across his face—a shadow of memory that Clara caught but couldn't interpret.

"You've seen this before? Outside the case files, I mean."

His jaw tightened almost imperceptibly. "Not exactly this, no."

The moment stretched between them, laden with things unsaid. Clara knew better than to push when that expression settled over her partner's features. It belonged to the part of Alan Hart that he kept locked away—the former academic whose brilliant career had ended in scandal and personal tragedy.

. . .

"Time of death is preliminary, but the ME's guessing between midnight and 3 AM," she offered instead, steering them back to safer territory. "No witnesses yet. The security camera on the corner was vandalised last week, and we are still waiting for city maintenance."

Alan nodded, standing to survey the scene from a different angle. The movement was fluid despite the hours he'd spent crouched beside the body. "The location is deliberate. Limited visibility, controlled access points." He gestured toward the alley's entrance. "He could observe from that apartment building without being noticed."

"I'll have officers canvass the residents."

"They won't find anything." The certainty in his voice wasn't arrogance but the weight of a well-considered conclusion based on experience. "Our killer doesn't make those kinds of mistakes."

Clara sighed, rubbing her temple. "You sound almost admiring."

"Respect for an opponent isn't admiration." Alan's gaze returned to the body, to the symbol that seemed to mock their efforts with cryptic precision. "It's recognition."

A young officer approached with evidence bags, hovering awkwardly at the edge of their conversation until Clara acknowledged him with a nod.

"No personal effects in a ten-meter radius, Detectives," he reported. "But we found this under the dumpster." He held up a bag containing what appeared to be a small, intricately folded piece of red paper.

Alan took the bag, holding it under his flashlight. The paper had been folded into a complex geometric form that echoed elements of the carved symbol. His expression remained neutral, but Clara caught the slight quickening of his breath, the narrowing of his eyes.

"It's an invitation," he said finally.

"To what?"

"To play." The words carried a weight that settled in the space between them. "He's getting bolder. The previous scenes were puzzles, but this—" he indicated the origami form, "—this is direct communication."

Clara watched her partner's face, noting the subtle shifts most would miss—the darkening of his eyes. This heightened focus transformed his features into something almost predatory. Alan Hart was slipping into the mental space that made him brilliant and concerning in equal measure, where obsession and insight blended until they became indistinguishable.

"Alan," she said quietly, "we'll figure this out, but not tonight. We need to process the scene properly.

He nodded, but his attention remained fixed on the folded paper, on the symbol carved in flesh. "He knows what he's doing, Clara. These aren't random killings—they're a sequence, building toward something."

"Building toward what?"

. . .

Alan carefully placed the evidence bag in his pocket, his expression distant. "That's what we need to determine."

The night air had grown colder, or perhaps it was just the chill of recognition spreading through Alan's veins. The symbol, the paper—they carried echoes of a past he had tried to leave behind, of classrooms and lecture halls traded for crime scenes and precinct walls, of a life unravelled by tragedy and suspicion.

"I'll meet you back at the precinct," he said, already walking toward his car. The leather notebook was clutched in fingers that had gone slightly numb despite the mild temperature. "There are files I need to review."

Clara watched him go, concerned but unsurprised. The case had hooked into Alan Hart with familiar ferocity, and she knew from experience that sleep and regular meals would become secondary considerations until they found answers. Until the puzzle was solved.

The victim lay forgotten behind her, another piece in a game that had begun long before tonight, his carved chest a message neither she nor Alan could yet fully decipher.

The precinct hummed with fluorescent efficiency, a sterile counterpoint to the crime scene's organic decay. Alan sat at his desk, which stood apart from the others like an island of controlled chaos. Case files formed neat stacks according to a system he understood, while photographs from the new crime scene were arranged in a precise grid before him. The origami paper, now carefully unfolded and preserved, lay at the centre of his attention like a strange flower blooming under glass.

His fingers traced the creases in the paper, each fold deliberate, purposeful. The red material proved to be high-quality card stock, not the type commonly found in ordinary stationery stores. Under magnification, the edges showed the clean precision of laser cutting rather than the roughness of manual scissors or tearing. Nothing about this was impulsive or unplanned.

Alan's reflection on his computer screen looked hollowed out, and the harsh overhead lighting deepened the shadows under his eyes. He'd been staring at the same evidence for three hours, making minute adjustments to the arrangement of photos and scribbling notes in his leather-bound book with a fountain pen that left ink stains on his fingertips.

The symbol from the victim's chest had been sketched and resketched a dozen times. Each iteration revealed something new— proportional relationships between elements, mathematical ratios that couldn't be coincidental. Alan had covered three pages with calculations and references, arrows connecting disparate elements into a coherent whole that only he could see.

"Package for Detective Hart."

The voice startled him from his concentration. A young officer stood awkwardly at the edge of his desk, holding a padded manila envelope with an expression suggesting he'd rather be elsewhere. The department knew Alan's reputation for intense focus when working on a case.

"Thanks," Alan murmured, taking the envelope without looking up. The officer retreated quickly like prey escaping a predator's notice.

The envelope was unremarkable—standard size, no return address, and his name typed rather than handwritten. It had passed through the department's security screening, and its weight felt significant in his hands.

. . .

Alan sliced it open neatly with an explicitly kept letter opener. Inside was a single card of the same red stock as the origami from the crime scene.

His heart stuttered slightly in recognition before resuming its rhythm.

The card held an elegant script in black ink that seemed to shimmer under the lights. Not printed—handwritten with a calligraphy pen, the strokes confident and precise:

> *"The first piece lies where shadows split,*
>
> *Where scholars failed, and silence fell.*
>
> *Seek the truth in numbers writ,*
>
> *In patterns, dead men cannot tell.*
>
> *Remember me, Professor Hart?*
>
> *This game has barely yet to start."*

The last two lines sent a chill down Alan's spine that had nothing to do with the precinct's aggressive air conditioning. He set the card down carefully, as though it might burn his fingers, and drew a slow breath.

"Alan? You look like you've seen a ghost."

. . .

Clara appeared beside his desk, two coffee cups in hand. She set one down near him, carefully avoiding the precisely arranged evidence.

"Not a ghost," he replied, sliding the card toward her. "A memory."

Her eyes narrowed as she read the elegant script. "Professor Hart? Is this—"

"Someone who knows about my past." Alan's voice remained calm, but there was a new tension in the line of his shoulders. "Someone is making it very personal.

Clara's concern deepened the fine lines around her eyes. "This changes things. We need to bring in protective detail, consider pulling you from the case—"

"No." The single word carried enough force to silence her suggestions. "This isn't a threat. It's an invitation."

"An invitation to what, exactly?"

Alan gestured to the crime scene photos. "The victim, the symbol, the origami—all elements of a larger puzzle. The killer is constructing something elaborate, designed specifically for me to unravel."

Clara set down her coffee with unnecessary force. "That's exactly why you shouldn't be involved. You're becoming part of the case rather than an investigator."

· · ·

"I already am part of it. I have been from the beginning." Alan stood, running a hand through his dark hair, disturbing its careful arrangement. "He's been watching me, studying me. The symbols weren't random—they were bait."

Before Clara could respond, a new voice entered their conversation.

"Detectives! I got those forensics you were waiting for." Officer Leo Chang approached with his youthful energy, starkly contrasting the tension between the two detectives. He wore a crisp button-up with the sleeves rolled precisely to mid-forearm, his dark eyes bright with the satisfaction of technological success.

"Please tell me you found something useful," Clara said, turning toward him.

Leo's smile faltered slightly at her tone. "Define 'useful'? Because I've got interesting, unusual, and downright bizarre covered."

Alan's attention sharpened. "Start with bizarre."

"The ink used in the origami paper? It contains trace elements of human haemoglobin." Leo swiped through screens on his tablet. "Not enough to be visible, but present in the molecular structure."

"Blood in the ink," Alan murmured. "Whose?"

. . .

"That's where it gets weirder. It's not from our victim." Leo handed Alan the tablet. "It doesn't match any samples in our database, but the DNA shows familial markers consistent with Eastern European ancestry."

Clara leaned over Alan's shoulder to view the results. "What about digital traces? Security footage from surrounding areas?"

"Someone wiped every camera within a six-block radius." Leo's expression mixed frustration and reluctant admiration. "Not just deleted footage—replaced it with looped clean feeds that would pass casual inspection. This wasn't amateur hour."

Alan handed back the tablet, his gaze distant. "He knows forensic procedures. He understands technology. He's familiar with academic cryptography and has access to specialised materials." He glanced at the red card. "And he knows me."

"That narrows it down to a few hundred people in your former academic circles?" Clara asked.

"Fewer." Alan returned to his desk, pulling open a drawer that Clara had never seen him access before. From it emerged a faded news-paper clipping, carefully preserved in a plastic sleeve. The headline read:

"UNIVERSITY CRYPTOGRAPHY DEPARTMENT SHAKEN BY SCANDAL AND TRAGEDY."

His fingers brushed the article with an uncharacteristic hesitancy. "This isn't just about puzzle-solving. It's about something that happened seven years ago."

.   .   .

Leo studied the article with undisguised curiosity. "What happened seven years ago?"

Alan didn't answer immediately. Instead, he returned to the red card, tracing the first line with his finger.

"The first piece lies where shadows split."

"He's directing us to the next crime scene," Alan said. "Or the next body."

"How can you be certain?" Clara asked.

"Because that's how the game is played." Alan pinned the card to his evidence board, connecting it with a red string to the crime scene photos and his symbol sketches. "He leaves a puzzle, I solve it, it leads to the next victim. Classical game theory applied to serial homicide."

His workspace had transformed during their conversation—the leather notebook lay open, filled with rapid calculations; the photos had been rearranged into a new pattern; the newspaper clipping sat prominently beside the red card. The effect was a mind made visible, connections forming and reforming frighteningly.

"I know where to look," Alan said suddenly, straightening with the alert tension of a predator catching a scent. "The first line—' where shadows split'—refers to the old Meridian Building at the university. The architecture creates a perfect shadow split at certain times of the day."

.   .   .

"And the 'scholars failed' part?" Leo asked.

A shadow passed over Alan's face. "That's where my research team was based. Where my wife—" He stopped abruptly. "Where everything fell apart."

Clara and Leo exchanged a glance that Alan pretended not to notice.

"I need to get to the Meridian Building," he said, already gathering his coat. "The killer is recreating something, finishing something that began years ago."

"Alan," Clara warned. This is precisely what he wants. You're playing into his hands."

He paused, one arm in his coat sleeve. "Yes," he agreed, his grey-blue eyes suddenly clear and focused. "And that's the only way we'll catch him."

The red card seemed to pulse under the fluorescent lights, its elegant script a challenge that reached beyond professional duty into the realm of personal demons that Alan Hart had spent seven years trying to outrun.

By midnight, the homicide department had undergone a transformation that reflected the inner workings of Alan Hart's mind. The conference room's glass walls disappeared beneath layers of crime scene photos, maps, and handwritten notes, connected by a red string that traced invisible relationships between seemingly disparate elements. The central table vanished under stacks of case files, from the current investigation and cold cases stretching back seven years. Alan moved between these stations with a conductor's practised choreography, his shadow elongated and contracting against the evidence-laden walls as he passed beneath the overhead lights.

Clara stood in the doorway, two fresh coffees in hand, observing the controlled chaos with admiration and concern. Alan's coat hung abandoned over a chair; his shirt sleeves rolled up to reveal forearms mapped with old scars he never explained. His tie had been repurposed as an impromptu marker, pinned between two photographs to indicate a connection only he fully understood.

"The captain's going to have an aneurysm when he sees what you've done to the conference room," she said, setting a coffee on the small clear space he'd left on the table.

Alan didn't look up from the red card he examined under a magnifying glass. "Then he shouldn't come in until we've solved it."

"That's not how departmental resources work, Alan." Clara stepped carefully over a line of string that ran along the floor, connecting a floor plan to a timeline. "There are protocols—"

"Protocols won't catch him." Alan finally glanced up, his eyes fever-bright with focus. "Look at this." He gestured to the card. "The paper stock is Fabriano Rosaspina, Italian-made, only available through specialised art suppliers. The ink contains trace elements of human blood, as Leo discovered. The handwriting shows characteristics of someone trained in traditional calligraphy."

When Alan entered this state, Clara sighed, recognising the futility of procedural arguments. Instead, she slipped into the role of sounding board, which had defined their partnership for three years. "So we're looking for an artistically trained killer with expensive taste and a flair for the dramatic."

"We're looking for someone who wants to be found—but only by the right person." Alan pinned the card to the wall, stepping back to observe the array. "Every element is deliberate, meaningful. The symbols at the crime scenes, the origami, and this riddle are all pieces of a larger statement."

"A statement about what?"

His gaze flickered to the newspaper clipping about the university scandal. "About unfinished business."

Hours passed. The precinct gradually emptied as the night shift thinned to a skeleton crew. The cleaners came and went, working around the conference room with the wary respect of those who recognised obsession when they saw it. Takeout containers accumulated in the trash can—Clara's doing, as Alan barely remembered to eat when focused. Coffee cups multiplied like ceramic mushrooms on available surfaces.

The red string network grew more complex, with Alan occasionally cutting sections to reroute connections as new patterns emerged. Clara maintained her system on a digital tablet, organising the evidence into categories that might be comprehensible to others when they eventually had to brief the captain.

. . .

"The answer is in the numbers," Alan muttered, more to himself than Clara. He had filled three pages of his notebook with calculations derived from measurements of the carved symbols. "The patterns dead men cannot tell…"

"Alan," Clara said softly, setting down her tablet. "It's almost three in the morning. We've been at this for sixteen hours straight."

"I'm close." His voice carried the rough edge of exhaustion. Still, his hands remained steady as he transferred measurements to a city map.

"You said that four hours ago." Clara stretched, her spine cracking after too long in the same position. Her practical ponytail had long since loosened, stray strands framing a face drawn with fatigue. "Even brilliant detectives need rest."

Alan paused, his pen hovering over the map. For a moment, Clara thought he might actually heed her suggestion. Instead, he said, "I had a dream about Rebecca last night."

The unexpected personal reference caught Clara off guard. Alan rarely mentioned his late wife by name in the three years of partnership.

"What was the dream?" she asked carefully.

. . .

"She was standing in our old university office, organising papers." His voice softened, losing its detective's precision. "She looked up and said, 'The patterns are repeating, Alan. Why aren't you seeing it?"

Clara watched him, recognising the rare moment of vulnerability. "Do you think your subconscious is trying to tell you something about the case?"

"Maybe." Alan set down his pen, rubbing his eyes with the heels of his hands. "Rebecca was brilliant at pattern recognition—better than me, though I never admitted it. She would have solved this hours ago."

"Was she part of your research team at the university?"

"She led it." A ghost of a smile touched his lips before fading. "We were developing novel cryptographic systems based on geometric algorithms. The applications were primarily theoretical, but there were potential military uses that attracted... attention."

Clara nodded, already knowing parts of this story from departmental gossip and news articles she'd researched after being assigned as Alan's partner. The scandal had involved allegations of stolen research, espionage, and ultimately, a suspicious death ruled as suicide.

"What happened to your research after...?" She left the question unfinished.

. . .

"Classified. Buried." His expression hardened. "Just like Rebecca."

The moment of openness passed as quickly as it had appeared. Alan returned to the map, marking locations with renewed intensity. Clara recognised his retreat into the case—his way of managing grief that remained raw despite the years.

The strings between the photos created a web extending to the map, forming connections between crime scenes, victims, and locations pulled from the riddle's cryptic lines. Four coffee cups later, with dawn beginning to lighten the windows, Alan suddenly straightened, his finger tracing a pattern on the map that only he could see.

"Meridian points," he murmured. "Not just the building—actual meridian lines."

Clara moved to his side, blinking gritty eyes. "What do you mean?"

"The victims were placed at locations that form a geometric pattern when connected." Alan's voice gained momentum as the pieces fell into place. "If we extend these lines according to the proportional relationships in the carved symbols..."

He drew rapidly on the map, extending lines from each crime scene according to his calculated measurements. The lines converged at a point near the industrial district.

"There." He circled the intersection. "That's where the next piece will be found."

. . .

Clara leaned closer, squinting at the location. "That's the old Blackwell Chemical warehouse. It's been abandoned for years."

"'Where shadows split, where scholars failed,'" Alan quoted from the riddle. "Blackwell Chemical was a major funder of our research program. They pulled out after the scandal broke."

Clara straightened, wincing as her stiff muscles protested. "So our killer is connecting victims to your past research, your university scandal, and now your former corporate sponsor?"

"It's not a coincidence." Alan gathered his notebook and coat with sudden urgency. "The warehouse is the next location. He's leading us through a sequence tied to my past."

"Wait." Clara placed a hand on his arm. "We need backup, a proper team. If this is as personal as it seems, you're walking into exactly what he wants."

"Of course I am." Alan didn't shake off her hand, but his body hummed with barely contained energy. "That's the point, Clara. He designed this entire sequence for me. The symbols, the locations, the riddle are all calibrated to my specific knowledge."

"Which makes you a target, not just an investigator." Her grip tightened slightly. "We do this by the book. Call tactical support, secure the perimeter, then approach cautiously."

. . .

Alan's expression suggested he'd already moved beyond such considerations, his mind racing ahead to the warehouse and whatever awaited. The physical toll of their marathon session showed in the shadows beneath his eyes and the pallor of his skin, but adrenaline and intellectual fervour overrode exhaustion.

"Fine," he conceded finally. "We'll call it in. But I need to be first through that door."

"Second," Clara countered. "Behind someone wearing proper tactical gear."

A ghost of a smile touched his lips. "Always the pragmatist."

"Someone has to be." She released his arm and reached for her phone. "While I arrange this, take fifteen minutes to clean up and get some caffeine that isn't cold. You look like something the crime scene techs should be photographing."

As Clara made the necessary calls, Alan stood before the evidence wall one last time. The red strings created a complex web that mirrored the connections forming in his mind—between past and present, between academic failure and current danger, between the brilliant woman he had lost and the elusive killer who seemed to know too much about both of them.

The warehouse waited, and with it, Alan suspected, another body —another message in what was becoming a conversation written in blood and cryptic symbols. A conversation seven years in the making, with a climax he could sense approaching but couldn't yet define.

He gathered his coat, checking that his service weapon was secure. The exhaustion of sixteen hours' investigation pressed against his consciousness, but the promise of answers pushed it back. Whatever waited at the Blackwell Chemical warehouse, Alan Hart would meet it with the same analytical precision that had defined his academic career and now guided his detective work.

Some puzzles demanded more than the solution. Some required confrontation.

2

THE FIRST RIDDLE

The alley exhaled the day's accumulated heat into the night, leaving behind a chill that seeped through Detective Alan Hart's coat as he knelt beside the body. Amber light from a distant street lamp caught the edges of the crime scene, casting long shadows that seemed to point accusingly at the victim splayed across the cracked pavement. Alan's breath formed thin clouds as he leaned closer, his eyes narrowing on what others might dismiss as random marks but which he recognised immediately as deliberate—a message meant for someone who knew how to read it.

The victim lay spread-eagled, limbs arranged with unnatural precision. He was a male in his mid-thirties, wearing an expensive suit now ruined by the grime of the alley and the dark stain spreading from his chest. Alan tugged a thin latex glove tighter and gently pulled back the torn fabric. The symbol carved into the flesh was unmistakable—a complex geometric pattern with sharp angles intersecting a perfect circle, all contained within what appeared to be a stylised eye. The precision of the lines suggested the work of someone with steady hands and infinite patience.

"Not the first time you've seen this," Alan murmured to himself, not a question but a statement of fact.

The symbol tugged at his memory—similar markings on victims from three years ago. These cases grew cold despite his obsessive pursuit—different victims, locations, meticulous attention to detail, and the same cryptic signature. He'd spent weeks decoding that first symbol, only to find it led to another puzzle and another, each taunting him with promises of answers that never materialised.

Alan pulled a small notebook from his pocket, its leather cover worn soft by years of handling. His fingers, though steady, felt distant as he sketched the symbol with quick, precise strokes. The familiarity of the act brought unwelcome comfort—this intellectual engagement, this puzzling through complexity—it reminded him of lecture halls and academic journals, of a life abandoned.

Behind him, tyres crunched on broken glass. Headlights swept the brick walls before extinguishing, plunging the scene back into its amber-shadowed state. Detective Clara Morgan's footsteps were even and unhurried as she approached, her silhouette resolute against the glow of distant streetlights.

"Same signature?" she asked, joining him beside the body. Her voice did not surprise or evoke the morbid fascination that often crept into others at scenes like this—just calm assessment and practical focus.

Alan nodded once, turning his notebook toward her. "Similar enough to be connected, different enough to mean something. The central eye is new."

Clara studied the drawing, then the body, her hazel eyes missing nothing. "Time of death estimated between midnight and 2 AM. No wallet, no phone, no ID. But those shoes cost more than my monthly rent, and that watch—" she nodded toward the victim's wrist, "—that's a Patek Philippe. Fifteen thousand minimum."

"Not a robbery," Alan said, his attention returning to the symbol. "The watch was left deliberately. A timepiece—time is significant somehow."

He glanced up at the walls surrounding them. The brick surface to the left was pockmarked with age and water damage, creating dark constellations across its face. The opposite wall, smoother and newer, bore faded graffiti tags. Neither showed signs of blood spatter or struggle.

"He wasn't killed here," Alan continued, his voice low as he circled the body. "No defensive wounds on his hands. There are no signs of a struggle in the alley. This was the display location, not the murder scene."

Clara knelt, examining the victim's fingernails. "Clean. Manicured. Whoever he was, he took care of himself."

"The blood pooling is inconsistent with the wound," Alan added. "The body was moved post-mortem, positioned deliberately." He gestured to the precise arrangement of limbs. "He's a message, Clara. A carefully composed message."

The wind shifted, carrying the scent of rain and urban decay. Alan's focus momentarily fractured, and behind it surged unwelcome fragments—the polished hallways of Cambridge University, equations scratched across whiteboards, a colleague's face contorted with betrayal, a funeral he couldn't bring himself to attend. The guilt bloomed in his chest, a physical presence he'd grown accustomed to carrying.

Clara's voice pulled him back. "You're doing it again," she said, not unkindly. "That looks like you're somewhere else entirely."

Alan closed his notebook with more force than necessary. "Just making connections."

"Between this and the Mercer Street cases?" Clara asked, standing and pulling off her latex gloves with practised efficiency. "Those went cold years ago, Alan. The department officially closed them."

"The department was wrong." The words came out sharper than he intended. He softened his tone. "The symbol is similar enough to suggest the same perpetrator, but deliberate variations exist. He's evolving his message."

Clara sighed, a small cloud dissipating in the cold air. "Or it's a copycat who studied the old case files. Or it's a coincidence that fits a pattern because that's what your mind is trained to find."

Alan's eyes returned to the victim's face, slack in death but still bearing traces of surprise rather than fear. "You know I don't believe in coincidences."

The crime scene technicians arrived, their equipment cases clacking against the pavement as they approached. The mechanical clicking of cameras began, flash illuminating the scene in stark, clinical bursts that stripped away the shadows and reduced everything to evidence.

"The blood patterns here," Alan said, gesturing to a subtle arc of droplets near the victim's left arm. "They're inconsistent with both the chest wound and the body position. There's a second injury we haven't found yet."

Clara crouched again, examining the pattern. "You're right. Likely from the actual murder location." She looked up at him, concern briefly crossing her face. "You're going to obsess over this one, aren't you? I can already see it."

Alan didn't answer immediately. His mind was already racing ahead, assembling and disassembling possibilities: the symbol, the precise arrangement, the expensive watch left behind. Each element was a piece in a puzzle explicitly constructed for someone who could appreciate its complexity.

For someone like him.

"I'll follow the evidence," he finally replied, knowing Clara would hear the evasion for what it was.

"Like you did before?" Her question hung between them, loaded with shared history and quiet concern.

The memory surfaced unbidden—Alan hunched over papers spread across his apartment floor, walls covered in photographs and string connections, sleepless weeks as the Mercer Street killer's puzzles consumed him. Clara brought food he wouldn't eat and insisted on rest he wouldn't take. The case had nearly broken him because it spoke his language, the language of academic cryptography he'd abandoned when Elizabeth died.

"I've learned since then," he said, though they both knew it wasn't entirely true.

Alan stood apart as the technicians continued their methodical documentation, staring at the symbol in his notebook. The killer had returned with a new puzzle, a new challenge. And despite everything —despite the cost he knew such obsession extracted—he felt the familiar quickening of his pulse, the clearing focus that came with a worthy intellectual problem.

"He's speaking to someone specific," Alan murmured, more to himself than Clara. "Someone who understands this language."

Clara's voice was soft but firm when she replied. "Just remember you're not alone in this one. Whatever he's saying, we'll figure it out together."

Alan nodded, but his mind was already elsewhere, tracing the angles of the symbol, seeking the hidden meaning inscribed in flesh and blood. The game had begun again, and whatever personal demons drove him, he couldn't deny the dark thrill of engagement, the sense that something—someone—worthy of his full attention had finally returned.

The precinct hummed with fluorescent efficiency, starkly contrasting the shadowed alley where Alan had spent the early morning hours. His desk stood apart from the others—not by physical distance but by the ordered chaos that colonised its surface: case files arranged in precise stacks, crime scene photographs aligned at perfect right angles, and at the centre, his notebook opened to the freshly sketched symbol. He'd barely spoken since returning, his mind still excavating the layers of meaning behind the killer's meticulous arrangement.

The coffee in his mug had grown cold, forgotten during his intense study of the preliminary forensics report, and three hours had passed without his notice. The bullpen's usual cacophony— ringing phones, keyboard clicks, casual conversation—registered only as distant static in the focused silence he'd created around himself.

The mail cart's squeaking wheel announced itself seconds before the department clerk dropped an unmarked manila envelope onto his desk.

"This came for you," the clerk said. "No postmark. Hand-delivered to reception."

Alan looked up, his attention momentarily pulled from his analysis. The envelope bore no markings beyond his name, which was written in an elegant script that suggested careful penmanship and the use of an expensive fountain pen. He reached for it, pausing just before contact. The weight of unseen eyes pressed against him.

"Did anyone see who delivered it?" he asked, his voice carrying a carefully controlled intensity.

"Reception says it was on the counter when they returned from break," the clerk replied with a shrug before continuing his rounds.

Alan pulled latex gloves from his pocket—a habit from the crime scene that now seemed prescient—and carefully lifted the envelope. It was too light for a bomb, had no suspicious powder residue, and was precisely sealed. His fingertips detected a card inside, a high-quality stock with a textured surface. Using a letter opener, he sliced the envelope with surgical precision.

The card that slid into his palm was the precise colour of freshly spilt blood. Its surface, smooth and calm, bore an intricate riddle written in the same elegant script as the envelope, the ink a metallic gold that caught the light as he tilted it:

"First came the disciple who betrayed with a kiss

Now comes the scholar who abandoned his bliss

Count the steps from betrayal to salvation.

Find where knowledge meets damnation.

The hour approaches when time will reveal

What sacred geometry cannot conceal

Your move, Professor Hart."

Alan's breath caught in his throat. *Professor Hart*. A title he hadn't used in years, abandoned when he'd left academia behind. The sender knew his past, knew precisely who he had been.

Within moments, Alan's desk transformed into the epicentre of a controlled frenzy. He spread papers across the surface, pulled reference books from his shelves, and quickly sketched geometric patterns. His mind accelerated, connections forming and dissolving as he muttered, testing theories against the riddle's structure.

"The first line references Judas," he whispered. "Betrayal with a kiss—thirty pieces of silver." He scribbled numbers in the margin of his notepad. "The second line is me. The scholar who abandoned his bliss. Academic life for detective work."

He didn't notice Clara approaching until her shadow fell across his notes. She stood beside his desk, arms folded, concern etched in the slight furrow between her brows.

"You've been at it for hours," she said. "Santos told me about the envelope. You should have called it in as evidence immediately."

Alan didn't look up. "It's addressed to me specifically. To Professor Hart."

"Which makes it even more concerning," Clara replied, her voice lowered to avoid drawing attention from the rest of the bullpen. "This isn't just about the case anymore, Alan. It's personal."

"It was always personal." Alan finally met her gaze. "The symbol, the precision, the academic references—it's all calculated to draw me in specifically."

"That's what worries me." Clara rested her palm on his desk, fingers splayed just inches from the blood-red card. "I've seen what happens when you disappear into a case. Last time—"

"Last time was different," Alan interrupted, more sharply than he intended.

Clara's expression didn't change, but her voice softened. "Was it? Three days without sleep. Hospitalisation for exhaustion. Captain nearly pulled you from active duty permanently."

Alan's retort was interrupted by the arrival of Officer Leo Chang, whose approach lacked the measured patience that characterised

Clara's. Leo moved with the perpetual energy of youth; his tablet clutched in one hand, wireless earbuds dangling from his collar, his entire demeanour suggesting excitement.

"Detective Hart," Leo began, then noticed the tension between the two detectives. "Uh, is this a bad time? Because this can wait like five minutes if you're in the middle of something, but then again, it's also time-sensitive and—"

"It's fine, Leo," Clara said, stepping back from Alan's desk. "What have you got?"

Leo's hesitation vanished instantly as he swiped across his tablet's screen, his enthusiasm for technology overtaking any social awkwardness. "So I ran the surveillance footage from the three-block radius around our crime scene. Nothing directly shows our victim being placed, but—" he tapped the screen and turned it toward them —check this out."

The tablet displayed a grainy image from a security camera, time-stamped at 1:47 AM. A figure in dark clothing, face obscured by the angle and a hood, walking with unhurried confidence, two blocks from the crime scene.

"Not exactly a smoking gun," Clara observed.

"Wait for it," Leo said, swiping to another image. "Same figure, seventeen minutes later, walking away from the direction of our crime scene. Now look at the hands."

Alan leaned forward. In the second image, the figure's right hand appeared to be wearing a dark glove.

"Could be blood," Leo continued. "And here's where it gets interesting. I ran the gait analysis algorithm; this person walks with a distinct rhythm and posture. Almost like they're—"

"Dancing," Alan finished, his eyes narrowing. "The steps are measured like they're moving to music only they can hear."

Leo blinked in surprise. "Exactly. How did you—"

"The riddle mentions steps," Alan explained, gesturing to the red card. "And sacred geometry often involves movement patterns. Our killer isn't just leaving puzzles; they're performing." He turned to Leo. "What about the victim's digital footprint?"

Leo set the tablet down, his fingers moving quickly across the screen. "That's the other thing. We got a preliminary ID from fingerprints. Victor Kazan, 42, professor of Religious Studies at Westmore University. Specialising in early Christian symbolism and iconography."

Alan felt the pieces shifting in his mind, forming new connection patterns. "Religious studies. The first line of the riddle references Judas. 'Count the steps from betrayal to salvation.'"

"There's something else," Leo added, his voice dropping slightly. "I pulled Kazan's professional background. Three years ago, he was on a university ethics committee. One that was investigating academic misconduct."

The silence that followed was powerful. Clara oversaw Alan, noting that his fingers were still reviewing his notes.

"You think this is connected to your past," she said. Not a question.

Alan didn't immediately respond. The precinct sounds receded further as his focus narrowed to the riddle, the crime scene, and the victim's identity—pieces of a puzzle designed specifically for him.

"The second line," he murmured. "'The scholar who abandoned his bliss.' He's referring to me leaving academia after Elizabeth's death." His voice remained clinical, divorced from the emotion such memories might normally evoke. "But the misconduct investigation was at Cambridge, not Westmore."

Clara leaned against his desk. "So either it's a coincidence, or—"

"Or our killer is combining elements deliberately," Alan finished. "Creating connections that only I would recognise."

The tension in the air thickened as the three contemplated the implications. Clara's expression hardened into the professional mask she wore when concerned but unwilling to show it.

"This changes our approach," she said firmly.

"That would be a mistake," Alan countered, his tone measured but unyielding. "He's challenging my intellect."

"That would be a mistake," Alan replied, his tone steady yet firm. "He's challenging me intellectually. If we change the parameters by introducing additional resources, we risk accelerating his timeline."

Leo shifted uncomfortably, feeling caught between the contrasting views of the two senior detectives. "For what it's worth, the digital evidence indicates that this individual is highly methodical. He navigated the camera blind spots perfectly and left no electronic traces behind."

Clara's frustration manifested in a quick, sharp exhalation. "By the book, Alan. That's how we stay safe. That's how we catch criminals without becoming casualties ourselves."

"Sometimes the book doesn't have the right chapter," Alan replied quietly.

The stalemate might have continued if not for the sudden shift in Alan's expression—a widening of his eyes, a subtle parting of his lips that signalled recognition. He reached for the red card, turning it at precisely a forty-five-degree angle under the light.

"The watermark," he breathed. "There's a watermark in the paper."

Leo and Clara leaned closer as Alan tilted the card to catch the fluorescent light at the right angle. Nearly invisible until that precise moment, the watermark revealed itself: a stylised compass and square, the ancient symbols of architecture and measurement.

"Masonic," Alan said, excitement bleeding into his controlled voice. "Combined with the reference to 'sacred geometry' and 'steps'—" His fingers traced across his city map. "There's an old Masonic temple on Riverview Drive. Abandoned since the 1970s but never demolished due to historic preservation laws."

Clara straightened, already reaching for her phone. "I'll get a tactical team assembled. If this is where he's leading us—"

"No," Alan interrupted, standing suddenly. "The riddle specifies 'the hour approaches when time will reveal.' He's set this up on a timetable. If we go in with a tactical team, we risk prematurely triggering whatever he's planned."

The tension between them crystallised into something sharp and dangerous—Clara's dedication to protocol versus Alan's intuitive approach to the puzzle-maker's psychology.

"You're suggesting we walk into an obvious trap?" Clara asked incredulously.

Alan's eyes held a glint that hadn't been there earlier—the spark of intellectual engagement, the thrill of a worthy challenge that both Clara and Leo recognised as dangerous.

"I'm suggesting," Alan said carefully, gathering his notebook and the blood-red card, "that sometimes, to catch someone who thinks three moves ahead, you have to stop playing by expected rules." He looked from Clara to Leo, and his decision was already made. "He's invited me to play. It would be rude to decline."

3

DESCENT INTO THE LABYRINTH

The note had been folded mathematically, creases sharp enough to draw blood. Detective Alan Hart studied it under the sickly fluorescent light, his eyes straining to decipher meaning from the seemingly random arrangement of symbols and numbers scattered across the pristine page. They resembled constellations—distant, cold, yet somehow deliberate in their chaos. Behind him, the empty apartment whispered of abandonment, of secrets hastily packed away, but the note spoke loudest of all.

Hart placed the paper on the small kitchen counter, careful not to smudge the ink with his gloved fingers. The apartment smelled of furniture polish and absence—the peculiar emptiness that occurs when a space is meticulously clean but rarely inhabited. Dust motes danced in the shaft of late afternoon sunlight that cut through half-drawn blinds, illuminating a room that appeared more like a museum exhibit than a home. Everything was arranged: books alphabetised, cushions at precise angles, and a single coffee mug left upside down on a drain board as if in patient anticipation.

"You're not random," Hart murmured to the symbols on the page, his voice barely audible. "You're trying to tell me something."

He withdrew a small, worn leather notebook from his trench coat pocket, its edges softened by years of handling. The pages contained his particular form of shorthand—half-cryptic notes, half-intuitive leaps—incomprehensible to anyone but himself. Hart began to copy the symbols, his pencil moving with practised precision. The action was meditative, allowing his mind to drift beneath the conscious act of recording.

Six numbers are arranged in a sequence. Three geometric shapes intersect at odd angles—a series of letters that failed to form any recognisable word in English. And yet, there was a pattern here—he could feel it like pressure behind his eyes, the familiar tension that always preceded insight.

Through the thin walls came the sounds of the forensics team working in the bedroom, their movements methodical and unhurried. This wasn't a murder scene—not yet—just a disappearance. A mathematics professor, Jeremy Winters, age 42, had been missing for three days. There were no signs of struggle, no indications of planned departure, just this note, these symbols, and the peculiar sensation that Hart was being watched from within the puzzle itself.

He closed his eyes, allowing the fragments to settle in his mind. The numbers—**6, 23, 8, 42, 15, 9**—seemed to pulse against his closed lids. They weren't phone numbers, not coordinates. Perhaps a code, a cypher? Something about them felt vaguely familiar, echoing something he'd encountered before.

"You're doing that thing again," a voice from the doorway said, warm with affection and mild exasperation.

Hart didn't need to open his eyes to recognise Clara Morgan's presence. Her light but purposeful footsteps crossed the laminate flooring as she approached. A subtle waft of sandalwood and coffee accompanied her—Clara's unchanging perfume and perpetual beverage of choice.

"What thing?" he asked, eyes still closed and mind half-submerged in numbers and patterns.

"That thing where you commune with the evidence like it's going to whisper secrets if you're quiet enough." There was no malice in her observation, only the comfortable honesty of a long partnership.

Hart opened his eyes, blinking away the afterimage of numbers. Clara stood beside him, her practical blazer and sensible shoes representing her grounded approach to detective work. Where he lost himself in abstractions, she remained firmly anchored in the tangible.

"Sometimes it does," he replied, gesturing to the note. "This isn't random, Clara. It's deliberately constructed to communicate something."

She leaned closer, hazel eyes narrowing as she studied the paper. "Our missing professor left us a math problem?"

"Not math. At least, not only math." Hart's finger hovered above the paper, tracing the arrangement without touching it. "These symbols have a rhythm to them, a syntax. It's less like an equation and more like..."

"Like what?" Clara prompted when he trailed off.

"Like a challenge." The word settled between them with unexpected weight. Hart felt a familiar tightness in his chest—the simultaneous thrill and dread of recognition. "Someone wants us to solve this."

Clara straightened, a slight furrow appearing between her brows. "You think this is connected to something else? Someone else?"

Hart didn't answer immediately. His mind had caught on a fragment of memory—green eyes behind stylish glasses, a voice smooth as polished stone: *Every puzzle has its solution, Detective. The question is whether you're clever enough to find it.*

His hands were suddenly cold, but his face felt warm—an uncomfortable heat he recognised as intuition-or perhaps fear. He pulled his notebook closer, flipping back through the pages until he found what he was looking for: similar symbols from a case three years earlier—not identical, but the style, the approach, the fingerprints of the same mind.

"Hart?" Clara's voice cut through his thoughts, concern evident in the single syllable.

"I think," he said slowly, carefully, as if the words themselves might trigger some unseen mechanism, "that Jeremy Winters didn't write this note. He became part of it—a piece moved on someone else's board."

He looked up at Clara, allowing her to see what he rarely showed: the unguarded apprehension behind his analytical façade.

"Remember Jonathan Price?" he asked.

Clara's expression shifted, recognition and wariness replacing curiosity. "The Riddler case? But he's—"

"Gone," Hart finished. "Not dead, not imprisoned—just gone. After the trial collapsed."

He turned back to the note, seeing it now with terrible clarity. It was not just a puzzle but a signature, a calling card, and the opening move in a game he thought had ended years ago.

"Price was obsessed with proving himself smarter than everyone else. Especially me." The last words came out quietly, almost reluctantly. "This—" he gestured at the symbols, "—this is an invitation."

Clara's hand came to rest on his shoulder, a steadying pressure. "We don't know that for certain yet."

But Hart did know. The certainty sat in his stomach like a stone. Jonathan Price had resurfaced, taking Jeremy Winters as his first move. The puzzle on the page wasn't just a clue to the professor's whereabouts—it was the opening gambit in a dangerous game of intellectual one-upmanship with potentially fatal consequences.

"We need to solve it," Hart said, folding the note along its original creases. "And we need to do it quickly."

As they left the apartment, Hart felt the note's weight in his pocket like a live coal. Outside, the afternoon had deepened toward evening, the sky bruised with approaching night. He paused at the threshold, glancing back at the empty apartment with its perfect angles and unnatural tidiness.

Somewhere, he knew, Jonathan Price was waiting, watching, anticipating Hart's next move with the patient certainty of a chess master who had already calculated twelve moves ahead. The game had begun again, and Hart could only hope he wouldn't be too late to save the man who had become its unwilling pawn.

Hart's office resembled the inside of a clock—meticulous, ordered chaos comprehensible only to its creator. Three cork boards dominated the far wall, layered with photographs, transcripts, and cards connected by varying-colour threads, a physical manifestation of neural pathways. Maps and diagrams covered another wall, while stacks of reference books formed precarious columns on the floor. The room smelled of coffee grounds and old paper, the academic perfume of obsession. Hart stood before the central board, the mysterious note pinned at its centre like the heart of a web, waiting to transmit its vibrations of meaning.

He had been standing there for hours, motionless except for his eyes, which darted between the note and his annotations surrounding it. The numbers—**6, 23, 8, 42, 15, 9**—had been transcribed onto index cards, arranged and rearranged in different sequences. The geometric shapes had been reproduced with exacting precision. The letters, isolated from their companions, stared back at him like abandoned children.

Dawn had come and gone unacknowledged. A coffee mug sat on his desk, contents long cold, a perfect ring of dark liquid marking the passage of time more reliably than the clock whose batteries had died weeks ago. Hart didn't believe in coincidences, yet the puzzle before him stubbornly refused to yield its secrets. It was deliberately opaque, designed to frustrate rather than illuminate—a taunt rather than a clue.

That was Price's signature. Jonathan Price had never been interested merely in hiding information but in transforming the act of concealment into a performance, a demonstration of intellectual superiority. His puzzles were mirrors, reflecting the solver's limitations at them.

The sound of the door opening broke Hart's concentration. Clara entered, bearing a fresh coffee and a folder under her arm. Her eyes scanned the room, taking in the evidence of Hart's sleepless night with practised assessment.

"I spoke with Winters' department chair," she said, placing the coffee beside its abandoned predecessor. "He confirmed that Winters was working on some theoretical paper involving encryption algorithms. Nothing classified, but innovative enough that several tech companies had expressed interest."

Hart nodded without turning from the board. "Anything on his personal life?"

"Divorced three years ago, lives alone, keeps to himself. By all accounts, he's brilliant but reserved. Not the type to have enemies." Clara moved beside him, studying the display. "You've been at this all night, haven't you?"

Hart's silence was confirmation enough. He reached for the fresh coffee, the cup's warmth a momentary anchor to physical reality.

"I've arranged for someone to help us with this," Clara continued. "Dr. Evelyn Shaw from the university. She specialises in ancient codes and cryptography. She studied under Jonathan Price before his... disgrace."

Hart turned at this, his attention finally diverted from the board. "Price's protégé?" A mixture of interest and wariness coloured his voice.

"Former protégé," Clara corrected. "She was the one who first raised concerns about his research methods. According to the background check, she's been rebuilding her academic reputation since the scandal. She'll be here in thirty minutes."

Hart returned to the board, taking a sip of coffee. His reflection in the window showed a man becoming a ghost—eyes shadowed, stubble darkening his jaw, hair mussed from repeated, unconscious raking of fingers through it.

"Price is playing a long game," he said. "The question is, why now? Why Winters?"

"Maybe it's not about Winters at all," Clara suggested. "Maybe he's just a means to an end."

Hart nodded; the thought had already occurred to him hours ago. "The bait."

A knock at the door announced Officer Leo Chang, the youngest member of their team. He entered with the easy energy of youth not yet burned down by years of grim cases, tablet in hand, earphones dangling around his neck.

"Got that background on Price you asked for," he said, swiping through screens. "Nothing on current whereabouts, but I tracked his financial activity until eighteen months ago when it just... stops. No credit card usage, no property records, nothing. It's like he walked off the digital map."

Hart wasn't surprised. "He would have prepared for that," he said. "Price thinks a dozen moves ahead."

Clara was examining the note again. "These shapes—they look almost like..."

"Glyphs," came a new voice from the doorway. "Specifically, they resemble Cretan hieroglyphs, though with distinctive modifications."

The woman who entered moved with the quiet assurance of someone who belonged in academic spaces. Dr Evelyn Shaw's dark auburn hair was secured in a loose bun, several strands escaping to frame a face that spoke of intense concentration and little concern for appearance. Wire-rimmed glasses magnified brown eyes immediately fixed on the note with undisguised fascination. She wore a cardigan over a simple blouse, an antique pendant hanging at her throat—a minor silver key on a chain.

"Dr. Shaw," Clara introduced. This is Detective Alan Hart."

Shaw approached the board without waiting for further formalities, focusing entirely on the puzzle. "Fascinating construction," she murmured as if speaking to herself. "The numerical sequence isn't random—it's using a modified Fibonacci principle where each number is derived from adding the digits of the previous two numbers, then taking their sum modulo 26."

Hart watched her, assessing. Her methodical approach reminded him of his own—a similar intensity and disregard for social niceties when engaged with a puzzle.

"And the letters?" he asked.

Shaw glanced at him, seeming to register his presence for the first time correctly. "That's where it gets interesting. If we apply the numerical sequence as a key, treating each number as a position in the alphabet..." She trailed off, her fingers moving as if typing on invisible keys. "May I?"

Hart handed her a marker. She wrote the alphabet on a clear section of the board, numbering each letter, and then began a rapid sequence of calculations. The room fell silent except for the squeak of the marker. Within minutes, she had produced a word:

ALEXANDRIA.

"The Library of Alexandria," she said, turning to them with bright eyes. "It's a reference to lost knowledge, destroyed wisdom. And if I'm right about the geometric shapes..." She traced them with her finger, not quite touching the paper. "These aren't just random angles. They're a star chart showing the position of specific celestial bodies on a particular date."

Hart felt a cold tremor of recognition—the Library of Alexandria —ancient knowledge lost to fire. His mind flashed back to another case, another time. A university library had been set ablaze, and rare manuscripts had been destroyed. Jonathan Price had been a suspect, though never charged due to insufficient evidence. The fire that had consumed centuries of knowledge had also destroyed the reputation of a young cryptographer named Alan Hart, whose security protocols had failed catastrophically.

"I know where he's taken Winters," Hart said, his voice flat with certainty. "And I know what happens next if we don't move quickly."

He turned to the others, his exhaustion burned away by sudden clarity. "The old Blackwood Library on the east side. It's been abandoned since the university built the new research facility. Price is recreating the scene of his original crime—with modifications."

"How can you be sure?" Clara asked, already reaching for her phone.

"Because that's where it all started," Hart said. "That's where Price and I first crossed paths, where he first challenged me. And now he's inviting me back to where it began." He grabbed his coat. "But this time, he's got a hostage."

Dr. Shaw was studying him with newfound intensity. "You're the one," she said quietly. "The cryptographer who became a detective after the Blackwood fire. I've read about your work."

Hart didn't acknowledge the recognition. "We need to go. Now."

As they hurried from the office, Shaw fell into step beside him. "Detective Hart," she said, her voice low enough that only he could hear, "there's something else about this puzzle. Something I don't think is coincidental."

"What?"

"The date indicated by the star chart," she said. "It's not just any date. It's today."

The Blackwood Library stood in architectural purgatory—too historically significant to demolish, too expensive to restore. Its neo-Gothic façade, once the university's pride, now wore decades of neglect like a shroud. Ivy had colonised the western wall, creeping through cracked windows. At the same time, the eastern side remained eerily bare, blackened stone still bearing witness to the fire that had devoured that wing fifteen years ago. Hart stared up at the building, his body physically present on the cracked sidewalk, his mind spiralling backwards through time. The place looked simultaneously familiar and foreign, like encountering an old friend after a disfiguring accident.

"I've arranged for backup," Clara said beside him, slipping her phone into her pocket. "They'll establish a perimeter but won't enter until we signal. If Price is watching, I don't want to spook him."

Hart nodded, his eyes tracking the broken line of windows along the third floor—the rare manuscripts section where the fire had begun, where everything had started.

"Officer Chang is bringing tactical equipment," Clara continued. "He should be here in ten minutes."

"We're not waiting," Hart said, already moving toward the entrance. Once polished by dedicated custodians, the massive oak doors had warped from years of rain and neglect. One hung partially open, like a mouth frozen mid-speech.

Dr. Shaw followed close behind, her academic curiosity visibly battling with apprehension. "The reference to Alexandria wasn't just about destruction," she said. "It was also about preservation. The Library of Alexandria wasn't just notable for being burned—it was notable for what was saved, what was hidden."

Hart paused at the entrance, scanning the dim interior through the gap. "Price wouldn't have brought us here just to find a body. That's not the game he plays."

"Then what is his game?" Clara asked, flashlight already in hand.

Hart didn't answer immediately. He'd been turning over the question in his mind since recognising Price's involvement. Jonathan Price had been brilliant and respected—until accusations of data manipulation tarnished his academic reputation. Hart had been among those who'd questioned his research methodology and demanded transparency. The subsequent investigation revealed deeper irregularities and Price's career imploded spectacularly.

"Vindication," Hart finally said. "Redemption on his terms. Price believes he was wrongfully accused, that his genius wasn't recognised." He stepped through the door into the library's cavernous foyer. "He wants to prove that he was right all along."

Inside, the building was a testament to faded grandeur. The marble floor, once gleaming, was now dull and cracked, with small puddles gathered where the roof had failed. Ornate pillars rose to a coffered ceiling where water damage bloomed like dark flowers. The air smelled of mildew and the peculiar, dusty scent of abandoned books.

"We should split up," Clara suggested, her flashlight beam cutting through the gloom. "Cover more ground."

"No," Hart and Shaw said simultaneously. They exchanged a look of mutual understanding.

"That's exactly what he would expect," Shaw explained. "He'd plan for it."

Hart nodded. "Price constructs scenarios like chess positions. Every move anticipated, every reaction accounted for." He withdrew his flashlight. "We stay together."

They moved past the hulking remains of the circulation desk toward the grand staircase. Each step groaned beneath their weight, the building keeping a creaking record of their progress. Hart led them upward, his movements becoming increasingly automatic as muscle memory overlaid present perception with past knowledge.

As a young cryptographer, he spent countless hours in this building before joining the police force. The Blackwood housed one of the country's finest collections of ancient manuscripts and coded texts. He was developing a digitisation protocol to preserve and secure the rarest volumes.

"The fire started there," he said, pausing on the landing to indicate an eastward corridor. "Special Collections. It spread quickly—too quickly to be natural. The investigation concluded it was arson, but they never identified the perpetrator."

"You suspected Price," Clara said. It wasn't a question.

Hart resumed climbing. "He had been denied access to certain manuscripts—his research credentials were questioned. A week later, the texts he wanted to examine were ash."

Dr. Shaw made a slight sound of recognition. "The Voynich facsimiles. Price was obsessed with them, believed he'd found a pattern in the text that everyone else had missed."

The third floor was a landscape of abandonment—reading tables askew, shelves partially collapsed, windows boarded or broken. Their footsteps echoed in the vast space, disturbing years of silence. Hart moved with increasing purpose toward the eastern wing, where the fire damage was most evident—blackened beams protruded from walls like exposed ribs. The floor transitioned from wood to concrete

—a structural reinforcement was added after the blaze, but it was never properly finished.

"Detective," Clara's voice cut through his thoughts. She pointed to the far wall, where a rectangle of cleaner space indicated something recently removed. "Something was hanging there."

As they approached, Hart saw that it wasn't just a cleaner wall—it was a deliberate marking. Numbers had been written in the dust: 15-25-18-1-13-9-4.

Dr Shaw was already working on the cypher, her lips moving silently as she translated. "It's a simple substitution. A=1, B=2...

It spells 'PYRAMID'."

Hart's flashlight caught something else—a small object placed precisely on the floor beneath the written numbers. He knelt to examine it without touching it: a miniature pyramid, meticulously crafted from what appeared to be the ashes of burned paper, hardened somehow into a solid form.

"He's not here," Hart said, the certainty settling into his bones. "Neither is Winters."

"How can you be sure?" Clara asked.

"Because this isn't the endgame. It's another move." Hart straightened. "Price is sending us on a journey. Each location and puzzle is a step in his designed sequence."

Dr. Shaw was examining the ash pyramid with undisguised fascination. "The Ancient Egyptians believed that knowledge was divine, that libraries were temples. The Great Library of Alexandria was an attempt to gather all the world's knowledge in one place."

"And the pyramid?" Clara prompted.

"A perfect geometric form," Shaw replied. "Mathematically precise, architecturally sound. But also a tomb." She looked up at Hart. "He's leading us somewhere specific."

Hart was already scanning the room for additional clues. His flashlight caught an anomaly on one of the remaining bookshelves— a single volume standing upright among collapsed and water-damaged companions. He moved toward it, somehow knowing what he would find before he even reached it.

The book was pristine, its cover unmarked by the decay affecting everything else in the building. Hart carefully removed it from the shelf. It wasn't a book at all but a hollow facsimile. A folded paper and a small electronic device with a blinking red light lay inside.

"Is that a—" Clara began.

"Tracker," Hart confirmed, unfolding the paper. On it was a simple message written in elegant script:

Clever as always, Detective Hart. The game continues. Your missing professor has much to contribute to our discourse on knowledge preservation. The next step awaits at the place where ancient wisdom meets modern folly. The clock is running. Tick tock.

"He's been watching us," Clara said, scanning the shadows as if Price might materialise from them.

Hart's attention had fixed on the tracker. "Not watching. Following." He held up the device. "This isn't for tracking Winters. It's for tracking us."

The realisation hit with crystalline clarity. The abandoned library wasn't the location of a hostage; it was a waypoint, a test of their ability to follow Price's path. Each puzzle solved advanced them to the next stage of whatever elaborate scenario he had constructed.

"But why?" Shaw asked. "Why this complexity?"

Hart's expression hardened. "Because Jonathan Price never believed in simple victories. He wants to prove that he's smarter than I and was right about his theories." He pocketed the tracker. "And he's using Winters as both bait and demonstration."

"The place where ancient wisdom meets modern folly," Clara repeated. "What does that mean?"

Hart was already moving toward the stairs, the others following. "It means Price has taken Winters to the new Technological Research Centre at the university—the building that replaced this one in function—the repository of knowledge for the digital age."

As they descended through the decaying library, Hart felt the weight of Price's game settling on his shoulders. This wasn't just about a missing professor or an old academic rivalry. It was about something larger, something Price believed would vindicate years of disgrace and exile.

And they were now irreversibly part of his demonstration.

The Technological Research Centre rose like a vision of tomorrow—all glass, steel, and mathematical precision. Sunlight fractured against its façade, creating prisms that painted the plaza with ephemeral rainbows. Where the Blackwood Library had been a temple to the past, this structure was an altar to the future—clean lines, uninhibited by ornament, functional to its core. Hart felt oddly exposed, approaching it as if the building's transparent walls stripped away concealment, leaving intentions bare. Somewhere within this crystalline hive of innovation, Price waited—or at least, the next breadcrumb on his meticulously plotted trail did.

"Security cameras everywhere," Clara observed, her eyes tracking the discreet black domes positioned at strategic intervals. "If Price came here, he's on film."

Hart doubted it would be so simple. "Price wouldn't allow himself to be recorded unless he wanted to be. He thinks too many steps ahead."

Officer Leo Chang, who had brought tactical equipment as requested, met them at the entrance. The young officer's usual energy was tempered by professional focus, and his tablet already displayed the building's floor plan.

"I've spoken with security," Chang reported. "They've agreed to give us access to their system, but they're unhappy. This place houses some serious intellectual property—corporate-funded research and prototype tech. They're nervous about police tramping through."

Dr. Shaw adjusted her glasses, studying the building with academic interest. "The contrast is deliberate," she said, almost to herself. The Blackwood was analogue, organic—wood, paper, and stone. This is digital, synthetic. Price is making a point about the evolution of knowledge storage."

Hart nodded. Price's puzzles were never just functional—they were symbolic, layered with meaning. "Where would he go in a building like this? What would draw him?"

Chang consulted his tablet. "The central server hub is on the fourth floor. It's the brain of the operation—it connects all the research labs and stores all the data."

"Too obvious," Hart said. "Price wouldn't choose the literal centre. He'd go for something with more... resonance."

Shaw was scanning the directory displayed near the entrance. "There," she said suddenly, pointing to a listing. "The Winters Algorithm Laboratory. It's named after Professor Winters—it must be where he conducted his research."

The connection was too perfect to be coincidental. Hart felt the familiar sensation of pieces clicking into place. "Which floor?"

"Basement level three," Chang read from the directory. "Looks like it specialises in physical implementations of encryption algorithms."

They took the elevator down, descending beneath the gleaming superstructure into the building's subterranean levels. The atmosphere changed perceptibly with each floor they passed—less glass, more concrete, and the aesthetic of innovation gradually yielded to utilitarian concerns of security and stability.

The elevator doors opened onto a stark corridor, brightly lit but windowless. Numbered laboratories branched off regularly, each secured with keycard access and biometric scanners. The air was noticeably cooler here, conditioned to accommodate the heat generated by servers and specialised equipment.

Hart approached the door marked "Winters Algorithm Laboratory" with measured steps. Unlike the other labs, this one had a numerical keypad beside its biometric scanner—an additional layer of security.

"We'll need authorisation," Clara said, reaching for her phone.

Hart held up a hand. "Wait." He examined the keypad more closely. Unlike standard models, this one had symbols etched beside each number—tiny glyphs that would be invisible to anyone not specifically looking for them.

"The pyramid," he murmured. "It wasn't just pointing us to this location. It was giving us the access code."

Dr. Shaw moved beside him, studying the symbols. "You're right. These match ancient Egyptian numerals, but they're paired with modern digits." She traced the sequence they had found at the library: 15-25-18-1-13-9-4. "If we convert from our numbering system to the Egyptian equivalent and then input those positions..."

Hart followed her logic, entering a seven-digit sequence. The keypad emitted a soft tone, and the door unlocked with a pneumatic hiss.

"Remind me to get you assigned to more cases," Clara said to Shaw with grudging admiration.

The laboratory beyond was a stark contrast to the abandoned library—immaculate, sterile, humming with dormant technology. Workstations encircled a central dais where a complex apparatus stood: a physical construction of metal and circuitry that resembled a modernist sculpture more than functional equipment.

"Winters' prototype," Shaw breathed, approaching it with reverent steps. "I've read about this. It's a physical implementation of his quantum-resistant encryption algorithm—designed to be unhackable even by quantum computers."

Hart scanned the room, looking for signs of disturbance or anything out of place. The laboratory appeared untouched and pristine—perhaps too pristine for a working research environment.

"Something's wrong," he said. "This place feels... staged."

His eyes caught on a computer monitor at the primary workstation. Unlike the others, which remained dark, this one displayed a screensaver—pulsing geometric patterns that shifted and reformed in hypnotic sequences.

As Hart approached, the screen changed, responding to his proximity. Text appeared:

Detective Hart. Right on schedule. Your consistency is your most admirable quality—or perhaps your most exploitable weakness. You now understand that Professor Winters' contribution to cryptography represents a significant evolution in knowledge security. You may not yet grasp why this matters to me, to us both. Activate the prototype. See what Winters has truly created.

Hart read the message twice, trying to discern the trap within the instruction. Price never gave straightforward directions without embedding some twist or some test.

"Should we call the bomb squad?" Chang asked, eyeing the prototype with newfound wariness.

"It's not a bomb," Hart said with certainty. "That's not Price's style. He destroys knowledge, not people—at least, not directly."

Shaw had moved to examine the prototype more closely. "This is incredible engineering. Winters was implementing theoretical concepts that most cryptographers only dream about." She pointed to a small interface panel. "The activation sequence would be here."

Hart hesitated, weighing the risk. Following Price's instructions felt like willing participation in his game, yet refusing to play could potentially result in losing Winters altogether.

"We need to know what we're dealing with," he decided finally. "Dr. Shaw, can you activate it safely?"

She nodded, fingers already moving across the panel with practised precision. "The basic principles are familiar to anyone in the field."

The prototype hummed to life, lights illuminating its intricate structure from within. The computer monitor changed again, displaying a complex visualisation—data flows represented as luminous streams, branching and converging in patterns too complex to follow.

"It's beautiful," Shaw murmured. "Winters' algorithm visualised as a physical process."

The visualisation suddenly froze, then reconfigured. A video feed appeared, showing a man seated in what seemed to be a small, windowless room. Though visibly exhausted, Professor Jeremy Winters was alive, his clothes rumpled, his expression dazed. He appeared to be reading from a prepared statement.

"My algorithm has been modified," Winters said, his voice thin and strained. "What was designed as a shield has been transformed into a key. Every digital security system built on standard encryption protocols can now be accessed. Banking systems, power grids, and communication networks are all vulnerable. This demonstration is being transmitted to select individuals who understand its significance."

Hart felt a cold certainty settling in his chest. "This isn't just about me or Winters. Price is advertising—showing off the breakthrough to potential buyers or allies."

On-screen, Winters continued: "The full implementation requires physical access to my prototype, which contains safeguards against remote exploitation. Dr. Price has arranged a demonstration for tonight at the Millennium Clock Tower. The prototype will interface with the tower's systems at midnight, initiating a cascading access sequence across networked municipal systems."

The video cut off, replaced by another text message:

The clock is indeed ticking, Detective. Midnight approaches. Will you attempt to stop the demonstration, save the professor, or perhaps accomplish both? Your move.

Clara was already on her phone, calling for backup. "We need to secure the Clock Tower immediately."

. . .

Hart stared at the now-dark screen, his mind racing ahead, analysing the game as it had evolved. "That's exactly what he expects us to do—rush to the tower with full tactical response. But Price wouldn't risk direct confrontation with police."

"You think it's another misdirection?" Chang asked.

"Not entirely," Hart replied. "The Clock Tower is significant—it's the perfect symbolic location for his demonstration. Time, precision, and public visibility. But he'll have contingencies, alternative access points."

Shaw had been scrutinising the prototype. "This has been modified," she said, pointing to newer components than the surrounding structure. "These aren't part of Winters' original design. They've been added recently—and look." She indicated a small port at the base of the device. "Something's been removed. A key component."

Hart felt the pieces connected. "Price has taken the core element—probably that makes Winters' algorithm functional. The prototype here is just a shell, a prop in his production."

"Then what's at the Clock Tower?" Clara asked.

"A performance," Hart answered. "But not the only one. Price operates on multiple levels simultaneously." He turned to Chang. "We need everything you can find on the Millennium Clock Tower—building plans, security systems, recent maintenance records."

As Chang worked on his tablet, Hart's mind continued assembling the puzzle. Price had chosen each location deliberately—the abandoned library representing the past, the research centre embodying the present. The Clock Tower would symbolise the future, the countdown to whatever Price believed would be his vindication.

"Got it," Chang announced. "The tower underwent maintenance last week. The contractor was a company called Egyptian Endeavours —specialising in 'preservation of timekeeping artefacts.'"

"Egyptian," Clara repeated. "Like the pyramid clue."

"A company that doesn't exist," Chang continued, still reading. "I just ran it through the database. It was incorporated three months ago, and there are no previous contracts."

Hart nodded grimly. "Price has been planning this for months. He created a fake company to gain access to the tower, probably installed whatever equipment he needed for tonight's demonstration."

"But why tell us?" Shaw asked. "Why give us time to respond?"

"Because he wants an audience," Hart replied. "Specifically, he wants me there to witness his triumph. This isn't just about proving his theory or selling his discovery—it's about validation."

The realisation struck him with sudden clarity. "And he's counting on me to approach this as a detective would—with tactical teams, formal responses, protocols. But that's not how this ends."

"What do you mean?" Clara asked, concern evident in her voice.

"This began as an academic rivalry, not a criminal case," Hart said. "It must end the same way—with a battle of minds, not forces." He turned to Clara. "I need you to coordinate with tactical to secure the Clock Tower, but keep them at a distance. Make it visible—let Price see the response he expects."

"While you do what?"

"What he doesn't expect," Hart replied. "I go back to the beginning —to what this is about."

Beneath the sterile lights of the laboratory, surrounded by the physical manifestation of the knowledge Price sought to control, Hart felt the game shifting. Price believed he was the grandmaster, moving pieces across the board of his design. But every chess player had blind spots—positions they couldn't see from their vantage point.

Hart intended to exploit those blind spots, to step off the board entirely. The clock was indeed ticking—but perhaps not in the way Jonathan Price anticipated.

The university courtyard lay empty in the twilight, between the abandoned Blackwood Library and the gleaming Technological Research Centre, a no-man's-land of carefully tended grass and ornamental trees. Hart stood at its centre, feeling the weight of years pressing down like accumulating snow. Behind him rose the blackened shell of the past; before him gleamed the sterile promise of the future. But Price, he was increasingly confident, would choose neither. A man obsessed with puzzles would select the perfect symbolic middle ground, where past and future are balanced on the knife's edge of the present moment. Hart turned slowly, his eyes drawn to the small observatory perched on the hill overlooking both buildings—the Department of Theoretical Mathematics, where he and Price had once been promising young academics before fire and disgrace had sent them on divergent paths.

His phone vibrated in his pocket: Clara was undoubtedly coordinating the tactical response at the Clock Tower. Hart silenced it without checking. Price would watch the police mobilisation with calculating eyes, measuring their response against his predictions. But he wouldn't be watching from the Clock Tower itself—that was merely the stage for his demonstration, not the control centre of his operation.

Hart began walking toward the observatory, its domed roof catching the last copper light of day. In his ear, the communication device he'd taken from Chang crackled with updates: a perimeter had been established around the Clock Tower, surveillance teams were in position, and technical experts were standing by to counter any digital intrusion. All proceeded according to procedure, according to expectation—all part of a performance that Price had scripted months ago.

The path up the hill was familiar, worn smooth by years of students trudging between classes. Hart had walked it countless times as a young cryptographer, his mind full of patterns and possibilities. Now, each step felt weighted with premonition. The observatory had been Price's favourite thinking space—he'd often claimed that cypher systems mirrored celestial mechanics, that the movement of information followed the same elegant laws as planets in orbit.

Hart paused halfway up, scanning the surrounding area for surveillance cameras, security personnel, or anything that might indicate a trap. The hilltop appeared deserted, the observatory's windows dark against the deepening blue of evening. Yet something about its silhouette struck him as subtly wrong—a minute alteration to its familiar outline that registered in his subconscious before his conscious mind could identify it.

An addition. Something was installed recently on the eastern edge of the dome—a small antenna array, barely visible against the darkening sky. The kind that could transmit a signal to a remote location. To the Clock Tower, perhaps.

Hart continued upward with renewed purpose, no longer concerned with concealment. If his intuition was correct, Price already knew he was coming. Would be disappointed if he didn't appear.

The observatory door stood slightly ajar, a thin line of light escaping from within. Hart approached cautiously, listening for movement, voices, and any indication of what awaited. Silence greeted him, broken only by the faint electronic hum of equipment. He pushed the door open with measured pressure.

The glow of multiple computer screens dimly lit the circular main room. The telescope that had once dominated the central platform had been removed, replaced by a workstation surrounded by monitors displaying various data feeds. One showed the Clock Tower, now surrounded by police vehicles, their lights painting the night in rhythmic pulses of blue and red. Another displayed what appeared to be a live feed of Professor Winters, still confined in his featureless room. The remaining screens showed scrolling code, system architecture diagrams, and real-time network traffic analytics across the city.

Jonathan Price sat at the centre of it all, his back to the door.

He didn't turn as Hart entered or acknowledge his presence except to say, "You're earlier than I calculated. Not by much—seventeen minutes, to be precise—but it's a meaningful deviation from your typical response pattern."

Price's voice was just as Hart remembered it: precise and measured, carrying an undercurrent of intellectual superiority that had once been annoying but now chilled the blood. He remained focused on the screens before him, fingers moving across a keyboard with fluid grace.

"The Clock Tower is a diversion," Hart said, stepping further into the room. "The real demonstration is happening from here."

Now Price turned, and Hart saw his face for the first time in years. He had aged selectively—his hair greyer at the temples, lines deeper around his mouth and eyes, but his gaze remained unnervingly bright, sharp with intelligence and something harder, colder. He wore stylish glasses and an impeccably tailored suit that seemed incongruous in the cluttered space.

"Not a diversion," Price corrected. "A component. Everything serves its purpose in an elegant system." His lips curved in what might have been mistaken for a smile if it had reached his eyes. "But you're essentially correct—the Clock Tower is merely the public face of tonight's demonstration. The visible symbol of invisible processes."

Hart took in the room, noting details—the fact that Price appeared alone, the small device on the desk that matched the missing component from Winters' prototype, the multiple exits, including a maintenance hatch in the dome that likely led to the roof.

"Where's Winters?" Hart asked.

Price gestured to one of the monitors. "Secure. Comfortable enough. Essential."

"Let him go, Price. He's not part of whatever grievance you're carrying."

"Grievance." Price spoke as if tasting it, finding it bitter. "Such a small word for such a comprehensive destruction. My research, reputation, and future are all reduced to ash, like the manuscripts in the Blackwood." He turned back to his screens. "Professor Winters is not merely collateral, Detective. He's fundamental. His algorithm is the key I theorised years ago—the unified approach to cryptographic systems that you and your academic colleagues dismissed as impossible."

Hart took another step forward, close enough to see the code scrolling across the main screen. It was beautiful in its complexity— elegant and efficient, unlike anything he'd seen before.

"You were right," Hart said quietly.

Price's fingers paused over the keyboard.

"About the unified theory," Hart continued. "Not about how you pursued it or what you're doing now. But I've had years to reconsider your core thesis. The concept was sound."

For a moment, Price remained perfectly still. Then, slowly, he swivelled his chair to face Hart fully. "An interesting tactical approach, Detective. Affirmation as a distraction technique."

"Not a tactic. A fact." Hart gestured toward the screens. "What I'm seeing here confirms it. Winters' algorithm appears to be a practical implementation of your theoretical framework. You should be published and credited, not planning whatever this is."

Something flickered across Price's expression—a momentary crack in his composure. "Publication? Credit? You think this is about academic recognition?" He stood abruptly. "This is about proving that knowledge—true innovation—cannot be controlled by institutions, by peer review, by the plodding consensus of lesser minds."

He gestured toward the window, where the Clock Tower was visible. "In forty-seven minutes, Winters' algorithm will unlock every digital security system in the city. Not to destroy or steal but to demonstrate the fundamental vulnerability of systems built on outdated cryptographic principles. The world will see that I was right —and that the protection they believe surrounds their most precious information is an illusion."

"And Winters becomes what—collateral damage to your vindication?"

"Winters becomes a footnote," Price said coldly. "A technical implementor of a theoretical breakthrough. History remembers the visionaries, not the engineers."

Hart studied the man before him—brilliant, damaged, dangerous in his certainty. "You've gone to elaborate lengths to prove your point, Jonathan. The puzzles, the symbolic locations, and the meticulous planning. All to ensure I would be here at this moment."

"You were always the most interesting opponent," Price acknowledged. "The one who came closest to understanding. The one whose validation would matter."

"Not validation," Hart said. "Witness. You needed someone who would understand the magnitude of what you've accomplished—and the magnitude of what you're about to destroy."

He took a deliberate step closer. "But you've miscalculated. I'm not here to stop your demonstration or to arrest you. I'm here to offer an alternative."

This caught Price's attention. His eyes narrowed slightly. "What alternative could compare to complete vindication?"

"Legacy," Hart said. "Real, lasting impact. Winters' implementation proves your theory works. Submit it properly, both of you. Revolutionise digital security by strengthening it, not by demonstrating its weaknesses."

Their eyes met across the observatory's dim interior. Something passed between them for a moment—a spark of mutual recognition, an acknowledgement of the thin line separating their divergent paths. Two minds capable of seeing patterns others missed, who had chosen different ways to employ that gift.

Price's hand moved toward the keyboard, hesitating just above the keys. For a heartbeat, Hart thought he might have reached him— might have found the one argument that could penetrate the armour of bitterness and obsession.

Then Price smiled, the expression never reaching his eyes. "An elegant attempt, Detective. Almost worthy." His fingers descended on the keyboard, executing a command. "But the demonstration has already begun."

Across the city, the Clock Tower's face illuminated, its hands freezing at their current position. Security systems began to flicker on the screens surrounding them, access protocols disengaging one after another.

"Now we'll see who history remembers," Price said softly. "The visionary or the footnote."

Hart's hand went to his phone to alert Clara, mobilise the technical response team, and do something to counteract what Price had set in motion. But as he watched the systemised chaos unfold on the screens, he realised that this was merely the opening move in a longer game. Price had orchestrated not just this moment but

what would follow—the response, the investigation, the consequences.

And somewhere in that carefully plotted sequence lay the opportunity to save Winters and stop whatever endgame Price was truly
planning. Because of this demonstration, Hart was suddenly sure that
it was just another puzzle piece—a distraction from something larger,
something still hidden.

"I will find him," Hart said, the words both promising and challenging. "Whatever you've done with Winters, wherever you've taken
him."

Price's smile deepened, satisfaction evident in every line of his
face. "I would expect nothing less, Detective. The game, after all, is
only interesting when played by worthy opponents." He gestured
toward the door. "You should hurry. The clock is ticking."

As Hart turned to leave, to rejoin the official response now scram-
bling to contain Price's digital infiltration, he felt the weight of the
challenge settling around him like a familiar coat. Whatever came
next would require more than police procedure or standard investigation. It would demand the full measure of his intellect, intuition, and
understanding of the complex, brilliant mind that had set these
events in motion.

Jonathan Price had resurfaced to prove a point about knowledge
and power—but in doing so, he had initiated a contest that extended
beyond algorithms and security systems to the very nature of truth
and vindication. A contest that had only just begun.

The real puzzle still awaited a solution. And time, as Price had so
pointedly observed, was running out.

4

THE ECCENTRIC ORACLE

Hart descended the observatory hill with measured steps, each footfall deliberate against the soft earth. Behind him, Price's digital assault radiated outward across the city's networks, invisible but catastrophic—a perfect crime for the modern age. No blood, no weapon, just the elegant dismantling of systems built on the illusion of security. In Hart's pocket, his phone vibrated with increasingly urgent messages. Still, his mind remained fixed on the puzzle that had revealed itself in the observatory. Price had shown his hand but not his whole game. The demonstration was spectacular but ultimately hollow—a diversion. The real threat, the real puzzle, lay elsewhere and with it, Professor Winters.

The night air had turned cold, stars emerging in the velvet darkness above. Hart paused at the base of the hill, looking back at the observatory's dome silhouetted against the sky. Price would be gone already—the confrontation had been calculated, every word measured, the timing precise. He wouldn't linger to witness the aftermath, not physically. That wasn't his style. He would watch remotely, analysing Hart's next moves, anticipating countermeasures.

Hart's phone vibrated again, more insistently. This time, he answered.

"Where the hell have you been?" Clara's voice was tight with controlled panic. "The entire city's going haywire. Traffic systems are failing, and emergency services communications are dropping in and out. The Clock Tower is just the beginning."

"I found Price," Hart said, already moving toward the university parking lot where he knew Clara would be waiting. "But he's already gone. The observatory was his control centre."

"The observatory?" Clara's confusion was audible. "We've got teams at the Clock Tower, at Winters' lab—"

"Exactly where he wanted them. The demonstration is automated now. Price doesn't need to be physically present." Hart quickened his pace. "Did you bring Dr. Shaw with you?"

"She's here. Working with Chang on trying to understand the algorithm's attack pattern."

"Good. I'm on my way to you."

The university grounds were eerily quiet, and the contrast between academic tranquillity and chaos unfolding across the city's infrastructure created a dissonance that pricked Hart's senses. In the distance, sirens wailed, their usual pattern disrupted, overlapping in uncoordinated urgency.

Hart found Clara, Chang, and Dr Shaw in the parking lot adjacent to the Technology Research Centre, their makeshift command post centred around Chang's SUV. Multiple laptops were arrayed on the vehicle's hood, screens flickering with data feeds and system alerts. Clara paced nearby, her phone pressed to her ear, voice low and intense as she coordinated with tactical teams. Shaw and Chang bent over the computers, their faces illuminated by the cold blue light of the screens.

"Hart." Clara ended her call and moved toward him. "Please tell me you have something we can use."

"Price confirmed what we suspected. Winters' algorithm has been modified to bypass security protocols rather than reinforce them." Hart joined Shaw and Chang at the computers. "What are we seeing?"

Chang gestured at one of the screens. "It's moving through the city's systems like nothing I've seen. It's adaptive and learning. Each security measure it encounters becomes part of its evolution."

Shaw nodded, her earlier academic fascination now tempered with grave concern. "The pattern suggests it's not just randomly attacking systems. There's a sequence, a deliberate progression."

Hart studied the data scrolling across the screens. Systems were failing not in order of vulnerability or importance but in what appeared to be a predetermined sequence: traffic control, then emergency services communication, followed by hospital security, banking systems, and water treatment controls—each falling precisely four minutes after the previous.

"It's a countdown," Hart said, the realisation crystallising. "Not random at all. Each system failure is a tick of the clock."

"Counting down to what?" Clara asked, rejoining them.

Hart's eyes moved to the distant Clock Tower, now visible above the city skyline, its illuminated face frozen when Price activated his program. "Not to midnight. That was misdirection. It's counting down to something specific." He pointed to the sequence of failures on the screen. "How many systems have been compromised so far?"

Chang consulted his data. "Seven major networks, twenty-three subsystems."

"And the pattern predicts how many totals?"

Shaw's fingers moved across the keyboard, calculating. "At this rate, forty-two systems before the sequence completes."

Hart felt a cold recognition settle in his chest. "Six, twenty-three, eight, forty-two... It's the numerical sequence from Price's first puzzle. The one we found at the abandoned library."

Clara's expression sharpened. "The numbers that led us to the pyramid clue?"

"Yes." Hart pulled out his notebook, flipping to his copy of the original sequence: **6-23-8-42-15-9.** "We've seen the first four numbers in the system failures. That means two more major networks will fall —fifteen and nine—before the sequence completes."

"What happens when it completes?" Chang asked, voicing the question hanging in the air.

Hart's mind raced ahead, assembling the puzzle pieces coherently. "The sequence was a countdown, but also an address. Each number corresponds to a letter in the alphabet. **F-W-H-P-O-I.**"

Shaw's eyes widened in recognition. "FWHPOI... The Frederick W. Harvey Physics and Optical Institute!"

"Another university building," Clara said. "Is that where Price is holding Winters?"

Hart shook his head. "Not Price's style to be so direct. But it's another clue, another step in his game." He turned to Chang. "What's the status of the Institute's security systems? Have they been compromised yet?"

Chang's fingers flew across the keyboard. "Not yet. It's not connected to the main university network—they run their isolated system due to the sensitive nature of their research."

"Which makes it the perfect place to hide something you don't want found when everything else is falling apart," Hart said. "Not Winters himself, but something related to him. Something Price needs us to find."

Shaw was already gathering her things. "The Institute specialises in quantum computing and advanced optics—fields directly related to Winters' encryption work."

Hart nodded, the pattern becoming clearer. "Price isn't just demonstrating the vulnerability of current security systems. He's leading us on a journey through the evolution of encryption itself. From ancient methods at the old library to modern digital security at the Research Centre—"

"To quantum cryptography at the Physics Institute," Shaw finished. "The past, present, and future of secure communication."

Clara was already on her phone, redirecting resources. "I'll have a team meet us there."

"No," Hart said sharply. "That's what Price expects—the official response, tactical teams, standard procedure. He's watching, waiting for us to follow the playbook." He gestured toward the chaos displayed on Chang's screens. "This entire demonstration is designed to fragment our attention, to force us to respond to crises across the city while he executes his real plan."

"Which is what, exactly?" Clara challenged.

Hart closed his eyes briefly, allowing the disparate elements to align in his mind. The puzzles, the symbolic locations, and the meticulous timing formed a pattern that spoke to Price's ultimate objective.

"Control," he said finally. "Not destruction. Price doesn't want to tear down security systems permanently. He wants to prove he can control them—access them at will. This demonstration isn't the end goal; it's a proof of concept."

He opened his eyes, his certainty solidifying. "Price wants to sell Winters' algorithm—or his modification. The countdown is leading to a demonstration for potential buyers."

"A black market auction," Clara surmised. "For a skeleton key to the world's digital infrastructure."

"Exactly. And the Physics Institute is where he's stored the complete version of the algorithm—the true prize." Hart was already moving toward his car. "We need to get there before the sequence completes."

Shaw hurried after him. "The algorithm in its complete form would be unstoppable—a digital master key."

Clara hesitated. "The city's systems are still failing. People could die if emergency services remain compromised."

Hart paused, understanding her dilemma. "Price won't let it go that far. This is theatre, not terrorism. The systems will restore once he's made his point—but only if we play along, follow his breadcrumbs to the Institute."

Clara's jaw tightened with frustration. "You're gambling with people's lives based on your assessment of a man who kidnapped a professor and paralysed a city."

"I'm gambling on knowing how Price thinks," Hart countered. "On understanding what this is really about for him. Vindication, not destruction."

A moment of tension stretched between them, years of partnership and trust balanced against the weight of the current crisis. Finally, Clara nodded.

"Chang, coordinate with technical services to implement manual overrides for critical systems. Focus on emergency services first." She turned to Hart. "You and Shaw head to the Institute. I'll join you once I've established contingencies here."

Hart knew this was as close to a compromise as he would get. "Understood. But move quickly. The countdown doesn't stop for contingencies."

As Hart and Shaw drove toward the Physics Institute, the city around them showed signs of Price's digital assault. Traffic lights flashed chaotic patterns, digital billboards displayed fragmented code instead of advertisements, and in one surreal moment, the street-lights along an entire avenue shut down perfectly, creating a wave of darkness rippled ahead of their car.

"It's beautiful, in a terrible way," Shaw observed quietly. "The precision of it. The math behind the chaos."

Hart's hands tightened on the steering wheel. "Price always had an aesthetic sense about his work. Even his academic papers were mathematically elegant."

"I remember," Shaw said. "I studied under him for a year before..." She trailed off, then continued with reluctant admiration. "He could see patterns that no one else could—connections between seemingly unrelated systems. It made him brilliant. And dangerous."

Hart glanced at her. "You were the first to question his research methods."

She nodded, her expression conflicted. "I admired him tremendously. However, there were inconsistencies in his data that couldn't be explained away. He dismissed them as irrelevant details when I brought them to his attention. When I persisted..."

"He accused you of intellectual inadequacy," Hart finished. "I remember the faculty hearing."

"He believed himself above conventional validation," Shaw said. "Above peer review, above accountability. The irony is that parts of his unified theory were genuinely groundbreaking. If he had been willing to subject his work to proper scrutiny, to collaborate rather than dictate..."

Hart understood the complexity of her feelings toward her former mentor. Price inspired both admiration and wariness—the tragedy of brilliance corrupted by hubris.

The Frederick W. Harvey Physics and Optical Institute loomed ahead, a modern concrete and glass structure situated on the eastern edge of the campus. Unlike the Research Centre's transparent façade, the Institute presented a more closed, secure appearance, befitting a facility that housed some of the university's most sensitive research.

As they approached, Hart noticed something unusual. The building's security lights were functioning normally despite the chaos affecting systems across the rest of the city. The electronic access panel at the main entrance glowed steadily, untouched by Price's digital assault.

"He's preserved this place," Hart observed. "Keeping it isolated from the attack."

Shaw approached the access panel cautiously. "Standard university credentials won't work if this system is isolated."

Hart studied the panel. Unlike at the Winters' lab, this one showed no apparent modifications, hidden symbols, or clues. It requested a simple numeric code.

"The final numbers in the sequence," Hart said. "Fifteen and nine."

Shaw entered the digits. The panel remained red, and access was denied.

Hart frowned. It couldn't be that simple, not for Price. The puzzle had to be more intricate and more personal.

"Wait," he said, a memory surfacing. "Not the numbers themselves. What they represent in the alphabet."

Shaw understood immediately. "O and I. Fifteen is 'O', nine is 'I'."

But when she entered these letters, the panel still refused access.

Hart stood back, considering the problem from different angles. Price designed his puzzles with multiple layers, each requiring insight into the pattern and its meaning. The sequence had led them here, but the final access required something more—something specific to this location and its significance.

"Optics," Hart said suddenly. "The Institute specialises in optics. Light."

Shaw's eyes widened with understanding. "Binary. The on-off pattern of digital information—the foundation of all computer systems."

She returned to the panel and entered the binary equivalents of the final sequence numbers: 1111 for fifteen and 1001 for nine.

The panel flashed green, and the door unlocked with a soft click.

The Institute was eerily quiet, emergency lighting casting long shadows down empty corridors. Most staff would have evacuated when the city's systems began failing, leaving the building in its secured state.

Hart and Shaw moved cautiously through the entrance hall toward the main research areas. Unlike the chaos visible throughout the city, everything here seemed precisely as it should be—untouched, waiting.

"Where would Price hide the complete algorithm?" Shaw whispered her voice unnaturally loud in the stillness.

Hart considered the building's layout, trying to think as Price would. "Somewhere symbolic. Somewhere that connects to the theme he's been developing."

They passed laboratories filled with complex optical equipment, quantum computing components, and experimental apparatus whose purposes Hart could only guess at. Each room stood dark and silent, offering no clues.

Then Hart noticed a door at the end of the corridor, marked with a simple plaque: "Advanced Encryption Laboratory." Unlike the other doors they had passed, this one stood slightly ajar, a thin line of light spilling from within.

Hart felt the familiar tension of insight building in his chest as they approached. This was it—the final destination in Price's elaborate game. Whatever waited inside would complete the puzzle, revealing Price's ultimate objective and, hopefully, Winters' location.

The room beyond contained a single computer terminal, its screen active and displaying a familiar sequence of symbols—the same pattern from the original note that had started their journey. But now the symbols were animated, pulsing with light that shifted between different spectrums, creating a hypnotic visual rhythm.

On the desk beside the terminal sat a small device about the size of a paperback book—sleek and metallic, with a single USB port and what appeared to be a miniaturised version of Winters' prototype embedded in its casing.

"The complete algorithm," Shaw breathed. "In portable form."

Hart approached carefully, scanning the room for traps or surveillance. "Too easy," he murmured. "Price wouldn't leave it unprotected."

The computer screen changed as they drew closer, the symbols rearranging themselves into a message:

Congratulations, Detective Hart. You've reached the end of the sequence ahead of schedule—a commendable performance. The device before you contains the complete implementation of Winters' algorithm, modified to serve as a shield or sword, depending on the user's intent. In thirty seconds, the transmission will begin to select parties who have expressed interest in acquiring this technology. Before you attempt to stop this transmission, consider one final puzzle: Winters remains secured in a location where time has already stopped. The answer lies in the meaning, not the sequence.

Hart's mind raced, the seconds counting down on the screen. The meaning, not the sequence. What was Price telling him?

"Time has already stopped," Hart repeated, then looked at Shaw. "The Clock Tower. That's where Price keeps Winters—inside the Clock Tower itself."

Shaw nodded urgently. "The demonstration was never separate from the hostage situation. They're the same."

Hart reached for the device but hesitated as the screen displayed a final warning:

Remove the device before transmission completes, and all affected systems will remain compromised. Allow the transmission to finish, and they will automatically restore. Choose wisely, Detective.

Twenty seconds remained on the countdown. Hart's hand hovered over the device, the decision weighing on him with physical pressure. Stop the transmission and save the algorithm from falling into dangerous hands, but leave the city's systems crippled. Or allow Price's demonstration to complete, restoring the systems but potentially releasing a digital skeleton key to whoever waited on the receiving end of the transmission.

In that moment of hesitation, Hart recognised the true elegance of Price's game. It was never about the technology itself but about forcing this exact choice—compelling Hart to decide between immediate safety and long-term security, between the pragmatic and the principled.

Price had constructed a puzzle and a moral dilemma customised specifically for Hart. A test of character disguised as a test of intellect.

Fifteen seconds.

Hart made his decision. He didn't touch the device. Instead, he pulled out his phone and called Clara.

"The Clock Tower," he said without preamble. "Winters is inside the Clock Tower itself. Get there now."

As the final seconds ticked away on the screen, Hart watched the transmission complete—a digital whisper carrying dangerous knowledge to unknown recipients. The moment it finished, the symbols on the screen rearranged themselves one last time, forming a simple message:

Systems restoring. Your priorities reveal more than you know. Winters await your arrival, Detective. Our game continues.

Hart's phone buzzed with incoming alerts—systems across the city were returning online, and emergency services resumed regular operations. Price had kept his word.

After completing its transmission, he picked up the device, which was now inert. The city had been saved, but at what cost? The knowledge it contained was now out there, beyond recall, a digital pandemic waiting to spread.

"We need to get to the Clock Tower," Hart told Shaw, pocketing the device. "And we need to understand exactly what Price has unleashed—because this game, as he says, is far from over."

As they hurried from the Institute, Hart felt the device's weight in his pocket—the physical manifestation of Price's vindication and compromise. He had chosen the immediate safety of the city over the abstract threat of the algorithm's release, exactly as Price had anticipated he would.

As they raced toward the Clock Tower and Winters, Hart realised that the real puzzle wasn't solving Price's clues but understanding what Price had learned about him in the process. Each solution revealed not just Hart's intellectual capacity but also his moral architecture, priorities, and limits.

And in a contest between minds, such knowledge was the most dangerous weapon.

5

DIGITAL BREADCRUMBS

The precinct's digital forensics lab existed in a permanent twilight state, illuminated not by windows or overhead fixtures but by the cold glow of screens that lined the walls like digital sentinels. Hart paused at the threshold, allowing his eyes to adjust to the dimness. Three days had passed since the Clock Tower, since they'd found Winters bound but alive in the maintenance room behind the massive gears, and three days since Price had vanished once again, leaving nothing but encrypted data and unanswered questions in his wake.

"Are you sure you're ready for this?" Clara asked beside him, her voice low enough that only he could hear. Although her concern was professional, it carried undertones of something more personal, more protective.

Hart didn't answer immediately, his attention caught by the semi-circle of monitors at the far end of the room, where Officer Leo Chang sat surrounded by technology like a conductor before an electronic orchestra. The hum of cooling fans provided constant white noise punctuated by the soft percussion of keystrokes. Cables snaked across the floor in organised chaos, bundled and labelled with the same meticulous attention that characterised everything Leo touched.

"Price is already planning his next move," Hart finally said. "We can't afford to wait."

Leo spotted them and sprang from his chair with the boundless energy of youth, his face brightening with undisguised enthusiasm. His glasses caught the light from the nearest screen, momentarily obscuring his eyes behind twin rectangles of code.

"Detective Hart! Detective Morgan! You're going to want to see this." He animatedly gestured them toward his workstation. "I've been running analysis on the device you recovered from the Physics Institute, cross-referencing the code patterns with known intrusions across the city's network."

Hart moved toward the screens, drawn by the promise of new insights, new patterns to decipher. The debriefing after Winters' rescue had been exhaustive, the professor himself still too traumatised to provide coherent details about his captivity. Price had left them breadcrumbs but no feast—just enough to suggest the case was far from closed.

"Professor Winters is still under police protection?" Leo asked, sliding back into his chair and typing commands with practised efficiency.

"Hospital security, round-the-clock," Clara confirmed, positioning herself to observe both the screens and Hart's reactions to them. "He's physically unharmed but disoriented. The doctors say it might be days before we get a coherent statement."

Leo nodded, then, with a theatrical flourish, tapped a final key. The monitors came alive with data visualisations—intrusion maps, timestamp logs, and security camera stills from five locations. "I found something you're not going to believe. Our mystery hacker—presumably Price—hasn't just been toying with university systems. He's been systematically infiltrating security networks at five historical landmarks around the city."

The screens displayed familiar locations: the Old Courthouse with its neoclassical columns, the Maritime Museum perched on the

Harbour's edge, the Central Library's imposing Gothic tower, the First National Bank building downtown, and the Pioneer Tower overlooking the river.

"At first glance, these intrusions look like standard security probes —the kind of automated scanning that happens thousands of times daily to any public network." Leo's fingers danced across the keyboard, highlighting sections of code. "But when you isolate the pattern signatures and overlay the timestamps..."

The data was rearranged on screen, and timestamps aligned in a sequence that quickened Hart's pulse. He pulled his worn notebook from his pocket, flipping through pages until he found handwritten notes from the Winters case.

"These dates," Hart said, finger tracing first his notebook, then the screen. "They match the sequence we found at the Blackwood Library. The original puzzle."

"Exactly!" Leo's voice rose with excitement. "Digital breadcrumbs like Hansel and Gretel, if Gretel were a criminal mastermind with a PhD in advanced cryptography. He's not just breaking in—he's signing his work."

Hart leaned closer, his attention wholly captured by the patterns emerging from what had appeared to be disparate data points. His mind began constructing connections, drawing invisible lines between intrusion points, matching methodologies to familiar signatures.

"The complexity escalates with each intrusion," Leo continued, comparing side-by-side. "First landmark, basic security override. By the fifth, he's implementing some version of the same algorithm he used to cripple the city's systems. It's like watching someone practice scales before playing a symphony."

Hart began to pace behind Leo's chair, energy building inside him like static electricity before a storm. "He's refining the method, testing its applications against different security architectures. The landmarks aren't random—they're selected for their varying security protocols."

"But that's not the wildest part," Leo said, unable to contain his excitement. "After each intrusion, nothing was stolen, nothing was damaged. The only consistent action was accessing the security cameras. He wanted to see something in each location."

Hart stopped pacing, a realisation dawning. "Not see. Be seen." He returned to the monitors, studying the camera angles. "These cameras overlook public spaces, areas with high visibility."

"Performance venues," Clara suggested, her voice cutting through Hart's accelerating thoughts.

"Yes, exactly." Hart's words tumbled out faster now, riding the crest of insight. "Price doesn't just want to prove his intellectual superiority —he wants an audience. Each landmark represents a different demographic and a different sector of society: legal, cultural, financial, educational, and historical. He's mapping the city's attention network."

Clara shifted her weight, arms crossing over her chest as she studied the displays with professional scepticism. "Before we go too far down this rabbit hole, I need to ask: how exactly did you access these security systems, Officer Chang? Do we have warrants for each of these locations?"

Leo's enthusiasm dimmed slightly. "Well, technically speaking, I didn't access their systems directly. I analysed suspicious traffic patterns in the city's network and identified matching signatures that happened to... intersect with these locations."

"So, no warrants," Clara stated flatly.

"I used publicly available data and some creative packet analysis," Leo offered, his voice taking on a defensive note. "Nothing that wouldn't stand up in court. Probably."

Hart continued his circuit of the room, barely registering their exchange. His notebook was open again, and his pencil moved across the page in swift, precise strokes as he copied timestamps, coordinates, and access patterns. The connections were undeniable, and the signature unmistakable.

"Price is building something," he murmured, almost to himself. "Each intrusion is a component of a larger construct."

"Alan," Clara said, using his first name to pull him back from the edge of obsession. "We need to consider the legal framework here. If we're building a case against Price, everything must be by the book. Admissible."

Hart looked up, his expression reflecting the internal battle between procedural constraints and the pure intellectual challenge of the puzzle. "Price doesn't operate within frameworks, legal or otherwise. He's already three moves ahead of conventional investigation methods."

Clara's mouth tightened. "That doesn't mean we abandon them. We need proper authorisation to pursue this angle."

Hart felt the familiar tension between them—Clara anchoring him to the procedure while his mind raced ahead, seeking patterns, solutions, and the elegant architecture of Price's design. They had worked this way for years, her pragmatism balancing his abstract leaps. However, in such cases, the friction between their approaches became more pronounced.

"The timestamps align perfectly with a modified Fibonacci sequence," he said, redirecting the conversation to the evidence. "The same mathematical principle Price used in his original puzzle. He's not hiding his identity—he wants us to know it's him. To recognise his signature."

Leo glanced between them, sensing the tension but pushing forward with his presentation. "There's more. Each intrusion left behind a small encrypted data packet bearing the same header structure. I'm still working on breaking the encryption, but they're messages. Or pieces of a larger message."

Hart nodded, his excitement mounting again. "Fragments of a whole. Price is assembling something, piece by piece, landmark by landmark." He tapped the screen, showing the Pioneer Tower—the final location in the sequence. "And whatever he's building, this is where it culminates."

Clara uncrossed her arms, a concession to Hart's reasoning if not his methods. "Fine. I'll start the warrant applications for these locations. But," she added, fixing Hart with a pointed look, "we proceed officially. No shortcuts, no unauthorised access."

Hart met her gaze, the familiar struggle between them—his relentless pursuit of intellectual truth against her unwavering commitment to legal process. Neither was entirely right nor wrong, but both were essential to the strange alchemy of their partnership.

"Price isn't finished," he said quietly. "This sequence is building to something bigger than either approach can contain."

In the artificial twilight of the forensics lab, surrounded by the soft electronic hum of machines cataloguing human behaviour, the three of them stood before the glowing screens—each seeing different aspects of the same emerging threat, each preparing for a confrontation that would test not just their methods but the very foundations of security in a digital age.

Leo's fingertips tapped across the keyboard with a pianist's light, precise movements, each keystroke revealing deeper layers of Price's digital infiltration. The main display shifted to show network architecture diagrams—skeletal maps of each landmark's security systems with glowing red nodes highlighting points of compromise. Hart's reflection ghosted across the screens as he leaned forward, his eyes narrowing at what the evidence suggested: not random breaches but surgical incisions, each cut made with the calculated precision of a master locksmith testing his skills against increasingly complex mechanisms.

"Here's where it gets exciting," Leo said, his voice dropping as though sharing a secret. "He didn't just breach their systems—he created persistent backdoor access at each location." His cursor circled a code cluster resembling a digital tumour grafted onto the otherwise healthy system architecture. "See these pathways? They're disguised as routine security updates but hidden tunnels leading directly to the security camera networks."

Clara stepped closer, her posture stiffening. "He can access their surveillance systems at will?"

"Not just access," Leo clarified, unable to completely mask his technical admiration. "He can control them. Pan, tilt, zoom—even loop pre-recorded footage to hide his activities. Classic Hollywood heist stuff, except he's not stealing diamonds or artwork."

Hart began pacing behind Leo's chair, his footsteps marking a metronomic path across the polished concrete floor. His lips moved in silent calculation, occasionally giving voice to fragmented thoughts that seemed disconnected until you understood the pattern connecting them.

"Camera positioning... sightlines... public gathering spaces..." He paused, pulling his notebook from his pocket and scribbling a series of symbols that bore little resemblance to conventional language. The pencil moved with frantic energy as though struggling to keep pace with the connections forming in his mind.

Leo continued his digital archaeology, bringing up security logs that tracked system access timestamps. "I compared these incursions with the city's event calendar. Each breach occurred exactly forty-eight hours before a major public gathering at that location. Old Courthouse: law school graduation. Maritime Museum: international trade conference. Central Library: mayoral debate. First National: Economic Summit. Pioneer Tower: upcoming tech innovation showcase."

Hart's pacing intensified, his path widening to encompass the entire lab. "He's not just accessing landmarks—he's targeting specific events. Gatherings of influence: legal, commercial, political, financial, technological." He stopped abruptly, turning to face them. "Price is assembling an audience. A specific audience."

Clara stood with arms crossed, her stance wide and planted like someone bracing against a strong wind. Her fingers drummed a controlled rhythm against her bicep—a tell that Hart recognised as her processing conflicting priorities.

"Before we go further," she said, her voice carrying the measured tone of someone choosing words with deliberate care, "we need to acknowledge the legal constraints here. These backdoors Leo found —we discovered them through an analysis that lacked proper authorisation. Any evidence gathered through these channels would be inadmissible in court."

She directed her gaze to Leo. "We need warrants, proper chain of custody documentation, and authorisation from each landmark's security team to access their systems directly."

Leo's boyish enthusiasm dimmed under her scrutiny. He adjusted his glasses, a nervous gesture that pushed them higher on his nose, only for them to slide back seconds later. "That could take days. Maybe weeks, given the sensitivity of these locations and their private security protocols."

"Then we start the process now," Clara replied firmly. We need to do this according to the book."

Hart halted his circuit around the room, his expression darkening. "The book doesn't account for someone this methodical. Price operates outside conventional parameters—he designed this puzzle knowing the procedural constraints we'd face."

His fingers tapped his notebook, where symbols and numbers formed connections that only he could fully interpret. "By the time we secure proper authorisations, he'll have progressed to the next phase. Whatever he's building toward, it's accelerating. The intervals between intrusions are decreasing."

Clara's stance shifted, professional concern overlaying personal worry. "Alan, I understand the intellectual appeal of this chase, but we can't abandon procedure just because the suspect is exceptionally intelligent. That's precisely when procedure matters most."

"It's not about intellectual appeal," Hart countered, though the intensity in his eyes suggested otherwise. "It's about preventing whatever comes next. The Price isn't done. The algorithm, landmarks, and events are building toward something."

He approached Leo's workstation, leaning over the young officer's shoulder to examine the network diagrams. "Can you access these backdoors directly? See what Price sees through these security cameras?"

Leo glanced uncertainly toward Clara, caught between conflicting authorities. "Technically, yes. The backdoors are still active. But legally..." He trailed off, looking deeply uncomfortable.

"Not," Clara interjected, her voice sharpening. "That would constitute unauthorised access to private security systems. We'd be committing the same crime we're investigating."

Hart straightened, his expression hardening into something that resembled Price's focused intensity more than either of them would care to acknowledge. "We're not dealing with a conventional criminal mind. Price has elevated this beyond standard categorisation. He's created an intellectual construct that demands an unconventional response."

"That sounds dangerously close to saying the end justifies the means," Clara observed, her words clipped and precise.

"Sometimes it does," Hart replied quietly.

The tension between them solidified, becoming almost a physical presence in the room. Leo hunched his shoulders slightly, fingers hovering indecisively over his keyboard as though unwilling to align himself with either approach.

"Um, I could potentially compile a report analysing the backdoor mechanisms without actually utilising them," he offered tentatively. "It wouldn't give us live access, but it might help us understand his methodology better."

Neither detective responded immediately, their attention locked in a silent confrontation transcending the immediate technical question. Years of partnership had given them an intimate understanding of each other's principles and breaking points. This wasn't their first philosophical impasse, but the stakes felt unusually personal.

"Alan," Clara finally said, her voice softening slightly, "you're getting pulled into his game again. That's exactly what he wants."

Hart's shoulders tensed. "Of course it is. Price designed this entire scenario as a challenge. But understanding his game is how we get ahead of it."

"Not by compromising our ethics. Not by becoming him." Clara's eyes reflected genuine concern now, professional boundaries momentarily thinning. "I've seen how these cases affect you. The way you disappear into the puzzle until everything else becomes secondary."

Hart turned away, returning to the network diagrams displayed across the screens. His silence was neither agreement nor rejection— merely acknowledging a truth he couldn't comfortably refute.

Leo cleared his throat, clearly searching for neutral ground. "Maybe there's a compromise? I could explain the situation to the security directors at each landmark. With their cooperation, we might get expedited access—properly documented but faster than formal warrants."

Clara nodded, recognising the olive branch. "That's a reasonable approach. Make those calls, focus on the urgency without revealing specific details about the backdoors."

Hart remained silent, studying the intrusion patterns with an intensity that suggested he was already several mental steps beyond the immediate procedural question. His fingers traced invisible connections between the glowing red nodes on the screen, following pathways that existed more in his mind than in the digital architecture displayed before him.

"He's showing off," Hart murmured, almost to himself. "Each intrusion is more sophisticated than the last. But why these landmarks? Why these specific events?" His hand moved to his coat pocket, unconsciously checking for the device they'd recovered from the Physics Institute. It was now secured in evidence but never far from his thoughts.

Clara watched him with the careful attention of someone monitoring a patient's vital signs, noting the slight tremor in his hands, the shadows beneath his eyes that spoke of sleep traded for obsessive analysis. Her posture remained rigid, and professional composure was maintained through discipline rather than natural inclination.

"Leo, continue your analysis, but stay within legal parameters," she instructed, her tone brooking no argument. "I'll expedite the warrant requests and make some calls to the district attorney's office. We'll find a way to accelerate the process without compromising the case."

Leo nodded, relieved to have a clear direction. "Yes, Detective Morgan. I'll compile everything we have so far into a formal briefing document."

Hart turned back toward them, his expression revealing that his mind had been travelling a separate track entirely. "Price isn't just testing security systems—he's testing responses. Each intrusion gauges technical vulnerabilities and human reactions: how quickly breaches are detected, what countermeasures are deployed, who becomes involved in the response."

He moved to stand directly beside Clara, close enough that she could see the constellation of notes scattered across the open page of his notebook. "He's mapping the city's response architecture—not just its digital infrastructure but human decision chains."

Clara studied the notebook, her professional frustration temporarily overshadowed by recognition of Hart's insight. Despite her concerns about his methods, she couldn't deny the value of his perspective—the ability to see patterns where others saw only chaos.

"If that's true," she said carefully, "we must ensure our response doesn't follow predictable patterns. We need to be unconventional— but within the framework of the law."

Hart's mouth tightened, a subtle acknowledgement of the compromise she was offering. It was not agreement, but not outright rejection either. In their long partnership, this was often as close to alignment as they achieved when principle collided with pragmatism.

Leo looked between them, sensing the détente. His fingers resumed their dance across the keyboard, pulling up additional data while carefully avoiding the temptation of the backdoor access points that pulsed like digital sirens on his screen.

"I'll have this analysis complete within the hour," he promised, youth and enthusiasm reasserting themselves. "And I'll immediately start those calls to the security directors."

In the artificial twilight of the lab, Hart returned to his restless circuit, the wheels of his mind turning with the strange, beautiful, dangerous architecture of Price's design. Clara watched him, concern evident in the slight furrow of her brow. At the same time, Leo continued his digital excavation—three approaches to the same looming threat, separated by methodology but united in purpose.

The screens continued to glow, reflecting their faces at them like modern oracles, hinting at patterns and connections that remained just beyond the edge of complete comprehension. Somewhere in that digital labyrinth lay Price's true intention—and the clock was ticking toward its revelation.

Leo's monitor emitted a soft ping that almost disappeared beneath the ambient hum of the lab's equipment. He might have missed it entirely had he not watched that particular data stream with such concentrated focus. His expression shifted from studious attention to puzzlement to something sharper—a quickening of interest that straightened his posture and brought his fingers to hover, momentarily suspended above the keyboard. Whatever he had expected to find in the labyrinthine data, this wasn't it.

"That's weird," he murmured, more to himself than to the detectives still caught in their tense orbit around the lab. His fingers descended in a flurry of keystrokes, pulling up command windows populated with scrolling text.

Hart paused his restless pacing, attention drawn by the change in Leo's tone. "What?"

"One of the backdoors just activated." Leo leaned closer to his screen, the blue light accentuating the angles of his face. "Not accessing historical footage—it's transmitting live data. Right now."

Clara moved toward the workstation, and professional disagreements were temporarily set aside. "Which location?"

"None of the five we've been monitoring." Leo's fingers flew across the keyboard with increasing urgency. "It's using the same signature and methodology but coming from somewhere new. A sixth location."

Hart was beside them instantly, his expression sharpening with predatory focus. "Can you trace it?"

"Working on it." Leo pulled up network mapping tools, digital tendrils extending through the city's tangled communications infrastructure. Windows multiplied across his screens, each displaying fragments of the data path. "The signal's bouncing through multiple proxy servers—classic misdirection technique."

He bit his lower lip in concentration, a habit from his younger days of solving puzzles for pleasure rather than survival. Code reflected in his glasses as he navigated the digital maze, following breadcrumbs that materialised and vanished with maddening elusiveness.

"Got a physical location," he announced after thirty seconds of intense, silent work. "It's an old building in the warehouse district— formerly some kind of club or bar, according to city records." He pulled up a property database entry. "The Whispering Door. Closed in 2018, currently listed as awaiting redevelopment."

"The speakeasy," Hart said immediately, a connection forming. "It was a Prohibition-era establishment, hidden behind a false store-front. Historical significance and architectural uniqueness fit Price's other targets."

Leo nodded, still tracking the signal. "Whatever's happening there, it's generating significant data traffic. This isn't passive surveillance; it's an active transmission."

His fingers executed a precise sequence of commands, attempting to isolate and capture the stream's contents. For a moment, nothing happened—then his primary monitor flickered, the display sput-tering like a candle in a draft before stabilising on a new image.

"Guys," Leo said, his voice dropping to an almost reverent whis-per, "this is happening right now."

The screen displayed a high-definition video feed of interior space—brick walls stained with decades of smoke and secrets, an ornate wooden bar clouded with dust, and brass fixtures tarnished to a dull gleam. Art Deco chandeliers hung precariously from a pressed-tin ceiling, casting skeletal shadows across what had once been a dance floor. At the centre of this decaying splendour sat a solitary chair, and bound to it with methodical precision was a figure whose head lolled forward in either exhaustion or unconsciousness.

Beside the chair, mounted on an antique bar cart, a digital display presented stark red numerals counting backwards: **27:46... 27:45... 27:44...**

The lab fell silent except for the soft, rhythmic beep that accompanied each decrement of the timer. The mechanical hum of cooling fans and the distant sounds of the precinct faded into irrelevance, leaving only the pulse of the countdown and their collective held breath.

Hart froze mid-gesture, his body becoming as still as the abandoned tables and chairs that surrounded the hostage on screen. His eyes narrowed, not in thought but in the physical manifestation of mental focus so intense it bordered on trancelike.

Clara's professional composure cracked momentarily, a sharp inhalation breaking her usual measured breathing. Her hand moved instinctively toward her service weapon, a reflexive response to a threat she couldn't physically confront.

Leo's earlier enthusiasm drained from his face, replaced by the sudden pallor of responsibility. His hands hovered above the keyboard, uncertain whether to continue excavating the signal or preserve what they'd already found.

"Can you get a clearer angle on the hostage's face?" Hart asked, his voice unnaturally flat, as though emotional inflexion required energy he couldn't spare.

Leo swallowed visibly before executing the command. The camera panned slightly, zooming toward the slumped figure. The image quality improved, revealing a man in his fifties, academic in appearance, with silver-streaked hair and wire-rimmed glasses askew on a face slack with unconsciousness.

"That's not Winters," Clara said, her trained eye cataloguing details for identification.

"Dr. Edmund Phelps," Hart supplied immediately. "Head of the

Mathematics Department. Price's former supervisor and the first to question his research methods."

The implications settled over them like a physical weight. Price wasn't randomly selecting targets—he was meticulously working through a list. Not landmarks, but people. Not demonstration, but retribution.

"We have twenty-seven minutes," Hart stated, already moving toward the door with the focused intensity of a bullet seeking its target.

Clara's training asserted itself through the shock, her voice finding its authoritative edge. "Leo, capture and secure this feed—full documentation, timestamp verification, everything we need for court. I want it streaming to my phone and to dispatch." She was already dialling as she spoke. "This is Detective Morgan. I need an immediate tactical response to 1437 Harbour Street, the old Whispering Door speakeasy. Confirmed hostage situation with countdown device visible. Requesting bomb squad, negotiator, and full perimeter control."

Leo's fingers blurred across the keyboard, executing her instructions while simultaneously pulling up building schematics for the speakeasy. "Sending floor plans to your phones now. The main entrance is on Harbour, but there's a service entrance on the alley side and a former smuggling tunnel in the basement that may or may not be collapsed."

Hart paused at the door, watching the hostage on the screen with an expression that combined analytical detachment with something darker, more personal. "Price doesn't expect us to find him there," he said.

"What do you mean?" Clara asked, already shrugging into her jacket, checking her weapon with practised efficiency.

"This is misdirection—another puzzle piece." Hart nodded toward the screen. "He wants us rushing to the speakeasy while he executes his actual plan elsewhere."

Clara's jaw tightened. "We don't have a choice. There's a man's life on that timer."

"I know." Hart's expression settled into grim determination. "And Price knows that, too. He's counting on our predictable response."

"Then we give him the predictable and the unpredictable," Clara decided, her tactical mind already formulating contingencies. "I'll lead the team to secure Phelps. You work with Leo to determine what Price's target might be."

For the first time in days, Hart nodded in complete agreement. Their methodological differences dissolved in the acid clarity of immediate threat. "The hostage situation could be Price's final move —or his opening gambit in something larger."

Leo continued his digital excavation, face illuminated by the glow of screens now filled with the speakeasy's interior from multiple angles. "I'm checking for additional transmission signals with the same signature. If this is a diversion, there might be other active feeds we haven't detected yet."

Clara was already at the door, her phone against her ear as she coordinated with tactical teams. "Approach with full stealth protocol. No sirens, no visible presence until we have eyes on all entrances. Assume sophisticated surveillance."

Hart collected his notebook, glancing at the countdown timer: 25:13... 25:12... The rhythmic diminishment of seconds seemed to fill the room with its soft, mechanical certainty. Each beep represented one less safety moment, one step closer to whatever Price had designed for them.

"I'll link my phone to the precinct system," Leo said, fingers still typing commands. "You'll have real-time updates on anything I find."

On every monitor in the lab, Dr. Edmund Phelps remained slumped in his chair, unaware of his role in Price's elaborate design. The timer continued its relentless descent, red numerals reflected in the glass surfaces of screens, windows, and eyeglasses—a digital heartbeat counting toward an unknown culmination.

The three of them moved with the coordinated efficiency of people who understood that their actions in the next twenty-five minutes would determine not just one man's survival but potentially the security of systems far beyond the abandoned speakeasy. Whatever game Price was playing had escalated from intellectual challenge to life and death—and the rules were still his to define.

As Hart followed Clara into the corridor, leaving Leo surrounded by his digital sentinel posts, he felt the weight of Price's intelligence pressing against him like a physical force. The man had calculated every response and anticipated every countermove. The question wasn't whether they could outthink him—it was whether they could disrupt his thinking enough to create an opening, a moment of uncertainty in his meticulously constructed design.

Twenty-five minutes to save a hostage. Twenty-five minutes to decipher Price's true intention. Twenty-five minutes to turn the game against its creator.

The countdown had begun.

6

SHADOWS OF THE CITY

Tunnel mouth gaped before them, a throat of crumbling brick and seeping moisture swallowing the beam of Hart's flashlight. He descended first, each step careful on the slick stone stairs, the worn leather of his notebook pressed against his chest as if it might shield him from whatever awaited below. Behind him, Clara's breathing came in measured intervals—the controlled respiration of someone accustomed to dangerous situations, someone who understood that fear acknowledged was fear controlled.

"Leo's coordinates led us here, but the transmission's origin could be anywhere in this network," Hart said, his voice immediately absorbed by the dense, damp air. "The city plans show these tunnels extending for miles beneath downtown."

Clara's flashlight joined his, cutting through the darkness like a surgical instrument. "And you're certain this is a separate lead from the speakeasy situation? Tactical is in position there, awaiting my command."

"Price wouldn't make it that straightforward," Hart replied, reaching the bottom of the stairs where the passage widened slightly. "The hostage situation is theatrical—designed to occupy our resources while he executes his actual plan elsewhere." He didn't add what both of them knew: that a man's life hung in the balance regardless of Price's larger schemes.

Above them, water dripped from ancient mortar, each drop marking the seconds of their borrowed time. The stone walls exhaled centuries of dampness, the air thick with mineral scents and the subtle rot of organic matter. Hart's flashlight illuminated patches of green-black moss clinging to the arched ceiling, thriving in this sunless world of perpetual twilight.

Hart withdrew his notebook, its pages slightly warped from the humidity, and compared the tunnel map Leo had transmitted to the passage stretching before them. The network resembled a spider's web—circular routes interconnecting at irregular intervals, and certain sections collapsed or sealed over the decades. According to Leo's analysis of the city's underground power grid fluctuations, the central chamber should lie approximately three hundred meters northeast.

"Price is deliberately leading us underground," Hart murmured, more to himself than to Clara. "Isolating us from communications, from backup. Creating an environment where his intellectual advantage is maximised."

Clara ran her hand along the tunnel wall, fingers testing the structural integrity with experienced precision. Small cascades of grit and powdered mortar followed her touch, gathering in miniature dunes at the base of the wall.

"Not exactly stable," she observed, wiping her dust-covered fingers on her jacket. "This section hasn't been maintained since the eighties, according to city records."

"That's why it's perfect," Hart replied, moving forward with measured steps. "Price appreciates symmetry, historical resonance. These tunnels were originally constructed as a transport network for goods between the harbour and inland markets, then repurposed during Prohibition for smuggling liquor." His voice took on the detached quality it often did when accessing his vast mental archive. "The precise engineering suggests German immigrant influence, probably around 1872."

Clara moved parallel to Hart, maintaining a careful distance between them. Their divided approach to the case was temporarily suspended in this claustrophobic environment where the partnership was survival.

"I understand your fascination with the historical context," she said, "but right now, I'm more concerned with whether these tunnels are about to collapse on our heads or if Price has left more immediate surprises for us."

Hart nodded, acknowledging the practical wisdom in her concern. His flashlight beam caught something embedded in the wall ahead—a circular outline of darker stone, incongruous against the uniform brick. He approached cautiously, Clara matching his pace on the opposite side of the passage.

"There," he said, directing his light. A rusted iron ring protruded from the wall, approximately chest height. Around its circumference, barely visible beneath a veneer of oxidation, intricate symbols had been etched into the metal.

Hart leaned closer, his breath fogging in the cool air as he examined the markings. The symbols formed a sequence he recognised immediately—a mathematical notation system used primarily in theoretical cryptography papers from the early 2000s. His papers. His notation.

"This is recent," he said, gripping the symbols. The iron was cold against his skin, but Hart felt a warmth in his chest, an uncomfortable heat that he recognised as anger mingled with reluctant admiration. "Price is using my academic work against me. This specific notation appeared in only one paper I published before leaving academia—a paper on the physical implementation of encryption methodologies."

Clara's light joined his, illuminating the ring from a different angle. "Can you decipher it?"

"It's not a code—it's a signature. A deliberate mockery." Hart's expression tightened, lines deepening around his mouth. "Price reminds me that he's read and understood my work more thoroughly than my colleagues. He's establishing intellectual dominance."

Clara didn't respond immediately, her attention shifting to the tunnel floor ahead. Her posture changed subtly—the almost imperceptible tensing of muscles Hart had learned to recognise as her sensing danger before consciously identifying it.

"Alan," she said quietly, using his first name—a rarity that instantly sharpened his focus. "Don't move forward."

He froze, following her gaze to the floor several paces ahead. At first, nothing seemed amiss—the same damp stone and scattered debris. Then he noticed what Clara had already seen: a subtle difference in the mortar lines, a slightly darker shade of stone forming a rectangular outline.

Clara reached out, her hand closing firmly around Hart's arm, pulling him back a half-step. The motion was protective but not patronising—the natural action of partners accustomed to safeguarding each other.

"Watch," she said, picking up a broken chunk of brick from the tunnel floor. She tossed it forward, the projectile landing precisely in the centre of the discoloured rectangle.

For a breath, nothing happened. Then, with a sound like dry bones breaking, the stone section collapsed inward, disappearing into darkness. The crash echoed through the tunnel, stone striking stone several meters below. Dust billowed upward, catching in their flashlight beams like spectral mist.

"Pitfall trap," Clara observed, her voice echoing in the confined space. "Someone knew we'd come this way."

Hart nodded, stepping carefully to the edge of the newly formed hole. His light revealed a pit approximately three meters deep, its bottom lined with debris and sharp fragments of broken stone—not bottomless enough to kill but certainly sufficient to incapacitate.

"This is deliberate engineering," he said, studying the clean edges of the collapsed section. "Not decay or structural failure. The supporting cross-beams were removed and replaced with temporary struts designed to fail under a specific weight."

Clara joined him at the edge, keeping a prudent distance from the crumbling perimeter. "Seems excessive just to slow us down."

"It's not about efficiency," Hart replied, making a notation in his book. "It's about historical resonance. This design precisely mirrors defensive mechanisms documented in the city archives—specifically, tunnel traps constructed during the Civil War to defend against potential invading forces." He closed the notebook with a decisive snap. Knowledge found only in rare historical texts. Texts catalogued in university collections."

"Academic resources," Clara concluded, "that only someone with Professor or research-level access would know about."

Hart's expression hardened as he calculated their route around the trap. "Price isn't just challenging our investigative abilities. He's reminding us that he's been planning this for years, accessing information, preparing each step." He gestured toward the narrow ledge that remained intact along one wall. "We proceed carefully. He's leading us somewhere specific."

They edged around the pitfall, backs pressed against the damp stone wall, flashlight beams cutting through the disturbed dust still hanging in the air. Ahead, the tunnel continued its gradual descent into the earth, shadows pooling in its recesses like accumulated secrets.

Hart felt the weight of Price's intellect pressing around him, as tangible as the stone above their heads. Each step forward was a move in a game whose rules remained partially obscured, a chess match played in three dimensions across time and space.

The pattern was there—he could sense its outlines forming in his mind. He just needed to see more pieces before the complete design would reveal itself.

The passage narrowed as they progressed, centuries of settling earth compressing the walls until Hart's shoulders occasionally brushed against the damp stone. Their twin beams of light carved elongated figures into the darkness ahead, the shadows dancing with each step like primitive cave paintings brought momentarily to life. The air grew thicker and heavier with each meter of descent as if the weight of the city above pressed it into a dense concentration of time and decay that filled their lungs with history.

Hart checked his watch—eighteen minutes remaining on Price's countdown. Somewhere across the city, tactical teams surrounded the speakeasy where Dr. Phelps remained unconscious, tethered to that merciless digital heartbeat. Yet Hart's intuition insisted that the proper solution lay in these forgotten arteries beneath the city streets.

"These tunnels predate the city's official founding," Hart said, his voice oddly clear in the confined space. "Dutch traders established the first smuggling routes in 1673, avoiding British taxation. The network was expanded during the Revolutionary War to move supplies past British blockades."

Clara's flashlight beam swept methodically from side to side, her practical mind assessing structural integrity while Hart catalogued historical significance.

"Fascinating lecture, Professor," she replied a gentle irony in her tone that acknowledged his tendency toward academic digression. "But unless Price is hiding behind one of these support beams, I'm more interested in where these tunnels lead us now."

Hart nodded, accepting the mild rebuke. "The historical context matters because Price chose it deliberately. He's not just leading us through physical space—creating a narrative, building connections between past and present."

His pocket vibrated—Leo had programmed their phones to pulse rather than ring when receiving messages, minimising sound while maintaining contact. Hart pulled out the device, its screen illuminating his face from below with ghostly blue light.

"Leo's analysis confirms unusual power usage in this sector," he read. "And he's found something else—city renovation plans from 1927 showing a junction chamber approximately seventy meters ahead. Three tunnels converge there."

Clara's flashlight beam swept upward, illuminating a section where moisture had crystallised into delicate mineral formations that resembled frozen tears.

"The structural degradation is worsening," she observed. "This section hasn't been maintained in decades."

They pressed forward, time hanging above them like the sword of Damocles. Hart's mind worked in parallel tracks—one following the immediate task of navigation, the other assembling the pattern of Price's design. The man's brilliance was undeniable, his planning meticulous. Each element carried multiple meanings and layers of significance that only someone with Hart's particular knowledge would appreciate.

The tunnel widened slightly before terminating in a crude T-junction. Three passages of nearly identical appearance branched outward, their entrances dark mouths awaiting their choice. Hart consulted the digital map Leo had sent. Still, the resolution wasn't detailed enough to distinguish which path corresponded to the original plans.

"The middle passage should lead toward the harbour," Hart said, studying the stonework around each entrance. "But these look like they've been altered more recently than the main tunnel."

Clara stepped forward, her expression shifting from a cautious assessment to a more intuitive focus. She moved slowly along the wall where the tunnels branched, her fingertips trailing across the damp stone. Years of partnership had taught Hart to trust these moments—when Clara's analytical mind yielded to something more instinctive, a perception that operated beneath conscious thought.

"Here," she said finally, pausing where the rightmost tunnel began. Her fingers pressed against an almost invisible marking scratched into the stone—a simple arrow, no larger than a thumbprint, pointing into the darkness of the right passage. "This isn't historical. The cut is fresher, edges still sharp."

Hart examined the marking, nodding. "Good catch. Too subtle for casual observation, but clear enough for someone who knows to look for it." He straightened, directing his light into the chosen passage. "Price is guiding us, step by step."

They entered the right tunnel, which descended at a steeper angle than the central passage. The ceiling lowered gradually until they were forced to duck their heads beneath protruding support beams. The air grew noticeably cooler, carrying a hint of open water —perhaps a connection to the underground drainage system that emptied into the harbour.

After fifty meters of careful progress, the passage abruptly opened into a larger chamber. Their flashlights revealed a circular space approximately six meters in diameter, with a domed ceiling that had partially collapsed on one side. Piles of brick and stone debris covered nearly a third of the floor, while the remaining area showed evidence of more recent human presence—scuff marks in the dust, the remains of a small fire in the centre.

"Someone's been using this place," Clara observed, approaching the fire site cautiously. "Recently."

Hart examined the collapse, noting the weathered edges of the broken ceiling. "This damage isn't fresh—it probably happened during the earthquakes ten years ago." He directed his light toward the debris pile, where something caught his attention—a glint of metal among the stones.

He moved carefully across the chamber, stepping around loose rubble until he reached the source of the reflection. Wedged between two fallen stones was a small metal box, its surface tarnished but intact. The container was approximately fifteen centimetres square, made of what appeared to be copper or brass, with a simple clasp securing its lid.

"Clara," he called softly. "I found something."

She joined him, her light adding to his as he carefully extracted the box from its stony embrace. The object was heavier than its size suggested, solid and cold in his hands.

"It was deliberately placed," Hart said, examining the positioning. "Not accidentally trapped by the collapse. Someone wedged it here recently, intending for it to be found."

Clara nodded, her expression guarded. "Open it. Carefully."

Hart released the clasp and lifted the lid. Inside lay two items: a faded photograph, its edges yellowed with age, and a folded piece of heavy cream paper. He removed the picture first, holding it in the beam of his flashlight.

The image showed a stone building with elaborate Gothic architecture—one of the university's oldest structures. Students in period clothing from the 1920s stood on its steps, their faces blurred by time and the photograph's degradation. But someone had circled one figure with red ink—a young man standing slightly apart from the others, his posture suggesting scholarly detachment.

Hart turned the photo over. The words were written on the back in a precise, angular hand: "Where knowledge was preserved when wisdom was illegal."

He unfolded the paper next. The handwriting matched that on the photograph—deliberate and meticulous, the script of someone accustomed to mathematical notation. It contained a short riddle:

"When laws ran dry, but spirits flowed,

Behind false walls, actual knowledge glowed.

The keeper's key turns twice in the wood,

Where scholars drank what they understood."

Clara read over his shoulder, her brow furrowing. "Prohibition," she said immediately. "When alcohol was illegal—' spirits flowed' behind 'false walls' in speakeasies."

Hart nodded, but his attention had fixed on the photograph, a cold realisation spreading through him. "This building is Hargrove Hall. It housed the university's rare manuscript collection until the new library was built." He looked up, meeting Clara's eyes. "During Prohibition, a group of professors established a secret gathering place in its basement—ostensibly a research archive, but an illegal drinking establishment. They called it 'The Scholar's Cup.'"

"How is that relevant to our case?" Clara asked, though her tone suggested she already suspected the answer.

Hart's expression tightened, the lines around his mouth deepening. "Because I wrote my doctoral thesis on the spatial acoustics of hidden rooms in Prohibition-era architecture. I used The Scholar's Cup as my primary case study." He tapped the photograph, his finger resting on the circled figure. "This isn't just about the city's history—it's about my history. My research. My past."

The personal nature of the connection settled between them like a physical presence. Price wasn't just creating intellectual puzzles—he was constructing a journey through Hart's academic life and the foundations of his identity before becoming a detective.

"Sixteen minutes left on the clock," Clara noted, checking her phone. "And Leo confirms the speakeasy situation remains unchanged."

Hart carefully returned the items to the box and secured them in his pocket. "The Scholar's Cup was located beneath Hargrove Hall on the university campus. If my thesis is guiding Price's design, that's where we'll find our next clue—and possibly understand what he's ultimately planning."

They retraced their steps through the chamber toward the exit tunnel, their lights catching dust particles suspended in the stale air. Hart felt a growing unease that had nothing to do with the crushing weight of the earth above them or the ticking clock of Dr. Phelps' predicament. It was the discomfort of recognition—of seeing his life's work twisted into something dangerous, weaponised against the city he'd sworn to protect.

Price wasn't just challenging Hart's detective skills. He was forcing Hart to confront the very foundations of his identity—the transformation from academic to investigator, from theorist to practitioner. Whatever awaited them at The Scholar's Cup would push that confrontation deeper into the spaces where intellectual fascination blurred with personal vulnerability.

The tunnel seemed to close as they hurried back toward the junction, the ancient stones witnessing yet another secret passage through their timeless corridors.

Hargrove Hall rose before them like a reproachful schoolmaster, its Gothic spires piercing the afternoon sky with accusatory fingers. The grandeur of its limestone façade had been dulled by decades of urban pollution, giving the building the appearance of an ageing aristocrat whose fine clothing had faded but whose posture remained impeccable. Hart stood momentarily frozen at the base of the worn stone steps, his gaze fixed not on the ornate main entrance but on the narrow service door half-hidden behind overgrown shrubbery—the untold entrance to a space few alive still remembered existed.

"Fourteen minutes," Clara noted, checking her phone. "Leo confirms tactical units are still in position at the Whispering Door speakeasy. No change in Dr. Phelps' condition."

Hart nodded, pulling his focus back to the immediate challenge. "The Scholar's Cup hasn't been accessed in years. The university sealed it after a partial collapse in the east wall and deemed it structurally unsound." He moved toward the concealed service entrance, memories of research visits surfacing like bubbles in still water. During renovation planning, I was granted special access for my doctoral research. I spent months documenting the spatial acoustics."

The service door wore years of neglect like a shield—its metal surface bloomed with rust, the keyhole stuffed with debris and spider silk. A weathered wooden board had been nailed across its frame, the official university seal stamped on a faded notice declaring the area condemned.

Clara examined the board and removed a compact pry bar from her jacket pocket. "Prepare to add breaking to our list of procedural violations," she said, wedging the tool beneath the rotted wood.

With a groan of protest, the board yielded, pulling free from rusted nails that had lost their grip on the crumbling doorframe. Behind it, the metal door stood partially ajar, as if someone had recently forced its ancient lock.

"Price has already been here," Hart said, producing his flashlight. "Recently."

Clara drew her sidearm, holding it alongside her light in a practised two-handed grip. "Stay behind me."

They entered a narrow utility corridor, the beam of their flashlights illuminating decades of undisturbed dust now marked with fresh footprints. The air hung heavy with the scents of mildew and decaying paper. Water stains mapped the ceiling like dark continents on a faded globe, a testament to years of neglected maintenance.

The corridor extended approximately fifteen meters before terminating at another door—this one crafted of solid oak with intricate panelling. Unlike the service entrance, this door was meticulously maintained during the speakeasy's operation and designed to impress even as it concealed illicit activities. Its surface was carved with imagery of open books and academic symbols, an intellectual façade for decidedly unscholarly pursuits.

Hart recalled the riddle from the metal box: "The keeper's key turns twice in wood." He examined the door's ornate brass handle, noting its unusual mechanism.

"It's a double-throw lock," he explained, running his fingers over the aged metal. "You turn the key around twice to engage or disengage the bolts."

Clara stepped back, allowing him access to the door. Do you know how to open it without a key?

Hart nodded, reaching up to run his hand along the door's upper frame. His fingers found what memory told him would be there—a small, recessed panel disguised within the carved wooden border. He pressed it firmly, and a soft click emanated from the lock mechanism.

"Prohibition-era speakeasies often had mechanical bypass systems," he said, pushing the door open. This was in case patrons needed to exit quickly during a raid."

The door swung inward on surprisingly silent hinges, revealing the Scholar's Cup in frozen glory. Their flashlight beams swept across a space suspended in time—an academic's imagination of a clandestine drinking establishment. Unlike traditional speakeasies with gaudy décor and jazz-age exuberance, the Scholar's Cup was designed to maintain intellectual pretences.

Bookshelves lined the walls, still populated with leather-bound volumes whose spines had cracked and faded with age and humidity. Oak tables, their surfaces bearing rings from countless forgotten drinks, stood arranged in conversational groupings. Behind a curved bar of polished mahogany, dusty bottles remained in neat rows— prohibition-era liquor that had escaped consumption and confiscation.

"This is exactly as I remember it," Hart murmured, moving into the room with the hesitant steps of someone encountering a vivid memory made physical. "I spent weeks measuring acoustic properties, documenting how the room's design allowed conversations to remain private despite the open floor plan."

Clara moved efficiently around the perimeter, checking corners and shadowing recesses professionally. "Clear," she announced, lowering her weapon but maintaining her alertness. "But someone's been here recently." She gestured toward several tables where the thick dust had been disturbed. "Multiple someones, from the look of these prints."

Hart approached the bar, his light revealing glasses still positioned as if awaiting patrons, stemware coated with decades of dust standing in neat rows like ghostly soldiers. Behind the bar, a large mirror reflected their flashlight beams at them, creating momentary pools of disorienting brightness.

Something about the mirror caught Hart's attention—an inconsistency in how it returned their light. He moved closer, directing his beam more deliberately. The surface wasn't a single pane but a collection of smaller panels arranged in a decorative pattern, some transparent and others opaque.

"These weren't part of the original design," Hart noted, examining the panels more closely. They have stained glass arranged in a seemingly random pattern of coloured sections. Each panel held a symbol etched into its surface—mathematical notations, astronomical signs, fragments of what appeared to be cartographic references.

"Price replaced the original mirror with these panels," Hart said, photographing each section with his phone. "The symbols are a code —or coordinates."

While Hart documented the stained glass, Clara continued her methodical examination of the room. Near one of the reading alcoves, her flashlight illuminated a section of flooring where the boards didn't quite align with their neighbours.

"Hart," she called. "I found something."

He joined her as she knelt beside the anomaly, her fingers probing the edge of a floorboard that appeared slightly raised compared to those surrounding it. With careful pressure, she lifted the board, revealing a shallow compartment beneath the floor. Inside lay a stack of yellowed newspaper clippings bound together with faded red string.

Hart carefully removed the bundle and untied the string. The top clipping dated from 1934, its headline announcing the dedication of the city's new public clock tower. Beneath it, articles spanning nearly a century documented the clock tower's history—its construction, renovation, and significance to the city's development. Each clipping had been meticulously annotated in margins and between columns, the handwriting matching that from the riddle they'd found in the tunnels.

"These annotations connect the clock tower's architectural elements to mathematical principles," Hart said, scanning the precise notations. "Specifically, to principles I explored in my paper on temporal representations in urban architecture."

Clara leaned closer, examining the most recent clipping, three weeks earlier. It announced the scheduled maintenance of the clock tower, including a complete shutdown of its mechanism for inspection.

"Where time stops," she said, connecting to Price's message about Dr. Phelps being kept "where time has already stopped."

Hart spread the clippings on the nearest table, aligning them chronologically. The annotated sections formed a pattern when arranged in sequence, deliberately highlighting specific architectural elements and technical specifications.

"He's not just leading us to the clock tower," Hart said, the realisation solidifying. "He's telling us exactly where within its structure to look." He tapped the annotations referencing the mechanism chamber, where the massive gears and weights controlled the clock's movement. "This is where we'll find whatever Price has planned next."

Clara studied Hart's face, noting the subtle tension in his jaw and his eyes' focused intensity, reflecting more than professional determination. "Whoever this is," she said quietly, "they know you. Personally."

Hart nodded, gathering the clippings and carefully returning them to their binding. "Price isn't just challenging the detective—he's challenging the academic I used to be. Every location has been connected to my research, papers, and intellectual history."

He straightened, pocketing the bound clippings. "He's leading me through my past, Clara. The abandoned library where I studied ancient texts. The tunnels I documented for historical preservation committees. This speakeasy is where I conducted acoustic research." His expression hardened with realisation. "And now the clock tower, which I used as a case study in urban architectural mathematics."

"Why?" Clara asked, though her tone suggested she already suspected the answer.

"Because Price believes our contest isn't just about crime and justice—it's about intellectual validation." Hart's voice carried a carefully controlled tension. "He's constructing a narrative where our confrontation becomes inevitable, where the ultimate puzzle can only be solved through our direct intellectual engagement."

They moved toward the exit, time pressing against them like a physical force. Twelve minutes remained before the countdown at the Whispering Door reached zero. But Hart now understood with certainty that Dr Phelps was merely one component in Price's elaborate design—a pressure point forcing Hart to follow this trail of intellectual breadcrumbs.

"The clock tower," Hart said as they emerged into the fading afternoon light. "That's where Price is orchestrating his endgame. Where all these threads converge."

Clara was already on her phone, coordinating with Leo and the tactical teams. "We'll need to split resources—maintain a position at the Whispering Door while establishing a new perimeter at the clock tower."

Hart gazed up at Hargrove Hall's weathered façade, the academic fortress that had once represented his future before tragedy and obsession redirected his path toward law enforcement. Price hadn't chosen these locations randomly—he had constructed a journey through the decisive points in Hart's life, the places that had shaped his transformation from theorist to detective.

"He's not just challenging my intelligence," Hart said quietly as they hurried toward their vehicle. "He's forcing me to reconcile who I was with who I've become."

The clock tower waited in the distance, its face momentarily visible between downtown buildings—a circular eye observing their progress with mechanical patience, counting down to whatever revelation Price had prepared for them at the intersection of Hart's past and present.

7

THE LOCKSMITH'S DILEMMA

The clock tower loomed against the pink-streaked dawn sky, its weathered limestone facade catching the first tentative rays of sunlight. Hart stood at its base, neck craned upward, studying the massive circular face that had witnessed a century of the city's evolution. Their initial investigation the previous evening had yielded nothing but locked doors and impenetrable darkness, forcing them to retreat and return at first light. As dawn pressed timid fingers through the morning mist, the tower stood revealed in all its ancient grandeur—patient, immovable, harbouring secrets beneath its corroded copper dome.

"Maintenance access is on the east side," Hart said, his voice unnaturally loud in the empty plaza. "Hidden behind decorative stonework—typical of architectural designs from this period."

Clara nodded, her breath forming small clouds in the cold morning air. She carried a tactical backpack containing tools, flashlights, and communication equipment—practical preparations for whatever awaited them inside. The contrast between them had never been more apparent: Hart, with only his worn notebook and pencil, and Clara armed with tangible solutions to physical problems.

They circled to the eastern face where Hart located the maintenance entrance—a narrow door disguised within a pattern of decorative stonework, nearly invisible unless you knew precisely where to look. The key from building management turned stiffly in the ancient lock, the mechanism resisting before yielding with a reluctant groan.

"Price would have come this way," Hart murmured, running his fingers over scratch marks around the keyhole. "Recent damage to the metal—someone forced entry within the last forty-eight hours."

The door opened to darkness and the smell of dust, oil, and forgotten spaces. Their flashlight beams cut through the gloom, revealing a spiral staircase of worn stone steps that disappeared upward into shadow. Each step had been hollowed in the centre by generations of footfalls, creating shallow depressions documenting human passage through time.

"Mind your step," Clara cautioned, taking the lead. "These weren't designed for modern safety standards."

They ascended in silence, broken only by their echoing footsteps and the increasingly audible mechanical heartbeat of the tower. With each revolution of the staircase, the ticking grew louder—a steady, methodical pulse that measured existence in perfectly calibrated intervals. Hart felt it resonating in his chest as if his heartbeat were gradually synchronised with the mechanism's rhythm.

"The main clockworks are located on the seventh level," Hart said, echoing against the stone walls. "The original builders designed the tower with separate chambers for the mechanical components, the bells, and an observation room for the clockmaster."

Clara paused on a landing, directing her light toward an inscription carved into the wall—dates and names documenting renovations spanning nearly a century. "Your research on this place was thorough."

"It represented mathematical precision translated into physical form," Hart replied, his tone taking on the detached quality it did when accessing academic memories. "Perfect intervals governed by mechanical principles that remain unchanged since its construction in 1896."

They continued upward, passing narrow windows that admitted

thin shafts of strengthening daylight. Dust particles danced in these beams like microscopic constellations, briefly illuminated before returning to darkness. The air grew thinner and cooler as they climbed, carrying the metallic taste of machinery and time.

The seventh-level landing opened onto a chamber dominated by the massive clock mechanism—a constellation of brass gears, counterweights, and pendulums that moved with hypnotic precision. The mechanism occupied the central space, surrounded by a narrow walkway that circled the room. Shafts connected to the external clock face translated the mechanism's movement into the steady rotation of enormous hands visible to the city below.

The ticking here was no longer sound but a physical presence—rhythmic percussion that vibrated through the floor, the walls, and their bodies. Each second announced itself with mechanical authority, the sound amplified by the chamber's architecture to create an atmosphere of relentless progression.

"There," Clara said, pointing to the northern wall where the walkway extended to a small landing. Unlike the rest of the chamber's weathered stone, this section featured a door that seemed incongruous—newer, its surface covered with symbols and equations rather than the expected patina of age.

They approached cautiously, flashlights revealing the door's elaborate decorations. Mathematical equations spiralled outward from the centre, interspersed with astronomical charts, geometric patterns, and cryptic pictographs that seemed to shift and change meaning depending on how the light struck them.

Hart's breath caught in his throat. His free hand unconsciously moved to his notebook, extracting it with practised efficiency. "This is it," he whispered, the words nearly lost beneath the mechanism's relentless ticking. "Price's ultimate puzzle."

While Clara methodically photographed the door from various angles, Hart instantly absorbed the symbolism before him. His fingers traced equations he recognised from his published works alongside astronomical calculations that mapped specific celestial alignments. Greek letters interlocked with numerical sequences, forming patterns suggesting cartographic coordinates and music notation.

"He's incorporated elements from at least four of my academic papers," Hart murmured, pencil flying across his notebook as he transcribed symbols and connections. "This equation here—it's from my work on spatial acoustics, but he's modified the variables to incorporate elements from my paper on architectural mathematics."

Clara circled the door, examining its edges and the surrounding stone for hidden mechanisms. "Do you know how it opens?" she asked, her flashlight beam searching for keyholes, pressure plates, or anything that might suggest a physical access point.

Hart barely registered her question, his mind fully engaged in the intellectual puzzle before him. "These astronomical symbols indicate specific stellar positions," he continued as if speaking to himself. "If we interpret them as temporal indicators rather than spatial coordinates..."

He stepped back suddenly, his eyes widening as a larger pattern emerged from the individual components. "It's a composite cypher," he said, his voice rising excitedly. Each symbol system independently means nothing—their relationships form the actual message."

Clara watched him with respect and concern as he paced before the door, muttering calculations and historical references. Her flashlight beam followed his movements, casting his shadow in elongated form against the far wall. The contrast between them had never been more pronounced—Hart pursuing abstract connections invisible to most, Clara analysing tangible reality with methodical precision.

"The pendulum," Hart said abruptly, turning toward the central mechanism. "The way it swings—seven degrees off true centre. That's not a mechanical error; it's deliberate calibration." He rushed to the railing separating the walkway from the clockworks, studying the massive pendulum's arc with newfound intensity. "Price adjusted it. He modified the mechanism to match a specific mathematical constant—my constant, from my paper on temporal distortion in historical architectural spaces."

Clara joined him at the railing, her expression sceptical yet attentive. "How does that help us open the door?"

Hart didn't answer immediately. He compared the pendulum's movement to the equations inscribed on the door. His lips moved silently, calculating intervals and measuring relationships between abstract principles and physical manifestation.

"Price isn't just testing my knowledge," he said finally. "He's testing whether I still think like a mathematician rather than a detective." His hands trembled slightly, not from fear but from intellectual stimulation more potent than he'd experienced in years. The ticking of the clock seemed to accelerate. However, Hart knew it remained perfectly consistent—his perception had shifted, time compressing as his mind expanded to encompass the entirety of the puzzle.

Clara moved back to the door, running her hands along its edge where metal met stone. "Whatever the solution, we need to find it quickly," she said, practical concerns asserting themselves. "Price's timing has been too precise to be coincidental. This door, this puzzle —it's all part of a larger design that's still unfolding."

Hart nodded absently, lost again in the symbols covering the door's surface. His fingers traced connections only he could see, his mind translating abstract patterns into concrete meaning. The massive gears continued their inexorable rotation above them, each tick marking another second in Price's meticulously orchestrated game.

The shadows stretched and shifted as the sun climbed higher, then slowly descended behind the city's skyline. Hart hadn't moved from the door in hours; his form silhouetted against the symbols like a man merged with the puzzle. Sweat darkened the back of his shirt despite the chamber's persistent chill, his body generating heat that his mind was too preoccupied to register. The clock mechanism continued its relentless rhythm, each tick now seeming to mock their lack of progress, each tock an accusation of intellectual inadequacy that Hart felt as physically as a blow.

Five hours had passed since they'd discovered the door. Five hours of Hart muttering equations, tracking patterns, and testing theories that blossomed and withered with equal rapidity. His appearance had degraded with each passing hour—tie loosened then removed entirely, sleeves rolled to the elbows revealing forearms mapped with blue veins that pulsed visibly beneath his skin. His fingers were stained with graphite from his pencil, which had worn down to a nub that he occasionally paused to sharpen with a small pocketknife, the shavings collecting around his feet like wood-curled question marks.

Clara checked her watch for the twelfth time that hour, her patience wearing thinner than the soles of her shoes from pacing the small landing. She had exhausted all practical approaches—examining the door's hinges, searching for hidden mechanisms, photographing the symbols from every conceivable angle to search for patterns visible only from specific perspectives.

"Alan," she said, her voice cutting through his mathematical murmuring. "We need to consider other options. Let me call Leo in on this. His digital analysis might reveal patterns we're missing."

Hart didn't look up from his notebook, which was now filled with calculations spilling from the lined pages onto the margins, creating a frantic cartography of thought. "No," he replied, the word clipped and final. This is meant for me to solve. He's testing my intellect specifically."

"That's exactly the problem," Clara countered, crossing her arms. "You're playing by his rules, dancing to his tune. We have resources, a team—"

"A team would just muddy the waters," Hart interrupted, finally turning to face her. His eyes were bloodshot, pupils dilated from hours of intense focus. "Price designed this puzzle as a direct intellectual challenge. If I bring in others, I'm acknowledging his superiority. I'm admitting defeat."

"This isn't about your academic pride," Clara said, frustration edging her voice. "It's about stopping whatever Price has planned next. We've been here for five hours, Alan. This could be another dead end while he's planning his next move."

Hart turned back to the door, his hands tracing connections between symbols with the reverence of a priest before an altar. "It's not a dead end," he said softly. "Everything we need is here. I just haven't assembled the pieces correctly yet."

Clara leaned against the wall opposite the door, the rough stone cool through her jacket. Through a narrow window, she could see the sun sinking toward the horizon, golden light giving way to the softer hues of approaching evening. They had arrived at dawn, and now dusk threatened—a full day consumed by Price's intellectual labyrinth.

The ticking of the clock had become more than background noise. It had insinuated itself into their consciousness, a metronome dictating the rhythm of their breathing, thoughts, and growing tension. In the enclosed space, the sound bounced from stone walls and metal gears, amplified and distorted until it seemed almost sentient in its persistence.

"We need to step back," Clara suggested after another thirty minutes of watching Hart trace and retrace the same symbols. Get some air, maybe food. Get a fresh perspective."

"There isn't time," Hart muttered, rubbing his eyes with the heels of his palms, leaving smudges of graphite that gave him a raccoon-like appearance. "Price is always three moves ahead. We might miss whatever he's set in motion if we leave now."

Clara pushed away from the wall, her patience finally exhausted. "Look at yourself, Alan. You're not solving this puzzle—you're becoming it. This obsession, this need to prove yourself against Price... It's exactly what he wants. He's not just testing your intellect; he's exploiting your psychological vulnerabilities."

Hart's head snapped up, his expression hardening. "And what would you suggest? Should we abandon the only solid lead we have? That we admit defeat and wait for his next victim to surface?"

"I'm suggesting we use all the tools at our disposal," Clara replied, her voice rising to match his. "That we remember we're detectives, not contestants in some twisted academic competition."

They stared at each other across the small landing, the clock's mechanism continuing its indifferent rotation above them. The space seemed to contract around their disagreement, the air growing thinner with each tense breath.

Hart ran a hand through his hair, causing it to stand on end like a crown of dark thorns. "You don't understand what this means," he said, his voice softer now but no less intense. "Price isn't just challenging my detective skills. He's forcing me to reconcile the academic I was with the investigator I've become. These symbols and equations are fragments of my former life, repurposed as weapons."

Clara's expression softened slightly, recognising the genuine pain beneath his frustration. "Then maybe that's the key," she said, modulating her tone to match his. "Not just solving the intellectual puzzle, but understanding why he's chosen these elements from your past."

Hart didn't respond, turning back to the door with renewed determination. His fingers traced an equation that spiralled outward from the centre of the door, connecting to astronomical symbols that formed a constellation pattern. "This sequence..." he murmured. "It's modelled after my paper on mathematical patterns in architectural acoustics, but he's replaced key variables with astronomical constants."

Clara watched him with a complex mixture of admiration and exasperation. Despite everything, she couldn't help but respect his brilliance. This singular focus allowed him to perceive connections invisible to others. His mind operated in realms she could access only peripherally, solving puzzles that would remain eternally opaque to most.

Yet that same brilliance was his vulnerability—the door through which Price had entered his psyche, manipulating his need for intellectual validation. She could see it in the tremor of his hands, the feverish intensity of his eyes, the way he unconsciously matched his breathing to the clock's ticking. Hart wasn't just solving a puzzle; he was engaging in a form of psychological combat with Price, each symbol a battleground where past and present collided.

The light through the narrow windows had faded to deep indigo, the last remnants of day surrendering to night. The chamber felt smaller in the growing darkness, more confined as if the walls were gradually closing around them. Clara switched on her flashlight, the beam catching dust particles that swirled in the disturbed air like miniature galaxies.

"At least let me get some additional lighting in here," she said, reaching for her backpack. "If we commit to staying through the night, we need better working conditions."

Hart nodded absently, his focus unbroken. His tie lay discarded on the floor, his shirt rumpled and partially untucked, sleeves rolled unevenly to expose forearms tensed with concentration. In the harsh beam of Clara's flashlight, he looked almost feral—a man stripped of social veneer, reduced to his essential intellectual core.

As Clara set up battery-powered lanterns around the perimeter of the landing, the clock continued its metronomic assertion of time's passage. Each tick marked another moment lost, another second claimed by Price's game. The pendulum swung with mathematical precision, its arc unchanged since the tower's construction—except for the seven-degree deviation Hart had identified hours earlier.

In this artificial twilight, surrounded by symbols and equations that mapped Hart's academic journey, Clara felt a growing certainty that they were approaching a critical juncture—not just in the case, but in Hart's ongoing internal struggle between the man he had been and the man he had become. Whatever lay beyond that door would force a reconciliation that had been years in the making.

The clock ticked on, indifferent to human drama, measuring moments with mechanical precision while beneath its massive gears, two detectives fought battles against time, against Price, and the limitations of their contrasting approaches to truth.

Night had claimed the tower completely, transforming the narrow windows into rectangles of perfect darkness. The lanterns Clara had positioned created islands of harsh light in a sea of shadow, their beams insufficient to fully illuminate the chamber yet strong enough to cast multiple overlapping shadows that danced with each movement. Hart stood motionless before the door, his silhouette fragmented by these competing light sources, creating the illusion of a man simultaneously present in multiple locations—an apt visual metaphor for his divided consciousness as he struggled to reconcile his past academic self with his present detective identity.

Clara sat on the bottom step of a maintenance ladder, her back pressed against cold metal rungs. Hours of tension and frustration had left her muscles coiled tight, a dull ache spreading from her shoulders to the base of her skull. She absently massaged her neck, eyes never leaving Hart's rigid form before the puzzle door.

"This reminds me of something," she said finally, her voice startling in the chamber that had known only the clock's ticking and Hart's occasional mutterings for the past hour. "A Chinese puzzle box my grandfather gave me when I was eight."

Hart didn't respond, seemingly lost in his internal calculations.

"Beautiful thing," Clara continued, speaking more to fill the oppressive silence than from any expectation of response. "Carved rosewood with inlaid jade. Supposedly contained a family secret." She smiled faintly at the memory. "I spent weeks trying to solve each panel individually, memorising sequences, tracking patterns."

Hart's shoulders tensed slightly—the first indication he was listening.

"The trick wasn't solving each side individually—it was seeing how they connected as a whole." Clara stretched her arms above her head, joints popping in protest. "When I finally understood the relationship between the panels, the solution revealed itself in seconds."

Hart froze, his pencil suspended above his notebook. Slowly, he turned to face her, his expression shifting from exhaustion to something sharper, more alert. "Say that again."

"Which part?"

"About the relationship between panels."

Clara straightened, recognising the change in his demeanour. "The puzzle couldn't be solved by treating each side as an independent challenge. The patterns only made sense when interpreted as parts of a unified whole."

Hart's eyes widened, a new understanding dawning in their depths. He spun back to the door but with a fundamentally different approach. Rather than focusing on individual symbols or equations, he began tracing connections between them, his fingers moving from one section to another, mapping relationships rather than isolated meanings.

"Of course," he breathed, the words barely audible. "Price wouldn't create a linear puzzle—that's too straightforward, too simplistic for his purposes." His movements quickened, energy-returning to his depleted frame. "It's a multidimensional matrix, each symbol system forming one layer of a composite whole."

Clara stood, approaching the door with renewed interest. "Like overlapping transparencies?"

"Exactly." Hart nodded vigorously, hair falling across his forehead. "Each equation, each astronomical reference—they're coordinate systems that only align when properly superimposed." His fingers traced an invisible grid across the door's surface. "The mathematical patterns provide the framework, the astronomical symbols provide temporal alignment, and the geometric designs provide spatial orientation."

Clara began following his logic, examining symbols she had previously dismissed as decorative elements. "So these pictographs here—they're not just ornamental?"

"They're positional indicators," Hart confirmed, standing beside her. "They tell us how to align the other systems."

Their shoulders nearly touched as they leaned forward, examining a sequence of interlocking geometric patterns near the door's centre. Both reached simultaneously for a circular symbol surrounded by radiating lines.

Their fingers brushed, and Hart felt a jolt pass through him—

undoubtedly static electricity from the dry air and wool carpet, but the sensation lingered longer than physics could explain. Clara withdrew her hand too quickly, suggesting she had felt it too. The intellectual puzzle before them receded briefly, replaced by an awareness of physical proximity that neither acknowledged directly.

Hart cleared his throat, focusing again on the door. "This central motif—it's a temporal anchor. All other systems must be interpreted relative to their position."

Clara nodded, her expression professionally composed, though a slight flush coloured her cheeks. "And these equations spiralling outward establish mathematical relationships between elements?"

"Yes, but not in isolation." Hart traced the spiral with newfound confidence. "They must be read with the astronomical symbols, which provide cyclical context."

Working together with their new understanding, they began mapping connections between previously isolated elements. Hart's theoretical framework and Clara's practical observations created a synergy that accelerated their progress. The tension that had separated them hours earlier transformed into a productive harmony, each supplying what the other lacked.

"The pendulum," Clara said suddenly, pointing to the clock mechanism above them. "You said earlier it was seven degrees off true centre. Is that an alignment indicator?"

Hart's expression brightened. "Yes! The seven-degree deviation isn't arbitrary—it's a calibration constant." He rushed to his notebook, flipping through pages until he found a specific calculation. "If we apply that adjustment to each coordinate system..."

He returned to the door, applying a consistent seven-degree rotation to each symbol cluster. Previously, discordant patterns suddenly aligned, creating new meanings that emerged from their relationship rather than their forms.

"There," Hart said, his finger resting on a sequence of symbols near the bottom edge of the door. "That's not an equation—it's a mechanical instruction. A physical key is hidden within the intellectual puzzle."

Clara knelt and examined the section he indicated. "These notches in the decorative border are not weathering damage." Her fingers probed the seemingly ornamental carvings, finding unexpected depth and precision in what appeared to be random deterioration. "They're pressure points."

Together, they identified seven distinct contact points arranged in a constellation pattern mirrored a mathematical sequence from Hart's earlier calculations. Clara applied pressure to each point in Hart's sequence, her fingers pressing against the ancient stone with precise, measured force.

At first, nothing happened. The door remained immovable, the chamber silent except for the clock's perpetual rhythm. Then, as Clara pressed the final point, a sound emerged from within the door —not the grinding of stone or the clanking of metal, but a series of musical tones, each corresponding to a specific pressure point.

The notes hung in the air for three seconds, then were answered by mechanical clicks from deep within the door's structure. Hart and Clara stepped back as the door began to move, sliding sideways into a hidden recess rather than swinging open as conventional doors would.

Beyond lay darkness, different from the shadows of the clock chamber—more complete, more expectant. Hart retrieved a lantern, holding it before him as they cautiously approached the threshold.

The room beyond was octagonal, its dimensions precise and symmetrical. Each wall consisted of a floor-to-ceiling mirror, creating an infinite regression of reflections that multiplied their images in all directions. The effect was immediately disorienting—dozens of Harts and Claras stretched into forever, each duplicate slightly different due to varying angles and light refraction.

In the centre of the room stood a pedestal of polished black stone, its surface holding a single item: an aged parchment, carefully rolled and sealed with red wax bearing the impression of an hourglass.

Hart approached the pedestal, his multiplied reflections moving in synchronised caution. The lantern light revealed other details of the room—a high-backed chair positioned to face the door, a delicate porcelain teacup on a small side table, and indentations in the thin layer of dust covering portions of the floor.

"Someone was here," Clara said, examining the teacup. She touched its surface cautiously. "Still warm. Hours old at most."

Hart broke the wax seal on the parchment, carefully unrolling it to reveal elegant script in the same precise handwriting as previous messages. He read the words aloud, his voice echoing strangely in the mirrored chamber:

"Clever detective, you've passed this test, but I remain three moves ahead on our chessboard. The queen's sacrifice draws attention, while the knight's manoeuvres are unseen. If you wish to prevent the next demonstration, look to where knowledge and commerce intersect. The timer has already started."

His voice reverberated from the mirrored walls, creating an eerie chorus of overlapping echoes that seemed to come from every direction simultaneously. The effect transformed his voice into something unfamiliar as if Price had momentarily possessed Hart's vocal cords to deliver his taunting message.

Clara knelt beside the chair, examining scuff marks on the floor. "He sat here watching the door, waiting. Not just waiting—anticipating." She looked up at Hart, her expression troubled. "He knew exactly how long it would take us to solve the puzzle. He calculated our arrival, our struggles, even our breakthrough."

Hart carefully rerolled the parchment, securing it in his pocket. "Price wasn't just testing our ability to solve the puzzle. He was calibrating his understanding of our investigative rhythm—how we work, think, and overcome obstacles."

He turned slowly, surveying the octagonal room with its infinite reflections. His dishevelled appearance confronted him in each mirror—a man pushed to intellectual extremes, transformed by hours of obsessive focus. But behind his reflection, multiplied into eternity, stood Clara—steady, practical, the necessary counterbalance to his theoretical approach.

"Where knowledge and commerce intersect," Clara repeated from the message. "The Financial District Library? The University Business School?"

Hart shook his head, moving to examine faint markings on the dusty floor near the pedestal—footprints preserved in the undisturbed powder that had settled over decades of isolation. "Those are too obvious. Price operates in more subtle domains." He traced the footprints with his eyes, reconstructing the movements of their author. "He stood here longer than necessary. Something about this specific position was important to him."

He positioned himself where Price had stood, looking down at the pedestal and then up at the mirrored walls, searching for what might have held the man's attention. He noticed something unusual in the reflection directly opposite—a slight distortion in the mirror's surface, a small area where the silvering had been deliberately altered.

"There," Hart said, pointing to the anomaly. "That's not random deterioration. It's a marker."

They approached the mirror together, examining the altered section. Up close, it revealed itself as a miniature map etched into the silver backing—streets and buildings forming a familiar pattern.

"The Old Market Exchange," Hart said with sudden certainty. "Where the city's first stock exchange met in the same building as the merchant guild's private library. Knowledge and commerce intersecting in a single historical location."

Clara was already reaching for her phone. "We need to move. If the timer has already started—"

"Wait." Hart touched her arm, a mirror image of her earlier restraining gesture. "Price didn't leave this message as a simple directional indicator. The form matters as much as the content."

"What do you mean?"

"An octagonal room of mirrors, creating infinite reflections." Hart gestured to the multiplied images surrounding them. "Price is telling us there are layers to his plan, reflections within reflections. Whatever we find at the Old Market Exchange will be another piece, not the complete picture."

Clara nodded slowly, understanding dawning in her eyes. "So we're still playing his game."

"For now," Hart acknowledged, pocketing the parchment. "But games have rules, patterns. The more Price's moves we witness, the more accurately we can predict his endgame."

They departed the mirrored chamber, their reflections diminishing like retreating ghosts. The clock mechanism continued its eternal measurement of passing moments, indifferent to the human drama unfolding beneath its massive gears. As they descended the worn stone steps, Hart felt the dual weight of Price's intellectual challenge and the city's vulnerability pressing upon him with each downward step.

The game continued, the chessboard expanding, pieces moving in patterns yet to be fully discerned. But for the first time since their pursuit began, Hart felt not just the pressure of keeping pace with Price's brilliance but the possibility of anticipating it—not as the academic he had been, but as the detective he had become.

8

THE RIDDLER'S GAME

The amber glow of a single floor lamp pushed weakly against the darkness of Hart's apartment, a battlefield where light and shadow fought for dominance, and shadow was winning. Hart sat hunched at his desk, the blue luminescence from his laptop screen casting his face in spectral relief, accentuating the hollows beneath his cheekbones and the shadows under his eyes. Three days had passed since the clock tower, since the discovery of the mirrored room and its cryptic message, and sleep had become a theoretical concept rather than a biological necessity.

A half-empty tumbler of whiskey sat untouched beside a stack of manila folders—case files pulled from archives, annotated with his precise handwriting, then discarded like spent ammunition. The Old Market Exchange had yielded nothing but dust and echoes, another misdirection in Price's elaborate game. Despite his methodical approach, Hart had returned to his apartment to regroup, recalibrate, and search for patterns that continued to elude him.

The email arrived at 2:17 a.m., announcing itself with the soft ping Hart had been waiting for without consciously acknowledging the anticipation. The sender's address was a complex string of characters —mathematical constants interspersed with astronomical references that formed a signature as distinctive as fingerprints. There was no subject line, only an attachment.

Hart's cursor hovered over the file for seventeen seconds—he counted each one, measuring time as Price would, with mathematical precision. His index finger descended on the mouse button with the deliberate pressure of someone defusing a bomb or signing a confession.

The video opened in full screen without prompting, as if the file had been designed explicitly for Hart's particular system configuration. The frame remained black for eight seconds before resolving into an image: a figure seated in shadow, only his hands visible in a pool of light that illuminated a desk surface resembling polished obsidian. The hands were elegant and academic—fingers long and precise in their movements as they arranged small metal puzzle pieces into geometric formations.

"Detective Hart." Price's voice emerged from the darkness, as measured and refined as Hart remembered. "Or should I say, Dr. Hart? Considering the intellectual nature of our ongoing exchange, the academic title seems more appropriate for our particular conversation."

The camera angle shifted slightly, revealing more of Price without fully illuminating him. His face remained in partial shadow, but Hart could discern the wire-rimmed glasses, the meticulously groomed hair now touched with distinguished grey at the temples, and the suggestion of a smile that never reached his eyes.

"I've been monitoring your progress with interest," Price continued, his fingers dancing among the puzzle pieces. "Your solution to the clock tower puzzle was elegant, if somewhat delayed. Seven hours and twenty-three minutes—approximately twelve per cent longer than my calculations predicted. Fatigue, perhaps? Or emotional interference?" The last question carried a subtle emphasis, the verbal equivalent of pressing on a bruise to gauge its tenderness.

Hart's hands flattened against the desk surface as if physically bracing against Price's intrusion into his psychological state.

"Our previous exchanges have necessarily been indirect—puzzles and patterns designed to calibrate our respective intellectual positions. But now, I believe, we've reached a stage where more direct communication is warranted." Price's hands completed their arrangement, forming a complex three-dimensional structure from the metal pieces. "After all, we share a history that predates your current profession, don't we, Alan? Academic collaborators, theoretical opponents, and then... something more personal."

Hart's breathing stopped momentarily, his body responding before his mind could intercept the reaction. Price noticed this—somehow, he saw, despite the impossibility of real-time observation—and his unseen smile widened.

"July 15th was unusually warm that year. Ninety-two degrees by mid-morning. The kind of heat that made the playground equipment too hot to touch and turned ice cream into soup before children could finish it. The kind of day that made supervision... difficult." Price adjusted his glasses with a single finger, a gesture Hart recognised from faculty meetings and academic presentations. "But we needn't discuss that yet. We have a game to complete first."

Price lifted a small notebook, opening it to reveal coordinates written in the same precise handwriting that had guided Hart through previous puzzles.

"The location where our first real puzzle awaits. Not a test or calibration, but the beginning of our actual contest." He tilted his head slightly, the light catching one eye that gleamed with intellectual hunger. "Come alone, Alan. Our mutual colleague Detective Morgan is admirable in many respects, but this exchange requires participants of similar... background."

The video continued for another thirty-seven seconds, Price sitting in contemplative silence as if studying Hart through the screen before terminating abruptly. The file deleted itself instantly, leaving no trace in the system—a digital ghost that Hart couldn't recall even if he wanted to share it with cybersecurity.

Hart carefully closed the laptop and sat motionless in the resulting darkness. His hands were numb, but he felt a warmth in his chest, an uncomfortable heat that he recognised as anger mingled with something more profound, more primal—a fear he hadn't allowed himself to acknowledge since beginning this case.

He rose slowly, moving to the living room where his case notes had migrated from desk to walls, transforming the space into a physical manifestation of his mental landscape. Crime scene photos connected by red string to city maps. Historical texts open to pages discussing cryptographic systems used during various periods. Printouts of Price's academic papers annotated with Hart's own observations. A timeline of events stretching back fifteen years to when both men had been promising academics with divergent approaches to the same theoretical problems.

And in the corner, partially concealed behind more recent case materials, a small photograph that Hart never allowed himself to look at directly but could not bring himself to remove: a smiling girl with his eyes and their mother's smile, holding a wrapped birthday present against a background of colourful decorations.

His phone sat on the coffee table, its screen dark and accusatory in its silence. Clara would be sleeping or perhaps still at the precinct reviewing evidence from the Market Exchange. She would want to know about Price's communication immediately. Protocol demanded it. Partnership required it.

Hart's hand hovered over the device, trembling slightly with exhaustion, emotion, or both. Price wanted him alone—isolated, vulnerable to whatever psychological game awaited at those coordinates. Going alone would be reckless, potentially career-ending, if the chief discovered the protocol breach.

Going with backup would mean Price changing the rules again, raising the stakes, and involving more innocents in their increasingly personal contest.

Hart grasped the phone and dialled Clara's number. The decision was made not from the procedure but from the recognition that isolation was exactly what Price wanted—and, therefore, precisely what Hart couldn't afford to give him.

She answered on the third ring, her voice alert despite the hour, suggesting she hadn't slept.

"Price made contact," Hart said without preamble, his voice controlled but tight with an undercurrent of tension he couldn't entirely suppress. "It's personal now. He knows about July 15th."

The silence that followed held more understanding than questions. Clara knew enough about his history to recognise the date's significance without elaboration.

"I have coordinates," Hart continued. "And we have very little time."

Morning light fell through the shattered skylights of the Westridge Gallery in precise geometric patterns, illuminating swirling dust motes that danced through the air like microscopic constellations. The space, once dedicated to celebrating beauty, now hosted a different kind of artistry—one of calculated malevolence designed to unsettle and challenge. Hart stood motionless before a wall covered in elaborate symbols painted in a substance that gleamed wet and dark red in the slanting light, his silhouette a study in rigid focus against the mathematical horror surrounding him.

The gallery had been abandoned for years, and its financial collapse was a footnote in the city's cultural history. Now, it served as Price's first true stage—a deliberate choice Hart recognised as symbolic rather than convenient. The building was a failed monument to aesthetic aspiration, its dreams crushed beneath economic reality—a metaphor Price would appreciate for its multiple layers of meaning.

Clara pushed through the makeshift police barrier at the entrance, Leo following close behind. Her footsteps echoed against marble floors once polished but now dulled by neglect. She wore dark slacks and a charcoal blazer with practical imprecision across her shoulders, her appearance a silent rebuke to the chaos surrounding them.

"You could have waited," she said, though her tone held more resignation than accusation. She knew waiting wasn't part of Hart's operational parameters regarding Price.

Hart didn't respond or turn, his attention held entirely by the equation before him—a sprawling mathematical statement covering nearly six feet of wall space, its components arranged with obsessive precision. His fingers traced invisible lines between symbols, his lips moving in silent calculation.

Leo whistled softly, taking in the scene with wide-eyed professional interest that hadn't yet been dulled by years of exposure to human depravity. His tablet cast a blue glow across his features as he began documenting the scene, fingers racing across the screen.

"The blood is porcine," he said, reading preliminary results from the forensic team that had arrived before him. "Not human. Lab-grade, actually—the kind used in controlled experiments."

In the gallery's centre stood a life-sized mannequin in a familiar but slightly altered pose—arms outstretched, one leg bent, head tilted at a precise angle. It took Clara a moment to recognise the reference: Rodin's "The Thinker," but twisted into a posture that suggested both contemplation and torment. Around the mannequin, more blood-red symbols had been painted on the floor in concentric circles, forming what appeared to be a protective barrier or target, depending on interpretation.

Forensic technicians moved through the scene with quiet efficiency, their white Tyvek suits making them appear like ghosts haunting the margins of this theatrical display. Camera flashes punctuated the dusty air irregularly, preserving evidence Hart had memorised and categorised in his mental database.

Clara approached Hart carefully, recognising the quality of stillness that indicated his mind was operating at maximum capacity. She positioned herself beside him, not interrupting his concentration but establishing her presence as a grounding force against the intellectual current that threatened to sweep him away.

"It's the Fibonacci sequence, but he's altered it," Hart said without turning, his voice carrying the distant quality it took on when he spoke from the depths of analytical immersion. "The deviations are the message."

Clara studied the equation, seeing only mathematical symbols arranged in patterns that held no inherent meaning for her. She understood numbers as tools for measurement and evidence, not as the philosophical language Hart and Price employed.

"How long have you been here?" she asked, noting the fine layer of dust that had settled on Hart's shoulders, suggesting hours of stillness.

"Three hours, twenty-seven minutes," he replied with characteristic precision. "The security guard discovered it at 4:15 a.m. during his rounds. I arrived at 5:03."

Across the gallery, Leo had connected his tablet to a small device attached to one of the remaining functional wall outlets. His expression shifted from concentration to surprise as data began populating his screen.

"You're not going to believe this," he called, looking up with the excitement of discovery animating his features. "The gallery's security system is fully operational. The cameras are active—have been this entire time."

Hart turned toward Leo for the first time, his attention momentarily diverted from the equation. "He left them functional deliberately."

"Not just functional," Leo continued, swiping through screens of technical data. "Enhanced. Someone installed high-definition replacements for the original cameras within the last week. They're transmitting to an external server, bouncing the signal through about twelve proxies."

"He's watching us," Clara said, the realisation settling cold against her skin. "Observing our reactions, our methods."

Hart nodded, returning his attention to the equation. "Of course he is. This isn't just a puzzle—it's a calibration device. He's measuring our response times, investigative approaches, and individual contributions to the solution."

The morning light strengthened, shifting the patterns on the floor as the sun climbed above the skylights. The blood symbols began to dry, darkening from bright crimson to the colour of old rust. Hart moved from the wall to the mannequin, circling it with predatory focus, analysing the precise positioning of its limbs and the symbols surrounding it.

"The Fibonacci sequence corresponds to growth patterns in nature," he explained, more to himself than Clara or Leo. "But Price has introduced deliberate errors—mathematical impossibilities that form a separate pattern."

He withdrew his notebook, flipping to a clean page where he began transcribing the equation, his pencil moving swiftly. "The errors, when isolated and converted using a modified alphanumeric substitution cypher, spell out coordinates."

"Another location?" Clara asked, already anticipating the extension of Price's game.

"A series of them," Hart confirmed. "He's mapping out a sequence of confrontations, each building on the previous one." He paused, studying his calculations with narrowed eyes. "But there's a secondary pattern embedded in the blood symbols around the mannequin. A separate message."

Leo joined them, his tablet displaying a freeze-frame from the security footage showing a figure in dark clothing working methodically on display. The image was carefully composed to reveal presence without identity—another deliberate choice.

"The timestamp on this footage is 2:43 a.m.," Leo said. "Exactly thirty-four minutes after the email was sent to Hart."

The implication hung between them: Price had prepared this elaborate scene before contacting Hart, confident in his ability to predict their arrival and investigative approach.

Clara watched Hart work, noting the subtle signs of his deepening obsession—the tight set of his shoulders, the way his eyes moved between the equation and his calculations with increasing velocity, the slight tremor in his left hand that appeared only when his mind was operating at its limits. She had seen this progression before in other complex cases, but never with this particular quality of personal engagement.

Hart was already disappearing into the puzzle, consumed by the intellectual challenge that Price had designed specifically for him. The abandoned gallery, with its shafts of light and swirling dust, became not just a crime scene but an arena—the first battlefield in what promised to be a war of minds in which the rules were known only to one participant.

As the forensic technicians continued their methodical collection of evidence, Clara recognised the uncomfortable truth: they were all pieces arranged on Price's chessboard, moved according to calculations made long before they entered the gallery.

The precinct's conference room had undergone a metamorphosis that mirrored the transformation of Hart's mind—ordered chaos replacing the sterile utility of its original design. Whiteboards commandeered from other departments lined the walls, their surfaces dense with equations, symbols, and photographs connected by a spiderweb of coloured lines that mapped the associations only Hart could fully perceive. The long central table had disappeared beneath case files, printouts of historical cypher systems, and three laptops running different analysis programs, their fans humming in discordant harmony like mechanical insects.

Hart moved between the boards with the intensity of a conductor before an orchestra, adding notations with different coloured markers, stepping back to absorb the composite image, and then moving forward again to adjust a symbol or connection. His movements had grown increasingly erratic over the past fourteen hours, his initial methodical precision deteriorating into something more frenetic, more desperate. His tie hung loosely around his neck like a forgotten appendage, and his shirtsleeves rolled unevenly to the elbows, revealing forearms mapped with blue veins that seemed closer to the surface than usual.

Clara leaned against the doorframe, a cup of coffee cooling in her hands as she watched him with quiet concern. She had left twice—once to coordinate with the forensics team processing the gallery scene, once to brief the chief on their progress—but Hart hadn't moved from the room except for necessary biological functions, even those begrudgingly.

"The equation from the gallery wall corresponds to specific locations throughout the city," Hart explained without turning, somehow sensing her presence through the fog of his concentration. "But the pattern is incomplete without understanding the symbolic language in the blood markings."

"You need to rest," Clara said, knowing the suggestion would be ignored but compelled to make it anyway. "Fresh perspective. A few hours of sleep."

Hart made a dismissive gesture with his marker, adding another notation to the rightmost board. "Price doesn't rest. Every hour we delay is an hour he uses to advance his position."

At the far end of the table, Leo sat surrounded by computer equipment, his workspace starkly contrasting with Hart's analogue chaos. Multiple screens displayed data streams, security footage from the gallery, and mapping software tracking the coordinates extracted from the Fibonacci deviations. His jacket had been discarded hours ago, his typically neat appearance giving way to the dishevelment that prolonged concentration demanded.

"I've got something," he announced, swivelling his chair toward them. "The security system recorded someone entering the gallery thrice over two days. Different access points each time, but similar movement patterns once inside." He gestured to one of his screens, which displayed a thermal motion mapping through the gallery space. "It's like watching someone rehearse a performance."

Hart nodded without surprise as if this confirmed what he had already calculated. "Price would approach the physical installation with the same precision as the intellectual puzzle. Every movement calibrated, every position optimised."

Leo opened his mouth to respond when the conference room

door swung open unexpectedly. Dr Evelyn Shaw entered like an academic whirlwind, her arms laden with books of various ages and sizes, a leather satchel hanging precariously from one shoulder. Papers protruded from her pockets and stuck at odd angles between book pages as if her mind generated more ideas than she could properly organise.

"Sorry I'm late," she said, though no one had been expecting her at a specific time. "The authentication process for removing these texts from the Special Collections vault was unnecessarily bureaucratic, even with my faculty credentials." She deposited her burden onto the only clear corner of the table, sending a minor avalanche of loose papers cascading to the floor.

Shaw could have been between thirty and forty, her age obscured by a peculiar timelessness that seemed to envelop academics who spent more time with ancient texts than people. Her dark auburn hair was gathered in a haphazard knot secured with what appeared to be a pencil, loose strands escaping to frame a face more striking than beautiful. Wire-rimmed glasses perched on a nose slightly too intense for conventional attractiveness, magnifying eyes that held the particularly intense focus of someone more comfortable with puzzles than social interaction.

"Dr. Shaw," Hart acknowledged without breaking his rhythm at the whiteboards. "Thank you for coming."

"When the department chair said Detective Hart needed consultation on historical cryptography, I assumed it was something straightforward—basic substitution cyphers or perhaps medieval merchant codes." Shaw was already unpacking her books, arranging them in an order comprehensible only to her. "But this..." She gestured toward the photographs of the gallery scene displayed on one of the boards. "This is extraordinary."

She moved directly to Hart's side, studying his notations with academic hunger, her social awkwardness momentarily forgotten in the face of intellectual stimulation. "Price is using a modified Vigenère cypher layered with astronomical symbols from medieval alchemy," she said, her fingers tracing patterns only she fully comprehended. "The combination is brilliant. The Vigenère was considered unbreakable for three centuries, and by integrating alchemical symbolism as a secondary encryption layer..."

Her voice took on the cadence of a lecture, technical terms flowing in a stream that washed over Clara but seemed to energise Hart. He turned toward Shaw for the first time, engaging directly with her observations, adding his insights that she absorbed and expanded upon with equal intensity. They spoke in the specialised language of cryptographers, a dialect composed of mathematical terms and historical references that excluded everyone else in the room.

Leo caught Clara's eye across the space. He pantomimed, drinking from a flask, rolling his eyes at the academic one-upmanship before them. Clara suppressed a smile—Leo's attempts at humour were often the only counterbalance to the oppressive intensity that complex cases generated.

Hours dissolved into a continuous flow of analysis, debate, and incremental progress. Night settled over the precinct, but within the conference room, time became an abstract concept measured only by the accumulation of coffee cups and the gradually decreasing space on the whiteboards. Clara periodically forced nutrition on Hart, placing sandwiches or energy bars directly into his hands and standing beside him until he mechanically consumed at least part of what she provided. He accepted these interruptions with distracted tolerance, and his mind never fully disengaged from the puzzle.

Shaw worked with similar single-mindedness, though her approach was more tactile. She spread ancient texts across her table section, cross-referencing symbols from the crime scene photos with illustrations from alchemical treatises and astronomical charts. Her fingers moved between books with practised efficiency, occasionally pausing to push her glasses higher on her nose or tuck an escaped strand of hair behind her ear.

"The integration of astronomical symbols isn't random," she explained sometime after midnight, spreading a star chart beside crime scene photos. "Medieval alchemists believed certain celestial alignments enhanced specific transformative processes. Price uses these symbols to indicate temporal relationships between the puzzle elements."

Dawn arrived with the grey inevitability of exhaustion, light seeping through the blinds in thin stripes that illuminated dust particles suspended in the conference room air. Leo had finally succumbed to fatigue, his head resting on his folded arms beside his keyboard, soft snores punctuating the keyboard's electronic hum. Clara had maintained her vigil, alternating between reviewing case notes and observing Hart's deteriorating condition with professional concern.

Shaw stood abruptly, her chair skidding backwards with enough force to wake Leo. Her eyes were wide behind her glasses, a flush of excitement colouring her cheeks.

"I've got it," she announced, reaching for one of Hart's markers. "The alchemical symbols form a secondary cypher key when arranged according to their astronomical correspondences rather than their chemical associations."

She moved to the central whiteboard, quickly sketching a circular arrangement of symbols with lines connecting specific points. "When the Vigenère cypher is applied using this key formation, it reveals not just coordinates but an embedded message."

Hart joined her at the board, his exhaustion momentarily forgotten as he followed her logic with growing intensity. Together, they completed the decryption, symbols transforming into alphanumeric characters, then words that Hart wrote in precise block letters across the bottom of the board:

COORDINATES 42.3791°N 71.1305°W + "REMEMBER JULY 15TH, ALAN? I DO."

The room fell silent, even the electronic hum of the computers seeming to recede as the personal message hung between them. Shaw looked from the message to Hart, her academic excitement giving way to confusion, then concern as she registered the words' effect on him.

Hart stood motionless before the board, marker still held in a hand that had gone white-knuckled with tension. The date—July 15th—pulsed in his vision like a wound suddenly reopened, raw and bleeding after years of careful suturing.

"Alan?" Clara's voice came from beside him, though he couldn't recall her crossing the room. "What does this mean?"

Hart cleared his throat, his voice emerging with forced control. "It means Price isn't just challenging my intellect. He's using something personal." He turned away from the board, capping the marker with deliberate precision. "We need to check these coordinates immediately. Whatever's waiting there will be time-sensitive."

But Clara had known him too long to be deflected by procedural focus. Her expression reflected the careful neutrality she employed when interviewing trauma survivors—gentle but insistent.

"July 15th," she repeated softly. "That's significant."

Hart met her gaze briefly, then looked away, his jaw tightening. "It's not relevant to solving the puzzle."

But everyone in the room, even the socially awkward Shaw, recognised the lie for what it was. The date wasn't just significant but central to the game Price played. It was a game that had suddenly expanded beyond intellectual challenge into something darker and more personal.

As they prepared to investigate the coordinates, the unspoken question lingered in the transformed conference room: What had happened on July 15th that connected Hart and Price in ways that transcended their academic rivalry? What memory was powerful enough to make Hart—controlled, analytical Hart physically recoil from its mention?

The Chronos Timepiece Emporium had once been a temple to precision. In this place, minutes and seconds were not merely measured but revered. Now it stood in decayed grandeur on a forgotten street corner, its elaborate façade crumbling, gilt lettering faded to ghostly impressions above a door that hadn't welcomed customers in over a decade. Yet from within its shuttered windows came a sound that raised gooseflesh on Clara's arms—the synchronised ticking of dozens of clocks, their mechanical hearts beating in perfect unison like a collective pulse counting down to something inevitable.

Hart approached the entrance first, his flashlight cutting through the early afternoon shadows. The coordinates from Shaw's decryption had led them directly to this abandoned business in the city's old commercial district—an area that time and economic progress had bypassed, leaving architectural remnants of a more elegant era to decompose slowly.

"The lock's been replaced," Hart noted, examining the door's modern security mechanism that starkly contrasted with the antique brass handle. "Recently."

Clara nodded to the uniformed officer who had arrived ahead of them to secure the perimeter. He stepped forward with bolt cutters, making short work of the padlock. The door swung inward with a protest of unoiled hinges, releasing a wave of dust-laden air and amplifying the ticking that the building's stone walls had previously muffled.

The sound washed over them with physical presence—dozens of timepieces marking seconds in perfect synchronisation, their combined precision creating a metronomic rhythm that seemed to adjust their heartbeats and breathing to its steady cadence immediately.

Shaw stepped through the doorway behind Hart, her academic composure momentarily shaken by the aural assault. "Remarkable," she whispered, her voice barely audible above the mechanical chorus. "The statistical improbability of this many antique timepieces maintaining such perfect synchronisation without digital assistance is—"

"Impossible," Hart finished for her, sweeping his flashlight across the shop's interior. "Which means Price has modified them."

The beam illuminated a scene of ordered decay—glass display cases lined the walls, their contents arranged with museum-like precision despite the thick dust covering every surface. Pocket watches, wristwatches, and small desk clocks occupied the cases. In contrast, grandfather clocks and wall-mounted timepieces stood sentry along the perimeter. At the centre of the space, a large work-bench had been cleared of dust and repurposed as the foundation for an elaborate mechanical construction.

Clara moved carefully around the perimeter, checking for traps or secondary mechanisms while Hart and Shaw approached the central workbench. The construction resembled a miniature solar system, with brass spheres of various sizes rotating on intersecting metal tracks, their movements governed by an intricate clockwork mecha-nism beneath the wooden surface.

"It's an orrery," Shaw said, adjusting her glasses as she leaned closer to the device. "A mechanical model of the celestial system. But this one's been heavily modified." Her fingers hovered above the rotating spheres, analysing their movements without touching the mechanism. "These aren't arranged according to our solar system— they're positioned according to an ancient cosmological model. Ptole-maic, I think, with elements of medieval astronomical theory."

Hart circled the workbench, studying the mechanism from multiple angles. "The rotation speeds have been deliberately cali-brated. Each sphere completes its circuit at a different rate, but there's an underlying mathematical relationship."

Shaw nodded, her initial social awkwardness dissolving as she immersed herself in the intellectual challenge. "It's a numerical system predating Arabic numerals—possibly Babylonian or early Greek." She pulled a small notebook from her satchel, quickly sketching the spheres' arrangement and relative positions. "Each position represents a value in a base-60 calculation method."

Clara watched them work, noting how seamlessly they had fallen into collaborative analysis. Hart and Shaw operated on a similar wavelength, their minds processing abstract patterns and historical references with a synchronicity mirrored by the ticking clocks surrounding them. Their shared intellectual approach created a bubble that excluded others, not deliberately but as a natural consequence of specialised expertise.

"The spheres are approaching alignment," Hart observed, checking his watch. "The current configuration began forty-seven minutes ago, according to the dust patterns on the tracks. If the cycle repeats, we have approximately thirteen minutes before they return to their starting positions."

Shaw had pulled several reference books from her seemingly bottomless satchel, flipping through yellowed pages with practised efficiency. "Here," she said, finding an illustration that matched the orrery's configuration. "This arrangement appears in a 9th-century astronomical treatise describing celestial influences on earthly events. Each planetary alignment was believed to govern specific types of human activity."

Her fingers moved with surprising dexterity among the delicate mechanisms, adjusting her position to examine components hidden beneath the primary structure. "A secondary system underneath is a series of geared discs with notched edges. They will be rotated into specific positions corresponding to the planetary alignment."

Hart nodded, already reaching beneath the workbench to locate these hidden components. Their hands moved in coordinated precision around the mechanism, neither impeding the other. Communication flowed through glances and minimalist gestures rather than words. Clara had seen Hart work with other specialists before, but never with this level of intuitive collaboration.

"This doesn't match standard astronomical notation," Shaw murmured, her fingers tracing symbols etched into one of the metal discs. "It's a hybrid system—astronomical symbols combined with..." She paused, her expression shifting from academic interest to recognition. "These are the same symbols from the gallery wall. Price is creating a consistent symbolic language across locations."

Hart adjusted one of the discs, rotating it until a specific symbol aligned with a marker on the workbench surface. "Each disc must be positioned according to the corresponding sphere's current location."

Together, they worked through the mechanism's logic, rotating discs and noting the resulting changes in the orrery's movement. The ticking of the surrounding clocks seemed to intensify as they progressed, the sound pressing against their eardrums with increasing urgency.

"Clara," Hart called without looking up from the mechanism. "Check the largest grandfather clock against the far wall. A hidden compartment in its base should be accessible by adjusting the pendulum weight."

She moved toward the indicated timepiece, a towering mahogany structure whose pendulum swung behind a glass panel with hypnotic regularity. Following Hart's instruction, she examined the pendulum mechanism, finding a small adjustment screw at its base that could shift the weight. As she rotated it, a nearly invisible seam appeared in the wooden panel beneath the clock face.

"Found it," she confirmed, carefully extracting a sealed envelope from the hidden compartment.

When she returned to the workbench, Hart and Shaw had aligned all seven discs with their corresponding celestial bodies. The orrery's movement changed subtly—spheres rotating on independent tracks now moved in harmonic relation to one another, their paths converging toward a central point.

"The system is seeking equilibrium," Shaw explained, her voice carrying the quiet intensity of scientific observation. "When all components align perfectly, it will reach its stable state."

As if responding to her words, the mechanism gradually slowed, spheres settling into their final positions with delicate precision. A soft click emanated from beneath the workbench, and a small drawer slid open on its side, revealing a brass key nestled on a velvet lining.

Hart carefully extracted the key, holding it up to examine its unusual design—the shaft inscribed with the same symbols that appeared on the orrery's discs, the head formed in the shape of an hourglass.

"It's a timepiece winding key," Shaw identified it. "Specifically designed for astronomical clocks of the late 18th century."

Clara handed Hart the envelope she'd retrieved from the grandfather clock. He carefully opened it, extracting a single sheet of cream-coloured paper covered in now-familiar handwriting. The team gathered around as Hart read the message aloud:

"Time measures all things equally, yet memory distorts its passage. Seven years can feel like yesterday when guilt preserves the moment in amber. The Observatory awaits at midnight, where stars once guided a child's imagination before darkness fell. Remember her fascination with the night sky, Alan? The way she clutched your hand as you named the constellations? The key opens more than doors."

The paper trembled almost imperceptibly in Hart's hands, a minute betrayal of emotion that would have been invisible to anyone who didn't know him as well as Clara. His expression remained controlled, but she saw the slight tightening around his eyes, the momentary cessation of breathing, and the microscopic tick at the corner of his jaw.

"The Observatory," Shaw said, seemingly oblivious to Hart's reaction as she focused on the practical implications. "He must mean the Hillcrest Observatory on the university campus. It's been closed for renovation for nearly a year."

Hart folded the paper with mechanical precision and pocketed it alongside the brass key. "Price is accelerating the timeline. Midnight gives us less than ten hours to prepare."

Clara studied him carefully, noting how he avoided direct reference to the message's personal elements. The mention of a child's fascination with stars and the reference to guilt preserved for seven years were significant. Still, Hart compartmentalised them behind the wall of professional focus he maintained during investigations.

Shaw continued examining the orrery, but her academic curiosity was not satisfied despite having solved its primary puzzle. "The precision of this mechanism is extraordinary," she commented, adjusting her glasses. "The mathematical relationships between rotation speeds, the integration of historical astronomical models with modern mechanical principles—Price must have spent months designing this."

"He did," Hart confirmed, already moving toward the door. "This isn't improvisation. Every element has been meticulously planned, every response calculated." He paused at the threshold, looking back at the synchronised clocks that continued their relentless ticking. "We need to get back to the precinct. Ten hours isn't much time to prepare for whatever he's arranged at the Observatory."

As they exited the shop, Clara noticed that Hart was walking slightly ahead of them, maintaining a physical distance that mirrored his emotional withdrawal. Shaw collected and followed her books, noting the theory's design principles. Her mind was already cataloguing the experience for potential academic application.

The clocks continued their synchronised countdown behind them, measuring seconds with mechanical indifference to the human drama unfolding within their tempo. And though he gave no outward sign, Clara knew that Hart was carrying more than the brass key in his pocket—he took the weight of whatever memory July 15th held, of a child who had once clutched his hand beneath the stars, of seven years of guilt preserved like an insect in amber.

The game had become deeply personal. Price was leading them step by methodically toward a confrontation that now seemed predestined—a convergence point that had been calculated long before the first puzzle appeared.

The yellow glow of streetlights filtered through Hart's equations scrawled across his living room windows, transforming mathematical formulas into amber hieroglyphics that projected onto the opposite wall. The apartment had evolved beyond mere disarray into something that resembled the internal architecture of Hart's mind. In this space, chaos adhered to principles comprehensible only to him. Case files lay open on every surface, their contents extracted and reorganised according to invisible connections. Coffee cups formed a chronological record of the past thirty-six hours, rings of evaporated liquid darkening from fresh brown to aged black, measuring time in caffeine consumption rather than hours.

Hart stood before the window, dry-erase marker poised against the glass, adding another variable to an equation that stretched from floor to ceiling. The marker squeaked against the smooth surface, the sound unnaturally loud in the midnight silence of his apartment. His reflection in the glass between equations revealed a man transformed by obsession—hair dishevelled from repeated agitated passes of his fingers, stubble darkening his jaw, eyes bloodshot and deeply shadowed. His usually impeccable dress shirt hung wrinkled and partially untucked, the sleeves rolled unevenly to expose forearms mapped with blue veins.

Six hours remained before the midnight meeting at the Observatory. Six hours to decipher whatever message lay beneath the surface of Price's puzzles—the actual pattern behind the patterns.

"The chronology is deliberate," he murmured, moving from the window to a wall where he had taped crime scene photos in sequence. "Gallery, clock shop, Observatory. Visual art, mechanical precision, and astronomical observation. A progression from aesthetic to scientific, from subjective to objective."

He traced the connections with a trembling finger, his body vibrating with the combined effects of exhaustion and excessive caffeine. Sleep had become an indulgence he couldn't afford, not with Price accelerating the timeline or each puzzle revealing more intimate knowledge of Hart's past.

A folder slipped from the edge of his desk, scattering contents across the floor. Hart knelt to gather the papers, his hand freezing as he encountered a photograph buried beneath case notes—a family portrait he kept as a reminder but rarely allowed himself to examine directly.

A sun-dappled backyard, birthday decorations hanging from tree branches, a cake with seven candles yet to be lit. A small hand reached for his, trusting fingers wrapped around his own with complete faith that they would always hold on, always protect.

The image flashed in his mind with such clarity that for a moment, he was there, feeling the summer heat on his skin, hearing childish laughter, and experiencing the particular weight of responsibility that came with being trusted completely. Then it was gone, pushed back into the compartment where he kept such memories locked away during investigations.

Hart returned the photograph to the folder with methodical care, sliding it beneath other papers where it wouldn't ambush him again. He moved to the kitchen, mechanically filling the coffee maker for what might have been the tenth time that day. As the machine gurgled to life, his gaze fell on a refrigerator magnet—a cheap souvenir from a museum gift shop, a plastic rendering of the solar system that had once delighted a child fascinated by stars.

Small hands clutched his as they looked upward through the Observatory dome, a high voice asking questions faster than he could answer them. "That one, Alan! What's that bright one called?" His patient explanation of stellar classifications and celestial mechanics was simplified for young understanding. The simple joy of knowledge was shared, and wonder was transmitted from generation to generation.

.   .   .

Hart blinked hard, dispelling the memory through sheer force of will. He abandoned the coffee, returning to the living room, where his case notes offered safer territory than the treacherous landscape of remembrance. He moved toward the wall covered with string connections—red for locations, blue for timing, and green for symbolic elements. The pattern was there; he could sense it forming at the edges of his comprehension, but it remained elusive.

His phone vibrated on the coffee table, the screen illuminating with Clara's name for the fourth time in two hours. Hart glanced at it with distant recognition as one might acknowledge an artefact from another life. Communication with the outside world seemed irrelevant in his current state of focused immersion. Whatever Clara wanted—updates on his analysis, concern about his absence from the precinct, reminders about basic human necessities like food or rest—would only distract from the essential task of understanding Price's valid message.

The phone eventually went silent, but the brief interruption had jolted something in Hart's thinking. He returned to the window, studying the equations he had written across the glass. The streetlights beyond transformed his mathematical notations into palimpsests—formulas superimposed over the nighttime city, symbols merging with distant buildings and moving cars.

"The alignments," he whispered, sudden understanding dawning. "He's not just creating puzzles—he's recreating significant moments."

Hart's hands moved with renewed purpose, pulling photographs from the gallery scene and the clock shop and arranging them beside his notes from the original sites. The positions, symbols, and specific references to stars and time weren't random elements chosen for intellectual challenge. They were reconstructions, physical manifestations of memories extracted from Hart's past with surgical precision.

He crossed to his desk, pulling out city maps and overlaying them with transparent paper on which he traced the locations of each puzzle site. When connected, they formed a pattern he recognised immediately—a constellation rendered not in stars but in urban geography. Cassiopeia. His sister's favourite constellation, the one she had identified with childish pride on their last night at the Observatory before—

Hart's hands trembled as he added the final connection—a line extending from the Observatory to a location he hadn't visited in seven years. The lake house where it had happened. July 15th had permanently altered the trajectory of his life.

His phone vibrated again, with a text message rather than a call. Hart glanced at it reflexively, his mind still partially submerged in revelation. Clara's message was brief and professional: "Meeting at the precinct, 7 a.m. Planning for Observatory. Need your input."

Hart didn't respond, his attention returning to the map and its implications. Price wasn't simply challenging him intellectually or emotionally—he was systematically reconstructing the events leading to July 15th, creating an elaborate path leading Hart back to the moment that had defined their lives.

He moved to the wall where he had taped photos of Price from academic journals and security footage, studying the man's face with new understanding. The intellectual rivalry, the criminal genius, and the elaborate puzzles were merely the framework supporting Price's true intention: forcing Hart to confront what he had spent seven years meticulously avoiding.

Hart stepped back, suddenly focusing on his apartment. The walls were covered with case notes, the windows transformed into transparent equations, and the floor was littered with coffee cups and discarded theories—all of it represented his desperate attempt to maintain intellectual distance from a case that had been personal from the beginning.

"He's not just playing with me," Hart whispered, his voice hoarse from hours of disuse. "He's recreating it. Step by step, puzzle by puzzle, he's leading me back to that day."

His hands were numb from exhaustion, but he felt a warmth in his chest, an uncomfortable heat that he recognised as a complex amalgam of fear, anticipation, and a strange, reluctant gratitude. Price offered what Hart had never been able to give himself: a path back through the labyrinth of guilt and regret to the truth at its centre.

Six hours until midnight. Six hours until the Observatory. Six hours until the next step toward a confrontation seven years in the making.

Hart returned to the window, adding one final equation to the glass—not a puzzle solution but a personal reminder written in a mathematical language that only he and Price would fully comprehend: the precise calculation of guilt's half-life, the decay rate of responsibility for a tragedy that had transformed two promising academics into the men they had become.

Rain fell in relentless vertical sheets, transforming the abandoned playground into a monochrome tableau of gleaming metal and saturated wood. Police floodlights cast harsh illumination across the scene, their beams catching raindrops in mid-descent, creating ephemeral curtains of light between the officers who moved with careful precision around the park's central feature. This chessboard should not have existed. The life-sized game board had been constructed overnight, its marble-like squares precisely measured and laid directly onto the playground's rubber matting, its pieces carved with unsettling detail and arranged in a configuration that defied standard rules and physical possibility.

Hart stood at the perimeter, rain streaming down his face, soaking through his coat and into the suit beneath. He hadn't bothered with an umbrella despite Clara's offered spare. The physical discomfort of cold water against skin provided a necessary sensory anchor, preventing his mind from floating untethered into the abstract realms of Price's design. Three hours had passed since the unexpected call had diverted them from the Observatory preparations—a patrolling officer discovering the elaborate construction in a park that had been empty and undisturbed during his previous rounds just six hours earlier.

Crime scene technicians hunched beneath plastic tarps, photographing the board and collecting evidence with increasing frustration as the rain intensified. Their usual methodical efficiency was compromised by weather that seemed determined to wash away whatever evidence Price might have left behind. Portable generators hummed beneath the percussion of rainfall, powering lights that pushed against the premature darkness brought by storm clouds.

Clara approached from the direction of the patrol cars, her practical navy raincoat beaded with water, a tablet protected within a waterproof case clutched against her chest. "The Observatory is still secure," she reported, positioning herself so the tablet remained sheltered. "Two uniformed officers on site, checking in every thirty minutes. Nothing's been disturbed there."

Hart nodded without shifting his gaze from the chessboard. "He's altered the timeline. Adding location before the Observatory." His voice carried the flat quality it assumed when he was processing multiple information streams simultaneously. "This wasn't part of the original pattern."

Leo worked beneath a hastily erected canopy at the far side of the playground, surrounded by electronic equipment he struggled to keep dry. "I've run the chess configuration through every database and analytical program available," he called, his usual enthusiasm dampened by the weather and the increasingly ominous progression of Price's puzzles. "It's not a standard opening, not a famous historical game position, not even a mathematically optimal arrangement."

Hart moved forward onto the board, his shoes leaving temporary impressions in the water pooling on the marble-like surfaces. The chess pieces stood immobile in their impossible arrangement—knights positioned where they couldn't have moved according to standard rules, pawns advanced in patterns that contradicted basic gameplay, and kings facing each other without being in check. Each piece had been carved with extraordinary detail, its features seeming to shift slightly in the unsteady light of the floodlamps.

"The configuration isn't the message," Hart said, circling the board with predatory focus, his fingers occasionally reaching out to touch a piece with feather-light precision. "It's the positioning relative to the surrounding elements."

The surrounding elements he referenced were symbols etched into the ground encircling the chessboard—complex geometric patterns that resembled those from the gallery and clock shop, but with subtle variations. These symbols had been carved directly into the rubber playground surface, deep enough to remain visible despite the rain pooling in their grooves.

Shaw joined Hart on the board, her academic aversion to inclement weather overcome by intellectual curiosity. She wore a transparent plastic poncho over her usual attire, the garment crackling with her movements as she examined the symbols.

"These incorporate elements from multiple ancient mathematical systems," she observed, crouching to trace one particularly complex etching. "Babylonian positional notation, Egyptian fraction representation, early Greek geometric proofs—all synthesised into a hybrid symbolic language."

Hart moved to the centre of the board, where the opposing kings faced each other across an expanse of empty squares. Unlike standard chess pieces, these kings had been carved with individualised features—one resembling Hart himself, the other unmistakably modelled after Price.

"It's a visualisation of our intellectual confrontation," Hart said, studying the pieces with detached analysis despite the unsettling nature of seeing himself rendered in miniature. "But the game state is impossible—it couldn't occur through any sequence of legal moves."

"Unless the rules have been changed," Shaw suggested, adjusting her glasses as rain speckled the lenses. "Many chess variants exist with modified movement patterns or additional pieces. Perhaps this configuration represents a game with different operational parameters."

Clara watched from the edge of the board, her expression reflecting professional concern rather than academic interest. She noted the tension in Hart's movements, the slight tremor in his hands that he controlled through sheer force of will, and the increasing pallor beneath his rain-streaked features. He hadn't slept in at least forty-eight hours, had barely eaten despite her persistent efforts, and was operating on a combination of caffeine and obsessive focus that couldn't be sustained indefinitely.

Hart crouched at the centre of the board, examining the space between the opposing kings. The rain had pooled in a slight depression there, forming a perfect circle of water that reflected the floodlights above. He reached forward, fingers breaking the water's surface to find something solid beneath—a small object embedded in the board.

With careful precision, he extracted what appeared to be a wooden box approximately four inches square. Its surface was carved with the same symbols that surrounded the chessboard. The wood was sealed against water damage, suggesting Price had meticulously planned the weather conditions.

"It's a music box," Hart said, turning the object in his hands to examine its construction. The craftsmanship was extraordinary—hand-carved from a single piece of dark wood, with a minor winding key of polished brass protruding from one side.

Shaw leaned closer, her scientific curiosity momentarily overwhelming social boundaries. "The carvings correspond to the symbolic system in the ground etchings. They're instructional—showing how to interpret the chess configuration."

Hart's fingers found the winding key, rotating it three complete turns with the careful precision of someone disarming an explosive device. For a moment, nothing happened. Then the box's lid opened automatically, revealing a miniature mechanical apparatus inside. A delicate melody began to play, the notes distorted by the rain but still immediately recognisable.

"Happy Birthday."

The tune struck Hart physically, and all protective compartmentalisation instantly shattered. The playground around him dissolved, replaced by a vivid cascade of memory fragments—

The lake house porch is decorated with streamers and balloons, a table set with birthday plates and party hats, and a cake with seven candles waiting to be lit. His sister's face was bright with anticipation, dark hair pulled into uneven pigtails she'd insisted on doing herself. "You promised you'd be here all day, Alan!" Her small hand tugged at his, pulling him toward the telescope he'd brought as a special gift. "You promised no phone calls from work today!" The reluctant vibration of his phone in his pocket, the university department chair calling about Price's research inconsistencies that couldn't wait, the weight of academic responsibility temporarily outweighing the birthday promise.

She expressed her disappointment as he stepped away to take the call, her voice following him: "But you promised, Alan!" The call extended longer than expected, with complex discussions of theoretical anomalies and potential research misconduct, and Price's name was repeatedly mentioned in concerned tones. Minutes stretched into a half hour as he paced the dock, academic concerns temporarily eclipsing his awareness of time passing, of supervision abandoned.

There was sudden silence when he ended the call. The absence of childish laughter registered a moment too late. The birthday cake was still unlit. The yard was empty. The open gate to the path leading down to the lake's edge. His voice called her name with increasing urgency, receiving no response but the lapping of water against the shore.

The music box continued its tinny rendition of "Happy Birthday" as Hart physically staggered, the memory overwhelming his defences with the force of floodwaters breaching a dam. His knees struck the chessboard with an impact he didn't feel, one hand reaching out to steady himself against a fall that seemed both physical and psychological—a plummet back through seven years of carefully maintained control.

Clara was beside him instantly, her hand on his arm to anchor the present moment. She signalled to the nearest officers to step back, to give him space, to maintain the dignity of a respected detective experiencing what appeared to others as a momentary physical weakness, but what she recognised as profound psychological trauma resurfacing.

"Alan," she said quietly, her voice pitched to reach only him, not the surrounding officers whose attention she worked to deflect. "You're here. Now. With me."

The music box finished its melody and fell silent, its mechanism winding down with a barely audible click. Rain continued to fall around them, drumming against the chessboard and pooling in the depressions left by Hart's knees. He remained crouched in the centre of the board, Clara's steady hand on his arm, his breathing gradually returning to the controlled rhythm.

When he finally looked up, his face had transformed—the mask of professional detachment momentarily stripped away to reveal raw emotion before being carefully reconstructed. In that unguarded moment, Clara saw what Hart had been hiding beneath layers of analytical precision—not just grief or guilt, but a deep, corrosive self-recrimination that had shaped every aspect of his life since whatever tragedy July 15th represented.

"He knows," Hart whispered, his voice barely audible over the rain. "He knows what happened to my sister."

Clara maintained her steadying grip on his arm, her presence offering silent support while respecting the fragile privacy of his momentary vulnerability. Shaw had retreated to the board's edge, recognising the intensely personal nature of what was unfolding. Leo had abandoned his equipment to move closer, concern evident in his youthful features.

Hart carefully closed the music box, securing it in his coat pocket as he regained his composure. When he rose to his feet, the professional detective had reasserted control. However, Clara could still see the aftershocks of memory trembling beneath his carefully maintained exterior.

"The chess configuration is a temporal map," he said, his voice steady despite the emotional earthquake that had just passed through him. "Each piece represents a specific moment in time, arranged to show not gameplay but chronological progression." He turned to face the surrounding team, rain streaming down his features like tears he would never allow himself to shed. "Price isn't just leading us to the Observatory. He's reconstructing a path that ends at the lake house."

"What lake house?" Leo asked, voicing the question that hung in the rain-soaked air.

Hart didn't answer directly, moving instead toward the edge of the chessboard with renewed purpose. "We continue as planned. The Observatory at midnight. That's the next coordinate in his sequence."

But as they departed the playground, the life-sized chess pieces witnessed what had transpired—when Price's game had transcended intellectual challenge to strike at the core of Hart's carefully guarded heart. The impossible configuration remained in the rain, kings facing each other across a battlefield where the actual stakes had finally been revealed.

Dr Shaw's university office resembled the nest of some academic magpie—a space where books, papers, and artefacts had accumulated in geological layers, their organisation following principles comprehensible only to their collector. Ancient texts shared shelf space with modern technology, papyrus fragments protected behind glass cases sat beside tablet computers running complex algorithms, and star charts from three centuries hung overlapping on walls barely visible beneath their scholarly burden. The room smelled of old paper and dust, and the particular alchemy of coffee transformed into intellectual energy through prolonged concentration.

Three hours remained before the Observatory meeting. Following the playground revelation, the team had retreated to Shaw's academic sanctuary, seeking shelter from the continuing downpour and a secure location to process what they had discovered. The chess puzzle, the music box, and the implications of both had fundamentally altered the investigation's trajectory, transforming what had begun as an intellectual challenge into something deeply, painfully personal.

Hart sat apart from the others, occupying an ancient leather armchair tucked into the farthest corner of the office. His rain-soaked clothing had dried, leaving wrinkles that mapped the contours of his prolonged stillness. His posture suggested not relaxation but a deliberate withdrawal, physical distance mirroring the psychological walls he had reconstructed following his momentary breakdown at the playground. The music box rested on his knee, its carved surface occasionally receiving a touch from his fingertips that seemed both reluctant and compulsive.

At the large oak desk that served as the room's gravitational centre, Shaw worked with quiet intensity, surrounded by reference books and historical texts she consulted in rotation, her glasses periodically pushed higher on her nose with an absent gesture that had become so habitual she no longer registered it. The chess pieces they had collected from the playground were arranged before her in their original impossible configuration, now complemented by pages of notes analysing their symbolic significance.

Leo occupied a corner desk cluttered with modern technology, his usual energetic movements subdued into uncharacteristic stillness. His fingers moved across his tablet's screen with mechanical precision, but his expression remained troubled. His typical stream of commentary was reduced to occasional murmured observations about data patterns. He glanced periodically toward Hart, then exchanged concerned looks with Clara, their wordless communication conveying shared worry about their colleague's state.

Clara stood by the single rain-streaked window, her posture suggesting a sentry positioned between Hart and the outside world. She had maintained a protective orbit around him since the playground, not hovering but remaining consistently within a supportive distance. Now, she watched raindrops trace irregular patterns down the glass, each following its unique path while ultimately arriving at the same destination—a metaphor for investigative work that would have amused her under different circumstances.

The office held the peculiar tension of people who had witnessed something profoundly private that could neither be acknowledged wholly nor directly ignored. The sound of turning pages, the soft click of Leo's tablet, and the persistent rhythm of rain against the window created an acoustic backdrop for unspoken thoughts.

Shaw finally looked up from her analysis, removing her glasses to rub tired eyes. "The chess configuration, when interpreted through the symbolic language established in the earlier puzzles, corresponds to a specific sequence of events rather than game moves," she said, breaking the extended silence. "Each piece's position represents a moment in time, with spatial relationships indicating causal connections."

No one responded immediately. Her academic analysis, though accurate, seemed to hover at the surface of something much deeper —the intellectual framework supporting an emotional architecture they had only glimpsed in Hart's momentary vulnerability.

Clara moved away from the window, crossing the room to sit in a chair adjacent to Hart's. She didn't speak, didn't attempt to draw him out, offered her presence as an anchor should he choose to reach for it. The silence between them stretched, not uncomfortably, but with the particular quality of space between people who understood that words weren't always necessary.

After several minutes, Hart spoke, his voice low and controlled in a way that suggested significant effort. "Elizabeth," he said, the name emerging like something preserved and rarely handled. "My sister. She would have been fourteen this year."

Clara nodded slightly, her expression open but undemanding. She had known fragments of this story through departmental rumours and occasional oblique references from Hart himself, but never the complete narrative.

"She was seven," Hart continued, his gaze fixed on the music box rather than on any of his colleagues. "July 15th was her birthday. We were at our family's lake house—our parents had been delayed in the city due to business matters, so it was just the two of us for the afternoon. She'd been looking forward to her party for weeks." A smile briefly touched his features, there and gone like sunlight through moving clouds. "She loved astronomy. I'd brought a telescope as a present. We were going to stargaze that night."

The rain's rhythm intensified against the window, providing a gentle percussion to his measured words. Leo had stopped working entirely, his attention now fully on Hart's quiet narrative, though he remained respectfully distant.

"I received a call from the university regarding academic integrity in the department. Price's research methods had raised concerns that couldn't wait." Hart's finger traced one of the symbols carved into the music box with precise pressure. "I stepped away to take the call. It lasted longer than expected. When I returned..." His voice maintained its even tone through what could only be years of practised control. "Elizabeth was gone. The gate to the lake path was open. We found her shoes by the water's edge."

The implications hung in the office air, heavier than the dust motes suspended in shafts of late afternoon light. Nobody mentioned that no closure was achieved—not death but the particular torment of permanent uncertainty, of questions without answers.

"They questioned me extensively," Hart continued after a moment. "My background is in academia rather than childcare, my decision to take the call, and the time unaccounted for. No charges were ever filed—no evidence of wrongdoing, just tragic circumstances. But the investigation changed me. I saw how patterns of behaviour, timelines, and physical evidence could be assembled to reveal the truth. Three months later, I left the university and entered the police academy."

Clara's hand moved slightly closer to his on the armrest, not quite touching but offering proximity. "And Price?" she asked gently. "What was his connection?"

"He was the subject of the call that day—his research methods, possible data manipulation. After the investigation, he was dismissed from the university for academic misconduct. My testimony was instrumental in that decision." Hart finally looked up, meeting Clara's gaze directly. "I always assumed he blamed me for his academic downfall. Now I understand it's more complex than that. This elaborate game, these puzzles—they're not just intellectual challenges. They're reconstructions of the path that led to that day."

From her desk, Shaw looked up suddenly, understanding dawning in her expression. "That's why each puzzle site corresponds to a location from your academic work," she said, academic detachment momentarily yielding to empathetic insight. "The gallery where you studied art history's influence on mathematical visualisation. The clockmaker's shop is near where you published your paper on temporal mathematics. The playground is adjacent to where you taught your first university class. He's not just challenging your intellect—he's forcing you to retrace the steps of your previous life."

"Leading to the Observatory," Leo added, comprehension spreading across his features. "Where did you take your sister for her birthday the previous year, according to the music box message?"

Hart nodded, replacing the music box in his pocket with deliberate care. "And ultimately to the lake house, where it happened. He's constructed an elaborate path back to the moment that transformed both our lives—my sister's disappearance and his academic disgrace occurring on the same day, connected by a phone call."

The rain continued its steady percussion against the windows as the implications settled over the team. Price's game had transcended an elaborate criminal puzzle to become something more profound— a psychological reconstruction forcing Hart to confront an unsolved case and his own unresolved guilt.

Shaw returned to her analysis of the chess puzzle, her movements more purposeful now that she understood the personal dimensions underlying the intellectual challenge. "If I'm interpreting these configurations correctly," she said after several minutes of concentrated work, "Price isn't just recreating past events. He's suggesting an alternative interpretation of what happened that day."

Hart's posture straightened slightly, the first change in his withdrawn stillness since he had begun speaking. "What do you mean?"

"These pieces," Shaw indicated specific elements on the chess board, "when viewed as a chronological sequence rather than game positions, suggest a narrative where certain events co-occurred rather than sequentially. It's as if he's presenting a counterargument to the established timeline."

A subtle tension gathered in Hart's shoulders, momentarily disrupting the controlled breathing pattern he had maintained throughout his narrative. "You think he knows something about Elizabeth's disappearance?"

"I think," Shaw said carefully, her academic precision extending to this delicate hypothesis, "that he believes he knows something. Whether that belief corresponds to actual events or represents his psychological reconstruction is impossible to determine without further evidence."

Hart stood slowly, the movement drawing everyone's attention. The withdrawn, emotionally vulnerable man who shared his sister's story was gradually replaced by the analytical, focused, and resolved detective. "Price isn't just challenging my mind," he said, his voice stronger now. "He's trying to break it by forcing me back through those events, making me relive each moment, each decision, each failure."

Clara rose beside him, her presence supportive but not protective —she recognised the return of Hart's professional capacity rather than his continued vulnerability. "What's our next move?"

"We change the game," Hart said. "Price has been anticipating my moves based on who I was then—the academic turned detective, driven by guilt and the need for certainty. He's calibrated each puzzle to that psychological profile." His expression hardened into a resolve that transformed his features. "So we introduce an element he hasn't calculated. We stop following his path and create our own."

Leo straightened in his chair, energy-returning to his posture. "How exactly do we do that?"

"We meet him at the Observatory as planned," Hart replied, "but not as passive participants solving his puzzles. We approach as investigators with new information—specifically, the understanding that this isn't just about intellectual challenge or vindication for his academic disgrace. It's about Elizabeth."

Shaw nodded, already gathering her notes. "I can complete the analysis of the chess configuration before the meeting. If there are specific clues about what he believes happened that day—"

"Do it," Hart confirmed. "And Leo, I need you to pull everything on Price from seven years ago—not just the academic misconduct case, but his whereabouts around July 15th, any connection he might have had to the lake house area, anything that might explain why he's fixated on reconstructing these events now."

The atmosphere in the cluttered office had transformed, academic analysis giving way to focused investigation. Hart moved to the window where Clara had stood earlier, watching the rain patterns with new awareness. For seven years, he had approached his sister's disappearance as a tragedy defined by his failure to pay attention. Now, Price's elaborate game suggested the possibility of a different narrative—one where academic disgrace and a child's disappearance might be connected by more than coincidental timing.

"He thinks I've been solving the wrong puzzle all these years," Hart said quietly, almost to himself. "The question isn't whether I'll meet his intellectual challenge. It's whether I'm prepared for what he believes is the solution."

The rain continued its steady rhythm against the glass, washing the world clean for whatever revelation awaited at midnight in the Observatory, where, seven years earlier, a little girl had gazed at stars with the wonder that only children and astronomers truly possess.

9

PRESSURE POINTS

Hart's consciousness returned in fragments—first, the smell of damp concrete, then the dull ache radiating from the base of his skull, and finally, the harsh flicker of fluorescent light against his closed eyelids. He remained perfectly still, a habit learned through years of detective work: assess before revealing awareness. The surface beneath him was unyielding except for a thin mattress, his body arranged with an unnatural precision that suggested placement rather than collapse. Someone had put him here, arranged him here, with deliberate intent.

He opened his eyes to a concrete ceiling crossed by hairline fractures, a single fluorescent tube suspended from rusted chains casting unsteady illumination that seemed to breathe with its arrhythmic pulse. The narrow cot beneath him protested as he shifted, its metal frame grinding against concrete. Hart pressed a palm to his forehead, finding the skin clammy. A faint tremor in his fingers suggested some chemical agent's lingering effects. Drugged, then. But by whom?

The room resolved itself around him—a three-by-five-meter chamber with walls of poured concrete stained with patches of moisture that mapped decades of neglect. A rusted metal door anchored one end, its surface pitted with corrosion. A small observation window cut into its upper half and covered by what appeared to be a sliding panel from the outside. The floor bore a palimpsest of footprints in dried mud, some fresh, others obscured by time.

Hart swung his legs over the edge of the cot, the movement sending a wave of nausea through him that he suppressed through practised control. The Observatory. He had gone to the Observatory as planned, arriving twenty minutes before midnight to secure the location before Price appeared. Clara had positioned officers at strategic points outside while Shaw analysed the astronomical alignment visible through the central dome.

He closed his eyes, straining to extract the final moments from memory:

The massive telescope angled toward Cassiopeia—Elizabeth's favourite constellation. The expected astronomical alignment is at precisely midnight. The sudden realisation that the officers outside had gone silent on their radios. The faint, sweet smell that had seemed out of place in the sterile observatory environment. Then... nothing.

Hart stood carefully, testing his equilibrium before stepping toward the cell's centre. His watch, phone, notebook, and service weapon were missing. Even his tie and belt had been removed, presumably to eliminate potential tools or weapons—classic isolation protocol. The only light came from the flickering bulb overhead, and no windows offered clues to the time of day or location.

A smear of dark red on the wall opposite the cot caught his attention—not random but precisely applied, its borders too defined for casual spatter. Beneath it, pinned by whatever substance created the red mark, hung a photograph. Hart approached carefully, studying the image before touching it.

The photo showed the interior of a café, its edges yellowed with age, a coffee stain marking one corner. Two men sat at a corner table, engaged in animated conversation—Hart recognised himself immediately, younger by perhaps eight years, his posture betraying the academic he had been rather than the detective he had become.

Across from him sat Price, equally transformed by time but unmistakable with his precise gestures and intent expression.

Hart carefully removed the photograph from the wall, turning it over to find a date written in familiar angular script: March 4th, fifteen years ago. This was their first meeting at an academic conference, the beginning of a collegial relationship that would eventually transform into intellectual rivalry, then something darker, more personal.

The substance holding the photo proved to be not blood but specialised red ink—the same formulation used in university department stamps for official documents—the same ink that had approved both their research grants all those years ago.

His fingertips brushed something at floor level—a loose floorboard, its edge slightly raised above its neighbours. Hart knelt, working a fingernail into the gap to lift the board. Beneath lay a minor brass key, its surface gleaming as if recently polished, its teeth arranged in a pattern he recognised immediately—a replica of the key to his university office from fifteen years earlier.

He pocketed the key and scanned the room for the third element he sensed was waiting. Price never employed fewer than three components in his intellectual constructions—the principle of triangulation that had been the subject of their first collaborative paper. The photograph established a past connection, and the key represented access, which meant the third element would indicate destination.

There, beside the frayed edge of a small rug near the door. A torn piece of paper lay positioned with deliberate casualness, its placement too precise to be accidental. Hart retrieved it, finding an address in the same angular handwriting:

1147 Westmoreland Avenue.

His pulse quickened with recognition. It was not a random location but the address of their former university department, specifically the building that had housed Hart's office—the office whose lock would accept the brass key in his pocket. This was another point on the constellation Price was constructing, another fragment of their shared past made physically manifest.

The three items—photograph, key, and address — formed a triangulation more precise than geographic coordinates, creating an intellectual map that transcended physical location. Hart turned slowly in the centre of the cell, reassessing its dimensions with a new understanding. The concrete walls suddenly seemed less like a prison and more like a puzzle box—a controlled environment to focus his attention on specific elements.

His fingers were numb from the lingering effects of whatever drug had rendered him unconscious. Still, he felt a warmth in his chest, an uncomfortable heat that he recognised as a complex amalgam of emotions: frustration at being manipulated, anticipation of the intellectual challenge, and beneath it all, a reluctant appreciation for the elegance of Price's design.

The fluorescent light flickered overhead, its rhythm matching the pulse of thoughts accelerating through Hart's mind. The photograph established temporal origin, the address provided a spatial destination, and the key offered the means of transition between them. Classic narrative structure: beginning, middle, end. Past, present, future.

But the red mark above the photograph suggested something more—not just an intellectual exercise but the implication of blood, of consequence—a symbolic representation of what had been lost between that first meeting and their current confrontation.

Hart returned to the cot, sitting with controlled precision as he arranged the items before him: three data points carefully selected to trigger specific cognitive processes, three breadcrumbs on a trail designed to be followed, and three pieces of a puzzle whose solution remained just beyond the edges of perception.

He closed his eyes, allowing his mind to shift into the analytical state that had been his refuge since childhood—the pure mathematics of pattern recognition, uncomplicated by emotion or physical circumstance. The cell around him receded, replaced by the abstract architecture of logical progression. Price was leading him through a specific sequence of memories, reconstructing their shared history with surgical precision, building toward some revelation he believed would alter Hart's understanding of what had happened on July 15th.

The door's observation panel slid open with a metallic scrape, admitting a thin shaft of brighter light that fell across Hart's face. Someone was watching, evaluating his response to the carefully arranged stimuli. Hart didn't look up, didn't acknowledge the observation. Instead, he continued his mental construction, assembling the puzzle pieces methodically.

The game continued, and the rules became clearer with each new element. And Hart—despite his physical confinement—felt the first stirrings of something approaching freedom. If Price believed this cell would constrain Hart's analytical abilities, he had fundamentally misunderstood the detective's mind. Walls could contain his body, but patterns, puzzles, and connections were where Hart moved without impediment.

He looked up toward the observation panel, a subtle change in his expression suggesting not defeat but acceptance of the challenge proposed. The panel slid closed immediately, but not before Hart caught a glimpse of an eye watching from the other side—an eye whose colour and intensity he would have recognised in absolute darkness.

Hart gathered the three items—photograph, key, and notepaper— and slipped them into his shirt pocket before approaching the door. Each step across the concrete floor produced a whisper of sound, his shoes leaving fresh prints in the dust accumulated since the previous visitor. He positioned himself precisely two feet from the metal surface, the optimal distance for observation without vulnerability, and waited. The figure would return; the observation panel had closed too quickly, suggesting not fear but tactical repositioning. Hart's mind calculated possibilities with mechanical precision: Price would reappear, speak, and offer the next coordinate in their intellectual chess match. Physical confinement was merely the board upon which this game was being played.

Three minutes and forty-seven seconds passed—Hart counted each one with internal precision despite his missing watch—before the panel slid open again. This time, no eye appeared in the narrow aperture. Instead, the opening remained empty, a rectangle of deeper shadow that suggested observation from a greater distance. Hart maintained his position, neither advancing nor retreating. The exchange of initiative was a move in their game, and he wouldn't concede the advantage of the first action.

The shadow shifted, and a tall figure stepped into view, positioning itself with careful deliberation before the slotted window. Hart's first impression was of meticulous composition—every element of the figure's appearance was designed for a specific psychological effect. A charcoal-grey coat fell to floor length, its fabric expensive but deliberately austere, buttoned from collar to hem with mathematical precision. The hood was drawn low, casting the upper portion of the face in shadow while allowing the lower half to remain visible—a directorial choice that emphasised certain features while obscuring others.

What remained visible was a pale, angular face with skin stretched taut over prominent cheekbones. The mouth formed a precise line, neither smiling nor frowning, but set in an expression of clinical interest—the face of someone observing a particularly complex equation resolving itself. A single lock of auburn hair coiled at the side of the jaw, escaping the hood's confines with what seemed calculated carelessness in an otherwise immaculate presentation.

Hart recognised Price instantly, not through obvious physical characteristics but through the particular quality of his presence—the absolute stillness that had always characterised him during moments of intense intellectual focus. Seven years had altered his appearance, adding subtle lines around his mouth and a new severity to his features. Still, the essential quality remained unchanged: the sense of a mind so intensely active that the body containing it became almost irrelevant.

"The results exceed expectations," Price said, his voice low and measured, each word precisely enunciated with the cadence of distant thunder. The academic accent remained subtle but distinctive, with consonants receiving slightly more emphasis than vowels, and a speech pattern developed through years of lecture halls and scholarly presentations. "Ninety-four seconds to locate all three items. Twelve minutes to extrapolate their significance."

Hart didn't respond immediately, analysing the statement's implications. Price had been monitoring him continuously, timing his actions with scientific precision. The concrete cell wasn't merely a holding area but a laboratory, Hart himself the experimental subject. He felt a familiar intellectual excitement stir despite his circumstances—the same response he had experienced during their academic debates years before the tragedy and obsession had transformed their relationship into something darker.

"The methodology is flawed," Hart replied, matching Price's formal cadence. "Variable conditions, insufficient control mechanisms. The data must be considered preliminary at best."

A slight movement at the corner of Price's mouth might have been a suppressed smile. "Your assessment is noted. However, this particular experiment is merely a larger research design component. The cumulative data remains statistically significant."

They observed each other through the narrow aperture, reverting to the scholarly language that had once been their common tongue. The concrete cell and metal door receded momentarily, replaced by the phantom architecture of university hallways, seminar rooms, and intellectual spaces where they had once moved as colleagues rather than adversaries.

"Remember the hourglass—every grain counts," Price said suddenly, his tone shifting to something more intimate, almost conspiratorial. "The transition from upper to lower chamber remains constant, but the accumulated weight increases with each passing moment."

Hart analysed the statement with automatic precision. It was not merely an aphorism about the fleeting nature of time but a specific reference to the pressure of accumulation—data points gathering, evidence mounting, revelation approaching with mathematical certainty. However, a secondary meaning was embedded in the choice of metaphor: the hourglass as an observation device, the grains as measured performance units, and success determined by completion within specific parameters.

"You're not working alone," Hart said, the realisation crystallising as he spoke. "The experimental design requires multiple observers. Independent verification of results."

Price's expression remained unchanged, but a subtle tensing around his eyes confirmed Hart's hypothesis. "Science demands rigorous methodology," he replied, neither confirming nor denying the specific allegation. "Particularly when the stakes extend beyond individual researchers."

Hart mentally recalibrated his understanding of the situation. It was not simply a personal confrontation between former colleagues but something more complex—a demonstration conducted for unseen evaluators. The concrete cell, the carefully placed items, and even Hart himself are all components in an elaborate proof Price was constructing to convince others of some larger theory.

"These observers," Hart continued, pursuing the thread, " are tracking specific metrics: response times, analytical approaches, emotional reactions." He paused, studying Price's expression for confirmation. "They have a particular interest in my connection to July 15th."

Price's hood shifted slightly as he inclined his head—not quite a nod, but an acknowledgement of accurate deduction. "They possess incomplete information," he said after a measured silence. "Their conclusions require adjustment based on empirical evidence only you can provide."

The statement carried multiple implications, each branching into possible interpretations. Price wasn't merely testing Hart; he was using Hart to prove something to these unseen observers—something connected to the events of seven years ago, Elizabeth's disappearance, and the academic disgrace that had transformed their lives.

"And if I refuse to participate?" Hart asked, though he already knew the answer. Within minutes of waking, his analytical mind had calculated the likely parameters of his confinement—the cell's location, the probable number of guards, and the security measures beyond the metal door.

Price's expression softened momentarily, a brief crack in his clinical demeanour revealing something almost like regret. "Refusal constitutes its form of data." He paused, the single auburn lock shifting against his jaw as he leaned closer to the aperture. "But I hypothesise you won't refuse. Your psychological profile suggests a 97.3% probability of continued engagement, particularly given the potential relevance to Elizabeth's case."

Hart maintained his outward composure despite the jolt that passed through him at his sister's name spoken aloud. Price was right, of course. The intellectual challenge alone would have ensured his participation; the connection to Elizabeth's disappearance made refusal impossible.

"Next stage preparations are complete," Price continued, his voice dropping lower, becoming almost intimate despite the metal barrier between them. "The data obtained here supports progression to more complex environments."

Hart nodded once, a tense, economical movement that acknowledged the rules of engagement without accepting their legitimacy. "The university address," he said. "Your former office. The brass key."

"The sequence matters," Price replied, a thin smile appearing and vanishing like a momentary glitch in a digital image. "As do the methods of transition between spaces."

With a final, assessing look, Price stepped back from the aperture. Hart caught a brief glimpse of the corridor beyond—concrete walls similar to his cell, suggesting an institutional structure repurposed for current needs. Then Price's hand appeared in the narrow opening, a slender, pale appendage with immaculately groomed nails and the faint callus on the middle finger that betrayed a lifetime of academic writing.

"The door is unlocked," Price said, his voice already receding as he moved away from the aperture. "The choice to open it is yours, though I calculate the probability of your remaining in voluntary confinement at less than 0.08%."

The observation panel slid closed with mechanical precision, leaving Hart alone once more with the flickering fluorescent light and the implications of their exchange. He remained motionless before the door, analysing not just Price's words but the subtle tells in his presentation—the careful positioning, the controlled revelation of specific features, the calculated balance between academic formality and personal intimacy.

Price wasn't merely continuing their intellectual contest; he was staging a performance for those unseen observers, using Hart as both subject and demonstration. The realisation should have been unsettling, but Hart felt a contrary response stirring within him—a professional appreciation for the complexity of the design combined with a personal determination to decipher its purpose.

He reached for the door handle, cool metal against his palm, and tested it with gentle pressure. It yielded as promised, the latch mechanism releasing with a soft click that echoed in the concrete chamber. Hart paused, considering one final time the implicit agreement he was making by proceeding, then pushed the door open to whatever stage Price had prepared for the next act of their intellectual drama.

The corridor stretched before Hart like the throat of some ancient beast, its damp stone walls glistening in the weak illumination cast by bare bulbs strung at irregular intervals along the ceiling. The air hung thick with moisture, and the peculiar mineral scent of long-buried things was finally exposed to oxygen. Hart stepped fully across the threshold, allowing the cell door to swing shut behind him with a sound like punctuation—the definitive end of one passage and the beginning of another. Price stood twenty meters ahead, his tall figure rendered in stark contrast by a light source beyond a bend in the passageway, the charcoal coat absorbing illumination rather than reflecting it. Without turning, Price began to walk forward, the coat's hem brushing the floor with each measured step, creating whispered conversations with the stone beneath.

Hart followed, maintaining a precise distance between them— close enough to track Price's movements, far enough to react if neces- sary. The corridor's stone walls pressed close on either side, their surfaces mottled with patches of pale green moss that thrived in the perpetual dampness. Limestone, Hart noted automatically, was water-carved and bore faint fossil impressions that suggested ancient marine deposits. It's not modern construction but something much older, repurposed for current needs. The slightly sloping floor confirmed his hypothesis: they were moving gradually downward, following the natural contours of what might once have been a subterranean water channel.

Overhead, exposed pipes ran in chaotic patterns, their rusted surfaces sweating droplets that fell with metronomic irregularity. Each drop struck the stone floor with a distinct pitch, creating an arrhythmic percussion that marked their passage through the space. Hart's mind automatically calculated the pattern, not random but complex, mathematical relationships between intervals that suggested deliberate calibration rather than natural occurrence. This was another of Price's controlled variables, another subtle manipula- tion of the environment to produce specific psychological effects.

Their footsteps echoed against the stone, Hart's sharper and more defined, Price's muffled by the heavy coat that seemed to consume sound as readily as light. The acoustics suggested a substantial struc- ture above them—thick walls, perhaps multiple stories, the weight of history or institution pressing down from above. A university build- ing? A government structure? The possibilities narrowed with each new data point Hart collected.

A sound like metal scraping against metal came from somewhere ahead, followed by a hollow thud reverberating through the corridor's confined space. The sequence repeated at irregular intervals, each occurrence slightly different from the last, as if someone were making minute adjustments to a mechanical apparatus. Hart catalogued the variations, constructing potential sources: pressure release valves, security mechanisms, or perhaps something more deliberate —another calculated element in Price's multisensory construction.

As they proceeded deeper into the corridor, the stone walls exhibited more extensive texturing—channels and grooves carved by water over centuries, creating a topographical record of geological processes. Hart's fingertips brushed against these features, reading the stone's history through touch. The tactile information registered alongside visual and auditory input, his mind assembling a comprehensive model of their surroundings even as it continued to process the intellectual implications of Price's puzzle.

A faint hiss emanated from a joint in the pipes overhead, releasing a wisp of steam that briefly obscured the passageway ahead. Through this ephemeral curtain, Price's figure seemed momentarily insubstantial, more theoretical construct than physical presence. The impression lasted only seconds before the steam dissipated. Still, it reinforced Hart's sense that this journey operated simultaneously in physical and abstract domains.

Rust flakes rattled on metal grates set at intervals in the ceiling, disturbed by air currents from their passage or perhaps by movement in spaces above. Each tiny sound registered in Hart's consciousness, adding to the acoustic profile of their surroundings. The combination of water drops, distant mechanical sounds, their footsteps, and these minute percussions created a complex soundscape that seemed almost composed—variations on a theme of confinement and antiquity.

"The corridor pre-dates the structure above by approximately 150 years," Price said suddenly, his voice carrying clearly despite its low volume. He didn't turn or slow his pace. "Originally designed for water management, later repurposed for storage, eventually forgotten until structural renovations revealed its existence."

The information aligned with Hart's observations, confirming his geological assessment while adding historical context. Price was establishing shared intellectual territory—a neutral ground where they could engage as analysts rather than adversaries. The strategy was familiar from their academic days: begin with verifiable facts, establish methodological common ground, and then progress to theoretical propositions.

"The university acquired the property in 1964," Hart replied, accepting the implicit invitation to dialogue. "Structural renovations occurred in 1978, 1992, and 2006. The last would have revealed this level during foundation reinforcement."

Price's hooded head inclined slightly in acknowledgement. "Your retention of institutional history remains impressive."

"As does your selection of symbolically resonant locations," Hart countered, maintaining the scholarly tone while advancing the underlying game. "A forgotten passage beneath the architecture of formal education. The hidden foundations supporting visible structures."

A soft sound that might have been appreciation escaped Price before he continued forward, his pace unchanging. The exchange had established parameters for their continued interaction—academic in form, adversarial in content, with multiple layers of meaning embedded in even the most factual statements.

The soft scrape of something sliding across stone drew Hart's attention to the floor near the wall. A small creature—perhaps a rat or other subterranean dweller—moved parallel to their path for several meters before disappearing into a crevice. Its presence confirmed Hart's assessment of their location: beneath ground level, connected to older systems that provided access to the outside world through routes unmapped by current architectural plans.

As they progressed, the floor's slope became more pronounced, and the descent more obvious. The temperature dropped perceptibly with each meter of depth, the air taking on the particular stillness of spaces rarely disturbed by human presence. Hart estimated they had travelled approximately seventy meters from his cell, moving in what his internal compass registered as a southeastern direction—toward the oldest section of the university campus.

The implication crystallised: Price was leading him literally beneath the foundations of their shared academic past through the hidden infrastructure that had supported their intellectual development. The metaphor was characteristic of Price's approach—physical space as a representational construct, geography as a narrative device.

Hart's mind worked simultaneously on multiple levels as they walked. One track analysed their immediate surroundings—calculating exit possibilities, mapping their route, and assessing potential threats or resources. Another track engaged with the symbolic architecture of Price's design, decoding the progression from cell to corridor as a transition from isolation to a guided journey. A third track maintained continuous awareness of the ultimate objective—discovering what Price believed he knew about Elizabeth's disappearance.

The final track, most deeply buried but never truly dormant, processed the emotional implications of following this path. Hart had spent seven years constructing rigorous compartmentalisation between his academic past and detective present, between the brother who had failed to protect Elizabeth and the investigator who solved others' mysteries as partial atonement. Price's elaborate game systematically dismantled those compartments, forcing the reintegration of fractured identities.

Ahead, the corridor bent sharply to the right before terminating at what appeared to be a heavy wooden door, its surface barely visible in the weak light cast by the final ceiling bulb. Price stopped several paces from this threshold, turning partially so his profile was visible to Hart. The single auburn lock remained coiled precisely at his jaw, the visible portion of his face as composed as it had been during their exchange through the cell door.

"The transition point," Price said, gesturing toward the door with a slight movement of his gloved hand. "From historical infrastructure to purposeful construction."

Hart understood immediately: while the corridor had been an

existing structure repurposed for current needs, whatever lay beyond the door had been created explicitly for this elaborate demonstration. He nodded once, acknowledging the information while maintaining his analytical distance.

The distant mechanical sounds had ceased, leaving only the water drops and their breathing to disturb the corridor's silence. The absence created a vacuum of expectation, a sense of suspended animation before some crucial revelation. Hart felt the weight of that anticipation pressing against him with almost physical force—the accumulated tension of intellectual challenge and personal history converging at this wooden threshold.

Price moved forward again, reaching the door and placing his palm against its ancient surface with a gesture that contained something almost like reverence. The wood beneath his hand seemed to respond, a barely perceptible vibration running through its grain as if awakening after long dormancy.

Hart followed, stopping precisely two steps behind Price—close enough to observe, far enough to react. The journey through the corridor had been both a physical and psychological preparation; the confined space and sensory elements conditioned his mind for whatever lay beyond. He was conscious of the manipulation but appreciated its effectiveness nonetheless. Price had always understood how the environment shaped cognition and how physical context influenced intellectual reception.

The soft rasp of Price's coat sleeve against the wooden door as he reached for its handle was the final sound in the corridor's acoustic composition—a concluding note in a passage of transition that had carried them from confrontation toward something not yet defined, but moving inexorably into existence with each step along this underground path.

Price pressed an almost invisible latch recessed within the oak panel's intricate carvings, his fingertips finding the mechanism with practised precision. The door swung inward on silent hinges, releasing a breath of warmer air scented with beeswax and some subtle herbal essence that Hart couldn't immediately identify. Light spilt from the opening—not the cell's harsh fluorescence or the corridor's weak electric glow, but the open flame's living amber warmth. Hart's pupils contracted against the sudden illumination, his vision adjusting to reveal a perfect circle of space beyond the threshold, its dimensions so precisely calculated that it created an immediate sensation of mathematical harmony. He followed Price through the doorway, crossing from ancient stone into what appeared to be a chamber constructed with deliberate ritual intent, its every element arranged to evoke specific psychological and symbolic responses.

The circular room measured approximately eight meters in diameter, its walls curving with flawless regularity to form an unbroken circuit. Twelve slender candles burned in stone niches spaced at thirty-degree intervals around the perimeter, their flames unnaturally steady in the still air. The light they cast created overlapping pools of illumination, the intersections forming complex patterns of brightness that shifted subtly with each minute movement of the flames. The ceiling arched overhead in a shallow dome, its surface painted matte black and embedded with tiny points of silver that Hart immediately recognised as an accurate celestial map of the northern hemisphere's night sky.

The walls between the candle niches were draped with black tapestries that absorbed light rather than reflected it, creating the illusion that the chamber extended indefinitely beyond its physical boundaries. Each tapestry was embroidered in silver thread with the same motif—an ouroboros, the ancient symbol of a serpent consuming its tail, rendered with meticulous attention to anatomical detail. The circular serpent encircled a crescent moon, its silver surface starkly contrasting the absolute black of the background fabric. The repetition of this emblem around the chamber's perimeter created a sense of being surrounded by identical windows into some parallel dimension where symbolism manifested as physical reality.

At the precise centre of the circular space stood a mahogany table, its surface polished to such perfection that it reflected the candlelight like still water. The wood's deep reddish-brown colouration appeared almost black in the chamber's soft illumination, creating a visual relationship with the surrounding tapestries while remaining distinctly organic in its subtle grain patterns. Upon this surface lay three objects arranged in triangular formation: a leather-bound tome whose cover was stamped with the same ouroboros and crescent emblem that adorned the wall hangings; a set of seven polished obsidian tokens, each carved with symbols that Hart recognised as alchemical notations for celestial bodies; and an ornate dagger whose handle was carved from what appeared to be ivory, its blade etched with angular runes that seemed to shift slightly when viewed from different angles.

Price moved to the table's far side, finally lowering his hood to reveal his face entirely. The change in illumination transformed his appearance from the austere, shadowed figure of the corridor into something more human yet simultaneously more disconcerting. The candlelight caught the sharp angles of his cheekbones, creating shadows that hollowed his cheeks and deepened the lines around his mouth. His eyes, which Hart saw clearly for the first time, reflected pinpoints of flame within irises of such pale grey that they appeared almost colourless.

"You analyse the symbolism," Price said, his voice assuming a different quality in this space, less clinical, more resonant, as if the chamber's acoustics had been specifically designed to enhance specific tonal frequencies. "The serpent consuming itself, perpetual destruction and creation. The crescent moon, with partial illumina-tion, suggests phases of revelation. The numerical significance of twelve candles, seven tokens, one blade."

Hart circled the room's perimeter, maintaining distance from the central table while cataloguing details professionally. The floor beneath his feet was polished stone—not the rough limestone of the corridor but something finer-grained, possibly marble, laid in concentric circles of alternating black and white that created a subtle labyrinthine pattern around the central table.

"Secret societies typically employ symbology from multiple historical traditions," Hart replied, his detective's instincts engaging with the evidence presented. "The ouroboros appears in Egyptian, Greek, Norse, and Hindu mythologies. The alchemical symbols date to medieval Europe. The runic script on the blade appears to be Elder Futhark, pre-Viking Era." He completed his circuit of the room, returning to stand opposite Price across the table. "An eclectic collection suggesting either comprehensive historical scholarship or deliberate misdirection regarding the organisation's origins."

Price's lips curved in what might have been appreciation for the analysis or amusement at its limitations. "The Order of the Eclipse pre-dates modern classification systems," he said, resting his fingertips lightly on the leather-bound tome. "Its membership has included individuals whose contributions to human knowledge remain largely uncredited in historical records—philosophers whose ideas were too dangerous for their time, scientists whose discoveries threatened established power structures, seekers who found truths that society wasn't prepared to accept."

Hart noted the present tense—*has included*, not *had included* —implying ongoing existence rather than a historical artefact. This claim was characteristic of secret society mythologies: ancient lineage, hidden influence, knowledge suppressed for the greater good or reserved for the worthy few. Such narratives typically elevated members' importance while justifying information asymmetry and hierarchical power structures.

"And now the Order concerns itself with the disappearance of a seven-year-old girl and the academic disgrace of a university professor," Hart said, the scepticism in his tone precisely calibrated— enough to establish critical distance without dismissing the possibility that something legitimate might underlie Price's elaborate presentation.

"The Order concerns itself with truth," Price replied, each word measured with scrupulous care. "Particularly truths obscured by those with vested interests in maintaining convenient narratives." He opened the leather-bound tome to a page marked with a silver ribbon, revealing text written in an unfamiliar script interspersed with astronomical diagrams and mathematical equations. "Seven years ago, two events occurred in apparent temporal proximity but without causal relationship: your sister's disappearance and my academic dismissal. The conventional narrative established these as coincidental personal and professional tragedies connected only by your involvement in both."

Price turned another page, revealing what appeared to be a map marked with locations Hart recognised from their puzzle trail: the gallery, the clockmaker's shop, the Observatory, and the university. "The Order has reason to believe these events share deeper connections—patterns invisible to those bound by conventional investigative methodologies. Patterns that, if properly understood, could reveal not just what happened to Elizabeth, but why it happened, and who benefited from her disappearance and my removal from the academic community."

Hart studied Price's expression, searching for telltale indicators of delusion or manipulation—the subtle signs revealing whether this elaborate construction was a genuine conspiracy or psychological compensation for professional failure. Price's features remained composed, his pale eyes steady, and his presentation neither too insistent nor too detached. Either he truly believed what he was saying, or he had achieved a level of deception that transcended standard analytical assessment.

"The Order of the Eclipse," Price continued, closing the tome with ceremonial precision, "has selected you for a mission capable of reshaping the fate of many. Not just Elizabeth's fate, mine, or yours—though these are certainly central to the immediate task—but potentially the fates of others affected by the same forces that converged seven years ago."

He lifted one of the obsidian tokens, rotating it between his fingers so candlelight played across its polished surface. "Our observers have monitored your progress through the preliminary trials. Your performance has confirmed what I argued from the beginning: that despite your scepticism and our complicated history, you possess the unique combination of skills and personal invest-ment necessary to uncover truths that have remained hidden for seven years."

Hart's mind worked with clinical detachment despite the charged atmosphere and personal implications of Price's words. The chamber, the symbols, the ritualistic presentation could be elaborate theatre designed to enhance the perceived significance of what might other-wise be recognised as a traumatised academic's conspiracy theory. Yet the resources required for such construction, the precision of the hidden mechanisms, and the comprehensive integration of mean-ingful symbols from Hart's past suggested something more substan-tial than individual obsession.

"You've gone to extraordinary lengths to arrange this meeting," Hart said, his gaze moving deliberately from the tokens to the dagger to the tome before returning to Price's face. "The cell, the corridor, this chamber—all constructed to create a specific psychological context for your proposal. The question remains: why not simply present your evidence directly? Why the elaborate puzzle trail leading to this moment?"

Price spread his hands in a gesture encompassing the chamber and, by extension, all that had preceded it. "Would you have believed me without experiencing the process? Would theoretical assertions about hidden connections have convinced you without demon-strating the intricate patterns underlying seemingly disparate events?" He shook his head slightly. "You required empirical evidence of my capabilities, tangible proof that I possess insights beyond conventional understanding. The journey was the evidence—each step revealing another layer of design invisible to others but percep-tible to you because of our shared intellectual foundation."

The explanation aligned with what Hart had already deduced: the elaborate construction served not just as psychological manipula-tion but as proof of concept, demonstrating that Price could indeed perceive and construct patterns of connection that others would miss.

Whether those patterns revealed actual conspiracy or merely the intricate architecture of obsession remained to be determined.

"And these observers from the Order," Hart said, gesturing toward the chamber's circular wall, "they're satisfied with my performance in your demonstration?"

"Sufficiently to proceed to the next stage," Price confirmed, adjusting one of the obsidian tokens to align precisely with a specific point in the celestial map painted on the ceiling. "The eclipse approaches, Detective Hart. The moment when hidden truth emerges from shadow into light, revealed not gradually but in sudden, complete illumination." He looked up from the token, meeting Hart's gaze with an intensity that transcended their complex history. "The question is whether you're prepared to stand in that revelation, regardless of what it might mean for your understanding of the past seven years."

The implication hung between them, weighted with the accumulated pressure of guilt, obsession, and the desperate hope that accurate answers regarding Elizabeth's fate might finally be within reach. The candles continued their steady burning, marking time through the consumption of wax rather than the mechanical progression of seconds. In this suspended moment, Hart felt the convergence of his past and present selves—the academic who had failed his sister and the detective who had spent seven years atoning through the solving of others' mysteries. Both versions of himself now stood at a threshold that promised integration or dissolution, revelation or deeper deception.

The choice remained genuinely his despite the elaborate stage management that had led to this moment.

Hart stood motionless before the table, the warm glow of twelve candles illuminating his choice. He closed his eyes, not in rejection of the moment but in a deliberate internal retreat—accessing memories he had filed away in the most secure vaults of his mind. The chamber around him receded as he excavated a specific recollection: afternoon sunlight streaming through kitchen windows, casting golden parallelograms across a wooden table cluttered with papers covered in childish handwriting. Elizabeth, six years old then, her dark hair escaping from hastily tied ribbons, bent over a puzzle he had created for her—a substitution cypher encoding a silly message about hidden cookies. Her small fingers traced letters, her brow furrowed in concentration, then the sudden brightness of her smile as understanding clicked into place. "I solved it, Alan!" Her voice's pure, uncomplicated pride as she revealed the decoded message made her delight in the process more significant than the trivial reward it led to.

The memory carried a sensory precision that belied its age—the particular quality of light, the scent of their mother's lemon cleaner on the wooden table, and the sticky residue of jam on Elizabeth's fingers from her afternoon snack. These details had been preserved with perfect fidelity in Hart's mind, unaltered by time or subsequent experience. What had changed was their context, transformed by tragedy from simple domestic happiness into artefacts of irretrievable loss.

Hart inhaled sharply, the chamber's warm air filling his lungs as another memory surfaced—Elizabeth at seven, her face serious with concentration as they sat together on the lake house porch, working through increasingly complex puzzles he designed to challenge her developing mind. These were their rituals: he created, she solved, both finding mutual satisfaction in the exchange. Even at seven, she had begun developing her puzzles for him, childish constructions with imprecise rules that he approached with exaggerated consideration, validating her nascent abilities through his careful attention.

"Your sister possessed remarkable pattern recognition abilities," Price said quietly, his voice penetrating Hart's reverie with unsettling accuracy as if he could observe the specific memories being accessed. "Genetic predisposition, perhaps, or environmental influence from your guidance. Either way, she demonstrated analytical capabilities far beyond her developmental stage."

Hart opened his eyes, the chamber returning to sharp focus. Price stood with uncharacteristic stillness, his usual precise gestures temporarily suspended as if recognising the delicacy of the moment. The ouroboros symbols on the tapestries shifted in Hart's peripheral vision; the serpents were neither fully static nor actively moving but existed in some intermediate state of potential motion.

"She left a message," Hart said, the words emerging with unexpected rawness despite his attempt at professional detachment. "The morning of July 15th. Before I took the call about your research irregularities. A cypher was written on her birthday card to me." He pressed a clenched fist against his chest, a physical gesture that externalised the constriction he felt whenever he accessed this memory. "I never solved it. I never decoded her final communication in all these years, with all my training."

The admission carried the weight of professional failure fused with personal guilt—the child's puzzle that had defeated the detective, the brother's inability to understand his sister's last message. Hart's jaw tightened against the surge of emotion accompanying this revelation, his shoulders stiffening as if physically bracing against the memory's impact.

"Perhaps," Price suggested, his voice modulating to perfect neutrality, "it remained unsolved because you lacked essential context —key information necessary for proper decryption."

The implication hung in the candlelit air between them: that the Order of the Eclipse possessed, or claimed to possess, the missing elements required to decode not just Elizabeth's final message but the larger mystery of her disappearance. The proposition was perfectly calculated to bypass Hart's considerable scepticism, targeting the point where intellectual curiosity intersected with his most profound emotional vulnerability.

Hart's analytical mind reasserted itself, conducting a rapid assessment of the situation despite the emotional undertow that threatened to overwhelm his professional judgment. The probability that Price had constructed this elaborate scenario based solely on delusional thinking remained significant. The resources required suggested either considerable personal wealth redirected toward obsessive purposes or the actual existence of an organisation backing his efforts. The precision of the psychological manipulation indicated either remarkable intuition regarding Hart's internal state or prior access to personal information that should have remained private.

None of these analyses, however, addressed the central question: what if Price was right? What if there truly were connections between Elizabeth's disappearance and Price's academic disgrace that conventional investigation had failed to discover? The cost of dismissing this possibility, however remote, was potentially abandoning his last chance to find his sister's fate.

Hart planted both feet firmly on the chamber's stone floor, physically grounding himself as his mind navigated treacherous currents of hope, scepticism, and the particular vulnerability accompanying potential revelation after years of uncertainty. His fingers trembled slightly as he extended his hand toward the leather-bound tome— not from fear but from the concentrated effort of maintaining control while approaching a decision that could irrevocably alter his understanding of the past seven years.

"If I accept this mission," Hart said, his voice steadier than his hands, "it's as a detective, not a convert. I retain my methodologies, my standards of evidence, my critical assessment of claims made by you or the Order." He met Price's gaze directly, establishing parameters with the same precision he would use to define terms in an academic debate. "I'll follow your trail of evidence, but I'll evaluate it according to investigative principles, not mystical revelations."

Price inclined his head in acknowledgement, causing candlelight to slide across his features like liquid gold. "The Order expects nothing less. Truth withstands scrutiny; only falsehood requires blind acceptance."

Hart exhaled, a decision crystallising within him not as sudden determination but as the natural conclusion of processes set in motion when he discovered the photograph in his cell. Every step since then—following Price through the corridor, entering this chamber, accessing memories of Elizabeth—had been a movement toward this inevitable point of commitment. The elaborate staging, the psychological manipulation, the symbolic presentation—all were secondary to the fundamental question that had driven him for seven years: what happened to Elizabeth?

His fingertips touched the leather cover of the tome, the material warm and responsive beneath his touch, as if the book possessed some form of awareness. The embossed ouroboros seemed to shift slightly against his fingers. However, Hart recognised this as a sensory illusion rather than a supernatural manifestation—a product of tactile perception and the interplay of candlelight on the textured surface.

"I accept," Hart said, the words carrying the weight of professional commitment and personal vulnerability. "Not out of belief in the Order or acceptance of conspiracy theories, but because unexplored possibilities regarding Elizabeth's case cannot be dismissed without investigation."

He rested both palms fully on the book's cover, the gesture carrying the solemnity of an unspoken vow. The symbolic significance wasn't lost on him—this physical connection to the tome represented intellectual engagement with whatever information the Order claimed to possess. Even as he committed, part of his mind maintained a critical distance, analysing his actions as a potential vulnerability and noting the emotional factors that influenced his decision.

Price nodded once, a precise, economical movement that acknowledged the significance of Hart's choice without celebrating victory. "The eclipse occurs in seventy-two hours," he said, revealing a slim leather case concealed there beneath the table. "This contains the initial documentation—evidence the Order has accumulated regarding both Elizabeth's disappearance and the academic investigation that led to my dismissal. Review it according to your detective's methodology. Identify the patterns that conventional investigation overlooked."

Hart accepted the case, its weight suggesting substantial contents despite its slender profile. The leather was cool against his fingers, strikingly contrasting the warmth of the tome's cover. This sensory distinction seemed engineered to underscore the transition from symbolic acceptance to practical investigation.

"When you've reviewed the materials," Price continued, "you'll understand why the Order believes these events share causal relationships beyond temporal coincidence. You'll recognise why we selected you specifically for this mission and why the eclipse represents our optimal window for revelation."

Hart nodded, already mentally preparing the analytical framework he would apply to the provided materials—the same rigorous methodology he employed in his detective work, now directed toward a case that blurred the boundaries between professional investigation and personal quest. Whatever truth lay buried in the connection between Elizabeth's disappearance and Price's disgrace, he would excavate it using the tools of evidence, logic, and pattern recognition that had defined his post-academic life.

As he prepared to leave the chamber with the leather case, Hart experienced a curious sensation—not quite hope, which he had carefully excised from his emotional repertoire years ago, but something adjacent to it. A tentative recognition that paths long thought permanently closed might contain previously unnoticed branches, that conclusions accepted as final might prove merely provisional.

The candles continued to burn steadily around the chamber's perimeter, twelve flames marking the boundary between the known and the unknown, between established narratives and possible revelations. Hart stood at this threshold, the leather case containing Price's evidence secure in his grip. His decision was made not in abandonment of scepticism but in service to a more fundamental imperative: the pursuit of truth, regardless of its compatibility with existing beliefs or the personal cost of its discovery.

Behind him, Price remained at the table, his tall figure rendered in dramatic chiaroscuro by the candles' glow, his pale eyes reflecting points of light that seemed to emanate from within. The Order of the Eclipse had selected its messenger carefully—a man whose intellectual history with Hart created the precise combination of rivalry and respect required to overcome initial disbelief. Whether the puppet master of an elaborate deception or agent of legitimate revelation remained to be determined. But Hart had committed to the investigation, and whatever path it revealed would be followed to its conclusion—for Elizabeth, for justice, and for the resolution of questions that had haunted him through seven years of uncertainty.

The quest began in a concrete cell with three carefully placed items now assumed formal structure, transforming from Price's elaborate puzzle into Hart's methodical investigation. The mysterious Order, the ritualistic chamber, the symbolic artefacts—all would be subjected to the same analytical scrutiny he applied to conventional evidence. And if legitimate truth regarding Elizabeth's fate awaited discovery beneath the layers of theatrical presentation, Hart would find it—not through mystical revelation but through the patient, precise application of the investigative skills he had spent seven years refining.

He left the candlelit chamber with steady steps, the leather case containing Price's evidence held securely against his side. His mind was already constructing the framework for assessment, analysis, and verification to determine whether the Order of the Eclipse offered genuine insight or merely elaborate misdirection in the case that had defined his life's trajectory.

10

THE SCHOLAR'S FALL

The evidence sprawled across three whiteboards like a patient's innards exposed during surgery—photographs pinned with clinical precision, red string connecting seemingly disparate elements, cryptic notations in Hart's increasingly unsteady handwriting stretching from edge to edge of the glossy white surfaces. The precinct's storage room had been hastily repurposed into a puzzle chamber forty-eight hours earlier, fluorescent tubes replacing the warm candlelight of Price's theatrical setting, institutional furniture standing in stark contrast to the ritualistic arrangements of the Order's underground sanctuary. Yet despite these differences, Hart recognised the space for what it truly was: another kind of temple, one dedicated to the methodical dissection of Price's elaborate game.

Hart sat hunched over a metal desk salvaged from the precinct's basement, his shoulders curved forward like parentheses around the open files before him. The leather case Price had given him lay empty beside his right elbow, its contents now dispersed across every available surface in the room. His tie hung loosened and askew, his collar darkened with perspiration despite the room's persistent chill. The muscles in his forearms twitched visibly beneath rolled sleeves—involuntary spasms born of caffeine saturation and sleep deprivation.

Seventy-two hours until the eclipse. Sixty-one remained, each minute devoured by the methodical consumption of Price's materials, each second tightening the coil of tension lodged beneath his sternum.

The door hinges protested with a metallic sigh as Clara entered, bearing two steaming cups that perfumed the stale air with the bitter promise of artificial alertness. She navigated the obstacle course of stacked file boxes and displaced furniture with practised ease, her movements suggesting this wasn't her first visit to Hart's improvised sanctuary since his return from Price's underground chamber.

"You should be wearing hazmat suits here," she said, placing one cup beside a stack of yellowed newspaper clippings. "The CDC probably has regulations against this level of caffeine concentration in enclosed spaces."

Hart's fingers continued their restless dance across a sheet of numerical sequences, tracing patterns only he could discern. His acknowledgement of Clara's presence manifested solely as a slight shift in posture, his shoulders relaxing infinitesimally as if her arrival permitted him momentary release from maximum vigilance.

"You need to rest," Clara said. It was not a suggestion, but a professional assessment was delivered with the detached concern of a doctor noting declining vital signs. "Your analysis degrades with each hour of sleep deprivation. Basic neuroscience."

"I'm fine." Hart's voice emerged rough from disuse, the words scraping against his vocal cords like rusted machinery returning to operation. He reached for the coffee without looking up, muscle memory guiding his hand to the cup with mechanical precision. "The eclipse timeline doesn't accommodate standard biological requirements."

Clara leaned against the desk's edge, deliberately casual yet strategically placed within Hart's peripheral vision. The soft lamp on the desk cast her shadow across the files, a gentle intrusion he couldn't entirely ignore.

"You've been avoiding talking about him," she said finally, the statement hanging in the air with quiet persistence. "About Price. Not just since you returned with that case, but for years."

Hart's shoulders tensed visibly, the muscles along his neck corded beneath his skin like ropes pulled to breaking tension. His pen stilled against the paper, a period in the middle of an unfinished sentence. The wall clock ticked into the silence, its hands indicating fifteen minutes past two in the morning—the indeterminate territory between yesterday's exhaustion and tomorrow's demands.

"There's nothing to discuss beyond what's relevant to the case," he said, each word measured and controlled, a man carrying volatile materials across uncertain terrain.

Clara waited, her silence more effective than further questioning. The tactic was familiar from countless interrogations they had conducted together—the power of an unfilled pause, the human instinct to populate emptiness with revelation.

After thirty-seven seconds, Hart counted each one with internal precision and carefully placed the pen on the desk. His fingertips drummed against the metal surface, a staccato rhythm that betrayed the controlled stillness of the rest of his body.

"We were colleagues," he said, his gaze fixed on a crime scene photograph rather than meeting Clara's eyes. "Intellectual rivals who became research partners. This was fifteen years ago, before I joined the department."

"Before Elizabeth," Clara said quietly, not a question but a gentle placement of the chronological marker they both recognised as the fulcrum upon which Hart's life balanced—before and after his sister's disappearance.

Hart nodded once, a tight, economical movement. When he finally looked up, his eyes revealed the particular hollowness that extended sleep deprivation carves into even the most disciplined minds. Against one wall, the evidence photos created a grim collage —body positions arranged in patterns that mimicked academic diagrams, blood spatter forming equations recognisable only to those with specific theoretical training.

"Price and I developed complementary theories regarding pattern recognition in seemingly random data sets," Hart continued, assuming the flat, instructional quality it took on when distance was required from emotional content. "His approach was intuitive, often brilliant, but methodologically questionable. Mine was systematic, rigorous, occasionally plodding. Together, we balanced each other's limitations."

His eyes darted away when Clara opened her mouth to ask a more personal question, his attention suddenly absorbed by a notation in one of the open files. The evasion was transparent but pointed —a boundary marked.

"Your academic background isn't in your personnel file," Clara observed, redirecting slightly. "Just that you transferred from academic research to law enforcement after your sister's disappearance. No specifics about your field or publications."

Hart's fingers resumed drumming against the desk, the rhythm changing to something more complex, almost musical in its mathematical precision. "I requested that those details be redacted when I joined the department. Too many questions otherwise. Too many assumptions about my motivations."

The scattered evidence photos cast morbid shadows across the room as the desk lamp's angle shifted with Clara's movement. The latest victim's face stared upward from a glossy 8x10, his body arranged in a position referencing a specific scientific apparatus. This detail would be meaningless to anyone without knowledge of Hart and Price's experimental work.

"He's reconstructing your shared research through these murders," Clara said, connecting threads Hart deliberately left unspoken. "That's why you recognised the patterns immediately and knew exactly which puzzles he was setting."

Hart's hands stilled, then flattened against the desk surface as if physically bracing against the weight of her observation. The wall clock's ticking seemed to intensify, each second hammering against the room's silence with metallic insistence.

"Yes," he acknowledged, the admission carrying the particular weight of a long-maintained silence finally broken. "Each victim is positioned according to specific experimental configurations we designed. Each puzzle incorporates elements from our theoretical models. He's not just killing people, Clara. He's rewriting our academic history in blood."

The fluorescent light overhead flickered momentarily, casting the room into partial shadow before reasserting its harsh illumination. Hart's face in that brief darkness had seemed to transform, revealing a glimpse of the younger man he had been before tragedy and professional reinvention had carved their signatures into his features.

"You've never talked about it," Clara said, her voice gentler now, offering a space for revelation rather than demanding it. "Any of it. Not Price, not your academic work, not the connection to Elizabeth."

Hart's gaze moved across the whiteboards where he had mapped connections between Price's evidence and the official case files from Elizabeth's disappearance. Red string linked academic papers to lake house photographs, experimental diagrams to search party maps. The pattern was incomplete, fragmented, but undeniably there—a constellation only half-charted, its full shape still hidden beyond the horizon of available information.

"I couldn't," he said, the words emerging with unexpected vulnerability. "Investigating Elizabeth's case as a brother nearly destroyed me. Approaching it as a detective required compartmentalisation."

His fingers traced the edge of a photograph showing Elizabeth on her seventh birthday, her smile reflecting a light that had left the world hours earlier. The image was worn at the corners, the only personal photograph in a room dedicated to clinical analysis.

"But Price is removing those compartments one by one," Hart continued, a new resolve hardening in his voice. "If I'm going to understand what he's trying to tell me about Elizabeth, I need to remember who we were before everything fell apart."

He looked up at Clara, decision crystallising in his expression. "You should know the whole story. Starting from the beginning."

———

The lecture hall swam into existence around him, not through the hazy distortion of typical remembrance but with the crystalline clarity of memories preserved through obsessive revisitation. Polished oak panels lined the walls, their warm honey tones absorbing the gentle illumination from brass light fixtures that had hung unchanged since the university's founding two centuries earlier. Tiered seating rose in a perfect semicircle around the presentation floor, each row filled with faculty members in formal academic attire, interspersed with graduate students clutching notebooks and recording devices. The air carried the particular quality of anticipation that precedes intellectual revelation—a collective inhalation held in suspension, waiting for the moment when new ideas would transform understanding.

Young Alan stood in the narrow antechamber beside the podium, adjusting his tie with precise, economical movements. His reflection in the small wall mirror showed a man just beginning to inhabit the role of academic pioneer—a freshly tenured professor still possessed the energy and conviction that sometimes erode with institutional security. His dark hair was cropped shorter than he wore it now, his face unmarked by the particular gravity that prolonged grief etches into human features. Beside him, Jonathan Price arranged presentation materials with theatrical deliberation, his movements suggesting an awareness of himself as a performer even in these preparatory moments hidden from the audience.

"Ready to make history?" Price asked, smoothing the lapels of a jacket that cost more than most assistant professors earned in a month. Unlike Hart's academic uniform of navy blazer and Oxford shirt, Price dressed with calculated distinctiveness—today a charcoal suit tailored to emphasise his height, paired with a crimson tie that drew attention to his animated gestures during presentations. His auburn hair curled artfully at his temples, styled to appear casually perfect in the way that requires significant effort.

"Ready to present empirically supported findings," Hart replied with the faint smile that characterised their professional repartee. "History can decide its parameters."

Price laughed, the sound rich with genuine affection beneath its patina of sophisticated amusement. "Always the methodological purist. That's why they need both of us up there." He tapped a finger against one of Hart's meticulously prepared slides. "You provide the foundation; I provide the vision. Structure and imagination in perfect balance.

They emerged onto the lecture floor together, their entrance triggering a subtle shift in the audience's collective posture—bodies leaning forward slightly, attention focusing with laser precision. Department heads nodded in professional acknowledgement, while graduate students watched with the particular hunger of those still believing in academic meritocracy, still convinced that brilliance alone determined trajectory.

Hart assumed his position first, organising his notes with surgical precision while Price arranged their visual aids with a showman's sense of timing. The wooden podium beneath Hart's fingertips was worn smooth by generations of scholars, its surface bearing the invisible imprints of countless nervous hands clutching at authority, certainty, or both.

"Our research addresses fundamental questions regarding pattern recognition in complex data environments," Hart began, his voice carrying the measured cadence of someone navigating between established knowledge and innovative proposition. He introduced their theoretical framework methodically, building from first principles through logical progressions, constructing a foundation of understanding beneath the audience's feet before guiding them toward more speculative territory.

His presentation slides reflected his approach—each masterpiece of informational efficiency, data visualised with elegant precision, unnecessary elements eliminated with almost ascetic discipline. His hands moved with controlled emphasis as he indicated key relationships in their findings, and his gestures were as economical as his speech patterns.

When Price stepped forward to present his portions, the contrast was immediately apparent yet perfectly complementary. Where Hart built methodical architecture, Price painted with bold theoretical strokes. His voice modulated dramatically, rising with excitement at pivotal concepts, dropping to conspiratorial intimacy when suggesting paradigm-shifting implications. His slides incorporated unexpected visual metaphors, his laser pointer dancing across the screen with flourishes that somehow clarified rather than distracted.

"The fundamental breakthrough," Price explained, leaning forward with infectious enthusiasm, "lies in our discovery that seemingly random datasets contain embedded geometric relationships invisible to conventional analysis methods. When viewed through our integrative framework—" he gestured toward Hart with genuine collegial respect, "—these patterns emerge not as statistical anomalies but as meaningful communicative structures.

They moved between their respective sections with choreographed precision, a scientific duet rehearsed through months of collaboration. Hart provided the empirical foundation for Price's theoretical flights, and Price illuminated unexpected applications of Hart's methodological innovations. Together, they created a presentation greater than either could have produced independently—rigour and inspiration in perfect balance, each strengthening rather than undermining the other.

The question period revealed the depth of their intellectual partnership even more clearly than the presentation itself. When a senior faculty member raised concerns about their statistical methodology, Hart responded with technical precision while Price translated the explanation into a compelling narrative. When a sceptical department chair questioned the practical applications, Price offered visionary possibilities while Hart grounded them in experimental parameters.

"The implications for cryptographic security alone justify continued research," Price concluded in response to a particularly challenging question, gesturing with elegant economy. "But as Dr. Hart's experimental protocols have demonstrated, the potential extends far beyond information security into pattern recognition applications ranging from early disease detection to predictive sociological modelling."

From the front row, the university president, who rarely attended departmental presentations, nodded with the particular expression administrators reserve for research likely to attract substantial grant funding. Department chairs exchanged glances weighted with professional assessment, while graduate students scribbled notes with the frantic energy of those witnessing a significant shift in their chosen field's landscape.

After the formal presentation concluded, colleagues gathered around them in concentric circles of academic hierarchy—senior faculty first, then junior professors, finally graduate students hovering at the periphery, hoping to absorb brilliance through proximity. Hart and Price accepted congratulations with their characteristic styles—modest professionalism and charismatic assurance that made each well-wisher feel particularly valued.

When the crowd finally dispersed, they stood alone in the lecture hall, surrounded by the silence that follows intellectual performance—a space filled with diminishing adrenaline and the peculiar vulnerability accompanying public revelation of private thought.

"That," Price said, gathering his presentation materials with satisfied deliberation, "was nothing short of triumphant." He glanced toward the empty seats, the expression on his face suggesting he was already imagining larger audiences, greater acclaim. "The foundation is laid. Next comes the actual construction."

Hart nodded, experienced enough to recognise a genuine breakthrough but too methodical to indulge in premature celebration. "The experimental protocols need refinement. Our sample sizes are still—"

"Details," Price interrupted, waving away methodological concerns with elegant dismissal. "Important details, certainly, but merely engineering at this point. The theoretical framework stands." He clapped Hart on the shoulder, the physical contact an uncommon breach of Hart's typical professional boundaries permitted by the moment's significance. "We're going to change the world, my friend."

Hart recalled perfectly how those words had filled him with uncharacteristic optimism—a momentary suspension of his natural caution, a belief that their partnership might produce something transformative. Price's certainty had been contagious, his vision compelling enough to temporarily override Hart's methodological reservations.

The lecture hall dissolved around him, oak panels and brass fixtures fading into the sterile fluorescence of the precinct's makeshift puzzle room. Clara watched him from her position against the desk, her expression revealing that something of that fifteen-year-old moment had translated through his retelling—some essence of possibility and potential now rendered tragic through subsequent events.

"We were brilliant together," Hart said, his voice carrying the particular weight of retrospective understanding. "That was the problem."

The laboratory materialised in Hart's memory with architectural precision—not the gleaming, windowed showcases featured in university promotional materials, but the actual research environment hidden two floors below ground level, where concrete walls and limited access points protected experiments too sensitive for casual observation. Brushed steel countertops stretched along three walls, their surfaces cluttered with equipment representing the awkward adolescence of technology—sophisticated enough to attempt unprecedented calculations but not yet elegant in design or interface. The specialised pattern recognition apparatus occupied the centre of the room, a hybrid construction of modified supercomputer components and custom-built analytical modules connected by a nervous system of fibre optic cables pulsed with subtle blue illumination.

Hart moved through the preliminary setup with methodical focus, his latex-gloved hands adjusting calibration settings with micrometre precision. Each movement followed the exhaustive experimental protocol he had developed over eighteen months of preliminary testing, his body navigating the laboratory's confined space with the unconscious efficiency of a surgeon in a familiar operating theatre. By contrast, Price paced the perimeter with barely contained energy, his movements suggesting a caged predator rather than a scientist preparing for controlled experimentation. He checked his watch every 47 seconds—Hart had counted—as if the passage of time constituted a personal affront.

"The university president is bringing the NSA grant committee at four," Price reminded him, adjusting equipment settings Hart had already verified. "We need preliminary results before they arrive."

Hart nodded without interrupting his calibration sequence. "The protocol requires 94 minutes for proper system stabilisation. We started at 1:17. That gives us an adequate margin if the process functions as designed."

The laboratory hummed with electronic life around it—cooling fans maintaining optimal operating temperatures, hard drives spinning at precisely regulated RPMs, and the environmental control system adjusting air circulation to compensate for the heat generated by their equipment. Beneath these mechanical sounds lay the subsonic vibration of the university's primary power conduits running beneath the floor, delivering the extraordinary electrical current their modified systems required. The air carried the distinct scent of ozone that accompanied high-energy computing, underlaid with the sterile emptiness of HEPA-filtered circulation.

Price's fingers drummed against a stainless steel counter, creating a rhythmic counterpoint to the laboratory's ambient sounds. "We've verified these calibrations three times already," he said, watching Hart complete another systematic check of their primary data collection modules. "The redundancies are excessive."

"The redundancies," Hart countered without looking up from his work, "separate legitimate research from theoretical gambling. Especially considering the security implications."

Their project had evolved significantly from its academic origins—what began as pure research into pattern recognition within random datasets had revealed unexpected applications for cryptographic security. The implications had attracted both substantial funding and intense scrutiny, elevating their work from departmental interest to institutional priority. Their apparatus could potentially identify embedded patterns invisible to conventional analysis, with applications ranging from medical diagnostics to signals intelligence.

Price moved to the central terminal, his reflection fragmenting across multiple monitoring screens. "Every significant scientific breakthrough in history came from researchers willing to accelerate beyond established protocols," he said, his voice carrying the particular timbre it assumed when delivering pronouncements he considered self-evident. "Galileo didn't triple-check his telescopic calibrations before challenging geocentrism."

Hart smiled thinly, continuing his systematic preparation. "Galileo also spent the latter part of his life under house arrest. I prefer our current laboratory access."

The specialized slides containing their test algorithms required precise handling. Each glass rectangle was etched with nano-scale circuit elements that would interface with the system's optical recognition components. Hart deliberately removed them from their protective case, inspecting each under magnification before positioning it in the analysis chamber. The slides represented months of painstaking development, each containing pattern-generation sequences designed to test specific aspects of their theoretical framework.

Price watched this process with visible impatience, checking his watch increasingly frequently as Hart continued his methodical preparation. When Hart began his third verification of the system's security protocols, Price's restraint finally collapsed.

"This is absurd," he said, moving to intercept Hart before he could initiate another diagnostic sequence. "We've established theoretical validity. We've constructed a functional apparatus. The only remaining step is execution, which you seem determined to postpone indefinitely."

Hart continued adjusting the security parameters, his focus unbroken despite Price's interruption. "The system connects directly to the university's primary data infrastructure. A malfunction could compromise every research database on campus."

"A remote possibility that doesn't justify this excessive caution,"

Price countered, his hand resting on Hart's shoulder firmly. "Greatness requires risk, Alan. You've verified the essential safeguards. The remaining protocols are bureaucratic redundancies imposed by administrators who don't understand our work."

Hart's fingers stilled on the keyboard as he considered Price's argument. The calibrations had indeed shown consistent stability across multiple preliminary tests. The additional security protocols were primarily designed to protect against worst-case scenarios whose probability vectors were vanishingly small. And Price was right about the grant committee—a successful demonstration today would secure funding to transform their research capacity.

"The quantum decryption module hasn't completed its full diagnostic cycle," Hart said, his tone suggesting this represented his final significant reservation. "Bypassing that verification introduces variables we haven't properly modelled."

Price's expression shifted from frustration to persuasive intensity. "The module has passed every previous diagnostic without issue. We're talking about a statistical anomaly probability in the ten-thousandth percentile." He gestured toward the central apparatus with the particular elegant emphasis that characterised his presentations. "This is the moment, Alan. The inflexion point where theoretical possibility transforms into demonstrated reality."

Hart studied the monitoring screens, each displaying stable parameters within expected ranges. His natural methodological caution wrestled with the compelling logic of Price's argument and the practical reality of their time constraints. The internal debate manifested physically in the minute tension of his shoulders, the controlled rhythm of his breathing as he calculated risk factors against potential benefits.

"Limited procedural adjustments," he conceded finally, entering commands that would bypass the extended security diagnostics while maintaining core safeguards. "But we maintain continuous monitoring of all primary systems, and at the first sign of instability, we initiate emergency shutdown."

Price's smile conveyed triumph, carefully modulated to avoid appearing excessive. "Sensible precautions for a reasonable probability assessment." He moved immediately to the central control station, initiating startup sequences before Hart could reconsider his decision. "History seldom remembers excessive caution, my friend. It remembers results."

The laboratory lighting dimmed automatically as the system drew additional power for its primary processing functions. Monitoring screens displayed cascading data as initialisation sequences progressed, each subsystem activating in carefully orchestrated succession. Hart monitored the process with heightened attention, compensating for the bypassed diagnostics with intensified personal vigilance. Price stood at the central console, his features illuminated by the blue glow of status indicators, his expression containing an almost religious quality of anticipation.

The system progressed through its abbreviated startup sequence without incident, each module coming online within acceptable parameters. The specialised slides were automatically loaded into the analysis chamber, their nano-etched surfaces scanned by precision optical sensors that translated physical patterns into digital information. Hart began to relax fractionally as the experiment proceeded according to design specifications, the initial data streams showing exactly the pattern recognition capabilities their theory had predicted.

"Perfect alignment between theoretical modelling and practical application," Price noted, his voice carrying the restrained excitement of validated hypothesis. "The security applications alone will—"

A soft chirp from the environmental monitoring system interrupted his assessment—a subtle alert indicating a minor temperature fluctuation in the quantum processing module. Hart moved immediately to the relevant terminal, fingers flying across controls as he assessed the deviation.

"Thermal regulation is showing anomalous readings," he reported, professional focus overriding any impulse toward recrimination. "The bypass may have affected cooling system integration."

"Minor fluctuation well within operational parameters," Price dismissed, focusing on the primary data output rather than system diagnostics. "The pattern recognition algorithms are performing exactly as predicted. Look at this differentiation capacity."

The temperature alert escalated from cautionary to warning, the soft chirp becoming more insistent. Secondary alerts activated in sequence—power consumption exceeding expected parameters, data throughput rates accelerating beyond modelled projections, security firewalls reporting probing attempts from within their system.

"Something's wrong with the quantum module's isolation protocols," Hart said, initiating emergency containment procedures with practised efficiency. "It's attempting to access external networks."

The overhead lights flickered as the system drew unexpected power surges, the laboratory's ambient hum rising to a discordant whine. Hart's fingers moved across three keyboards in synchronised urgency, attempting to contain cascading failures across interconnected systems. Price remained at the central console, his expression transformed from triumph to disbelief as monitoring screens displayed increasingly erratic behaviour from the core processors.

"This is impossible," Price insisted, attempting his override commands that conflicted with Hart's containment protocols. "The recognition algorithms can't generate autonomous execution sequences."

Warning alarms activated in full emergency mode, piercing the laboratory's typical acoustic environment. Red warning lights rotated at the ceiling corners, revolving crimson illumination across the increasingly chaotic scene. Sparks erupted from an overloaded circuit panel, the acrid scent of electrical fire cutting through the filtered air. Hart abandoned the manual containment attempts and slammed his palm against the emergency shutdown control—a physical killswitch designed to sever all power connections instantly.

Nothing happened.

The system continued accelerating, displaying data transfer rates that their existing hardware shouldn't have prevented. The specialised slides began to vibrate increasingly in the central analysis chamber, their nano-etched surfaces glowing with unnatural blue luminescence. Hart moved toward the manual override panel on the far wall, but before he could reach it, the analysis chamber emitted a high-pitched whine followed by the distinctive sound of shattering glass.

The primary slide had disintegrated under impossible internal pressure, its fragments spraying across the laboratory in a glittering constellation of technologically enhanced glass. Price's face contorted in shock and rage as the university's security system finally activated, emergency containment doors slamming closed as external monitoring stations detected the catastrophic failure.

The last image before the security team burst through the doors was Price standing motionless amid the chaos, illuminated by sparking equipment and emergency lighting, his expression containing not fear or confusion but something Hart recognised with disturbing clarity: the particular fury of a man whose vision of personal greatness had been thwarted by forces he refused to acknowledge as beyond his control.

Three days after the laboratory incident, the university administration arranged what they carefully termed an "informational briefing" rather than a press conference. This semantic distinction fooled no one but established the desired tone of controlled disclosure rather than crisis management. The Chancellor's conference room had been selected for its imposing architectural gravitas—oak-panelled walls lined with portraits of distinguished former administrators, a massive table of polished mahogany that positioned university officials in a literal elevation position above the assembled press representatives. The room's windows were strategically curtained to admit dignified natural light while preventing the more aggressive illumination that might have revealed the strain evident on the officials' faces had they been subjected to direct sunlight.

Chancellor Edwards occupied the central position, his silver hair and tortoiseshell glasses projecting calculated wisdom, his navy suit and burgundy tie suggesting institutional stability through traditional academic semiotics. He was flanked by the university's general counsel—a woman whose tailored charcoal suit and pearl necklace visually translated legal caution into professional elegance—and the Dean of Sciences, whose slightly rumpled appearance communicated academic credibility uncompromised by public relations concerns.

"The university takes matters of research security with the utmost seriousness," Edwards began, his voice modulated to project concern without alarm. "The incident in our Advanced Computational Laboratory represents an unfortunate technical malfunction that has been fully contained, with no risk to ongoing academic operations or student safety."

Hart stood at the room's periphery, positioned just far from the officials' table to establish visual separation from administrative decision-making while remaining close enough to indicate continued institutional affiliation. His appearance had been carefully negotiated through three separate meetings with university counsel—a fresh haircut, a conservatively cut suit provided by the university's public relations team, all visible bandages from the laboratory incident removed regardless of healing status. He maintained the neutral expression he had practised before his bathroom mirror for forty-seven minutes that morning, a carefully constructed mask of professional composure that revealed neither culpability nor defensiveness.

"Preliminary investigation indicates that the experimental apparatus experienced a catastrophic system overload," the Dean of Sciences explained, reading from a prepared statement that Hart knew had been revised seventeen times before this presentation. "This malfunction appears to have created a temporary vulnerability in our network security infrastructure, which was exploited by unknown external entities to access certain research databases."

Newspaper headlines spread across the laps and notebooks of the assembled journalists told a different story. The technology section of the morning's Tribune lay visible on the nearest reporter's notepad: **"UNIVERSITY QUANTUM COMPUTING EXPERIMENT**

COMPROMISES NATIONAL RESEARCH DATABASE." The more
sensationalist Metro had opted for directness: "ACADEMIC AMBI-
TION LEADS TO MASSIVE DATA THEFT." Even the conservative
Journal had abandoned restraint: "RECKLESS RESEARCHERS
EXPOSE SENSITIVE INFORMATION THROUGH PROCEDURAL
NEGLIGENCE."

The conspicuous absence of Jonathan Price had not gone unnoticed
by the press contingent. Questions about his whereabouts were
deflected with institutional precision—"Professor Price is cooperating
fully with the ongoing investigation"—a technically accurate statement that omitted his current location in a university-owned guest
house, isolated from press contact and collegiate interaction. At the
same time, separate teams of legal and public relations specialists
assessed damage control strategies.

"The affected systems have been isolated and secured," the university's chief information officer explained, having been summoned to
the table to provide technical gravitas. "Enhanced security protocols
have been implemented across all research networks, and we are
working closely with federal authorities to address potential data
compromise."

What remained unspoken in this carefully constructed narrative
were the actual consequences already unfolding behind administrative doors: suspended research grants, withdrawn federal funding
applications, inquiries from three separate oversight agencies, and
preliminary discussions of academic censure that would eventually
lead to Price's dismissal and Hart's professional purgatory. These real-
ities existed in a parallel conversational universe, one conducted
through confidential memoranda and closed-door meetings where
terms like "catastrophic reputation damage" and "liability exposure"
replaced the sanitised language of "unfortunate incidents" and "technical malfunctions."

The press conference concluded with practiced efficiency, the
Chancellor reading a final prepared statement that promised trans-

parency while committing to nothing specific, then standing to indicate the non-negotiable conclusion of questions. Hart was escorted
from the room through a side door before journalists could approach
him. He was guided by a public relations assistant whose sympathetic
smile failed to mask the institutional directive to remove him from
potential unscripted interactions.

Forty-seven minutes later, Hart stood in the empty faculty lounge
of the Physics Department, a neutral territory selected for its privacy
after regular hours yet public enough to discourage extreme displays
of emotion. The wall clock's second hand moved with mechanical
indifference. It measured the increasing tension as Hart waited for
Price to arrive for their first direct contact since university security
had separated them in the damaged laboratory.

The door opened with unnecessary force, its solid oak frame
absorbing the impact against the wall without visible damage. Price
entered like a carefully controlled storm system, atmospheric pressure dropping noticeably in his wake. His appearance testified to a
fundamental rejection of the university's damage control aesthetics—
unshaven, hair uncombed, wearing the same shirt he had worn
during the experiment. However, it had been perfunctorily cleaned of
obvious debris. The angry red laceration along his left cheekbone
remained undisguised by the bandage Hart knew the medical team
had applied and Price had removed.

"You were notably silent at the press conference," Price said
without preamble, each word carved from ice then polished to
dangerous sharpness. "Though I suppose maintaining silence is
easier than explaining betrayal."

Hart maintained his position by the conference table, neither
advancing nor retreating. "I followed established security protocols
after the system showed signs of instability. That's not betrayal; it's
basic research safety."

"You initiated emergency shutdown against my direct instruction!"
Price's voice escalated beyond his typical controlled modulation,
revealing the extent of his emotional compromise. "The pattern
recognition sequences were achieving unprecedented differentiation

capabilities. Another three minutes and we would have demon-strated conclusive proof of concept."

"Another three minutes and we might have compromised every research database on the eastern seaboard," Hart countered, main-taining the factual tone that had always been his emotional bulwark. "The quantum module was attempting to establish unauthorised external connections. The security breaches were originating from within our system."

Price moved further into the room, his physical presence expanding to fill the space between them with the particular density of academic fury—a specialised form of rage composed of equal parts intellectual dismissal and professional humiliation. "A properly designed quantum system establishes search parameters across networked databases. What you interpreted as 'unauthorised connec-tions' were precisely the breakthrough applications we've been theorising."

"Applications that required proper security protocols, ethics committee review, and external system authorisation." Hart felt his composure fraying at the edges, the careful neutrality he maintained throughout the administrative aftermath giving way to the genuine convictions that had motivated his emergency shutdown attempt. "We were witnessing system behaviour we couldn't predict or control."

"We were witnessing the future of pattern recognition technolo-gy!" Price slammed his palm against the conference table, the sound sharp and final in the otherwise empty room. "A future now compro-mised because you panicked at the first sign of unexpected results."

The accusation hung between them, transforming the air into something dense with unspoken subtext. In the silence that followed, Hart recognised the fundamental fracture that had always existed beneath their productive partnership—not merely different method-ological approaches, but essentially opposed views on the relation-ship between intellectual advancement and responsible research governance.

"The university investigation will establish the actual sequence of events," Hart said, his voice quieter now, the professional distance he had maintained giving way to personal disappointment. "The system logs will show—"

"The system logs will show whatever narrative best protects this institution's funding relationships and legal exposure," Price interrupted, his voice dropping into a register Hart had never heard from him before—something colder and more dangerous than academic disagreement. "But we both know what happened. You were always jealous of my insights, my intuitive leaps beyond your plodding methodology. You couldn't stand me pushing boundaries, you were too afraid to cross."

The accusation was so fundamentally disconnected from Hart's actual motivations that he momentarily lost his response capacity. Price pressed his advantage in that silence, stepping closer until only the corner of the conference table separated them.

"You've built your entire academic identity on methodological purity," Price continued, each word precisely aimed. "The careful researcher, the responsible scientist, the trusted authority. My approach threatened that identity—showed that true breakthroughs come from intuitive risk, not procedural caution. When the moment of genuine innovation arrived, you couldn't bear to be proven wrong."

"I followed established safety protocols to prevent exactly the kind of breach that occurred," Hart replied, his own anger finally surfacing through his carefully maintained composure. "Protocols we both agreed to when designing the experiment."

"Protocols that become irrelevant when standing at the threshold of transformative discovery!" Price's hand formed a fist against the polished wood of the conference table, his knuckles whitening with restraint that seemed increasingly tenuous. "Now, instead of recognition, I face academic censure. Instead of advancement, professional death. All because you lacked the courage to see our work through to its logical conclusion."

The faculty lounge's wall clock continued its mechanical measurement of their disintegrating partnership, each tick marking another irretrievable moment in a relationship that had once promised intellectual revolution and now lay shattered beyond repair. Price straightened suddenly, his posture shifting from confrontational to more contained, more precisely controlled. When he spoke again, his voice had regained its characteristic modulation, though now it carried a new undertone that raised primal warning signals in Hart's hindbrain.

"You've ruined me, Alan," he said with disturbing quietness. "My research, my reputation, my academic future—all destroyed because you couldn't transcend your methodological limitations at the crucial moment." He adjusted his cuffs with deliberate precision, a gesture incongruously formal amid the emotional devastation surrounding them. "And one day, I'll return the favour."

Hart recognised the statement not as an empty threat but as a sincere promise—a declaration of intent delivered with the same conviction Price had once applied to their shared research vision. The realisation settled in his stomach with leaden certainty: this was not merely the end of their academic partnership but the beginning of something darker that would extend beyond institutional walls into territory neither of them had yet mapped.

Price departed without further comment, leaving Hart alone in the faculty lounge with the broken pieces of their intellectual collaboration scattered invisibly around him like the glass fragments of their shattered experimental slides. Outside the window, afternoon sunlight continued to illuminate the campus with indifferent beauty, students crossing the quad with no awareness of the seismic shift that had just occurred in a quiet room where two men who once sought to change the world together had instead altered each other in ways neither had anticipated nor desired.

Alan closed the case file with a deliberate precision that belied the tremor in his hands, the folder's edge aligned exactly parallel to the desk's metal rim. The room had grown colder as his narrative progressed, or perhaps it was simply that speaking the past aloud had depleted whatever warmth his body still contained after forty-eight hours without proper rest. The fluorescent lights continued their dispassionate illumination of the puzzle room, revealing with clinical clarity the scattered evidence of Price's elaborate game—photographs of precisely positioned victims, cryptic messages written in mathematical notation, murder scenes arranged with the methodical care of academic presentations.

His voice had grown quieter as he approached the conclusion of his story, the words emerging with the careful control of someone handling fragile artefacts that might shatter under excessive pressure. The muscles along his jaw had tightened into visible relief beneath three days of stubble, and the skin beneath his eyes had darkened to the particular bruised shade that accompanies prolonged sleep deprivation. When he finally fell silent, the absence of his voice created a vacuum that seemed to draw oxygen from the room.

Clara remained seated at the edge of the desk, her posture suggesting the practised stillness of someone accustomed to receiving harrowing testimonies without contaminating them with premature response. She had maintained this supportive silence throughout his account, interrupting only with occasional clarifying questions when his narrative threatened to disappear into technical terminology or academic shorthand. Now she watched as he methodically straightened a stack of photographs, his fingertips lingering on each image as if they contained tactile information invisible to everyday observation.

"The university cleared me eventually," Hart continued after the extended silence, his tone shifting to the more distant register he employed when discussing institutional matters. "Their internal investigation concluded that I had attempted to follow proper security protocols during the system malfunction. My academic record was officially unblemished, though there were unspoken consequences—research partnerships that dissolved, grant applications that received unprecedented scrutiny, informal exclusion from certain collaborative opportunities."

He reached for the coffee cup Clara had brought hours earlier, now containing a cold and bitter liquid. He consumed it anyway, the physical discomfort seemingly irrelevant compared to the psychic effort of excavating memories he had so carefully interred.

"Price lost everything," he said, replacing the empty cup with mechanical precision. "His position, his reputation, his future in academia. The investigation found evidence of previous security violations, unauthorised system access, and experimental protocols conducted without proper oversight. My testimony was instrumental in those findings—not from malice but factual necessity."

Clara nodded, her expression conveying understanding without justification or condemnation. The puzzle room had transformed during Hart's narrative, its sterile institutional architecture overlaid with the invisible residue of past traumas and present implications. The whiteboards covered with evidence photos and cryptic notations seemed to pulse with new significance, connections previously obscured now illuminated by the context of Hart's revelations.

"Three months later, my sister disappeared," Hart concluded, the transition delivered with such careful neutrality that its emotional weight registered only in the minute adjustment of his breathing pattern. "I left academia and joined the department. Price also disappeared—institutional rumour suggested private sector work in Asia, though nothing was confirmed. Until now."

His hands moved to a manila envelope containing the most recent crime scene photographs, not yet displayed on the whiteboards with the others. The folder's tab was marked with yesterday's date and a case number in precise administrative handwriting. Hart's fingers rested on the sealed edge without opening it, as if gauging whether he possessed sufficient strength for what lay within.

"You think these puzzles, these murders—all about revenge?" Clara asked her question precisely calibrated to neither lead nor dismiss.

Hart nodded slowly, the movement revealing the weight of certainty settling across his shoulders. "It's not just a game. It's not merely an intellectual challenge." His fingers finally broke the envelope's seal, extracting the photographs with the care one might apply to unexploded ordnance. "It's personal. Price is recreating our academic history, transforming theoretical conflict into physical consequence."

The photographs emerged in sequence, each revealing another angle of the previous day's discovery—a victim seated at a desk constructed from particleboard and metal pipe, the surface covered with printed pages positioned in precise order. The man's hands had been placed on a keyboard, his head tilted slightly downward as if examining the screen of a laptop computer that was conspicuously absent. Around him, red string had been strung from floor to ceiling in complex geometric patterns that intersected at specific points marked with silver thumbtacks.

"Every riddle, every victim—they're all part of a message meant for me," Hart said, arranging the photographs in a semicircle before him, their edges touching with mathematical precision. "The first victim was posed exactly as Price stood during our initial joint presentation. The second recreated my position during the experimental calibration process. The third..."

His voice trailed into silence as he studied the latest images, something shifting in his expression—not the confusion of continued puzzlement but the particular clarity accompanying significant pattern recognition. He moved to the whiteboard where he had mapped the locations of each murder, his finger tracing connections between points that formed a geometric shape identical to the quantum processing module from their laboratory experiment.

"He's not just killing random victims," Hart said, his voice acquiring the focused intensity it assumed when an analytical breakthrough displaced emotional consideration. "He's recreating our experiment through human tableaux. Each murder corresponds to a specific component in our original apparatus design."

He returned to the desk, spreading the photographs of all victims chronologically. What had previously appeared as separate, though stylistically similar, crime scenes now revealed themselves as components of a larger construction. The positioning of each body, the specific arrangement of surroundings, the precise geometric relationships between key elements—all formed a macabre reproduction of the experimental architecture Hart and Price had designed fifteen years earlier.

"The string patterns at each scene," Hart continued, moving with renewed energy despite his physical exhaustion, "are not decorative or randomly symbolic. They're physical representations of our theoretical data flow models, showing how information was meant to move through the system." He indicated specific intersection points in the crime scene photographs. "These marks correspond exactly to the connection nodes in our original design. He's constructed a perfect replica of our experimental apparatus, with human beings replacing electronic components."

Clara joined him at the desk, studying the photographs with fresh understanding informed by his explanation. "And this latest victim represents what specific component?"

"The user interface terminal," Hart replied, his finger hovering above the photograph of the seated man before the missing laptop. "The human access point where experimental parameters were entered and results were displayed." His expression darkened as the implication crystallised. "Which means the next murder will represent the quantum processing module itself—the component that catastrophically failed, the element whose malfunction initiated the cascade that destroyed both our careers."

The fluorescent lights buzzed overhead, one tube flickering in irregular rhythm as if providing visual punctuation to Hart's revelation. He studied the photographs with the particular intensity of someone recognising not just intellectual pattern but personal threat —these were not merely evidence of Price's methodology but prophecy of his intentions, a roadmap leading inexorably toward whatever culmination he had designed for their renewed confrontation.

"He's not just recreating history," Hart said, his voice dropping to a register Clara had never heard from him before, containing equal measures of professional assessment and personal dread. "He's correcting it. Completing the failed experiment fifteen years ago, but with human components arranged according to his theoretical model." He looked up from the photographs, his eyes reflecting a clarity purchased at significant psychological cost. "And if the pattern holds, the final victim will represent the quantum module's catastrophic failure—when the system attempted to establish unauthorised external connections, when a theoretical breakthrough transformed into practical destruction."

His hands were numb from exhaustion and the room's persistent chill, but he felt a warmth in his chest, an uncomfortable heat that he recognised as the complex fusion of professional insight and personal reckoning. Price's elaborate puzzle had been deciphered, the pattern revealed, the message received with terrible clarity. Now the only remaining question was whether this understanding had come soon enough to prevent the experiment's final, fatal conclusion —or whether recognition would arrive precisely too late to avert catastrophe as in their original collaborative work.

11

ECHOES OF BETRAYAL

The fluorescent lights hummed overhead, their sterile glow casting harsh shadows across the room where Hart had spent the past seventy-two hours. His hands were numb from exhaustion, and his skin was dry and cracked from constant contact with paper and ink. Still, he felt something stirring beneath his ribcage—an uncomfortable heat that he recognised as the first embers of horrified understanding. The pattern was there—it had always been there—waiting patiently for him to see what Price had hidden in plain sight.

Hart hunched over the desk, shoulders curved into a question mark of concentration. The makeshift puzzle room had once been a storage closet at the precinct's far end, requisitioned when the scale of The Riddler case had outgrown his office walls. Three whiteboards stood sentinel around him, their white surfaces nearly obliterated by photographs, notes, and the red strings that connected them—physical manifestations of synaptic connections forming in his mind. Crime scene photographs formed a gruesome gallery: bodies arranged with meticulous precision, each positioned to replicate a component in the quantum computing experiment that had ended his academic career.

The room was silent except for the scratch of his pen across paper and the occasional whispered calculation that escaped his lips without conscious permission. His voice had taken on a ragged quality after days without proper rest, the words emerging like sandpaper against wood. The air smelled of marker ink, cold coffee, and the particular staleness that accumulates when a single human being occupies an enclosed space for too long without proper ventilation.

"Seven points of connection," he muttered, his fingertips trembling slightly as he traced a line between two photographs. "Seven death tableaux forming a perfect circumscription of the original quantum modelling parameters."

His hands bore the evidence of his obsession—ink stains had worked their way into the whorls of his fingerprints, turning them into smudged approximations of the very patterns he was attempting to decode. He hadn't bothered with sleep since the laboratory records arrived yesterday afternoon, their dusty manila folders containing fifteen-year-old diagrams of the apparatus he and Price had constructed. Those diagrams now lay spread across the desk, their edges aligning with crime scene photographs in perfect, terrible symmetry.

The room had acquired layers during his occupation, like geological strata, each marking a distinct phase in his investigation. Nearest the door lay discarded coffee cups and the remains of sandwiches Clara had forced him to unwrap at least, if not consume. The centre area held meticulously organised current case materials, while the far corner, where Hart now worked, contained the historical archives —academic papers, laboratory notes, and fifteen-year-old police reports from a case that had never been solved.

The Lowell homicide.

Hart's fingers stilled above a photograph he had deliberately placed face-down hours earlier, unable then to confront what it might reveal. Now, with dawn's grey light beginning to seep through the room's single high window, he turned it over with the careful precision of someone handling unexploded ordnance.

Professor James Lowell was found in his university office fifteen years ago, three weeks after Price's academic disgrace. Arranged at his desk as if working, hands positioned on a keyboard, throat cut with surgical precision—the first crime Hart had encountered after leaving academia for police work. The first case he had failed to solve.

Outside, the city was stirring to life. Morning light crept across the whiteboards, illuminating connections his mind had subconsciously formed for days. The tremor in Hart's hands intensified as he lifted the Lowell crime scene photograph and placed it beside the image of Price's most recent victim. The positioning was identical, not merely similar, but precise to the centimetre. The head's angle, the hands' placement, and even the overflow of blood that had dried on the desk surface followed the same pattern.

"No," Hart whispered, the word escaping as denial and recognition. His breathing shifted, becoming shallow and rapid as if the room's oxygen content had suddenly diminished. "No, it can't be..."

But it was. His eyes rushed between the photographs, confirmation building with each detail he absorbed. The Lowell murder hadn't been a random killing or professional dispute as they'd theorised fifteen years ago. It had been the first component in Price's human reconstruction of their failed experiment—the initial node in a pattern that had lain dormant for over a decade before resuming with the current sequence of killings.

Cold sweat broke across Hart's forehead as he pulled open the bottom desk drawer. He extracted a file he'd requested but has avoided examining it until now. The original investigators' notes on the Lowell case included a reference to a symbol found carved into the underside of the desk—a simple geometric shape they'd dismissed as unrelated graffiti. Hart spread the photograph on the desk, revealing a design identical to the connection nodes in their quantum apparatus schematics.

"He's been playing this game for fifteen years," Hart said aloud, horror building in his chest like pressure against a faulty valve. "The current murders aren't the beginning—they're the completion."

His hand reached for his coffee cup, the movement automatic rather than deliberate. His mind was too consumed with implications to coordinate fine motor control. His elbow struck the cup, sending dark liquid cascading across the desk, seeping into the paper with the same inexorable spread as blood across laboratory tiles. The coffee formed rivulets between photographs, creating inadvertent connections that seemed as deliberate as Price's design.

Hart made no move to stop the spread, watching instead as the liquid formed a pattern across his notes that mirrored the theoretical data flow they had mapped for their quantum module all those years ago. The symmetry was too perfect to be coincidental, too precise to be anything but designed. Price hadn't just been killing random victims; he had been recreating their experiment with human components, beginning fifteen years ago with Lowell, then pausing— why?—before resuming the pattern now.

"He was watching me," Hart whispered, insight striking with the force of physical impact. The coffee had reached the edge of the desk, drops falling to the floor in a rhythm that matched his heart pounding. "Waiting until I joined the police. Waiting until I was in the position to recognise what he was doing."

The full implication hit him with nauseating clarity. This wasn't random. This wasn't primarily about the failed experiment or Price's academic disgrace. This was about him—Alan Hart specifically. Every murder, every puzzle, every cryptic message had been designed with one recipient in mind. Price had spent fifteen years constructing an elaborate trap, baited with human lives, waiting for Hart to recognise the pattern and become ensnared in its logic.

Hart pushed back from the desk, the chair's metal legs scraping against linoleum with a sound like distant screaming. The walls of photographs and evidence suddenly seemed to pulse with malevolent intent, the red strings connecting them transformed from investigative tools to predatory webs. His vision narrowed, tunnel-like, focusing on the final photograph in the sequence. In this position, the quantum module would have been in their original apparatus, which remained empty in Price's human reconstruction.

The final killing was yet to come. And Hart knew, with sickening certainty, exactly who the intended victim would be.

The door opened with barely a sound. Clara's presence was announced instead by the subtle shift in air pressure that accompanied her entry. She paused at the threshold, absorbing the scene before her with the practised assessment of a detective who had learned to read rooms the way others read facial expressions. The coffee pooled across the desk, dripping steadily onto the floor. Hart stood with his back to the door, shoulders rigid beneath a shirt that appeared to have aged years in the past seventy-two hours, its once-crisp fabric now a topographical map of exhaustion and revelation.

"Alan," she said quietly, her voice neither startling nor soothing, simply present.

He didn't turn immediately. His hand remained extended toward the photographs spread across the desk, fingers frozen mid-gesture like a conductor who had lost his place in the score. When he finally acknowledged her presence, the movement was mechanical, as if his neck had temporarily forgotten its proper range of motion.

Clara crossed the threshold fully, closing the door behind her. The overhead light caught the tired shadows beneath Hart's eyes, the faint stubble that had progressed from deliberate neglect to unintentional beard. His shirt wrinkled beyond redemption, bore the telltale stains of someone using his clothing as an impromptu napkin. Ink marks decorated his fingers like primitive tattoos, and a smudge of black across his left cheekbone suggested he had been rubbing his face with stained hands.

"You look like a pack of fountain pens has interrogated you," she said, her tone matter-of-fact rather than judgmental. Without waiting for a response, she moved to the desk, gathered the scattered papers, and lifted them carefully above the spreading coffee. Her movements were precise and methodical, countering the chaos surrounding her.

Hart watched her organise what he had disorganised, his expression curiously blank, as if his features had temporarily forgotten their default arrangement. Something flickered behind his eyes—perhaps relief or simply a recognition that another human being was now sharing the burden of whatever revelation had struck him moments before.

"The first victim wasn't three weeks ago," he said finally, his voice hollow and clinical, each word emerging with the careful neutrality of someone reporting findings rather than experiencing them. "It was fifteen years ago. Professor James Lowell. He was found in his university office with his throat cut, positioned at his desk exactly like our third victim."

Clara continued sorting papers, creating neat stacks in dry areas of the desk. Still, her attention remained focused on Hart, allowing his words to settle into the space between them. She did not rush his explanation or fill the silence between sentences. Her shoulder occasionally brushed against his as she moved, the contact brief but deliberate—a physical reminder of presence without the presumption of comfort.

"I was still in academia then," Hart continued, reaching for one of the photographs Clara had rescued from the coffee. "It was the first homicide case I consulted on after leaving the university. We never solved it." His finger traced the edge of the image, stopping at a detail almost invisible in the lower corner. "There was a symbol carved underneath Lowell's desk that the original investigators dismissed as unrelated graffiti. It's identical to the connection nodes in the quantum apparatus Price and I designed."

Clara placed the last stack of papers on a dry corner of the desk and turned to face him fully. The fluorescent light cast her features in stark relief, emphasising the intelligence in her eyes as she processed this information. She had known fragments of Hart's academic history, pieced together from departmental gossip and the occasional oblique reference from Hart himself. Still, the whole picture had remained obscured by his careful compartmentalisation.

"This isn't a coincidence," Hart said, his finger moving between the Lowell photograph and the images of recent victims. "He's been planning this for years. The current murders aren't the beginning—they're the completion of a sequence he started fifteen years ago, then suspended until I was in a position to recognise what he was doing." His voice maintained its clinical detachment, but his hands betrayed him, trembling slightly as he arranged the photographs chronologically.

Clara stepped closer, her shoulder deliberately maintaining contact with his, a physical anchor in the current of revelation threatening to carry him away. "Then we have something he doesn't expect," she said, her voice carrying the measured pragmatism that had always balanced Hart's analytical intensity. Foreknowledge of his game. Suppose he's spent fifteen years constructing this pattern. He assumes you'll only recognise it at whatever moment he's designated —not before his endgame."

Her fingers moved to one of the whiteboards, rearranging several notes that had been placed haphazardly during Hart's moment of realisation. "What exactly is he reconstructing?" she asked, the question precise and procedural, guiding him back to the familiar territory of methodical investigation.

Hart's breathing steadied slightly as his mind engaged with the analytical challenge. "Our quantum computing experiment," he said, standing beside her at the whiteboard. "The one that failed catastrophically and ended both our academic careers. Each murder victim is positioned to represent a specific component in the apparatus we designed."

His hand moved across the board, indicating connections between photographs with a surety that had been absent moments before. "The first victim, Lowell, represented the data input terminal. The second was the primary calibration module. The third..." He paused, swallowing audibly. "The third was the user interface where the experimental parameters were entered and results displayed."

Clara watched his hand move across the board, absorbing both the information and the slight steadying of his movements as he reclaimed the familiar territory of pattern analysis. "And the next victim?" she asked quietly.

Hart's composure fractured momentarily, his features contracting with something more profound than professional concern or intellectual engagement. "The quantum processing module itself," he said, his voice dropping to a register she had never heard from him before. "The component that catastrophically failed fifteen years ago. The element whose malfunction initiated the cascade that destroyed both our careers."

His hand remained still on the board, pressing against a blank space where no photograph existed. "And when it failed," he continued, the clinical detachment slipping further, "it attempted to establish unauthorised connections to external systems. It reached beyond its containment parameters, beyond anything we had designed or anticipated."

Clara placed her hand on Hart's shoulder, the gesture neither maternal nor romantic but collegial—professional recognition of psychological burden. His muscles tensed briefly beneath her touch before releasing a fraction of their held tension.

"Whatever Price is planning," she said, her voice low but firm, "it's still bound by physical reality, not academic abstraction. His experiment requires real people, locations, and real-time constraints. Those are variables we can identify and interrupt."

Hart's breathing steadied further under her steady gaze, his mind visibly transitioning from the paralysis of revelation to the momentum of action. "You're right," he said, straightening slightly beneath her hand. "If he's recreating our experiment, only specific configurations would satisfy his design parameters. We can use that to predict his next move."

He returned to the desk, retrieving a notebook that had escaped the coffee flood. "We need to pull the complete laboratory records from university archives," he said, his voice regaining its professional cadence. "And we need Leo to analyse the digital surveillance price that has likely been established."

Clara nodded, already moving toward the door, her notebook appearing as if conjured. "I'll organise both," she said, pausing with her hand on the doorknob. "And Alan? Change your shirt. You look like you've been sleeping in a library recycling bin."

The shadow of something almost resembling a smile crossed Hart's features—not happiness but recognition of Clara's supportive pragmatism. As she left, he turned back to the whiteboard, his shoulders slightly altered—still burdened, but no longer solely by the weight of isolated realisation.

The digital forensics lab hummed with the precise electronic symphony of high-performance computing—cooling fans whirring at variable frequencies, hard drives clicking in arhythmic patterns, and the occasional soft ping of completed processes. Leo Chang sat surrounded by six monitors arranged in a semicircle, their blue-white glow painting his features in stark contrast, transforming his usually animated expression into something more sombre, more focused. His fingers moved across three separate keyboards with the fluid precision of a concert pianist, each keystroke deliberate, each command sequence executed with mathematical efficiency.

The room resembled the interior of some advanced technological organism—server racks lined the walls like metallic ribs, network cables traced paths like neon veins, and the glass partitions separating workstations reflected endlessly repeating images of screens and their human operators. Leo's station occupied the corner position, affording him privacy and the additional space required for his expanded hardware configuration. A half-empty energy drink can be stood at a precise right angle to his primary keyboard, condensation gathering at its base in a perfect circle of moisture.

Leo's usual workspace energy—the perpetual motion, the spontaneous exclamations, the desk adorned with action figures and tech memorabilia—had been replaced by something altogether different. His body remained perfectly still except for his fingers, his breathing regulated to minimal necessity, his eyes fixed on the scrolling data with unwavering attention. The transformation was so complete that the junior technician who delivered a requested file folder approached with uncharacteristic caution, placing the documents silently at the edge of the desk before retreating without attempting conversation.

He had been tracking The Riddler's digital presence for seventy-two hours without interruption, following electronic breadcrumbs through the labyrinthine architecture of the internet's less visible regions. What had begun as the standard forensic procedure had evolved into something far more complex—a digital archaeology expedition excavating layers of carefully concealed activity stretching back years rather than months.

Leo's eyes widened slightly behind his glasses as a pattern emerged from the seemingly random data points displayed across his central monitor. His posture straightened incrementally, the movement subtle but significant in a body that had maintained near-perfect stillness for hours. His typing pace accelerated, fingers now striking keys with the urgency of someone who had glimpsed something significant disappearing around a corner.

"That's impossible," he whispered, the first words he had spoken aloud in over three hours. The data flowing across his screen suggested an extensive, meticulously constructed infiltration pattern that its execution would have required resources and patience beyond ordinary criminal capability.

The glass door to the forensics lab opened with a pneumatic sigh, admitting Hart and Clara. They moved through the space with the particularly focused efficiency of detectives on a deadline, navigating between workstations without unnecessary acknowledgement of other technicians. Hart's shirt was different—Clara's influence evident—though it already showed the beginning creases of someone who considered clothing merely functional rather than presentational.

Leo sensed their approach before seeing them, and his peripheral awareness was maintained despite his screen focus. He spoke without turning, his voice lacking its usual enthusiastic cadence. "I found it," he said. "All of it."

Hart and Clara positioned themselves behind him, their reflections appearing as ghostly overlays on his monitors. Leo gestured toward the central screen with a precision that mimicked Hart's economic movements.

"He's been watching you for years," Leo explained, his fingers executing a command sequence that transformed the chaotic data display into a chronological timeline. "Not just casual observation—systematic surveillance, comprehensive monitoring, deep data collection." The timeline expanded across three screens, its earliest entries dating back fourteen years. "He's been studying every aspect of your professional and personal life since you left academia."

The screens displayed evidence of methodical electronic intrusion—hacked email accounts, compromised home networks, surveillance footage collected from public cameras near Hart's apartment and the precinct, academic database queries tracking Hart's publications and citations, and even medical record access points showing when Hart's encrypted patient files had been viewed.

"The technical sophistication is..." Leo paused, searching for the appropriate term, uncharacteristically avoiding the pop-culture reference that would typically have served as explanatory shorthand. "Exceptional. Military-grade in some implementations, custom-designed in others. He's been refining his methods, adapting to new security protocols as they emerged."

The reflection of the screens in Leo's glasses created the unsettling impression of data flowing across his eyes as if the information had become physically internalised. "He established the primary surveillance architecture approximately six months after you joined the police department," he continued, highlighting a cluster of activity points on the timeline. "The initial focus was exclusively professional—case files, departmental communications, and performance evaluations. The personal surveillance component was added three years later, coinciding with your first public lecture on investigative methodology."

Hart's expression remained carefully neutral as he absorbed this information. Still, Clara noted the slight tensing of muscle along his jaw and the fractional narrowing of his eyes, which signalled controlled anger rather than surprise. "What specific elements of my casework received the most attention?" he asked, his voice maintaining professional detachment despite the deeply personal nature of the violation being detailed.

Leo's fingers danced across the keyboard, pulling up a heat map visualisation that displayed the intensity of surveillance focus across different categories. "Consistent monitoring of all cases, but particular emphasis on those involving pattern recognition, cryptographic elements, or academic connections." He highlighted a specific cluster. "Highest concentration on the Henley homicides three years ago—the ones with mathematical equations carved into the victims."

"I consulted on that case but wasn't the lead detective," Hart noted, leaning closer to the screen. "What else?"

"He maintained persistent access to your personal computer," Leo said, pulling another data set. "Keystroke logging, screen captures at five-minute intervals, complete browser history." His voice remained clinically detached, but a hint of his usual empathy surfaced in the slight hesitation before continuing. "He has copies of your private research notes, correspondence, and search history. Everything."

Clara's hand moved slightly toward Hart's arm. Still, it stopped short of contact, recognising that professional space rather than comfort was required. "Can you determine his physical location from the digital footprint?" she asked, redirecting toward actionable intelligence.

Leo shook his head, frustration briefly breaking through his careful composure. "He's using a sophisticated proxy network—traffic routed through at least seventeen countries, dynamic IP addressing, multiple virtual machines." He gestured toward a world map on the rightmost screen, red lines tracing convoluted paths between server locations. "However, the timing of certain activities suggests physical presence within the city limits for extended periods during the past six months."

Hart studied the surveillance timeline with analytical precision, and his initial reaction was now completely submerged beneath professional assessment. "He's been gathering data for his reconstruction," he said, indicating specific points on the timeline that corresponded with the current sequence of murders. "Each surveillance escalation preceded a killing by approximately three weeks—he was studying my movements and schedules, ensuring I would encounter his puzzles at precisely the moments he designated."

"There's more," Leo said, his fingers executing a final command sequence. A new window opened, displaying a three-dimensional rendering of what appeared to be architectural blueprints. "I found these in an encrypted partition. They're detailed schematics for some constructed environment—multiple connected chambers with elaborate technological integration. Based on the power requirements and materials specified, this isn't theoretical. He's built this somewhere."

Hart leaned closer, recognition dawning in his expression. "It's a physical recreation of our quantum laboratory," he said quietly. "Every dimension is perfect to the millimetre, every component exactly as we designed it fifteen years ago." His finger traced the central chamber on the screen. "But with one significant modification —there's an observation gallery that didn't exist in the original."

Clara's expression tightened as the implication registered. "He's built a theatre," she said. "A stage for whatever finale he's planning."

Leo nodded, the screens' reflection shifting in his glasses as he looked up at them. "And based on the digital calendar I extracted," he said, "the performance is scheduled for tomorrow night."

The precinct corridor stretched before Hart like the final passage of some ancient labyrinth, its fluorescent tubes flickering at irregular intervals, creating momentary pockets of shadow that seemed to pulse with the rhythm of his exhaustion. He moved with the careful precision of someone navigating by muscle memory alone, his mind too overwhelmed by the day's revelations to spare processing power for something as mundane as walking. His private office waited at the corridor's end—a temporary sanctuary where the walls didn't pulse with photographs of murdered human beings arranged in patterns only he and Price fully understood.

The building had emptied hours ago, and the day shift was replaced by the skeletal crew that maintained the precinct's nocturnal functions. Their presence manifested as distant sounds that travelled through the building's circulatory system of corridors and stairwells—a file cabinet closing two floors below, the soft electronic chime of the booking desk computer, occasional fragments of conversation from the dispatch room carried through ventilation ducts. These ambient noises only emphasised the profound solitude surrounding Hart as he unlocked his office door.

The space beyond was modest but meticulously organised—a desk facing the door and the window, bookshelves containing reference texts arranged by subject rather than author, and a single chair for visitors placed at the precise angle that allowed observation without intimacy. The walls held no personal photographs, no commendations, nothing that would reveal the occupant's identity beyond professional function. The only concession to individuality was a small, smooth stone that sat at the corner of his desk—a piece of the lakeshore where Elizabeth had disappeared, polished by years of unconscious handling during moments of deep thought.

Hart sank into his chair, the familiar contours of the seat conforming to his body with the particular intimacy that develops between objects and their long-term users. He closed his eyes, allowing himself this momentary abdication of vigilance. The revelations of the past twenty-four hours arranged themselves in his mind with mathematical precision: Price's fifteen-year surveillance campaign, the elaborate reconstruction of their failed experiment using human components, the architectural plans for what amounted to a theatre of scientific revenge.

His hands were numb from exhaustion, but he felt a warmth in his chest, an uncomfortable heat that he recognised as a complex fusion of anger, violation, and the peculiar responsibility of being the object of someone's obsessive attention. Price had transformed human lives into experimental components simply to create a puzzle only Hart could solve—they had murdered six people over fifteen years to construct this elaborate intellectual confrontation.

The laboratory plans Leo had discovered suggested that tomorrow's "performance" would involve the quantum module itself. This component had catastrophically failed fifteen years ago, resulting in system crashes and data breaches in their original experiment. In Price's human recreation, the implications were unspeakable.

A soft knock at the door interrupted Hart's thoughts. He opened his eyes, momentarily disoriented by the intrusion of external reality into his analytical space. "Yes?" he called, his voice roughened by fatigue and disuse.

The door opened to reveal a uniformed courier, not police personnel but a commercial service provider, a young man in a pressed grey uniform holding a tablet for signature verification. "Delivery for Detective Alan Hart," he said, his practised professional tone suggesting this was merely one of the dozens of packages he had delivered that evening, nothing to distinguish from restaurant receipts or business contracts.

"I'm Hart," he confirmed, rising from his chair with the careful movements of someone whose muscles had begun to stiffen from sustained stillness.

The courier nodded, offering the tablet while retrieving an envelope from his shoulder bag. "Signature required," he said, watching Hart scrawl his name's approximation across the screen. "Sender specified hand delivery directly to the recipient only."

Hart accepted the envelope, its weight and texture immediately registering as anomalous—too heavy for standard stationery and too precisely crafted for commercial correspondence. The courier departed with rehearsed efficiency, closing the door behind him with a soft click that seemed to seal Hart alone with whatever message the envelope contained.

He carried it to his desk, positioning it beneath the direct light of his desk lamp for proper examination. The envelope was constructed from heavy cream stock with a subtle texture that suggested artisanal production rather than mass manufacturing. No postmark or shipping label marred its surface—only his name and title, "Detective Alan Hart," rendered in flowing calligraphy executed with a precision that suggested years of practice. The ink possessed a particular sheen that changed subtly as he tilted the envelope beneath the light—not standard commercial formulation but something custom-blended, perhaps containing metallic elements that created the appearance of depth within each character.

Hart retrieved latex gloves from his desk drawer, pulling them on with practised efficiency before carefully breaking the envelope's seal —a small circle of deep crimson wax impressed with what appeared to be a custom signet. The seal separated cleanly from the paper, suggesting expensive materials designed to release without tearing. Inside, a card of matching cream stock rested against the envelope's lining, which he noted was constructed of silk rather than paper—an unnecessary extravagance that communicated wealth and obsessive attention to detail.

He extracted the card using forensic tweezers, placing it on a clean sheet of paper on his desk. The message consisted of three elements arranged with precise symmetry across the card's surface: an address in the industrial district at the city's eastern edge; a time— 9:47 PM tomorrow; and below these, a message in the same flowing calligraphy as the envelope's exterior:

"The final examination awaits, Professor. Come alone, or others will answer for your absence."

At the card's bottom edge, rendered in ink so dark it seemed to absorb rather than reflect the desk lamp's light, was a small insignia —a geometric configuration of intersecting lines forming what appeared to be a stylised quantum gate symbol. Hart recognised it immediately as identical to the marking found carved beneath Professor Lowell's desk fifteen years ago—the first victim in Price's human recreation of their failed experiment.

Hart's hand closed around the card, his fingers tightening involuntarily, creating a network of creases across its previously immaculate surface. The action was uncharacteristic—he typically handled evidence with meticulous care—but something in the presumptuous formality of the invitation had triggered a response beyond his usual professional restraint. The creases radiating from his fingertips resembled the pattern of fractures created when a quantum field collapses under observation—a visual metaphor Price would have appreciated with his typical intellectual vanity.

He placed the crumpled card back on the desk, smoothing it with careful pressure that failed to eliminate the evidence of his momentary lapse in control. The address corresponded to a location he knew —an abandoned manufacturing complex that had once produced specialised electronic components for university research laboratories. The time, 9:47 PM, carried specific significance in their shared history—the exact moment when their quantum experiment had initiated its catastrophic failure sequence fifteen years ago.

Hart's reflection in the window opposite his desk revealed the tension that had taken residence in his features—not merely fatigue or concern, but the weight of a decision that stretched beyond professional obligation into the territory of personal reckoning. Price had constructed an elaborate trap baited with human lives, designed a performance with Hart as the intended audience, and created a puzzle only he could solve. The proper procedural response was clear —involve tactical teams, establish perimeter containment, and approach with overwhelming force.

But Price had anticipated this. "Come alone, or others will answer for your absence." The threat wasn't idle—Price's surveillance would have provided a comprehensive understanding of police response protocols, allowing him to prepare countermeasures that would result in additional casualties. Moreover, the elaborate puzzle trail leading to this moment suggested Price wanted more than a simple confrontation—he sought specific forms of recognition and understanding that only Hart could provide.

Hart's fingertips brushed against the smooth lake stone at the corner of his desk, its familiar contours grounding him in the physical world as his mind processed abstract threat calculations. The past twenty-four hours had revealed how completely Price had integrated himself into Hart's life, how thoroughly he had studied every aspect of his former colleague's existence. Whatever awaited at the industrial complex tomorrow night would be calibrated precisely to Hart's psychological and intellectual profile—a customised confrontation fifteen years in the making.

His expression in the window's reflection shifted subtly, fatigue and uncertainty giving way to something more challenging, more defined—the particular clarity that comes when competing options resolve into a single necessary path. He would go to the address alone as instructed, not out of obedience to Price's demands but from recognition that the alternative ensured additional casualties. He would engage with whatever "final examination" awaited, not as Price's audience but as the detective who had spent seven years developing skills his academic self had never possessed.

Hart carefully placed the card and envelope into an evidence bag, labelling them with precise notation despite knowing he would likely be the only person ever to examine their contents. The action was neither surrender nor compliance but preparation—establishing the documentary foundation for whatever conclusion awaited tomorrow night's performance. His reflection watched him from the darkened window, his shoulders now set with the particular straightness that accompanies difficult decisions finally made, the burden of uncertainty replaced by the cleaner weight of determined action.

12

AMBUSH IN THE ARCHIVES

The city archive loomed before them, its weathered limestone facade darkened by decades of exhaust and neglect. Built in an era when public records demanded cathedral-like reverence, the structure rose four stories above street level, while rumour suggested its basement levels descended at least as deep. Alan studied the building with professional wariness, his eyes tracing the ornate cornices where stone gargoyles peered down through accumulated grime. The sun had begun its late afternoon descent, casting long shadows across the archive's worn steps and rendering its recessed entrance a mouth of perfect darkness. Beside him, Clara checked her watch with measured precision, her gesture communicating the unspoken pressure of remaining daylight.

"Dr. Shaw was specific about the date range," Clara said, retrieving a small notebook from her jacket pocket. "Municipal records from 1897 through 1904, with particular emphasis on land acquisitions in what's now the eastern industrial district." Her voice carried the flatness that emerged when translating academic information into investigative parameters. "She believes the original property titles may contain coded information about underground structures that aren't on modern surveys."

Hart nodded, his mind already calculating search methodologies against probable archival organisation systems. "The industrial complex where Price is staging his 'final examination' was built over the foundations of something much older." His fingers absently brushed the folded paper in his pocket where he'd copied the address from Price's invitation. "Shaw thinks whatever's beneath that building is significant to his reconstruction."

"This could give us an advantage," Clara added, her tone suggesting practical strategy over academic curiosity. "If there are access points he doesn't know about or structural weaknesses we could exploit."

They climbed the worn granite steps together, their footsteps echoing in the cavernous entrance hall beyond. The building's interior existed in a perpetual twilight—weak sunlight filtering through high windows clouded by dust, supplemented by ancient fluorescent fixtures that hummed and flickered with irregular periodicity. The air carried the distinct perfume of institutional neglect—paper slowly surrendering to entropy, leather bindings exhaling microscopic decay particles, metal oxidising in the peculiar microclimate created by massive stone walls and inadequate climate control.

A lone archivist occupied the reception desk, his ancient frame mirroring the building's architectural decrepitude. He examined their identification with rheumy eyes that nevertheless missed nothing, his fingers trembling slightly as he recorded their names in a leather-bound visitor log that looked like it might have been in continuous use since the building's construction. After consulting a desktop computer whose beige plastic case had yellowed with age, he directed them towards the municipal records section with instructions delivered in the particular unhurried cadence of someone who had long ago surrendered to institutional time.

"Why didn't we bring a team?" Clara asked quietly as they navigated through the initial gallery of reference materials, her voice pitched just above the silence between the towering shelves.

Hart's expression subtly tightened. Price's surveillance is extensive. If he notices a strong police presence, he'll speed up his plans." He glanced at the numbered indicators at the end of each row, mentally mapping out the archive's complex layout. "Two individuals could pose as researchers instead of law enforcement. This offers us the best opportunity to gather information without activating his backup measures."

They proceeded deeper into the archive's recesses, passing from the moderately maintained public section into increasingly neglected territories. The ceiling rose to accommodate three levels of metal catwalks and narrow stairways connecting stack levels, creating a three-dimensional maze of information storage. Dust motes danced in the angled light from clerestory windows, giving substance to the air. The shelves towered over them like canyon walls, their contents arranged according to an organisational logic that had calcified into institutional habit generations earlier.

Hart moved with the focused intensity that characterised his investigative process, his fingertips tracing along leather-bound spines as he decoded archive numbering systems against their search parameters. Clara positioned herself at intersections between stack rows, maintaining sightlines in multiple directions while Hart excavated potential sources. They communicated in the abbreviated language of long-term colleagues—quick gestures, truncated sentences, and shared references requiring no elaboration.

Hours passed with growing frustration as each promising source was only close to their needs but never quite aligned. The weak natural light gradually faded toward evening, forcing them to rely on inconsistent overhead fixtures that cast more shadows than actual light. Clara's posture showed the first signs of fatigue, although her alertness remained strong. Hart's focus intensified with each setback; his movements became more deliberate, and his expression hardened as he transformed the analytical challenges from professional puzzles into personal challenges.

"This organisational system defies logical reconstruction," he muttered, closing yet another ledger whose contents referenced adjacent years to their target range but never intersected with their specific requirements. "There are deliberate gaps in the sequence as if certain records were systematically removed or recategorised under non-standard parameters."

Clara glanced at her watch and then toward the darkening windows overhead. "It's almost closing time," she noted, her tone conveying the practical limitations they faced rather than discouragement. The archivist mentioned restricted collections in the east wing basement—materials requiring special handling or containing sensitive information.

Hart nodded, adjusting his mental map of the search area. They descended narrow metal stairs, each step creaking in protest as they moved deeper into the building's substructure. The basement level existed in a perpetual artificial twilight, illuminated by widely spaced incandescent bulbs that created islands of weak yellow light surrounded by expanses of shadow. The air hung heavier here, carrying the distinct mineral scent of old stone and subterranean moisture.

The restricted collection occupied a section separated from the main stacks by a heavy metal fire door that should have been locked but stood slightly ajar. Hart paused, his hand hovering over the door's push bar, eyes narrowing at this deviation from institutional protocol.

Clara stood beside him, her right hand subtly moving toward the service weapon concealed beneath her jacket. After a brief assessment, Hart pushed the door open with controlled pressure, minimising its movement against the aged hinges.

The space beyond felt different from the rest of the archive—the shelving was older, wooden rather than metal, arranged in concentric circles around a central reading area rather than rectilinear grid patterns. The highest shelves required rolling ladders to access, their uppermost levels disappearing into shadow beyond the reach of the sparse lighting. Hart recognised the organisational logic immediately, and his academic background translated the archaic system into navigable parameters.

"These are arranged chronologically by acquisition date rather than content categorisation," he said, moving directly toward the northwest quadrant. "Pre-1920 municipal records would be..." His voice trailed off as his eyes located the appropriate section, where a gap in the shelving revealed a heavy oak cabinet set into the wall itself.

The cabinet was approximately one-metre square, its surface decorated with elaborate carvings that incorporated the city's founding seal among stylised representations of infrastructure development—bridges, buildings, and water systems. A sturdy brass lock secured the doors, its surface darkened by age yet revealing signs of recent tampering in its accumulated patina. Hart knelt before it, pulling a slender leather case from his inner jacket pocket. To his surprise, the lock's mechanism yielded easily to his manipulation, indicating that it had been accessed regularly despite its hidden location.

The cabinet's interior contained a single item—a leather folio approximately forty centimetres square, its surface embossed with the same city seal that decorated the cabinet door. Hart lifted it with careful reverence, recognising the particular fragility of leather exposed to decades of environmental fluctuation. He carried it to the central reading table, positioning it beneath the brightest available light before carefully unfastening the tarnished brass clasps that secured its contents.

Inside lay carefully organised documents—surveyors' maps on translucent drafting paper, property transfers inscribed on heavy-weight parchment, and engineering specifications rendered in faded blue ink on yellowed linen. Hart's fingers hovered above the brittle pages, tracing the information they contained without touching their fragile surfaces.

"These are the original plans for the underground infrastructure," he said, his voice tight with the controlled excitement of significant discovery. "Not just sewers and utility tunnels, but a complete subterranean network beneath what's now the eastern industrial zone. Look at these depth specifications—three levels below current foundation depth."

Clara leaned closer, her attention divided between the documents and their surroundings. "Why would they build so deep in the 1890s? The technology would have made it prohibitively expensive without a specific purpose."

"There are notations here in the margins, some kind of technical shorthand." Hart indicated faint pencil markings that formed complex patterns along the main tunnels' paths. "And these sections are marked with the same quantum gate symbol Price has used."

Clara's response died unspoken as a slight movement registered in her peripheral vision—a shadow shifting between distant shelves where no shadow should have existed. She straightened slowly, her posture communicating alert assessment rather than alarm. Hart continued examining the documents, absorbed in their revelation, while Clara's gaze methodically tracked the movement's origin.

. . .

"Alan," she said quietly, the single word carrying specific warning tones he had learned to recognise through years of partnership.

Before he could respond, figures emerged from multiple directions between the concentric shelving rings—three, five, then seven individuals moving with coordinated precision toward the central reading area. They wore dark clothing and face coverings that revealed only their eyes, each carrying improvised weapons fashioned from archive materials—a metal shelf bracket transformed into a bludgeon, a paper cutter's blade mounted on a wooden handle, a length of chain that might once have secured reference volumes.

Hart's hand moved towards his service weapon, but Clara's slight head shake stopped him. They found themselves outnumbered in confined spaces with limited visibility, and their position was already compromised. The attackers continued advancing, their movements indicating professional coordination rather than opportunistic aggression. They maintained precise spacing between themselves, establishing containment sectors rather than confrontation, cutting off potential escape routes with methodical efficiency.

The circle tightened around the reading table, trapping Hart and Clara between the advancing threat and the fragile historical documents that might hold the key to Price's elaborate puzzle. Hart's eyes met Clara's in momentary silent communication—assessing options, calculating risks, preparing for the inevitable transition from investigation to survival.

Hart moved with the explosive precision of someone who had visualised this moment before it arrived. His hand closed around the leather folio as he upended the reading table violently, creating momentary chaos in the advancing semicircle of assailants. Clara was already moving, and her trajectory was calculated to exploit the narrowest gap in their containment formation. They broke through the initial encirclement together, Hart cradling the fragile documents against his chest as they sprinted towards the shelving labyrinth beyond. Behind them, the disciplined silence of their pursuers dissolved into the percussion of multiple footsteps, the metallic scrape of weapons dragging against shelves, the soft exhalation of controlled breathing that marked trained professionals rather than common thugs.

They plunged into the first narrow corridor between towering shelves, Hart leading with Clara half a step behind. The wooden floors amplified their footfalls despite their attempts at controlled movement, each step echoing through the cavernous space like auditory breadcrumbs for their pursuers. Hart's mind calculated routes as they ran, transforming the archive's three-dimensional maze into a mental schematic that revealed optimal escape paths and likely interception points.

"Left," he instructed as they approached an intersection, his voice compressed to essential information only. They veered between stacks of bound newspapers whose yellowed edges blurred into streaks of amber as they passed.

Clara glanced backwards, assessing pursuit vectors with professional efficiency. "Three following, others flanking," she reported, her breathing controlled despite their pace.

Hart nodded once, acknowledging the tactical assessment without breaking stride. His eyes tracked the numbered indicators at each shelf end, correlating their position with his mental map of the building's layout. The folio pressed against his chest like a living thing, its contents potentially worth the lives these assailants had been dispatched to risk. He tucked it more securely inside his jacket as they rounded another corner.

A dark figure appeared at the corridor's end, weapon raised. Clara reacted first, her hand closing around a heavy reference volume on a nearby shelf. She pulled the book free in a single fluid motion, sending it skidding along the polished floor toward their adversary's

feet. The assailant adjusted professionally, sidestepping the improvised projectile—exactly as Clara had anticipated. Her follow-up
movement targeted the now-destabilised shelf itself, her shoulder
leveraging against its frame with her full body weight behind the
impact.

The ancient wooden shelving unit shuddered, then tipped slowly
before surrendering to gravity's insistence. Books cascaded in a
literary avalanche, their bound spines and loose pages creating a
hurricane of paper and leather. The pursuing figure disappeared
beneath the collapsed shelving, a muffled impact suggesting temporary incapacitation rather than serious injury.

"Alternate route," Hart said, veering at the next junction. Clara
followed without hesitation, her complete trust in his navigational
instincts manifested in physical synchronisation.

They moved deeper into the archive's recesses, each turn calculated to maximise distance from pursuit while progressing towards
potential exit points. The air grew thicker with dust disturbed by
their passage, motes swirling in the weak light and catching in their
lungs. Books crashed to the floor behind them as unseen pursuers
navigated the same narrow passages, occasionally dislodging
volumes in their haste.

Rather than seeing the presence ahead, Hart felt a subtle shift in air
currents that suggested human movement was disrupting the
archive's stagnant atmosphere. He raised his hand in silent warning,
and Clara flattened herself against the nearest shelf. They froze in
position, controlling their breathing despite oxygen demand,
listening as footsteps approached from the intersection ahead.

They waited, heartbeats stretched into seconds that felt like
minutes until the footsteps receded down an adjacent corridor. Hart
exhaled silently, exchanging a glance with Clara that conveyed relief
and recognition of continued danger. They proceeded with greater

caution, a pace moderated by tactical necessity rather than diminished urgency.

"Southeast stairwell," Hart whispered, indicating a direction with a slight tilt of his head. "Access to upper catwalks."

They moved toward this objective with renewed purpose, sensing pursuit closing from multiple vectors. The stairwell appeared as a metal spiral ascending through a circular opening in the ceiling, its wrought iron construction suggesting original architectural elements rather than modern additions. As they approached this potential escape route, Hart's mental mapping faltered—a corridor that should have continued instead terminated in a solid wall of shelving, creating an unexpected dead end.

"Recent renovation," Clara observed, identifying the newer wood and different organisational markers in this section.

Pursuit sounds intensified behind them, at least three movement patterns converging on their position. Hart's eyes tracked upward, locating a maintenance ladder attached to the shelving unit—a metal framework rising towards a narrow access space between the top shelf and the ceiling. He gestured towards this potential escape route, calculating load-bearing capacity against their combined weight.

Clara nodded once, understanding without explanation. Hart transferred the folio to his inner jacket pocket, securing it with careful efficiency before approaching the ladder. The metal felt cold and damp beneath his palms, suggesting the building's moisture management issues extended beyond visible evidence. He ascended with deliberate speed, testing each rung before transferring full weight, aware that ageing infrastructure in a neglected public building represented its threat category.

Clara maintained her position below, her weapon now drawn and held with professional discipline as she covered their retreat. Hart reached the top of the ladder, leveraging himself onto the narrow access platform along the upper shelving level. He turned immediately, extending his hand to assist Clara's ascent.

She holstered her weapon and began climbing, her movements economical despite the awkward vertical orientation. Hart tracked the pursuit sounds, calculating the remaining time against Clara's ascent rate. The margin was dissolving—footsteps and controlled breathing were now close enough to distinguish individual pursuers.

Clara had nearly reached the top when the first assailant appeared at the corridor's end. The figure assessed the situation with practised efficiency, immediately recognising their escape route. With a speed that confirmed professional training, the pursuer closed the distance to the ladder's base, one gloved hand reaching upward to grasp Clara's ankle.

Hart's hand closed around Clara's wrist, securing her position as the assailant attempted to drag her downward. Clara's face revealed nothing but focused determination as she maintained her grip on the ladder despite the opposing forces threatening to dislodge her. With her free foot, she delivered a precisely targeted kick to her attacker's forearm, creating a momentary release that allowed her to climb one rung higher.

The assailant adjusted strategy, abandoning direct physical contact to ascend the ladder behind them. Clara reached the top platform, Hart pulling her to relative safety as she extracted a heavy leather-bound encyclopedia from the nearest shelf. With calculated timing, she dropped the massive tome directly onto the pursuer below. It struck with mathematical precision, impacting the assailant's face with an audible crack that suggested nasal cartilage surrendering to physics. The figure lost grip, falling backwards into two additional pursuers who had reached the ladder's base.

· · ·

"Move," Clara instructed, already turning toward the narrow catwalk that extended from their position across the open space above the archive's main floor. The metal walkway swayed slightly under their weight, its structural integrity compromised by decades of institutional maintenance neglect. They proceeded with necessary caution despite the urgency of pursuit, each step calculated to minimise oscillation that might further destabilise the precarious pathway.

Halfway across, Hart paused, his attention captured by movement on a parallel catwalk twenty metres distant. A dark figure traversed the connecting bridge with practised efficiency, its trajectory calculated to intercept them at the far junction where multiple walkways converged. The assailant moved with the particular economy of someone who had memorised the environment in advance, suggesting pre-mission reconnaissance beyond casual familiarity.

"Interception point ahead," Hart noted, his voice carrying the detached, analytical quality it assumed when processing tactical information.

Clara nodded once, her stride lengthening slightly as they approached the junction. The catwalk's metal grid pattern allowed partial visibility of the archive floor four metres below—concrete rather than wood at this point, promising unforgiving impact in case of structural failure. Their pursuer reached the junction first, positioning himself with a tactical advantage. A metal bookend transformed into an improvised weapon with practised comfort in his gloved hand.

Without verbal coordination, Clara stepped slightly ahead of Hart as they approached the junction, her body position shifting to place herself between him and the waiting assailant. Hart recognised her intention a fraction of a second too late, his hand reaching towards her shoulder as she moved into the protective formation that prioritised his safety above hers.

The assailant struck with professional efficiency, the metal edge of the improvised weapon arcing towards them with calculated force. Clara partially deflected the blow with a forearm block that redirected its trajectory, but the bookend's sharpened edge sliced through her jacket sleeve and into the flesh beneath. Blood appeared immediately, darkening the fabric in an expanding circle around the wound.

Hart registered multiple sensory inputs simultaneously—the soft hiss of Clara's controlled exhalation as she absorbed the pain without vocal expression; the metallic scent of fresh blood mingling with the archive's established odours of paper and dust; the subtle vibration of the catwalk as additional pursuers reached the ladder they had ascended. These details were processed in the fraction of a second between the assailant's initial strike and the beginning of his follow-up movement.

Despite the injury, Clara maintained her protective position, her unaffected arm raised in a defensive posture, and her weight shifted to compensate for the compromised limb. Blood dripped between her fingers where she pressed her hand against the wound, each crimson droplet falling through the catwalk's metal grid to mark its position on the concrete below. The assailant adjusted his grip on the weaponised bookend, preparing for a second strike with the tactical recalibration of someone who had assessed an opponent's weakened condition.

Hart moved before conscious thought fully formed, years of analytical hesitation compressed into instinctive action. His hand closed around a fire extinguisher mounted on the catwalk's support column, wrenching it free with a single violent motion. The extinguisher's weight felt substantial in his grip as he swung it in a controlled arc that terminated against the assailant's temple with mathematical precision. Impact translated through metal and bone, the figure crumpling instantly, unconscious body suspended momentarily before collapsing through the catwalk railing into space. The sound of impact on the concrete below provided terminal punctuation to their confrontation.

. . .

"Exit," Hart said, his voice tight with controlled urgency as he assessed Clara's condition. Blood continued seeping through her fingers despite the pressure she maintained on the wound, her complexion displaying the first indications of physiological response to fluid loss.

She nodded once, teeth clenched against the pain as they continued across the catwalk toward the emergency exit now visible at the far wall. Behind them, pursuers had reached the upper level, their coordinated movements suggesting tactical reformation rather than abandoned objective. Hart placed his hand beneath Clara's uninjured elbow, providing subtle support that respected her autonomy while acknowledging the reality of her compromised condition.

Blood continued marking their path as they moved toward potential safety, each drop leaving evidence of their passage like a macabre trail of breadcrumbs leading into the archive's forgotten recesses.

The service corridor stretched before them like a forgotten artery, its concrete walls sweating with decades of accumulated moisture. Emergency lighting cast irregular pools of sickly yellow illumination at fifteen-metre intervals, revealing floors stained with the particular patina that develops when industrial cleaning products interact with ancient grime. The air hung heavy with the mingled scents of mildew, floor wax, and the metallic tang of Clara's blood as it continued seeping through her fingers despite the pressure she maintained on her wounded arm. Hart supported her with careful attention to balance, providing necessary assistance without undermining her professional dignity even in a compromised condition.

. . .

"Maintenance exit should be thirty metres ahead," Hart said, his voice carrying the particular flatness that accompanied intense concentration. His free hand remained near his service weapon, anticipating a potential ambush despite the corridor's apparent emptiness. Each doorway they passed received momentary tactical assessment— threat evaluation compressed into fractions of seconds as they proceeded toward potential safety.

Clara nodded once, her breathing controlled despite the pain radiating from her lacerated arm. Blood had soaked through her sleeve from shoulder to wrist, the fabric now adhering to her skin with macabre intimacy. "They'll have covered the main exits," she noted, professional analysis uncompromised by physical distress. "This route was not in their initial containment strategy."

"Suggests incomplete building reconnaissance," Hart agreed, their exchange falling into the familiar pattern of shared analytical processing that characterised their partnership. "Or priority on document retrieval rather than capture or elimination."

They reached the maintenance exit—a heavy metal door whose institutional green paint had faded to the particular non-colour that develops when industrial pigments surrender to time and neglect. A push bar mechanism promised egress without keys, though the layer of dust suggested infrequent use by actual maintenance personnel. Hart positioned Clara against the wall adjacent to the door, providing support while freeing his weapon hand in case the exit revealed additional threats.

"On three," he said, meeting her eyes briefly to confirm mutual preparation. "One, two—"

The door yielded to controlled pressure, swinging outward with a protesting groan of rarely used hinges. Beyond lay an alleyway rendered in monochrome by early evening darkness and persistent rainwater sheeting from rooftops, gathering in depressions in the uneven pavement, transforming distant streetlights into wavering constellations of reflected illumination. Hart scanned their surroundings with professional thoroughness, identifying potential cover positions, sightlines from adjacent buildings, and approach vectors for possible pursuit.

They emerged into the rain's embrace, the sudden transition from stagnant indoor air to a water-cleansed atmosphere momentarily disorienting. The precipitation immediately began diluting the blood on Clara's sleeve, creating pale crimson rivulets that traced paths along her fingers before joining the rain's downward journey toward storm drains. Hart secured the door behind them, jamming a discarded metal pipe through the push bar's external housing to prevent pursuit through this exit.

"Car's four blocks northwest," he said, orienting himself against the urban landscape now rendered unfamiliar by darkness and precipitation. Clara nodded, her uninjured arm reaching inside her jacket to ensure her weapon remained accessible despite their waterlogged condition. They moved with deliberate efficiency despite Clara's compromised state, each step calculated to maximise progress while minimising visibility from primary thoroughfares.

The rain intensified as they navigated through secondary alleys and service passages, the downpour providing acoustic cover for their movement while reducing visibility for potential observers. Water plastered Hart's hair against his forehead, ran in continuous streams inside his collar, and transformed his shoes into sodden weights that complicated each step. Beside him, Clara maintained pace through what appeared to be pure professional determination, her injured arm now cradled against her body, her expression betraying nothing beyond focused concentration.

Hart's sedan waited where they had left it hours earlier, its nondescript government-issue appearance rendering it functionally invisible among similar vehicles lining the residential street. They approached from the rear, Hart's eyes scanning for surveillance devices or signs of tampering before unlocking the doors with a single electronic chirp immediately swallowed by the rain's persistent percussion.

Inside, the air felt suddenly, artificially still—the rain's constant motion was now reduced to rhythmic impacts against metal and glass, creating a contained environment that emphasised their ragged breathing and the soft sound of water dripping from saturated clothing onto upholstery. Hart activated the vehicle's heating system before focusing on Clara's condition.

"Let me see," he said, his voice softening from tactical assessment to something adjacent to personal concern. Clara extended her injured arm with reluctant compliance, her professional composure momentarily fractured by a wincing contraction around her eyes as the movement aggravated damaged tissue.

Hart examined the wound with clinical precision, gently rolling back the saturated sleeve to reveal a laceration approximately twelve centimetres long extending from mid-forearm towards her elbow. The cut was clean-edged but deep, suggesting the weaponised bookend had been deliberately sharpened for maximum effectiveness. Blood continued seeping from the wound despite the temporary pressure reduction provided by the rain's natural cleaning action.

"Needs medical attention," Hart concluded, reaching into the glove compartment for the emergency kit standard in all department vehicles. "At a minimum, proper cleaning and closure. The hospital would be preferable."

Clara shook her head once, a decision already made. "The hospital creates records. Records create administrative questions. Questions create delays." She accepted the gauze pads Hart extracted from the kit, applying them to her wound efficiently. "Field dressing will suffice until we conclude immediate investigative priorities."

Hart knew better than to argue when Clara had transitioned to this particular register of professional determination. Instead, he unbuttoned his shirt, the fabric surrendering with a wet sucking sound as he pulled it away from his skin. The white undershirt beneath contrasted with the rain-darkened outer garment as he began tearing the shirt into strips suitable for bandaging.

"We've lost the folio," Clara noted as Hart carefully wrapped the improvised bandage around her arm, securing the gauze pads in position with methodical precision. She delivered this assessment with the same neutral tone she might use to report cloudy weather or traffic conditions—a factual observation requiring neither emotional embellishment nor self-recrimination.

Hart's hands stilled momentarily, his eyes lifting to meet hers with the intensity that accompanied significant realisation. "When did you notice?" he asked, resuming the bandaging with increased focus as if the physical action might compensate for the intellectual failure.

"During the catwalk confrontation," Clara replied, her uninjured hand automatically moving to check her weapon's condition despite the car's apparent security. "Your jacket was partially open when you swung the fire extinguisher. The inner pocket was empty."

Hart completed the bandage, securing the final knot with precise tension, firm enough to maintain pressure without compromising circulation. His mind reconstructed their flight through the archive, calculating moments when the document might have been extracted without his awareness. "The initial escape through the shelves," he concluded finally. When we broke their containment circle, one of them must have extracted it during the physical contact."

Clara nodded, her analysis reaching similar conclusions. "Their objective was the folio, not us," she said, professional assessment overriding physical discomfort. "We were incidental complications rather than primary targets. The attack pattern emphasised containment and acquisition rather than elimination."

"Not common criminals," Hart agreed, starting the car's engine while continuing their shared analytical process. "Professional operatives with specific mission parameters and advanced intelligence regarding our investigation."

"The Riddler," Clara said, giving voice to the conclusion they had both reached. She adjusted the bandage slightly, blood already beginning to seep through the layered fabric. "Price has resources beyond what we initially estimated. Personal surveillance is one thing; deploying specialised tactical teams suggests organisational infrastructure."

Hart guided the vehicle away from the curb, windshield wipers struggling against the persistent downpour. His reflection in the rain-streaked driver's window revealed the tension that had taken residence in his features—not merely the concentration of active investigation but something deeper, more personal. "We need to revise our approach," he said, his voice carrying the weight of professional reassessment balanced against escalating threat parameters.

"The hospital first," Clara countered, her tone leaving minimal room for negotiation despite her compromised physical condition. "Brief medical intervention, then the immediate continuation of the investigation." She met his sideways glance with the particular expression that had ended countless previous disagreements in her favour. "I'm fully operational despite peripheral damage."

Hart recognised the futility of argument, adjusting their route with a single turn that would carry them toward the university medical centre rather than department headquarters. The dashboard clock displayed 7:23 p.m.—approximately twenty-six hours before Price's scheduled "final examination." The rain continued falling with mechanical persistence, transforming the city beyond its windows into impressionistic architecture suggestions rather than defined structures.

"Leo may have extracted usable information from the archive's security system," Hart noted, his mind already calculating alternative investigative approaches despite the setback. "And Dr. Shaw might have additional insights regarding the underground structures."

Clara nodded, her uninjured hand moving automatically to check her phone for messages despite knowing the device had been powered down before entering the archive. "We still have a tactical advantage through the foreknowledge of his timeline," she confirmed, their shared professional determination creating a momentary suspension of the physical reality of her injury.

The rain-slick streets reflected traffic signals and headlights in wavering approximations, creating a liquid mirror world beneath their wheels. Hart navigated with mechanical precision, his external focus on traffic patterns and potential surveillance maintaining perfect separation from the internal current that threatened to over-whelm professional detachment. His hands were numb from the car's aggressive air conditioning, but he felt a warmth in his chest, an uncomfortable heat that he recognised as guilt. Clara's blood continued seeping through the improvised bandage he had applied, each expanding crimson bloom a silent indictment of his decision to pursue this investigation without adequate departmental support.

Clara caught him studying the bandage during a prolonged stop at a traffic signal, her expression shifting to the particular configuration that indicated she had correctly identified his psychological state. "This was my choice," she said, the statement neither absolution nor accusation but precise recalibration of perspective. "Price's game, his rules, his responsibility. Not yours."

Hart nodded once, acknowledgement rather than agreement, his attention returning to the road as the light changed. The windshield wipers continued their metronomic rhythm, measuring their progress through the storm-darkened city toward whatever conclusion awaited at the end of Price's elaborate puzzle—now less than twenty-six hours away, with the rules suddenly and drastically altered by the loss of crucial intelligence and the shedding of Clara's blood.

13

BROKEN PIECES

The fluorescent lights of the University Medical Centre cast Hart's shadow in sharp relief against the polished linoleum floor, his pacing figure elongating and contracting with metronomic regularity as he moved between ceiling panels. Twenty-four hours until Price's "final examination," and here he stood, trapped in the antiseptic purgatory of a hospital corridor while the case—his case—ticked relentlessly forward without him. His hands were numb from excessive caffeine and insufficient sleep. Still, he felt a familiar warmth in his chest, an uncomfortable heat that he recognised as guilt mixed with something more dangerous: the particular frustration of a puzzle solver separated from his puzzle.

The hospital corridor stretched before him like an institutional gauntlet—walls painted the particular shade of off-white designed to suggest cleanliness while concealing accumulated grime, interrupted only by occasional framed prints of watercolour landscapes selected for their complete absence of emotional content. A nurse's station stood at the corridor's midpoint, staffed by professionals whose practised efficiency included acknowledging his police credentials without engaging with the uncomfortably damp, visibly exhausted man who had been pacing their corridor for ninety-seven minutes.

Hart's fingertips traced a hairline crack in the wall plaster as he passed it for the thirty-fourth time, the imperfection becoming a physical anchor in the homogenous environment. His shirt, changed at Clara's insistence before they'd left the car, already displayed the characteristic rumpling of expensive fabric worn by someone who considered clothing merely a necessary concession to social convention. He attempted to straighten the collar, his fingers trembling slightly against the cotton—a physiological betrayal that annoyed him more than the persistent ache in his shoulders or the grinding fatigue behind his eyes.

Through the half-open door of Room 307, monitors maintained their electronic vigilance over Clara's still form, each steady beep an algorithmic assurance of continued life wrapped in medical measurement. The doctors had used phrases like "significant blood loss" and "potential nerve damage," delivered with the particular cadence of medical professionals accustomed to translating bodily trauma into palatable terminology. Clara herself had remained stubbornly conscious throughout their initial assessment, insisting on calling the laceration a "peripheral inconvenience" before the administered sedative had finally overcome her professional composure.

Hart paused at the door's threshold, unwilling to enter yet unable to depart entirely. Clara's reposed features displayed no tension that typically accompanied her waking professionalism—the perpetual alertness that characterised her detective work temporarily suspended by medical necessity. Her injured arm lay elevated on a precisely arranged pillow, pristine white bandages replacing his improvised shirt strips that now resided, blood-soaked, in a hospital waste receptacle.

This was his responsibility. Not directly—he hadn't wielded the weapon that sliced through her flesh—but through the particular transitive property of partnership and protection. He had led them into the archive without adequate backup, pursuing Price's puzzle with the same obsessive focus that had characterised his academic collaboration with the man who now orchestrated this elaborate game of murder and manipulation.

Hart's jaw clenched, his teeth grinding momentarily against the unwelcome realisation forming in his consciousness since they'd fled the archive—a crystallising awareness that his analytical methods and Price's shared a dangerous symmetry. Both men transformed human experiences into abstract patterns, both sought solutions with a singular focus that excluded peripheral concerns, and both possessed the particular intellectual arrogance that justified means through anticipated ends.

The primary difference, the distinction Hart had relied upon for professional identity and personal absolution, suddenly seemed insubstantial—merely that Price's patterns were constructed to destroy while Hart's were assembled to protect. However, the methodological architecture, the fundamental approach to human complexity, remained disturbingly similar.

Hart turned abruptly from the doorway, steps carrying him toward the elevator before a conscious decision fully formed. The motion caught the nurse's attention, her expression suggesting that she intended to provide an update on Clara's condition. Hart averted his gaze with deliberate precision, his body language communicating unavailability for interaction with such clarity that the nurse altered her trajectory without verbal exchange.

The elevator doors opened immediately as if the machine had anticipated his approach. Hart entered the empty car, finger hovering over the control panel as competing imperatives battled for prioritisation. The precinct represented procedural correctness—reporting the archive attack, mobilising resources, and establishing containment strategies for Price's apparent operational network. Standard investigative protocol demanded this course of action.

His finger remained suspended, and uncharacteristic indecision manifested as physical hesitation.

· · ·

The university campus contained a different set of resources—Dr. Evelyn Shaw, with her cryptographic expertise, academic databases containing the research history he shared with Price, and environmental familiarity that might illuminate his former colleague's psychological architecture. This direction offered no procedural justification but promised intellectual alignment with Price's constructed puzzle—the ability to approach the final examination through a shared academic context rather than standard police methodology.

Behind him, the hospital corridor continued its institutional functions—medication carts wheeled by efficient technicians, monitors transmitting vital statistics to central nursing stations, and family members navigating the suspended reality between everyday life and medical crisis. Clara's unconscious form remained under electronic supervision, and her professional competence was temporarily replaced by pharmaceutical sedation and medical protocol.

The elevator chimed softly, a gentle electronic insistence on decisional resolution. Hart's finger descended toward the control panel, then stopped again as Price's invitation manifested in his mind with photographic clarity: "Come alone, or others will answer for your absence."

Clara had already answered. Her blood had already been extracted as collateral in a game she hadn't chosen to play.

Twenty-four hours remained before Price's scheduled performance. The standard investigative approaches—tactical teams, containment strategies, negotiation protocols—would trigger whatever contingencies Price had established to maintain his advantage. Different methods were required, approaches that existed beyond procedural frameworks and ways of thinking that accessed the particular intellectual architecture Hart shared with his former colleague.

Hart pressed the button for the ground floor, the decision crystallising into action. The elevator descended with hydraulic precision, each floor marked by a soft electronic tone that seemed to count down toward some predetermined conclusion. As the doors opened onto the main lobby, Hart moved with renewed purpose, his footsteps no longer aimless pacing but directed movement.

Through the hospital's automatic doors, grey afternoon light painted the exterior world in monochromatic gradients—concrete sidewalks, asphalt roadways, and granite building facades all rendered in variations of institutional colourlessness. Hart paused momentarily, orienting himself against the urban landscape before turning not toward police headquarters but in the direction of the university campus, his stride reflecting the particular determination of someone who had transformed uncertainty into resolve, even as the uncomfortable heat of guilt continued to warm his chest beneath his rumpled shirt.

Dr Evelyn Shaw's office was a physical manifestation of her mind—a space where organisational systems battled against entropy and consistently lost. Books formed precarious geological formations on every horizontal surface, their spines displaying a linguistic diversity that suggested impressive polyglotism or aspirational acquisition. Ancient texts with cracked leather bindings shared space with spiral-bound journals containing her cramped handwriting, while the walls disappeared beneath overlapping cryptographic charts, mathematical equations, and historical timelines connected by coloured threads pinned directly into the plaster. The air itself seemed saturated with academic fervour, particles of dust and knowledge suspended in the shaft of late afternoon sunlight that penetrated the room's single window.

Hart knocked hesitantly against the partially open door, his knuckles making inadequate contact with the wood due to the multiple layers of academic conference schedules and departmental notices affixed to its surface. He stood awkwardly in the resulting aperture, neither entirely present nor absent, watching as Shaw hunched over her desk like a medieval scribe. Her attention remained fixed on a magnifying glass positioned above what appeared to be a weathered parchment covered in spiralling text, her auburn hair escaping from a haphazard bun secured by what looked suspiciously like two pencils. She wore a cardigan selected for pocket capacity rather than aesthetic consideration, its mismatched buttons suggesting multiple emergency repairs performed with whatever materials were within reach.

"The substitution cypher appears non-standard but contains regularised character groupings suggesting Kabbalistic influence rather than pure cryptographic intent," she announced without looking up, her words emerging in the particular rapid cadence of someone accustomed to vocalising thoughts without expectation of response. "The medieval tendency toward mystical rather than math-ematical encryption creates fascinating inconsistencies that—" She finally glanced upward, her sentence terminating abruptly as recog-nition registered in her expression. "Detective Hart. You're not here about the Voynich manuscript, are you?"

Her transition from academic absorption to interpersonal aware-ness occurred with the elegant efficiency of someone who had learned to navigate between intellectual passion and social obliga-tion. She immediately began clearing books from a chair opposite her desk, creating a small avalanche of academic texts that she redi-rected to the floor with practised movements.

"Please sit. Sorry about the..." She gestured vaguely toward the chaos surrounding them, the unfinished sentence suggesting even she lacked adequate terminology for the room's particular brand of disar-ray. "Tea? I have a kettle somewhere beneath this... well, beneath something."

Hart remained in the doorway for several seconds before his body seemed to remember its ambulatory function. He moved carefully through the narrow pathway between stacked papers and balanced books, his typically precise movements now sluggish with exhaustion. The chair accepted his weight with an ominous creak of protest, positioning him beneath a wall section where medieval alchemical symbols had been meticulously charted against modern chemical formulas.

His gaze fixed on a cracked teacup that occupied a small clear space on Shaw's desk—a delicate porcelain vessel whose blue-and-white pattern remained visible despite a spiderweb of fine fractures extending from rim to base. Despite structural compromise, the cup's continued functionality captured his attention with unusual intensity.

"I've been analysing those underground structural plans we discussed yesterday," Shaw continued, her words accelerating to fill Hart's silence. "Fascinating engineering anomalies in the eastern industrial zone. The subsurface levels incorporate symbolic elements consistent with several esoteric traditions, suggesting the original architects embedded cryptographic meaning directly into the architectural design. I've identified at least three distinct numerical sequences in the foundation measurements alone."

Her hands moved continuously as she spoke, rearranging papers, adjusting reference materials, and occasionally pushing escaped hair strands back into their tenuous confinement. The movements possessed a frenetic grace that contrasted sharply with Hart's uncharacteristic stillness.

"The historical pattern recognition suggests..." Her voice gradually decelerated as she fully registered Hart's appearance—his rumpled clothing, the shadows beneath his eyes, the slight tremor in his hands that he attempted to conceal by keeping them flat against his thighs. "You haven't slept," she observed, her typically scattered attention suddenly focused with surprising precision. "And Detective Morgan is not with you."

Hart's jaw worked silently for several moments before words emerged. "Clara's in the hospital. She was injured during our archive investigation." His voice carried the flatness that suggested emotional content deliberately compressed into factual reporting. "Laceration to her right arm. Significant blood loss."

Shaw's expression shifted through several configurations—surprise, concern, analytical assessment—before settling into focused attentiveness. She said nothing, creating a silence that functioned not as an absence but as space deliberately provided.

"I'm becoming like him," Hart said, the words emerging with the particular difficulty of a confession extracted against internal resistance. "Like Price." His eyes remained fixed on the cracked teacup as if the object provided safer focus than direct human contact. "Obsessed. Willing to sacrifice..."

The sentence remained incomplete, but its intended conclusion hung between them. Shaw's typically restless movements stilled completely, her body adopting the careful stillness of someone approaching wounded wildlife.

"I recognised the pattern too late," Hart continued after several heartbeats of silence. "I should have anticipated the archive ambush, should have requested proper backup, should have..." His voice fractured slightly on the final word. "Clara was protecting me. I was so focused on the intellectual puzzle that I failed to recognise the physical threat until she was already bleeding."

The shaft of late afternoon sunlight had shifted during their conversation, now illuminating a section of wall where ancient numerical sequences had been carefully transcribed onto yellowing paper. Dust motes continued their suspended dance in the golden light, moving with the subtle air currents created by their breathing and speech. The room smelled of old parchment, tea leaves, and the complexity of books stored too densely for proper air circulation.

"My analytical mind is both my greatest asset and my fundamental flaw," Hart said, his voice steadying as he transitioned from emotional admission to intellectual assessment. "The same pattern recognition capacity that makes me effective as a detective also creates dangerous similarity to Price's methodology." His fingers traced the edge of the chair arm, following a groove worn into the wood by years of similar contact. "Both of us transform human elements into abstract patterns. The primary distinction is merely application rather than approach."

Shaw's typically animated features had assumed an uncharacteristic gravity, her academic enthusiasm temporarily replaced by something more personal, more grounded. "You think intellectual similarity creates moral equivalence," she said, not a question but a precise identification of his underlying concern. "That your shared cognitive architecture with Price necessarily leads to shared ethical outcomes."

Hart's eyes finally lifted from the cracked teacup to meet hers directly, the movement requiring visible effort. In that eye contact, Shaw seemed to read something that shifted her approach entirely. She leaned forward slightly, her posture communicating a transition from an academic colleague to something adjacent to a friend.

"Tell me more about what you're seeing in his puzzle," she said, her voice quieter now, its usual rapid pace moderated to match his fatigue. "What patterns have you recognised that trouble you so deeply?"

"The mind that deciphers a puzzle and the mind that creates one appear identical in structure but differ fundamentally in purpose," Shaw said, her voice assuming an unexpected clarity that contrasted with her typical academic tangents. She rose from her chair with deliberate movements, navigating the cluttered topography of her office with the confidence of someone who understood the method within apparent madness. Her hands selected the cracked teacup from her desk, holding it toward the light where its fractures created a network of fine lines across the delicate porcelain. "Form and function exist in relationship, not equivalence," she continued, her eyes meeting Hart's with surprising directness. "The Riddler uses puzzles to control, to hurt. You solve them to protect, to heal."

The academic fervour that typically animated her features had been replaced by something quieter, more grounded—a stillness that suggested emotional insight rather than intellectual abstraction. She located an electric kettle partially hidden beneath a stack of medieval linguistic journals, filling it from a water bottle before setting it to boil with practised efficiency.

"This cup has been broken for three years and four months," she said, returning to her desk with the teacup still cradled in her palm. "A student knocked it over during a particularly enthusiastic debate about Mayan numerical systems." Her fingers traced the enormous fissure that ran from rim to base. "By conventional assessment, it's damaged beyond proper function. Yet it still holds tea."

The kettle signalled with a soft click that echoed in the momentary silence between them. Shaw carefully moved the tea, measuring loose leaves into the cracked cup before adding steaming water. The liquid immediately sought the cup's weakest points, exploring the fracture network without quite breaching its boundaries.

"The cup still functions despite its imperfections," she said, offering it to Hart with steady hands. "Your analytical mind isn't your flaw—how you use it matters."

Hart accepted the cup with uncharacteristic hesitation, his fingers registering both the heat of the liquid within and the textural irregularity of the fissures beneath his fingertips. The cup felt simultaneously fragile and resilient—a physical paradox within simple porcelain.

"Let me show you something," Shaw said, moving to a side table where a complex cypher filled several pages of yellowed paper. The characters appeared as a combination of alphabetical and mathematical symbols arranged in patterns that suggested linguistic structure without revealing immediate meaning. "I've been working on this for eleven months. Not for publication or academic recognition, but because these documents contain the only surviving records of a refugee family's genealogy across seven generations."

Her fingers traced the cryptographic patterns with the same care she had shown the teacup's fissures. "The family was separated during their escape from political persecution. The grandfather carried these documents for thirty years, believing they contained information about property holdings that might someday be reclaimed. He died never knowing what they recorded—the family's complete history, including members whose existence had been officially erased by the regime they fled."

Hart sipped the tea, its warmth spreading through his chest to counter the guilt that had resided there. The liquid found the cup's structural boundaries without breaching them, and function was maintained despite imperfection. "You're using cryptographic analysis to restore their history," he said, understanding registering in his voice.

"The puzzle exists not for itself but for what it protects," she confirmed, returning to her chair with movements that had lost their earlier frenetic quality. "Your analytical mind functions the same way. Price creates puzzles to demonstrate his intellectual superiority, to control narratives, and to inflict specific forms of suffering. You solve puzzles to prevent harm, create justice, and protect lives."

Hart's shoulders gradually straightened as he absorbed her words, the physical manifestation of psychological weight being redistributed rather than removed. He studied the teacup in his hands with new attention, running his index finger deliberately along the enormous fissure before taking another sip.

"Price and I approach intellectual problems with similar methods," he acknowledged, his voice steadier now. "We both seek patterns where others see randomness; both extract meaning from seemingly unrelated data points." His posture continued its subtle transformation, tension giving way to a more balanced alertness. "But methodology doesn't determine morality. The application does."

"Precisely," Shaw nodded, her typically scattered attention focused entirely on their conversation. "The difference lies not in cognitive architecture but in purpose. The same analytical capacity that makes you effective against Price also prevents you from becoming him— because you've directed that capacity toward protection rather than harm."

Hart carefully placed the teacup on the desk's edge, his movements conveying respect for both the object and the metaphor it represented. "The case has specific parameters I still can't resolve," he said, transitioning from philosophical concern to practical application. Price's puzzles contain references to our shared academic history, but the selection pattern suggests specific emphasis I haven't fully decoded."

Rather than offering solutions, Shaw posed questions that reframed his approach. "What elements appear consistently across different murder scenes? Which academic references receive repeated emphasis? Are there components deliberately excluded from his reconstruction?"

These questions didn't provide answers but created alternative perspectives—intellectual scaffolding that allowed Hart to reorganise his understanding of the puzzle's architecture. As he responded, articulating patterns and connections he had observed, his voice gradually reclaimed its natural analytical cadence, free from the flattened effect of guilt and exhaustion.

The office's lone window now displayed the deepening blue of approaching evening, the shaft of sunlight having migrated across the room during their conversation. Shaw's academic chaos remained unchanged, but Hart moved through it with greater ease, his body reclaiming its natural economy of motion as he traced patterns on the cryptographic charts that covered one wall.

"I should return to the hospital," he said finally, the statement emerging not as an obligation but as a chosen direction. "Clara will regain consciousness soon. There are case developments she needs to know."

Shaw nodded, not attempting to extend the conversation beyond its natural conclusion. "The difference between obsession and dedication," she said as Hart prepared to leave, "is that obsession serves only itself, while dedication serves something beyond."

Hart paused at her cluttered doorway, his posture now containing none of the uncertainty that had characterised his arrival. The rumpled clothing, the shadows beneath his eyes, the physical evidence of prolonged strain remained unchanged, yet something fundamental in his bearing had shifted. His hand rested briefly against the doorframe, fingertips tracing a pattern only he could discern in the wood's grain.

"Thank you for the perspective," he said, the words containing multitudes beneath their surface restraint.

As Hart navigated the corridor outside Shaw's office, his steps carried the particular purpose of someone who had relocated their centre of gravity after prolonged imbalance. The late afternoon light through the university's arched windows transformed the institutional hallway into something more dignified, more intentional—not unlike the transformation occurring within Hart himself as he turned toward the hospital with renewed resolve, the analytical mind that had been his perceived weakness now reclaimed as his essential strength.

14

RALLY OF ALLIES

The hospital room door yielded to Hart's touch with clinical indifference, its weight perfectly calibrated by pneumatic hinges designed for silent operation. He paused at the threshold, allowing his eyes to adjust to the fluorescent brightness that rendered everything in the room, from the mechanically adjustable bed to the transparent IV tubes, in shades of unforgiving clarity. The electronic monitors maintained their vigilant symphony, translating Clara's vital signs into steady green lines and numerical reassurances that she remained firmly tethered to the world despite the bandages visible beneath her hospital gown.

Clara's eyes were closed, but the particular stillness of her body suggested consciousness rather than sleep—the deliberate immobility of someone conserving energy rather than the abandoned posture of unconsciousness. Her injured arm lay elevated on precisely arranged pillows, white bandages absorbing the harsh overhead light and reflecting it with almost painful brightness. The skin visible around these medical restraints appeared unnaturally pale, as if her body had redirected blood away from superficial concerns to focus on the essential work of internal repair.

Hart moved toward the bed with the careful economy that characterised his professional movements, his shoes making only the slightest whisper against the polished linoleum. His hand drifted to his coat pocket, fingers closing around the smooth lake stone that had travelled with him through seven years of police work. The stone's familiar contours, worn by water long before his handling added polish, provided tactile grounding as he approached his wounded partner.

"The doctors say you lost just under a litre of blood," he said by way of greeting, his voice pitched to the particular register he used when translating medical information into investigative parameters. "The laceration required twenty-three stitches and minor nerve repair, but they anticipate full recovery of motor function within six to eight weeks."

Clara opened her eyes at his words, the movement deliberate and controlled like everything else about her. "Their estimate fails to account for my superior recovery metrics," she replied, her voice slightly roughened by recent sedation but containing its character-istic pragmatism. "I'll be field-ready in four weeks—five at most."

Hart positioned himself at the precise angle to monitor Clara and the room's entrance without obvious vigilance. The chair beside her bed creaked slightly as he settled his weight, the sound amplified by the room's hard surfaces. He placed the case folder from Shaw's office on the bedside table, its edges aligned with mathematical precision to the table's boundaries.

"The archive incident has caused major complications for the case," he stated, sticking to his role as a professional. "The loss of the folio is a tactical drawback; however, Dr Shaw has identified alternative research pathways utilising university resources."

Clara studied him with the particular intensity that had charac-terised their partnership from its beginning—her gaze cutting through his carefully constructed professional façade to the underlying currents he preferred to keep submerged. "We're not doing this," she said quietly, her uninjured hand making a small gesture encompassing his rigid posture and clinical detachment. "Not now. Not after I've had twenty-three stitches put in my arm because we went into a situation without backup."

Hart's fingers tightened around the lake stone in his pocket, its smooth surface warming to his touch. The familiar heat in his chest expanded, guilt mingling with something more complex—a recognition that Clara's injury represented not just physical damage but a breach in his carefully constructed methodology.

"I miscalculated," he admitted, struggling to express himself as he stepped outside his usual analytical comfort zone. "In focusing on the intellectual aspects of the puzzle, I overlooked the necessary physical security measures. Your injury is a direct result of my—"

"Stop," Clara interrupted, her voice carrying surprising strength despite her compromised physical condition. "Your guilt doesn't serve this investigation. What happened at the archive wasn't a failure of your analytical approach but a success of Price's operational planning. He has resources we didn't anticipate, so we need to adjust our approach, not abandon it."

Hart's hand emerged from his pocket, leaving the stone behind as he leaned slightly in the uncomfortable hospital chair. His posture shifted subtly, the rigid self-containment giving way to something more receptive, more present. "I've been treating this case as a puzzle to be solved rather than a threat to be contained," he said, his voice softening toward a register rarely heard beyond their private consultations. "The intellectual challenge became the primary focus, obscuring the human implications."

Clara's eyes never left his face, her gaze steadying him like a physical anchor. "That's not the whole truth, Alan," she said, using his first name with the deliberate intimacy she reserved for moments of particular significance. "You've treated it as a personal reckoning with Price rather than a collaborative investigation. You've been carrying this alone because you believe it's your responsibility."

The monitors continued their electronic vigilance, the steady beep marking cardiac rhythms providing a counterpoint to their conversation. Outside the room, the hospital continued its perpetual operations—medication carts wheeled by efficient personnel, intercoms summoning doctors to various emergencies, the particular institutional percussion that formed the backdrop to all healing and dying within these walls.

"I see the symmetry between Price's methodology and my own," Hart confessed, the words emerging not in his usual precise diction but with the rougher edges of genuine vulnerability. "Pattern recognition is the abstraction of human experience into analysable components, the singular focus that excludes peripheral concerns. The primary difference appears to be application rather than approach."

"The difference is everything," Clara countered, her uninjured hand moving to adjust her position with careful deliberation. "You transform patterns into protection. He weaponises them for destruction. The similarity in cognitive architecture doesn't create moral equivalence."

Hart recognised Shaw's essential insight reflected in Clara's words, the parallel framing suggesting a universal truth he had been circling but unable to embrace fully. "Shaw said something similar," he acknowledged, his posture gradually transforming from rigid self-containment to receptive attention.

"Because it's true," Clara said. "But there's something else you're overlooking that I've noticed throughout our partnership." She paused, closing her eyes briefly to gather her thoughts before continuing. "Your analytical mind isn't your greatest asset, Alan. Rather, you can empathise, which often comes across as pattern recognition. You solve puzzles not for intellectual satisfaction but because you can't stand the suffering they represent when left unresolved."

The silence that followed her words contained no awkwardness that typically accompanied emotional revelations between them. Instead, it held a quality of expansion, as if the sterile hospital room had suddenly grown larger by adding this new perspective.

"I've been approaching this case incorrectly," Hart said finally, his voice carrying the particular weight of significant realisation. "Not because I've been treating it as a puzzle, but because I've been trying to solve it alone. Price anticipates my methodology, but he can't predict how our combined perspectives might reframe his game."

Clara's expression shifted toward the subtle configuration representing her version of a smile—more evident in her eyes than her lips, a momentary softening of perpetual alertness. "Now you're thinking like a detective rather than an academic," she said, approval warming her typically pragmatic tone. "So tell me what you've learned from Shaw, and let's reshape this investigation together."

Hart reached for the case folder, opening it with renewed purpose rather than burdened obligation. As he began sharing Shaw's insights, his body language completed its transformation, turning toward Clara rather than the door, hands gesturing with cautious animation rather than controlled precision, voice modulating to include questions rather than only assertions. The lake stone remained in his pocket, its presence felt but no longer clutched like a talisman against uncertainty.

The rhythmic beeping of medical monitors provided a technological counterpoint to Clara's steady breathing as Hart sat beside her hospital bed, his mind methodically sorting through the case's evolving complexities. The squeak of rubber-soled shoes against polished linoleum announced Leo Chang's arrival before the young officer appeared in the doorway, his arms laden with laptop, external drives, and tangled cables – digital investigation tools that had become extensions of his analytical capabilities. The confidence in his stance suggested a transformation more profound than the mere passage of months since joining the department; he carried himself with the earned assurance of someone who had found his professional footing.

"Detective Hart," Leo acknowledged with a nod that conveyed professional respect without the eager deference that had characterised his earlier interactions. His gaze shifted to Clara, who had regained consciousness an hour earlier, her complexion still carrying the particular pallor that accompanies significant blood loss. "Detective Morgan. The doctors say you'll fully recover, but I brought reinforcements anyway." He lifted his tech-filled arms slightly, and a ghostly smile appeared at the corners of his lips.

Clara adjusted her position against the inclined hospital bed, wincing slightly as the movement disturbed her bandaged arm. "Please tell me those reinforcements include actual case developments and not just sympathetic emojis," she said, her professional acerbity reassuringly intact despite her medical circumstances.

Leo moved to the small table near Clara's bed, optimistically setting his equipment. Each device found its place within an invisible organisational system, cables arranged to minimise interference, and power supplies positioned for optimal access. His movements displayed none of the scattered enthusiasm that had once marked his technical preparations—this was a professional establishing his workspace with methodical precision.

· · ·

"I've been reconstructing Price's digital architecture," he explained, his fingers moving across the laptop keyboard with the particular fluency that develops when technology becomes an unconscious extension of thought. The screen illuminated his features from below, creating shifting patterns of light and shadow that emphasised the intensity of his concentration. "Not just the surveillance network monitoring Detective Hart, but the entire information ecosystem he's constructed over the past fifteen years."

Hart watched Leo with careful attention, noting the evolution in the young officer's presentation style – technically precise but accessible, confident without overreaching. Where the earlier Leo might have peppered his explanation with movie references and technical jargon, this version had found the professional balance between expertise and communication.

"His surveillance operation goes deeper than we initially thought," Leo continued, turning the laptop so both detectives could view the screen. A three-dimensional visualisation rotated slowly, showing interconnected nodes and data pathways that resembled neural networks more than conventional surveillance architecture. "It's not just electronic monitoring. He's created an integrated system that combines digital surveillance, human intelligence, and physical observation points throughout the city."

Clara leaned forward despite her injury, her eyes narrowing as she studied the visualisation. "Those distribution patterns match patrol routes," she noted, her index finger tracing a sequence of connected nodes. "He's mapped police movement protocols."

"Exactly," Leo affirmed, his head bobbing with controlled enthusiasm. "And not just standard patrol patterns. He's mapped shift changes, response protocols, even the particular routes individual officers prefer." His fingers executed a precise command sequence, transforming the display to show a time-lapse representation of data collection patterns. "He's been gathering this intelligence for years, building a predictive model of departmental behaviour that would make our analysts jealous."

Hart's expression tightened almost imperceptibly as the implications registered. "He can anticipate our standard tactical responses."

"Down to the minute," Leo confirmed, the gravity in his voice momentarily overshadowing his youth. Then, with a quick sideways glance at Clara, he added, "Though I doubt he predicted Detective Morgan deciding to redecorate the city archive with her blood. That probably threw off his calculations."

"I aim to be unpredictable," Clara replied dryly, her uninjured hand adjusting the IV line attached to her wrist. "What else have you found?"

Leo's fingers danced across the keyboard, bringing up a new display that showed intercepted communications – fragments of encrypted messages, data packets captured from network traffic, snippets of voice recordings that appeared as waveform visualisations. "He's been communicating with multiple operatives through a custom encryption protocol. Most of it is still locked down, but I managed to crack parts using pattern analysis based on his academic publications."

Hart noted the particular methodological precision in Leo's explanation – no longer the impulsive technological showmanship of his early days with the department, but the measured confidence of a specialist who had grown into his expertise. Leo had always possessed the technical skills, but now he wielded them with professional discipline and investigative purpose.

"This is the most interesting part," Leo continued, extracting a specialised flash drive from his collection of devices. He carefully inserted it into the laptop as if its contained data might be volatile. "Price has been accessing historical city records dating back to the 1890s – property titles, infrastructure plans, municipal development proposals. The same records we were looking for at the archive."

A series of digitised documents appeared on screen–aged paper rendered into high-resolution scans, faded ink transformed into searchable text through advanced character recognition. Leo highlighted sections where handwritten notes appeared in the margins, annotations that hadn't been part of the official documentation.

"These are from private collections, not public archives," he explained, his voice carrying the particular satisfaction of someone presenting a significant breakthrough. "Price has been compiling a parallel historical record of the city's development, focusing specifically on underground structures in the eastern industrial zone."

Hart leaned closer, his eyes tracking the digital reproductions with analytical intensity. "The same location where he's scheduled his 'final examination,'" he noted, the connection crystallising in his mind. "How did you obtain these?"

A ghost of the old Leo – the eager officer with a touch of mischievous tech wizard – flickered across his features. "Let's just say I followed his digital breadcrumbs home and borrowed his research notes while he was out." The playful expression vanished almost immediately, replaced by professional seriousness. "I traced his data exfiltration patterns back to their source and established a passive monitoring connection that allowed me to mirror his historical database. Completely admissible in court," he added with a glance at Clara, "assuming we want to prosecute him for illegal data access after we deal with the multiple homicides."

Clara exchanged a look with Hart, the subtle shift in her expression registering impressed approval. The young officer who had once enthusiastically announced his findings with pop culture references and technical jargon had evolved into a sophisticated digital investigator whose work demonstrated technical excellence and investigative discipline.

"There's more," Leo said, bringing up another visualisation showing three-dimensional architectural plans overlaid with data flow patterns. "Price's surveillance network isn't just monitoring external targets. It also feeds information to a centralised processing system beneath the industrial complex. These power consumption patterns suggest he's built something significant down there – something that draws as much electricity as a small research facility."

As Leo continued his presentation, the blue light from the laptop screen caught the angles of his face, emphasising the maturity that had emerged in his features. His hands moved with precise economy between the keyboard and external devices, each gesture purposeful, each explanation clear and concise. The enthusiastic rookie remained visible in moments of technical excitement, but these flashes now existed within a framework of professional competence that commanded genuine respect.

Hart watched this evolution with quiet acknowledgement – another piece in the complex puzzle of human potential and growth, a reminder that while some patterns led to destruction, others led to development and contribution. In Leo's transformation from eager assistant to essential team member, Hart recognised another counterpoint to Price's destructive brilliance – the constructive application of intelligence toward protection rather than harm.

The door to Clara's hospital room burst open with such unexpected force that Leo nearly dropped his laptop. Dr Evelyn Shaw appeared in the doorway like an academic whirlwind, her arms struggling to contain an architectural impossibility of ancient texts, rolled papers, and what appeared to be at least three different colours of string dangling from between leather-bound volumes. Her cardigan—different from yesterday's but equally distinguished by its abundance of pockets—appeared to serve as auxiliary storage, bulging with markers, folded papers, and what might have been a partial archaeological map protruding from the left breast pocket.

"Detective Hart! The subsurface symbolism is Hermetic rather than purely Masonic!" she announced without preamble as if continuing a conversation that had been momentarily interrupted rather than initiating an entirely new one. Her auburn hair had escaped whatever temporary containment system she had attempted that morning, creating a halo of academic intensity around features animated by intellectual discovery. "The geometric proportions follow the Golden Ratio when measured from the central access point rather than the cardinal directions, which completely transforms the interpretive framework!"

She navigated into the room with the specialised spatial awareness of someone accustomed to moving through cluttered environments, her trajectory carrying her to the small table where Leo had established his digital command centre. Without apparent notice of the delicate electronic equipment, she began depositing her academic burden across any available surface—ancient texts with bookmarks protruding at improbable angles, rolled architectural plans that immediately attempted to curl themselves, loose papers covered in handwritten notations that appeared to follow no consistent organisational system.

With its calculated neutrality and antiseptic simplicity, the sterile hospital environment seemed to recoil from this sudden invasion of academic chaos. The fluorescent lighting that had previously rendered all surfaces in uniform illumination now created dramatic shadows beneath stacked books and highlighted the vivid colours of string, markers, and Post-it notes that had materialised across formerly pristine surfaces.

"The underground passageways weren't designed merely for practical purposes but as physical manifestations of alchemical principles," Evelyn continued, extracting a battered leather journal from one of her cardigan pockets. "The founders incorporated esoteric knowledge into the literal foundations of the city's infrastructure, embedding symbolic references that remain actively significant rather than merely historical."

She opened the journal to reveal densely packed handwriting interspersed with diagrams resembling architectural schematics and obscure mathematical formulas. Coloured threads had been taped to specific pages, creating a three-dimensional reference system that extended beyond the book's physical boundaries.

Leo glanced at Hart with an expression eloquently communicating professional respect tangled with complete bafflement. Despite her medication and injury, Clara had managed to prop herself higher against her pillows, her analytical mind visibly attempting to extract actionable intelligence from Evelyn's academic tempest.

"Dr. Shaw has been researching the historical context of the eastern industrial zone," Hart explained, his voice stabilising counterpoint to Evelyn's intellectual flurry. Where previously he might have dominated the analytical space, he now created conversational bridges between team members, translating academic complexity into the investigative framework. "The underground structures connect to the city's founding families and contain embedded codes that may reveal Price's ultimate objective."

Evelyn looked up from her journals with momentary surprise as if reminded that communication requires shared context rather than merely shared enthusiasm. "Yes, exactly," she confirmed, her rapid speech decelerating slightly toward comprehensibility. "The architectural anomalies I identified in yesterday's discussions reveal a complex symbolic system integrated into the physical infrastructure."

She extracted a large roll of yellowed paper from beneath a stack of books, spreading it across the foot of Clara's bed with careful movements that contrasted with her general kinetic energy. The document revealed itself as a hand-drawn map of subterranean passages, annotated with numerical sequences and geometric symbols that appeared initially as decorative elements rather than functional notation.

"These passages weren't merely utilitarian," Evelyn explained, retrieving coloured markers from various pockets with the unconscious efficiency of someone whose clothing had evolved into specialised tool storage. "They were constructed according to proportional systems derived from Renaissance cryptographic traditions, primarily Trithemius and later Kircher." She circled specific architectural elements with a green marker, her other hand reaching for a red marker behind her ear. "The numerical sequences embedded in structural measurements correspond to substitution cyphers when correctly identified."

"The passage dimensions encode actual messages," Hart translated, noticing the flicker of understanding beginning to illuminate Leo's expression. "The physical architecture itself contains encrypted information."

Clara leaned forward despite her injury, her analytical focus overriding physical discomfort. "Those numerical patterns," she said, gesturing toward the map with her uninjured hand, "match the surveillance node distribution in Leo's digital model."

Leo immediately pulled his laptop closer, fingers moving across the keyboard with practised efficiency. "You're right," he confirmed after a moment, turning the screen to display his surveillance network visualisation alongside Evelyn's historical map. "The geographic distribution of Price's modern surveillance points mirrors these historical passage configurations almost exactly."

"He's not just using the underground structures," Hart said, the connections crystallising in his mind. "He's reactivating the original system for its intended purpose."

Evelyn nodded vigorously, auburn hair bouncing with each movement. "The founders created these passages for information transmission and security," she explained, now drawing connecting lines between specific points on her map with the red marker. "A nineteenth-century surveillance network disguised as mundane infrastructure, designed to protect certain families' interests and monitor potential threats."

The room had transformed during their exchange, hospital sterility giving way to a vibrant investigative hub centred around Clara's bed. Evelyn's manuscripts and maps now covered every available surface, creating a palimpsest of historical information layered with Leo's digital displays. Coloured strings connected key documents, creating a three-dimensional representation of intellectual connections that mirrored the physical networks they were uncovering.

Clara pointed toward a specific intersection on Evelyn's map, her movement causing a momentary wince as it disturbed her injured arm. "This junction corresponds with the location Price selected for his 'final examination,'" she noted, professional focus overriding physical discomfort. "It's not randomly chosen—it's the central node in the original network."

"The primary information processing point," Evelyn confirmed, manuscripts cascading from her lap as she leaned forward to circle the location with emphatic green strokes. "All communication lines converge at this nexus, allowing monitoring of the entire system from a single position."

Leo's fingers moved across his keyboard with increasing urgency, his screen displaying various data visualisations that shifted and reformed as he tested hypotheses against the available evidence. "The power consumption patterns I detected are concentrated at exactly that location," he reported, professional excitement animating his features. "Whatever he's built down there, it's drawing massive electrical resources through carefully concealed channels to avoid triggering utility company notifications."

Hart observed the intellectual exchange around him, consciously restraining his tendency to direct and control. Instead, he watched as Evelyn gestured with coloured markers clutched between her fingers like some academic conductor's baton, her explanations punctuated by the rhythmic waving of writing implements that occasionally left unintended marks on nearby papers. Her academic fervour manifested physically—leaning forward when emphasising connections, eyebrows rising when establishing theoretical frameworks, and hand movements becoming increasingly elaborate when tracing cryptographic patterns.

The contrast between team members created a productive tension —Leo's digital precision complementing Evelyn's academic expansiveness, Clara's investigative focus providing structural coherence to their shared analytical process. Where Hart would once have imposed methodological uniformity, he now recognised how these diverse approaches created a more comprehensive understanding than any perspective could provide.

.   .   .

"The nineteenth-century designers used architectural symbolism as information security," Evelyn continued, extracting yet another text from the diminishing pile beside her. This volume appeared significantly older than the others, its binding cracked with age, pages yellowed by centuries rather than decades. "Geometric patterns that appear decorative represent coded access protocols—specific pathways that must be followed in precise sequence to reach the central chamber without triggering defensive mechanisms."

"Defensive mechanisms?" Leo echoed, his attention momentarily diverted from his screen. "In an underground tunnel system built in the 1890s?"

Evelyn nodded with the particular enthusiasm of an academic sharing specialised knowledge. "Primarily mechanical rather than electronic—pressure plates triggering structural collapses, false passages leading to dead ends or hazardous areas, water management systems that could be redirected to flood specific sections." She traced these elements on her map with a blue marker, creating a new layer of information across the complex document. "Quite sophisticated for their era, and potentially still functional if maintained or restored."

The four of them had unconsciously formed a circle around Clara's bed, and their diverse materials and methodologies combined to create a unified investigative approach that transcended individual limitations. As they continued working, the steady beeping of Clara's heart monitor provided a metronomic backdrop to their collaborative analysis—a reminder of both human vulnerability and resilience in the face of carefully constructed threats.

The evidence board dominated the far wall of Clara's hospital room, transforming the sterile medical space into something between crime scene investigation headquarters and an academic conference. They had requisitioned a wheeled whiteboard from the hospital's teaching department, supplementing its limited surface with taped papers that extended the analytical canvas onto the adjacent wall. The fluorescent lights cast harsh shadows across the assembled evidence—crime scene photographs arranged in chronological sequence, Leo's surveillance network visualisations rendered in precise digital clarity, Evelyn's historical maps with their cryptographic annotations, and at the centre, Hart's carefully maintained case timeline linking each element into a narrative of escalating precision.

The murder tableaux formed a particularly disturbing constellation across the upper portion of the board—each victim positioned with the meticulous care of an artist arranging figures in a grotesque exhibition. The photographs had been deliberately placed at precise intervals, mirroring the spatial relationships of the original quantum experiment components they represented. Red strings connected each crime scene to its corresponding element in Hart's quantum apparatus schematic, reconstructed from memory and university archives.

The four of them had arranged themselves around this central focus with unconscious symbolism—Hart standing slightly apart, his posture suggesting analytical assessment rather than directive control; Clara propped against elevated pillows in her hospital bed, which had been wheeled closer to the evidence wall; Leo seated with his laptop balanced on his knees, digital displays supplementing the physical evidence, and Evelyn moving between documents with the particular kinetic energy of someone whose thoughts travelled faster than her ability to articulate them.

The hospital room's standard medical equipment continued its quiet technological vigilance—the IV pump administering Clara's prescribed fluids, the heart monitor maintaining its steady rhythmic beeping, and the oxygen saturation sensor glowing softly on her uninjured hand. These mechanical constants provided a strangely appropriate counterpoint to their investigation—precise measurements of physical parameters existing alongside their attempt to quantify the patterns of a disturbed, brilliant mind.

"The murder locations aren't random," Clara observed, her professional focus undimmed by medication and injury. Her uninjured arm extended toward the crime scene photographs, index finger tracing an invisible pattern between them. "They form a specific geometric configuration when mapped against the city grid."

Hart remained deliberately silent, resisting his instinct to direct the analytical process. The posture required conscious effort—his body contained the particular tension of someone intentionally restraining an established pattern of behaviour. This restraint wasn't an absence of engagement but a different form of participation, creating space for collaborative insight rather than individual direction.

Leo's fingers danced over the keyboard, executing commands with practised efficiency. "I'm plotting the murder coordinates against the historical subway infrastructure," he explained. His screen displayed a three-dimensional map of the city, with illuminated points marking each crime scene. The display rotated slowly, highlighting spatial relationships that weren't immediately obvious in a two-dimensional view. "There's a pattern here."

"Compare it with the quantum experiment schematic," Hart suggested, his contribution offered as a possibility rather than an instruction. His voice carried the particular modulation of someone who had recalibrated his approach to the collaborative process—still analytical but no longer dominating.

Leo nodded, fingers already implementing the suggestion before Hart completed his sentence. The display transformed, overlaying the murder locations with a ghostly blue representation of the quantum apparatus Hart and Price had designed fifteen years earlier. The correspondence between physical crime scenes and experimental components revealed itself with chilling precision—each murder occurring at a location that corresponded precisely to a specific element in their failed experiment.

"The architectural alignment is even more precise than we initially recognised," Evelyn added, spreading one of her historical maps across the foot of Clara's bed. Her finger traced specific structural elements marked on the yellowed paper. "Each murder occurred directly above one of the primary nodes in the original underground network."

The hospital room's fluorescent lighting flickered momentarily, casting brief, unnatural shadows across the evidence board before resuming its harsh, steady illumination. The effect created a fleeting impression of movement among the crime scene photographs as if the positioned victims had momentarily shifted before returning to their arranged tableaux.

Clara's heart monitor maintained its steady electronic rhythm—a metronomic counterpoint to the intellectual intensity filling the room. The sound had become so integrated into their environment that they registered it only subconsciously, its regular beeping providing temporal structure to their analytical process.

"The quantum experiment was designed to identify patterns within apparently random data," Hart explained, gesturing toward the apparatus schematic without touching it as if the diagram itself might retain some dangerous essence of their failed project. "Price has recreated each component as a murder tableau but also positioned each victim at a location corresponding to a node in the historical underground surveillance network."

. . .

"He's not just recreating our experiment," Clara said, understanding illuminating her features despite the persistent pallor of blood loss. "He's integrating it with the city's original surveillance architecture."

Leo's screen displayed a new visualisation—a hybrid representation showing the quantum experiment structure and the nineteenth-century tunnel system overlaid onto the modern city grid. The integration revealed a more complex and precise pattern than either system would have suggested.

"The founders' tunnel network was designed according to Renaissance cryptographic principles," Evelyn elaborated, her academic precision momentarily overriding her typical tangential tendencies. "Specific geometric relationships that encoded information within the architectural structure itself." She retrieved one of her ancient texts, holding it open to display a diagram of concentric circles intersected by radial lines. "These same proportional systems appear in your quantum experiment design, though I suspect neither recognised the historical precedent."

Hart's expression shifted subtly as this connection registered—another layer of pattern emerging from what had appeared to be separate analytical tracks. "Price would have discovered this correspondence during his research," he said, his voice carrying the weight of significant realisation. "He's not simply recreating our experiment with human components; he's integrating it with an existing system designed for surveillance and information control."

Under this analytical framework, the crime scene photographs took on new significance. Each victim was not merely a component in Price's revenge scenario but a node in a larger pattern that extended forward into his planned "final examination" and backward into the city's historical foundations.

Clara shifted against her pillows, wincing slightly as the movement disturbed her injured arm. "The city's founding families created the historical network," she noted, her analytical mind extracting connections from the assembled evidence. "The same families whose descendants still control significant portions of the city's infrastructure, government, and financial systems."

Leo had fallen unnaturally still, his typical energy temporarily suspended as he studied the pattern on his screen. "There's more," he said, voice uncharacteristically quiet. "The power consumption patterns I've been tracking are not just concentrated at the central node. They're distributed throughout the entire historical network." His fingers executed a command sequence, causing the display to pulse with colour-coded intensity markers. "He's not just built something at the examination location. He's reactivated the entire underground system."

The heart monitor's steady beeping continued its rhythmic measurement, the consistency of its electronic vigilance contrasting with the escalating implications of their discoveries. Hart moved closer to the evidence board, studying the arranged photographs with renewed attention—each victim's positioning, each crime scene's particular details now illuminated by expanded contextual understanding.

"The quantum experiment was designed to identify embedded patterns within seemingly random datasets," he said, his mind reconstructing the theoretical framework he and Price had developed years earlier. "If Price has integrated that capability with the historical surveillance network..."

"He could extract patterns from the city's information flow that would otherwise remain invisible," Evelyn completed his thought, academic enthusiasm momentarily overshadowing the grim implications.

"Identifying connections, correlations, and causalities that conventional analysis would never detect."

Clara's gaze moved deliberately across the evidence board, her professional assessment uncompromised by her medical condition. "The murder tableaux aren't just recreating your experiment," she said, the steady beeping of her heart monitors punctuating her observation. "They're calibrating the system—each victim positioned to initialise a specific component in whatever he's constructed beneath the city."

The fluorescent lights continued their unforgiving illumination of the assembled evidence, casting harsh shadows across photographs of meticulously arranged death. The contrast between the hospital room's clinical sterility and the intellectual horror they were assembling created a dissonance that manifested as a particular tension in the air—the sense of something monstrous taking shape through their collective understanding, each analytical contribution bringing Price's design into sharper focus.

Leo's screen displayed the integrated pattern with mathematical precision, while Evelyn's historical documents provided context and precedent. Clara's investigative insights connected disparate elements into a coherent narrative, all building upon the foundation of Hart's reconstructed quantum framework. Their diverse methodologies had converged into a unified analytical approach transcending individual limitations—precisely the collaborative synthesis that Price had failed to achieve in his isolation and arrogance.

The heart monitor maintained its steady rhythm, measuring Clara's continued life in consistent electronic intervals that seemed, at that moment, to count down toward whatever culmination awaited at Price's "final examination"—now less than eighteen hours away.

The manila envelope arrived via hospital courier at precisely 4:17 p.m., its unremarkable appearance belying the significance of its contents. Hart accepted the delivery with the careful neutrality he maintained during all professional interactions, signing the receipt with mechanical precision while his mind calculated probabilities regarding its source and purpose. The envelope bore the department's official stamp. Still, the handwriting inscribed his name across its surface belonged to the records clerk whose grandfather had been the city's commissioner during the initial construction of the eastern industrial zone—a historical connection suddenly rendered relevant by their evolving understanding of Price's design.

Hart carried the envelope to the evidence board, where Leo and Evelyn continued refining their integrated model of Price's system. Clara watched from her elevated position in the hospital bed, her analytical focus undiminished by medication or injury. The room had grown warmer throughout the afternoon as their collective intellectual intensity seemed to generate physical heat that the hospital's climate control system struggled to disperse.

"The archival photos I requested," Hart explained, opening the envelope with careful movements that respected both the potential fragility of its contents and the forensic implications of its handling. From within, he extracted a single black-and-white photograph approximately fifty years old, its edges slightly yellowed with age, its surface bearing the particular patina that develops when chemical development processes begin their slow surrender to time.

The image depicted a clock tower rising above the eastern industrial district, its architectural details rendered with the stark contrast characteristic of mid-century municipal photography. The tower's stone façade displayed elaborate carvings partially obscured by industrial grime, while its clock face remained pristine—four Roman numerals positioned at the cardinal points around a central mechanism whose internal workings remained invisible behind leaded glass.

Hart placed the photograph at the centre of their evidence board, his movements carrying the deliberate precision of someone who recognised its significance without fully understanding its implications. The image exerted a gravitational pull on the surrounding materials, creating a new focal point around which their previous analysis might reorganise itself.

Clara gasped—a sound so uncharacteristic that all three others turned towards her immediately. Her complexion, already pale from blood loss, had acquired an additional shade of pallor that suggested revelation rather than medical distress. "The clock tower," she said, her voice unusually tight. "It's not just architecturally significant—it's the central processing node of the entire historical network."

Leo immediately turned to his laptop, fingers rapidly moving across the keyboard. His screen displayed digital signal patterns that shifted and realigned as he implemented new search parameters. "There's a transmission source at exactly that location," he confirmed, professional excitement momentarily overriding the sombre implications of their discovery. "It's broadcasting on a frequency that wouldn't register on conventional scanning—I only caught it because I was specifically looking for anomalous patterns in the electromagnetic background noise."

Evelyn had begun frantically rifling through her stack of historical texts, auburn hair falling across her face as she hunched over the volumes with uncharacteristic focus. Her typical academic tangents had disappeared, replaced by methodical urgency as she searched for specific information. "The tower wasn't in my original research because it wasn't designated as part of the underground network in the official records," she explained, fingers tracing down a page covered in cramped handwriting. "But it appears in these private journals belonging to one of the founding architects."

She extracted a weathered leather-bound volume, opening it to reveal pages covered in faded ink diagrams interspersed with text in an archaic hand. "The tower was constructed as the central monitoring station for the entire surveillance system," she continued, her voice acquiring the particular cadence of significant academic discovery. "Its height provided line-of-sight to all major city districts, while its basement levels connected directly to the primary underground junction."

The four fell into sudden, complete silence, each absorbing the implications from their particular analytical perspective and recognising the pattern that had emerged with terrible clarity from their combined investigation. The only sound in the room was the steady electronic beeping of Clara's heart monitor, measuring the moments of their collective realisation with medical precision.

The hospital room seemed to contract around them, its dimensions suddenly inadequate to contain the weight of their understanding. The fluorescent lights buzzed with subliminal intensity, their harsh illumination emphasising the grim expressions that had settled across four faces now united in comprehension. Outside the window, afternoon shadows lengthened across the hospital grounds, stretching toward evening with the particular inexorability that marks transitions beyond human capacity to halt or redirect.

"The clock mechanism isn't merely decorative," Hart said finally, breaking the silence with words that seemed to crystallise their shared understanding. "It's the physical interface for the original surveillance system—a nineteenth-century information processing device disguised as municipal architecture."

Leo nodded, his screen displaying a three-dimensional rendering of the tower's internal structure based on electromagnetic scanning data. "The signal patterns suggest he's modified the original mechanism," he explained, highlighting specific anomalies in the digital visualisation. "Integrated modern technological components while maintaining the historical framework."

"The founding families constructed the surveillance network to maintain their control over the city's development," Evelyn added, her academic expertise providing historical context for their contemporary discovery. "They monitored political opposition, tracked financial transactions, intercepted communications—all through this seemingly antiquated system that operated beneath official governance structures."

Clara's uninjured hand gripped the hospital bed railing with white-knuckled intensity, her professional composure momentarily fractured by the scale of what they were uncovering. "And these families still control significant portions of the city's infrastructure," she said, her voice carrying the particular weight of an investigator recognising conspiracy beyond individual crime. "Banking, real estate, municipal contracts, political appointments—their descendants maintain influence through ostensibly legitimate channels."

"Price isn't just targeting me," Hart said, the realisation spreading through his consciousness with cold clarity. "My persecution is merely the mechanism, not the objective." His hand moved unconsciously to his pocket, fingers closing around the smooth lake stone that had become his tactile anchor during moments of significant stress or revelation. "He's using our quantum pattern recognition technology to expose the entire historical surveillance network and the power structures it has protected for generations."

The stone felt cool against his palm, its polished surface grounding him in physical reality as his mind processed the implications. Price's elaborate game of murder and manipulation had never been merely personal revenge—it was the initialisation sequence for something far more comprehensive, more destructive, and more transformative than mere individual retribution.

"His 'final examination' isn't just for you," Leo said, understanding registering in his expression. "It's for the entire city power structure. He's using the pattern recognition capabilities you developed to extract evidence of corruption, collusion, and conspiracy from historical and contemporary data sources."

Evelyn nodded vigorously, the academic implications aligning with investigative reality. "The quantum processing capacity integrated with the historical surveillance architecture would allow him to identify connections invisible to conventional analysis," she confirmed, her fingers tracing patterns in the architectural diagrams spread before her. "Correlating seemingly unrelated data points across municipal development and governance generations."

"He's planning to expose them all," Clara said, her professional assessment cutting through academic complexity to practical implications. "Not through conventional evidence but through pattern recognition so comprehensive it constitutes its form of proof."

Hart studied the clock tower photograph, and his analytical mind now processes it through multiple contextual frameworks simultaneously—architectural significance, historical function, contemporary threat, and philosophical implication. The regular beeping of Clara's heart monitor provided rhythmic accompaniment to his thoughts, each electronic tone marking another moment closer to Price's scheduled performance.

"The quantum experiment was designed to identify embedded patterns within seemingly random datasets," he said, his voice acquiring the particular clarity that accompanies significant recognition. "Price has spent fifteen years refining that technology while researching the historical power structures that have shaped this city since its founding. He's not just targeting me. He's using me to expose them all."

The weight of this understanding settled across the room like invisible sediment, altering the atmospheric pressure of their shared space. Price's elaborate game had revealed itself as something far beyond personal vendetta—a comprehensive architecture of revelation designed to collapse structures of power that had persisted for generations beneath the city's visible governance.

Hart's gaze moved deliberately across the faces of his team members, registering the particular configuration of features that accompanied profound realisation in each—Leo's widened eyes betraying youth momentarily overwhelmed by implication; Evelyn's furrowed brow signalling academic frameworks struggling to accommodate real-world consequence; Clara's tightened jaw indicating professional determination reasserting itself after momentary shock.

"We have less than sixteen hours," Hart said, his voice steady despite the magnitude of what they now faced. "Price has designed his 'final examination' not merely as a personal confrontation but as a public revelation. Whatever evidence he's accumulated, whatever patterns he's identified through his integrated system—he intends to release it all from the clock tower at precisely 9:47 tomorrow night."

The team exchanged looks of determined understanding—four different analytical approaches now aligned toward a common purpose, four distinct methodologies integrated into a coherent response. Where Price operated in isolated brilliance, they functioned as collaborative counterpoint; where his genius served destruction and exposure, theirs would be directed toward protection and containment.

Clara adjusted her position against the hospital pillows, professionalism overriding physical discomfort. "The department needs to secure the clock tower immediately," she said, tactical considerations already forming in her expression. "Whatever transmission mechanism he's established must be neutralised before he can activate it."

Leo nodded in agreement, fingers moving across his keyboard to initiate necessary communications. "I can establish a counter-broadcasting protocol that might disrupt his signal," he offered, technical expertise transforming immediately into a practical contribution.

Evelyn gathered her historical materials with uncharacteristic organisation, and her academic knowledge was now directed toward immediate application. "The architectural plans show multiple access points to the tower's substructure," she noted, extracting specific diagrams from her collection," some of which wouldn't appear on modern city planning documents."

Hart silently acknowledged this mobilisation, recognising how their diverse capacities had integrated into a unified response. His hand held the lake stone in his pocket, its smooth surface a reminder of both personal loss and professional purpose—the particular weight of responsibility that comes from standing at the intersection of individual justice and collective protection.

Outside the window, the evening had begun its transition toward night, city lights illuminating against deepening darkness. Somewhere across that urban landscape, Jonathan Price completed his preparations for tomorrow's performance—the culmination of fifteen years' planning, the integration of a brilliant mind and a wounded spirit, the terrible perfection of revenge expanded beyond personal target to societal revelation.

The heart monitor continued its steady electronic rhythm, measuring each moment that brought them closer to confrontation with a precision that neither hastened nor delayed the inevitable. Hart's fingers closed more tightly around the lake stone in his pocket, its solid reality anchoring him as he prepared to face not merely his former colleague but the expanded architecture of consequence Price had constructed around their shared history.

15

THE CIPHER'S KEY

lara's once pristine medical hospital room became a disorganised mess of notes, papers, diagrams, and computer displays. Replacing it with a combination of coffee, marker ink, and Evelyn's old books, the antiseptic smell became almost intellectual. Harsh shadows from the institutional fluorescent lights fell across the makeshift war room, where the battle focused mainly on pattern recognition and historical cryptography.

The wall-mounted digital clock, acquired from the nurses' station using Leo's charm and my badge, showed 4:23 p.m. in uncompromising red numerals. Price's "final examination" was five hours and twenty-four minutes away. The regular electronic countdown felt like a physical weight as they worked, growing heavier each minute.

With deliberate purpose, Hart paced the narrow path between workstations, his movements contrasting with the aimless anxiety typical of hospital waiting. Hart carefully planned each step to bridge different analytical regions. His fingers occasionally brushed against the evidence pinned to the walls, establishing physical connections between Evelyn's historical discoveries and Leo's digital architecture as if tactile contact might extract additional meaning from the materials themselves.

Observing the yellowed architectural drawing Evelyn had spread on an equipment cart, he noted that the geometric proportions in the foundation measurements weren't purely structural.

"They incorporate the Golden Ratio in sequences that suggest intentional embedding rather than coincidental occurrence."

From her hunched position over a Renaissance manuscript, Evelyn looked up, her auburn hair escaping its hastily arranged confinement. Her nose was something that no one felt compelled to mention.

"That's exactly what I've been tracking," she replied, moving toward Hart with the particular animated energy that characterised her intellectual excitement.

"The sequence appears repeatedly throughout the founding documents, always concealed within seemingly decorative elements or marginal notations." Her finger trembled slightly as she traced a pattern of numbers hidden within the ornate border of a city planning document. Observe identical numerical sequences within this notarial seal, expressed via varied symbolic notations.

Leo sat cross-legged on the floor near Clara's bed, his laptop on his knees. Three external drives connected to his computer via a nest of cables that resembled some technological organism spreading across the linoleum. His posture suggested the particular concentration of someone whose physical body had become secondary to his digital engagement—shoulders slightly hunched, neck bent at an angle orthopaedists would disapprove of, fingers moving across the keyboard with percussion-like precision.

"I've modified the pattern recognition algorithm to incorporate historical cypher structures," he said without looking up, his voice carrying the tight focus of someone translating between mental conception and digital implementation. "Running a comparative analysis against the surveillance data extracts from the last fifteen years of Price's activity."

Clara observed their efforts from her elevated position in the hospital bed, her injured arm carefully positioned on a precisely arranged pillow, fresh white bandages concealing the stitches beneath. The IV stand remained beside her bed, its medical necessity a physical reminder of her compromised condition, but her eyes carried none of the pharmaceutical sedation from earlier—her gaze moved across the assembled evidence with the particular incisiveness that had characterised her detective work since Hart had known her.

"The numerical sequence correlates with specific locations in the city grid," she noted, her uninjured hand gesturing toward the map Leo had printed and mounted on the movable table beside her bed. "If you translate the values into geographical coordinates using the original city planning metrics rather than modern GPS parameters."

Clara's remark immediately captured Hart's attention, halting his pacing. Studying the pattern she'd found, his eyes narrowed, his mind clearly readjusting its analytical processes.

"He proposed the sequence could be used to locate members of the underground network and strode towards the map with renewed determination. 'Architectural detailing that doubles as a navigation structure."

Evelyn's excitement manifested as a small, involuntary hop that sent several loose papers fluttering to the floor. She ignored them, hurrying to extract another document from her seemingly bottom-less portfolio case. The parchment she produced appeared significantly older than her previous references. Its edges were irregularly worn, and its surface bore the particular patina that develops when human hands transmit oils to paper across centuries of handling.

"This manuscript fragment belonged to one of the original city architects," she explained, carefully spreading it beside Clara's map. "It contains a numeric sequence embedded within what appears to be a simple measurement table." Her finger traced the columns of faded numbers, some barely visible beneath centuries of discolouration. "But the pattern isn't architectural—it's cryptographic. These aren't measurements but a codified addressing system for information transmission."

Hart and Clara exchanged a glance of shared recognition. This silent communication develops between long-term partners who process information along parallel tracks. "Price would have discovered this during his research," Hart said, the statement carrying the weight of significant realisation. "He's not just targeting the founding families' descendants—he's using their own hidden system against them."

Leo's laptop emitted a soft electronic tone that immediately drew everyone's attention. He straightened from his hunched position, his expression shifting from concentrated focus to surprised validation. "The algorithm found a match," he announced, turning the screen toward the others. The historical sequence Evelyn identified correlates perfectly with anomalous metadata patterns in Price's surveillance records."

Data streams shown on a city map as coloured lines between nodes on the screen visualised know data streams are displayed on a city map as coloured lines between nodes on the screen that visualised knowledge flow. Volumes or specific importance in the general design. The pattern precisely mirrored the numerical sequence Evelyn had extracted from the historical documents, the digital validation of the academic hypothesis rendered in glowing pixels.

"The pattern appears consistently across multiple data categories," Leo continued, his fingers executing commands that transformed the visualisation to show different information streams. "Financial transactions, communications intercepts, surveillance footage—all channelled through pathways that follow this same numerical progression."

Clara leaned forward despite her injury, eliciting a slight wince that she immediately suppressed. "He's using the original surveillance architecture as a framework for his modern system," she said, professional analysis overriding physical discomfort. "The founding families created a hidden network for monitoring and controlling the city's development. Price has reactivated it using contemporary technology."

Hart studied Leo's screen with analytical intensity, his mind extracting patterns and implications with characteristic precision. "The quantum experiment we designed should identify embedded information within random datasets," he said, the connections crystallising in his expression. "Price has applied that method to the historical surveillance network, extracting patterns of influence and control that would otherwise remain invisible."

Evelyn nodded vigorously, her glasses sliding down her nose with the movement. "The founding families encoded their activities within legitimate municipal records," she confirmed, academic excitement momentarily overtaking the grim implications. "Price has created a system capable of decoding centuries of hidden governance."

Leo's algorithm emitted another alert tone, drawing their attention back to his screen. A new pattern had emerged from the digital analysis—a geometric configuration that pulsed with particular intensity at the city's eastern edge. The visualization automatically zoomed in on this anomaly, revealing what appeared to be a concentrated nexus of information flow centered on a single location.

"That's it," Hart said quietly, recognition dawning in his expression. "That's where his final examination will take place."

The digital visualisation continued pulsing on Leo's screen, the concentrated nexus of information flow demanding their collective attention like a beacon. Clara's eyes, however, had shifted to a different focus—a barely visible notation in the margin of a yellowed parchment that Evelyn's more dramatic manuscripts had partially obscured. The handwritten note, rendered in faded brown ink that had once been black, contained two phrases that vibrated with sudden significance against the backdrop of their emerging understanding: "eastern sentinel" and "ninth hour".

"Look at this," Clara murmured, her voice soft but with a specific urgency that instantly focused the audience.

Leo immediately returned to his keyboard, fingers executing commands with intensified purpose. The visualisation on his screen was transformed, and timeline data appeared alongside the geographical display. "Confirmed," he said, the professional satisfaction in his voice tempered by the implications of their discovery.

"Anomalous power surges at the eastern tower complex, consistently occurring between 9:45 and 9:50 p.m. since Tuesday. Each event lasts approximately seven minutes before returning to baseline levels."

Hart froze mid-stride, his pacing abruptly terminating as connections crystallised in his consciousness with almost audible clarity. His eyes widened slightly—the physical manifestation of intellectual revelation too significant to be contained entirely within his typically controlled expression. Without speaking, he moved to the whiteboard they had positioned near Clara's bed, snatching a marker with uncharacteristic abruptness. His hand began moving across the smooth surface with urgent precision, sketching lines and symbols that initially appeared abstract but gradually coalesced into recognisable patterns.

The room fell into complete silence, the only sounds being the rhythmic beeping of Clara's heart monitor, the soft clicking of Leo's keyboard as he continued extracting supporting data, and the marker's squeaking progress across the whiteboard as Hart translated mental architecture into visible schematics. They watched his work with a collective intensity that seemed to physically compress the air in the hospital room, each person recognising that they were witnessing the assembly of a puzzle whose completed image would irreversibly alter their understanding of the case and the city's hidden power structures.

Hart's diagram grew more complex with each passing moment— the historical cypher Evelyn had identified from founding documents overlaid with the digital patterns Leo's algorithms had extracted, both integrated with the architectural proportions of the eastern clock tower. He added numerical sequences along specific pathways, coordinates at junction points, and transmission frequencies beside communication nodes. His typical methodical approach had accelerated into something more fluid, more intuitive—the particular state of concentrated productivity where a conscious analytical process gives way to deeper pattern recognition operating just beneath the threshold of articulation.

Evelyn gasped as the completed diagram revealed itself, her hand rising to cover her mouth in a gesture of academic astonishment. "It's a Renaissance-stacked cypher," she said, her tone barely above a whisper yet carrying the weight of significant discovery. "Several encryption layers operating simultaneously, each concealing different aspects of the same fundamental message." "The architectural specifications of the tower itself form the primary encryption key, with the clock mechanism serving as the physical interface for decoding and transmission."

Hart stepped back from the whiteboard, his face pale but possessed of a focused determination that had replaced his earlier uncertainty. The marker remained in his hand, uncapped, forgotten as his attention remained fixed on the pattern he had externalised from mental conception into visible structure.

"The eastern clock tower," he announced, his voice carrying the particular weight of certainty derived from comprehensive understanding rather than mere hypothesis. "That's where Price will be at 9:47 tonight." He turned toward the team, his posture suggesting a man who had finally located solid ground after traversing uncertain terrain. "And he's not just planning revenge against me—he's going to expose the founding families' secret society and the conspiracy they've maintained for centuries."

Clara's expression shifted subtly as the implications registered—professional assessment modulating from case-specific focus to recognition of a much larger societal impact. "The founding families created the underground surveillance network to maintain their control," she said, bridging historical discovery and contemporary threat. "Their descendants still occupy positions of influence throughout the city's government, financial system, and infrastructure management."

"Price has spent fifteen years gathering evidence of their continued operations," Hart continued, moving closer to the whiteboard again, his marker indicating specific pathways in the diagram. "The murders were never the primary objective—they were calibration points for his integrated system, physical initialisations of the pattern recognition technology we developed together."

Leo looked up from his laptop, his expression reflecting the particular discomfort of someone whose technological expertise enabled clear recognition of both method and magnitude. "He's created a quantum-enhanced information extraction system," he said, the technical terminology failing to obscure the underlying implication. "Capable of identifying connections and conspiracies invisible to conventional analysis, extracting patterns from centuries of deliberately obscured activity."

Evelyn nodded, her academic perspective providing historical context for Leo's contemporary assessment. "The founding families embedded their communications within seemingly legitimate municipal functions," she explained, gesturing towards her collection of ancient texts. "Architectural specifications, city planning documents, infrastructure development—all containing hidden layers of information exchange accessible only to those with the correct decryption protocols."

"And Price has reverse-engineered those protocols," Hart concluded, the final piece settling into position in their collective understanding. "He will use the original surveillance network to expose its creators' descendants, revealing centuries of concealed manipulation and control."

Clara shifted carefully against her pillows, her uninjured hand unconsciously checking the security of her bandages as if preparing for movement beyond hospital constraints. "The eastern clock tower was the original monitoring hub for the entire system," she said, a professional strategy already forming in her expression. "Its height provided a line of sight to all major city districts, while its clock mechanism served as both an encryption device and a transmission technology."

Hart nodded, his gaze returning to the digital clock displaying 4:37 p.m. in unwavering red certainty. The countdown to Price's "final examination" continued its relentless progression, each minute bringing them closer to a confrontation whose implications extended far beyond individual justice into territories of historical revelation and institutional collapse.

"Price's pattern recognition system will extract evidence of corruption and conspiracy from centuries of accumulated data," he said, his voice carrying the particular quality of someone accurately assessing personal and societal threats. "He isn't testing me; " He's exposing them," he said.

Leo closed his laptop, his movement suggesting a transition from analysis to action. "Five hours until he initiates the sequence," he said, requiring no additional emphasis to communicate its urgency. "Whatever he's built inside that tower connects to the entire underground network and the modern surveillance infrastructure he's integrated with it."

The team exchanged glances that contained no triumph despite their investigative breakthrough—only the shared recognition that they had decoded Price's puzzle only to discover a more comprehensive and potentially destructive mechanism than they had initially imagined. Their collective expression reflected the tension of impending confrontation and the weight of understanding that Price's revenge had expanded beyond personal grievance into something approaching historical judgment.

The makeshift war room transitioned from discovery to deployment with practised efficiency and investigative theory, giving way to tactical planning as they prepared to confront Price's endgame. Hart spread the architectural plans of the eastern clock tower across the foot of Clara's bed, his fingers tracing structural elements with the precision of someone who understood that dimensions and access points had transcended academic interest to become matters of life and death. The blueprints, extracted from city archives by Leo's digital excavation, revealed aspects of the tower that modern renovation records had systematically obscured—substructures beneath the publicly accessible areas and chambers that appeared on no contemporary documentation.

"There's a hidden chamber beneath the main clock mechanism,"

Hart said, indicating a circular room under the tower's central axis. "Approximately eight metres in diameter, accessible only through this narrow spiral staircase behind the maintenance panel." His finger traced the sole ingress point, an architectural bottleneck that would force any approach into a tightly controlled corridor. "The original plans designated this space as the 'Synchronisation Chamber'— though its actual function appears to have been the primary monitoring hub for the entire surveillance network."

Leo had positioned himself at the small table beside Clara's bed, his laptop now connected to a portable projector borrowed from the hospital's education department. The device cast a three-dimensional rendering of the tower onto the blank wall opposite Clara's bed, the digital model rotating slowly to reveal structural details from multiple perspectives. His fingers moved across the keyboard efficiently, enhancing specific visualisation sections as Hart referenced them.

"I've incorporated power consumption data into the model," Leo explained, executing commands that added a heat-map overlay to the rendering. Certain areas glowed with intensity, most notably the hidden chamber Hart had identified. "These readings indicate significant electrical activity centred in that substructure—consistent with advanced computing equipment drawing power through concealed infrastructure." The visualisation zoomed in to highlight the spiral staircase, and its dimensions were displayed in precise numerical values beside the rendering. "There's only one access point, as Alan noted, and it's barely wide enough for single-file descent."

Clara struggled to sit up straighter, her face tightening momentarily with the particular tension that accompanies movement against physical pain consciously suppressed. Her uninjured arm braced against the mattress for support as she leaned forward to study Leo's visualisation more carefully. "The restricted access works both ways," she observed, professional strategy emerging through medical discomfort. "It limits our approach options and restricts Price's potential escape routes."

Her fingers reached toward the digital rendering, passing through the holographic staircase with ghost-like interaction. "The timing is significant beyond merely recreating your failed experiment," she continued, her analytical focus undiminished by injury or medication. "According to Evelyn's historical documents, 9:47 was when the founding families signed their original pact—the agreement that established both their public governance and hidden control mechanisms."

Evelyn nodded vigorously, her features animated by the particular excitement of academic validation. "Tonight is the anniversary of that signing," she confirmed, extracting a journal page marked with multiple coloured tabs from her seemingly bottomless portfolio. "May 17th, 1847—exactly one hundred and seventy-five years ago. The founders commemorated the occasion by commissioning the clock tower, its mechanism designed to serve as both a physical reminder and a functional component in their surveillance architecture."

Hart's expression tightened as these historical details integrated with their contemporary understanding of Price's design. "He's selected the timing for maximum symbolic impact," he said, the statement carrying the weight of recognition rather than mere speculation. "The mechanism will activate precisely when the original pact was signed, creating a symmetry between establishment and exposure."

Leo continued manipulating his digital model, adding another information layer representing signal transmission patterns detected over the past three nights. "These test activations suggest he's established a broadcasting capacity that extends well beyond the tower itself," he explained, the visualisation now displaying concentric circles radiating outward from the central chamber. "Whatever he's planning to reveal, it's designed for wide dissemination rather than controlled disclosure."

Hart studied these transmission patterns with the intensity of someone recognising a familiar methodology applied to an unfamiliar purpose. "He's adapted our quantum pattern recognition technology to function as an information extraction and distribution system," he said, a professional assessment briefly coloured by a flicker of something adjacent to admiration despite the circumstances. "Capable of identifying hidden connections and broadcasting them through the city's existing communication infrastructure."

Clara's uninjured hand moved unconsciously to check her bandages, suggesting preparation for activity beyond her current medical constraints. "He's not just planning to reveal the conspiracy," she said, her voice quiet but carrying the particular authority that had always balanced Hart's analytical intensity. "He's designed a system that will extract and expose centuries of hidden manipulation in a single synchronised transmission—a complete dismantling of power structures that have operated beyond public awareness since the city's founding."

The digital clock displayed 4:52 p.m. in unwavering red certainty —less than five hours before Price's mechanism would activate. The team's collective focus had acquired the particular sharpened quality that emerges when theoretical understanding transitions to imminent confrontation, each person mentally preparing for their role in whatever intervention they might still orchestrate.

Hart's phone vibrated against his hip, the silent alert drawing his attention downward. He extracted the device with the careful movements of someone who anticipated significant information, his expression remaining neutral as he registered the notification of a text message from an unknown number. The screen displayed a single line against a black background, the white text rendered in the same serif font Price had used for his formal invitation days earlier:

"Are you ready for your final examination, Professor?"

Hart held the phone where the others could see it, the shared observation creating a momentary suspended silence in the hospital room. The message carried no elaborate construction or cryptic references that had characterised Price's previous communications— just a direct question that functioned simultaneously as a taunt and confirmation.

"He knows we've figured it out," Leo said quietly, requiring no additional evidence beyond the message's timing and content. "He's monitoring us somehow, tracking our investigation in real-time."

Hart nodded once, his posture straightening with the tension that precedes decisive action. "He's always been at least one step ahead," he acknowledged, returning the phone to his pocket. "But he wants me there at the appointed time—consistent throughout his design. The examination requires a witness who understands the full significance of what he's revealing."

His hand moved to the inner pocket of his jacket, extracting the smooth lake stone that had accompanied him throughout the investigation. He studied its polished surface momentarily before returning it to his pocket with the unconscious ritual that had become second nature over years of carrying it. "We have less than five hours to prepare," he said, already reaching for his coat draped over the visitor's chair. "Price isn't just exposing a conspiracy—he's planning to destroy the evidence and anyone connected to it once the revelation is complete."

Clara's expression hardened with a particular determination that had characterised her throughout their partnership. "I'm coming with you," she said, the statement presented as fact rather than proposal despite her obviously compromised physical condition. She continued with precision before Hart could respond, preventing immediate contradiction. "Leo can provide remote technical support from here, coordinating with Evelyn on historical context as needed. But you need direct backup at the tower."

Hart met her gaze with a particular intensity that developed through years of professional partnership—a silent communication more efficient than verbal exchange. After a moment's assessment, he nodded once, acknowledging rather than enthusiastically. "Limited mobility in close quarters might be advantageous," he conceded, the tactical observation serving as an oblique acceptance of her participation despite her injury.

Leo was already establishing a more permanent workstation, connecting additional equipment to his laptop with the focused efficiency of someone preparing for extended remote operations. "I can access the city's surveillance network to monitor approaches to the tower," he said, fingers moving across his keyboard without requiring visual guidance. "And I've developed a potential signal disruption protocol if we need to interrupt his transmission."

Evelyn gathered specific historical documents with uncharacteristic organisation, selecting only those most relevant to their immediate needs rather than her usual comprehensive approach. "The founding families embedded fail-safe mechanisms within their system," she explained, securing the selected papers in a slender portfolio. "If we can identify the original control protocols, we might be able to use them against Price's adaptations."

The team exchanged looks of determined understanding—four perspectives integrated into a coherent purpose, four distinct methodologies aligned toward a common objective. Where Price operated through isolated brilliance, they functioned as a collaborative counterpoint; where his genius served exposé and destruction, theirs would be directed toward containment and protection.

Hart held the door open as Clara carefully disconnected herself from the monitoring equipment. Her movements were slow but deliberate as she prepared to leave medical safety for investigative necessity. The digital clock continued its unwavering countdown, each minute bringing them closer to confrontation with the man who had transformed academic competition into elaborately constructed revenge—and who now stood poised to collapse centuries of hidden governance through the perfect integration of historical discovery and technological innovation.

Clara's hospital room, once sterile and medical, was now buried under a chaotic jumble of notes, documents, diagrams, and digital displays. The antiseptic smell, replaced by a mix of coffee, marker ink, and Evelyn's old books, created an almost academic fragrance. Harsh shadows from the institutional fluorescent lights fell across the makeshift war room, where the battle focused mainly on pattern recognition and historical cryptography.

The wall-mounted digital clock, acquired from the nurses' station using Leo's charm and my badge, showed 4:23 p.m. in uncompromising red numerals. Price's "final examination" was five hours and twenty-four minutes away. The regular electronic countdown felt like a physical weight as it worked, growing heavier each minute.

With deliberate purpose, Hart paced the narrow path between workstations, his movements contrasting with the aimless anxiety typical of hospital waiting. Each step is carefully planned to bridge different analytical regions. His fingers occasionally brushed against evidence pinned to the walls, establishing physical connections between Evelyn's historical discoveries and Leo's digital architecture as if tactile contact might extract additional meaning from the materials themselves.

Observing the yellowed architectural drawing Evelyn had spread on an equipment cart, he noted that the geometric proportions in the foundation measurements weren't purely structural. "They incorporate the Golden Ratio in sequences that suggest intentional embedding rather than coincidental occurrence."

From her hunched position over a Renaissance manuscript, Evelyn looked up, her auburn hair escaping its hastily arranged confinement. She pushed her glasses up with an ink-stained finger, leaving a small smudge on the bridge of her nose that no one felt compelled to mention.

"That's exactly what I've been tracking," she replied, moving toward Hart with the particular animated energy that characterised her intellectual excitement. "The sequence appears repeatedly throughout the founding documents, always concealed within seemingly decorative elements or marginal notations." Her finger trembled slightly as she traced a pattern of numbers hidden within the ornate border of a city planning document. Observe identical numerical sequences within this notarial seal, expressed via varied symbolic notations.

Leo sat cross-legged on the floor near Clara's bed, his laptop on his knees. Three external drives connected to his computer via a nest of cables that resembled some technological organism spreading across the linoleum. His posture suggested the particular concentration of someone whose physical body had become secondary to his digital engagement—shoulders slightly hunched, neck bent at an angle orthopaedists would disapprove of, fingers moving across the keyboard with percussion-like precision.

"I've modified the pattern recognition algorithm to incorporate historical cypher structures," he said without looking up, his voice carrying the tight focus of someone translating between mental conception and digital implementation. "Running a comparative analysis against the surveillance data extracts from the last fifteen years of Price's activity."

Clara observed their efforts from her elevated position in the hospital bed, her injured arm carefully positioned on a precisely arranged pillow, fresh white bandages concealing the stitches beneath. The IV stand remained beside her bed, its medical necessity a physical reminder of her compromised condition, but her eyes carried none of the pharmaceutical sedation from earlier—her gaze moved across the assembled evidence with the particular incisiveness that had characterised her detective work since Hart had known her.

"The numerical sequence correlates with specific locations in the city grid," she noted, her uninjured hand gesturing toward the map Leo had printed and mounted on the movable table beside her bed. "If you translate the values into geographical coordinates using the original city planning metrics rather than modern GPS parameters."

Clara's remark immediately captured Hart's attention, halting his pacing. Studying the pattern she'd found, his eyes narrowed, his mind clearly readjusting its analytical processes.

"He proposed the sequence could be used to locate members of the underground network and strode towards the map with renewed determination. 'Architectural detailing that doubles as a navigation structure."

Evelyn's excitement manifested as a small, involuntary hop that sent several loose papers fluttering to the floor. She ignored them, hurrying to extract another document from her seemingly bottomless portfolio case. The parchment she produced appeared significantly older than her previous references. Its edges were irregularly worn, and its surface bore the particular patina that develops when human hands transmit oils to paper across centuries of handling.

"This manuscript fragment belonged to one of the original city architects," she explained, carefully spreading it beside Clara's map. "It contains a numeric sequence embedded within what appears to be a simple measurement table." Her finger traced the columns of faded numbers, some barely visible beneath centuries of discolouration. "But the pattern isn't architectural—it's cryptographic. These aren't measurements but a codified addressing system for information transmission."

Hart and Clara exchanged a glance of shared recognition. This silent communication develops between long-term partners who process information along parallel tracks. "Price would have discovered this during his research," Hart said, the statement carrying the weight of significant realisation. "He's not just targeting the founding families' descendants—he's using their own hidden system against them."

Leo's laptop emitted a soft electronic tone that immediately drew everyone's attention. He straightened from his hunched position, his expression shifting from concentrated focus to surprised validation. "The algorithm found a match," he announced, turning the screen toward the others. The historical sequence Evelyn identified correlates perfectly with anomalous metadata patterns in Price's surveillance records."

The screen visualised information flow—data streams represented as coloured lines between nodes on a city map. Specific pathways glowed more brightly than others, their intensity suggesting higher transmission volumes or particular significance in the overall architecture. The pattern precisely mirrored the numerical sequence Evelyn had extracted from the historical documents, the digital validation of academic hypothesis rendered in glowing pixels.

"The pattern appears consistently across multiple data categories," Leo continued, his fingers executing commands that transformed the visualisation to show different information streams.

"Financial transactions, communications intercepts, surveillance footage—all channelled through pathways that follow this same numerical progression."

Clara leaned forward despite her injury, eliciting a slight wince that she immediately suppressed. "He's using the original surveillance architecture as a framework for his modern system," she said, professional analysis overriding physical discomfort.

"The founding families created a hidden network for monitoring and controlling the city's development. Price has reactivated it using contemporary technology."

Hart studied Leo's screen with analytical intensity, his mind extracting patterns and implications with characteristic precision. "The quantum experiment we designed was intended to identify embedded information within seemingly random datasets," he said, the connections crystallising in his expression. "Price has applied that methodology to the historical surveillance network, extracting patterns of influence and control that would otherwise remain invisible."

Evelyn nodded vigorously, her glasses sliding down her nose with the movement. "The founding families encoded their activities within seemingly legitimate municipal records," she confirmed, academic excitement momentarily overtaking the grim implications. "Price has created a system capable of decoding centuries of hidden governance."

Leo's algorithm emitted another alert tone, drawing their attention back to his screen. A new pattern had emerged from the digital analysis—a geometric configuration that pulsed with particular intensity at the city's eastern edge. The visualisation zoomed automatically to focus on this anomaly, revealing what appeared to be a concentrated nexus of information flow centred on a single location.

"That's it," Hart said quietly, recognition dawning in his expression. "That's where his final examination will take place."

The digital visualisation continued pulsing on Leo's screen, the concentrated nexus of information flow demanding their collective attention like a beacon. Clara's eyes, however, had shifted to a different focus—a barely visible notation in the margin of a yellowed parchment that had been partially obscured by Evelyn's more dramatic manuscripts. The handwritten note, rendered in faded brown ink that had once been black, contained two phrases that vibrated with sudden significance against the backdrop of their emerging understanding: "eastern sentinel" and "ninth hour".

"Look at this," Clara said, her voice quiet but carrying the particular urgency that immediately redirected the room's attention. She winced as she reached towards the document with her uninjured arm, the movement pulling against her bandages with a discomfort she refused to acknowledge beyond a momentary tightening around her eyes. Her fingers trembled slightly as they traced the faded script, whether from pain or the significance of her discovery remaining unclear. "This marginal note references' eastern sentinel' and 'ninth hour'—and Leo's data shows unusual activity at the eastern clock tower at precisely 9:47 p.m. for the past three nights."

Leo immediately returned to his keyboard, fingers executing commands with intensified purpose. The visualisation on his screen was transformed, and timeline data appeared alongside the geographical display. "Confirmed," he said, the professional satisfaction in his voice tempered by the implications of their discovery. "Anomalous power surges at the eastern tower complex, consistently occurring between 9:45 and 9:50 p.m. since Tuesday. Each event lasts approximately seven minutes before returning to baseline levels."

Hart froze mid-stride, his pacing abruptly terminating as connections crystallised in his consciousness with almost audible clarity. His eyes widened slightly—the physical manifestation of intellectual revelation too significant to be contained entirely within his typically controlled expression. Without speaking, he moved to the whiteboard they had positioned near Clara's bed, snatching a marker with uncharacteristic abruptness. His hand began moving across the smooth surface with urgent precision, sketching lines and symbols that initially appeared abstract but gradually coalesced into recognisable patterns.

The room fell into complete silence, the only sounds being the rhythmic beeping of Clara's heart monitor, the soft clicking of Leo's keyboard as he continued extracting supporting data, and the marker's squeaking progress across the whiteboard as Hart translated mental architecture into visible schematics. They watched his work with a collective intensity that seemed to physically compress the air in the hospital room, each person recognising that they were witnessing the assembly of a puzzle whose completed image would irreversibly alter their understanding of the case and the city's hidden power structures.

Hart's diagram grew more complex with each passing moment—the historical cypher Evelyn had identified from founding documents overlaid with the digital patterns Leo's algorithms had extracted, both integrated with the architectural proportions of the eastern clock tower. He added numerical sequences along specific pathways, coordinates at junction points, and transmission frequencies beside communication nodes. His typical methodical approach had accelerated into something more fluid, more intuitive—the particular state of concentrated productivity where a conscious analytical process gives way to deeper pattern recognition operating just beneath the threshold of articulation.

Evelyn gasped as the completed diagram revealed itself, her hand rising to cover her mouth in a gesture of academic astonishment. "It's a Renaissance-stacked cypher," she said, her tone barely above a whisper yet carrying the weight of significant discovery. "Several encryption layers operating simultaneously, each concealing different aspects of the same fundamental message." "The architectural specifications of the tower itself form the primary encryption key, with the clock mechanism serving as the physical interface for decoding and transmission."

Hart stepped back from the whiteboard, his face pale but possessed of a focused determination that had replaced his earlier uncertainty. The marker remained in his hand, uncapped, forgotten as his attention remained fixed on the pattern he had externalised from mental conception into visible structure.

"The eastern clock tower," he announced, his voice carrying the particular weight of certainty derived from comprehensive understanding rather than mere hypothesis. "That's where Price will be at 9:47 tonight." He turned toward the team, his posture suggesting a man who had finally located solid ground after traversing uncertain terrain. "And he's not just planning revenge against me—he's going to expose the founding families' secret society and the conspiracy they've maintained for centuries."

Clara's expression shifted subtly as the implications registered—professional assessment modulating from case-specific focus to recognition of a much larger societal impact. "The founding families created the underground surveillance network to maintain their control," she said, bridging historical discovery and contemporary threat. "Their descendants still occupy positions of influence throughout the city's government, financial system, and infrastructure management."

"Price has spent fifteen years gathering evidence of their continued operations," Hart continued, moving closer to the whiteboard again, his marker indicating specific pathways in the diagram. "The murders were never the primary objective—they were calibration points for his integrated system, physical initialisations of the pattern recognition technology we developed together."

Leo looked up from his laptop, his expression reflecting the particular discomfort of someone whose technological expertise enabled clear recognition of both method and magnitude. "He's created a quantum-enhanced information extraction system," he said, the technical terminology failing to obscure the underlying implication. "Capable of identifying connections and conspiracies invisible to conventional analysis, extracting patterns from centuries of deliberately obscured activity."

Evelyn nodded, her academic perspective providing historical context for Leo's contemporary assessment. "The founding families embedded their communications within seemingly legitimate municipal functions," she explained, gesturing towards her collection of ancient texts. "Architectural specifications, city planning documents, infrastructure development—all containing hidden layers of information exchange accessible only to those with the correct decryption protocols."

"And Price has reverse-engineered those protocols," Hart concluded, the final piece settling into position in their collective understanding. "He will use the original surveillance network to expose its creators' descendants, revealing centuries of concealed manipulation and control."

Clara shifted carefully against her pillows, her uninjured hand unconsciously checking the security of her bandages as if preparing for movement beyond hospital constraints. "The eastern clock tower was the original monitoring hub for the entire system," she said, a professional strategy already forming in her expression. "Its height provided a line of sight to all major city districts, while its clock mechanism served as both an encryption device and a transmission technology."

Hart nodded, his gaze returning to the digital clock displaying 4:37 p.m. in unwavering red certainty. The countdown to Price's "final examination" continued its relentless progression, each minute bringing them closer to a confrontation whose implications extended far beyond individual justice into territories of historical revelation and institutional collapse.

"Price's pattern recognition system will extract evidence of corruption and conspiracy from centuries of accumulated data," he said, his voice carrying the particular quality of someone accurately assessing personal and societal threats. "His 'examination' isn't designed to test me—it's designed to expose them."

Leo closed his laptop, his movement suggesting a transition from analysis to action. "Five hours until he initiates the sequence," he said, requiring no additional emphasis to communicate its urgency. "Whatever he's built inside that tower connects to the entire underground network and the modern surveillance infrastructure he's integrated with it."

The team exchanged glances that contained no triumph despite their investigative breakthrough—only the shared recognition that they had decoded Price's puzzle only to discover a more comprehensive and potentially destructive mechanism than they had initially imagined. Their collective expression reflected the tension of impending confrontation and the weight of understanding that Price's revenge had expanded beyond personal grievance into something approaching historical judgment.

The makeshift war room transitioned from discovery to deployment with practised efficiency and investigative theory, giving way to tactical planning as they prepared to confront Price's endgame. Hart spread the architectural plans of the eastern clock tower across the foot of Clara's bed, his fingers tracing structural elements with the precision of someone who understood that dimensions and access points had transcended academic interest to become matters of life and death. The blueprints, extracted from city archives by Leo's digital excavation, revealed aspects of the tower that modern renovation records had systematically obscured—substructures beneath the publicly accessible areas and chambers that appeared on no contemporary documentation.

"There's a hidden chamber beneath the main clock mechanism," Hart said, indicating a circular room under the tower's central axis. "Approximately eight metres in diameter, accessible only through this narrow spiral staircase behind the maintenance panel." His finger traced the sole ingress point, an architectural bottleneck that would force any approach into a tightly controlled corridor. "The original plans designated this space as the 'Synchronisation Chamber'— though its actual function appears to have been the primary monitoring hub for the entire surveillance network."

Leo had positioned himself at the small table beside Clara's bed, his laptop now connected to a portable projector borrowed from the hospital's education department. The device cast a three-dimensional rendering of the tower onto the blank wall opposite Clara's bed, the digital model rotating slowly to reveal structural details from multiple perspectives. His fingers moved across the keyboard efficiently, enhancing specific visualisation sections as Hart referenced them.

"I've incorporated power consumption data into the model," Leo explained, executing commands that added a heat-map overlay to the rendering. Certain areas glowed with intensity, most notably the hidden chamber Hart had identified. "These readings indicate significant electrical activity centred in that substructure—consistent with advanced computing equipment drawing power through concealed infrastructure." The visualisation zoomed in to highlight the spiral staircase, and its dimensions were displayed in precise numerical values beside the rendering. "There's only one access point, as Alan noted, and it's barely wide enough for single-file descent."

Clara struggled to sit up straighter, her face tightening momentarily with the particular tension that accompanies movement against physical pain consciously suppressed. Her uninjured arm braced against the mattress for support as she leaned forward to study Leo's visualisation more carefully. "The restricted access works both ways," she observed, professional strategy emerging through medical discomfort. "It limits our approach options and restricts Price's potential escape routes."

Her fingers reached toward the digital rendering, passing through the holographic staircase with ghost-like interaction. "The timing is significant beyond merely recreating your failed experiment," she continued, her analytical focus undiminished by injury or medication. "According to Evelyn's historical documents, 9:47 was when the founding families signed their original pact—the agreement that established both their public governance and hidden control mechanisms."

Evelyn nodded vigorously, her features animated by the particular excitement of academic validation. "Tonight is the anniversary of that signing," she confirmed, extracting a journal page marked with multiple coloured tabs from her seemingly bottomless portfolio.

"May 17th, 1847—exactly one hundred and seventy-five years ago. The founders commemorated the occasion by commissioning the clock tower, its mechanism designed to serve as both a physical reminder and a functional component in their surveillance architecture."

Hart's expression tightened as these historical details integrated with their contemporary understanding of Price's design. "He's selected the timing for maximum symbolic impact," he said, the statement carrying the weight of recognition rather than mere speculation. "The mechanism will activate precisely when the original pact was signed, creating a symmetry between establishment and exposure."

Leo continued manipulating his digital model, adding another information layer representing signal transmission patterns detected over the past three nights. "These test activations suggest he's established a broadcasting capacity that extends well beyond the tower itself," he explained, the visualisation now displaying concentric circles radiating outward from the central chamber. "Whatever he's planning to reveal, it's designed for wide dissemination rather than controlled disclosure."

Hart studied these transmission patterns with the intensity of someone recognising a familiar methodology applied to an unfamiliar purpose. "He's adapted our quantum pattern recognition technology to function as an information extraction and distribution system," he said, a professional assessment briefly coloured by a flicker of something adjacent to admiration despite the circumstances. "Capable of identifying hidden connections and broadcasting them through the city's existing communication infrastructure."

Clara's uninjured hand moved unconsciously to check her bandages, suggesting preparation for activity beyond her current medical constraints. "He's not just planning to reveal the conspiracy," she said, her voice quiet but carrying the particular authority that had always balanced Hart's analytical intensity. "He's designed a system that will extract and expose centuries of hidden manipulation in a single synchronised transmission—a complete dismantling of power structures that have operated beyond public awareness since the city's founding."

The digital clock displayed 4:52 p.m. in unwavering red certainty —less than five hours before Price's mechanism would activate. The team's collective focus had acquired the particular sharpened quality that emerges when theoretical understanding transitions to imminent confrontation, each person mentally preparing for their role in whatever intervention they might still orchestrate.

Hart's phone vibrated against his hip, the silent alert drawing his attention downward. He extracted the device with the careful movements of someone who anticipated significant information, his expression remaining neutral as he registered the notification of a text message from an unknown number. The screen displayed a single line against a black background, the white text rendered in the same serif font Price had used for his formal invitation days earlier:

"Are you ready for your final examination, Professor?"

Hart held the phone where the others could see it, the shared observation creating a momentary suspended silence in the hospital room. The message carried no elaborate construction or cryptic references that had characterised Price's previous communications— just a direct question that functioned simultaneously as a taunt and confirmation.

"He knows we've figured it out," Leo said quietly, requiring no additional evidence beyond the message's timing and content. "He's monitoring us somehow, tracking our investigation in real-time."

Hart nodded once, his posture straightening with the tension that precedes decisive action. "He's always been at least one step ahead," he acknowledged, returning the phone to his pocket. "But he wants me there at the appointed time—consistent throughout his design. The examination requires a witness who understands the full significance of what he's revealing."

His hand moved to the inner pocket of his jacket, extracting the smooth lake stone that had accompanied him throughout the investigation. He studied its polished surface momentarily before returning it to his pocket with the unconscious ritual that had become second nature over years of carrying it. "We have less than five hours to prepare," he said, already reaching for his coat draped over the visitor's chair. "Price isn't just exposing a conspiracy—he's planning to destroy the evidence and anyone connected to it once the revelation is complete."

Clara's expression hardened with a particular determination that had characterised her throughout their partnership. "I'm coming with you," she said, the statement presented as fact rather than proposal despite her obviously compromised physical condition. She continued with precision before Hart could respond, preventing immediate contradiction. "Leo can provide remote technical support from here, coordinating with Evelyn on historical context as needed. But you need direct backup at the tower."

Hart met her gaze with a particular intensity that developed through years of professional partnership—a silent communication more efficient than verbal exchange. After a moment's assessment, he nodded once, acknowledging rather than enthusiastically. "Limited mobility in close quarters might be advantageous," he conceded, the tactical observation serving as an oblique acceptance of her participation despite her injury.

Leo was already establishing a more permanent workstation, connecting additional equipment to his laptop with the focused efficiency of someone preparing for extended remote operations. "I can access the city's surveillance network to monitor approaches to the tower," he said, fingers moving across his keyboard without requiring visual guidance. "And I've developed a potential signal disruption protocol if we need to interrupt his transmission."

Evelyn gathered specific historical documents with uncharacteristic organisation, selecting only those most relevant to their immediate needs rather than her usual comprehensive approach. "The founding families embedded fail-safe mechanisms within their system," she explained, securing the selected papers in a slender portfolio. "If we can identify the original control protocols, we might be able to use them against Price's adaptations."

The team exchanged looks of determined understanding—four

perspectives integrated into a coherent purpose, four distinct methodologies aligned toward a common objective. Where Price operated through isolated brilliance, they functioned as a collaborative counterpoint; where his genius served exposé and destruction, theirs would be directed toward containment and protection.

Hart held the door open as Clara carefully disconnected herself from the monitoring equipment. Her movements were slow but deliberate as she prepared to leave medical safety for investigative necessity. The digital clock continued its unwavering countdown, each minute bringing them closer to confrontation with the man who had transformed academic competition into elaborately constructed revenge—and who now stood poised to collapse centuries of hidden governance through the perfect integration of historical discovery and technological innovation.

16

BATTLE OF WITS

The Eastern Clock tower stood against the twilight sky like a forgotten sentinel, its stone facade stained by decades of industrial grime and acid rain. Hart paused at the iron gate that separated the tower's small courtyard from the surrounding district, his eyes tracing the structure's angular ascent toward the darkening heavens. The tower's four clock faces glowed with unnatural brightness against the gathering gloom, their synchronised hands frozen at 9:47 despite the time being nearly two hours earlier. His fingers closed around the lake stone in his pocket, its smooth surface warmed by his body heat, as he contemplated the man waiting at the summit of this architectural anachronism—a brilliant mind whose trajectory had twisted from colleague to nemesis through a series of choices, Hart was still struggling to fully comprehend.

The gate yielded to his touch with a protesting shriek of rusted hinges, the sound carrying across the deserted courtyard with unsettling clarity. Behind him, Clara's voice came through his earpiece with characteristic precision despite the static interference generated by the tower's unique electromagnetic properties.

· · ·

"Signal strength is fluctuating but holding," she reported from her position in the surveillance van parked three blocks away, her professional detachment maintained despite her recent injury. "Leo has established partial access to the building's electrical systems, but Price has isolated the upper levels on a separate circuit."

Hart acknowledged with a soft affirmative as he crossed the cracked paving stones toward the tower's main entrance. Shadows lengthened around him like reaching fingers, the last horizontal rays of sunlight fragmenting through broken windows to cast elongated patterns across the courtyard. The heavy oak door stood slightly ajar, an invitation that felt simultaneously welcoming and threatening— the ambiguity that had characterised all of Price's communications throughout this elaborate game.

The entrance hall stretched before him, its vaulted ceiling disappearing into shadows despite the weak illumination provided by ancient sconces now retrofitted with modern LED bulbs. Dust motes floated in the slanting light that streamed through the shattered windows, making the air feel tangible as Hart moved cautiously across the marble floor. His footsteps echoed with a hollow persistence, announcing his presence to whatever surveillance systems Price had surely set up throughout the building.

"I'm proceeding to the central staircase," he murmured, knowing Clara would relay his position to the tactical team staged six blocks away—close enough to respond if necessary but distant enough to avoid triggering Price's contingency plans. The earpiece crackled with a brief acknowledgement before falling silent again.

The spiral staircase wound upward through the tower's core like an architectural spine, each step worn into a shallow depression by generations of maintenance workers and municipal timekeepers. Hart ascended with a measured pace, conserving energy for whatever confrontation awaited above while allowing his analytical mind to process the symbolic significance of this location. The founding families had designed this tower not merely as a functional chronometer but as the central hub of their surveillance network—a physical manifestation of their control over the city's temporal and informational dimensions.

And now Price had reclaimed this historical mechanism, integrating their quantum pattern recognition technology with infrastructure designed for nineteenth-century conspiracy. The particular elegance of this appropriation—using the founders' own system to expose their descendants' continued manipulation—carried Price's intellectual signature. Even in his apparent madness, the man's methodological brilliance remained intact.

Hart's ascent terminated at a heavy metal door marked with the municipal seal that appeared on historical documents Evelyn had shown them—the same emblem that had decorated the leather folio stolen during the archive attack. The door stood unlocked, its security apparently unnecessary given the elaborate game Price had orchestrated. Beyond lay a circular chamber occupying the tower's entire upper level, directly beneath the massive clock mechanism whose steady ticking permeated the space with metronomic insistence.

The room's periphery disappeared into shadow, but its centre blazed with the harsh illumination of multiple monitors arranged in concentric rings around a central workstation. The screens displayed real-time footage of locations throughout the city—a hospital entrance, the central library steps, the university quad, and the eastern industrial district's main intersection. Each location featured a small red indicator in the corner of its display, and numerical countdowns synchronised to reach zero simultaneously at precisely 9:47.

Jonathan Price stood with his back to the door, his attention apparently focused on adjustments to the central console. His silhouette appeared simultaneously familiar and foreign—the physical frame Hart remembered from their academic collaboration now transformed by the particular tension that accompanies single-minded obsession. His clothing maintained the meticulous precision that had always characterised his professional presentation—tailored dark suit, polished shoes—though his hair had developed a dishevelled quality that suggested personal grooming had become secondary to intellectual purpose.

"Eight minutes and forty-three seconds early, Alan," Price said without turning, his voice carrying the same cultured articulation Hart remembered from university seminars and late-night research sessions. "You've always preferred arriving ahead of schedule—a habit I anticipated in my planning." He completed whatever adjustment had occupied his attention, then turned slowly to face his former colleague.

Price's features remained recognisable despite the transformation wrought by years of isolated preparation. His eyes retained their unsettling intensity behind stylish glasses, though now they carried a particular coldness that suggested emotional detachment rather than the intellectual enthusiasm Hart recalled from their academic partnership. A subtle scar bisected his right eyebrow—a new addition since their last encounter, its origin unknown. However, its presence somehow emphasised the psychological distance between the man Hart had known and the figure who now called himself The Riddler.

"Jonathan," Hart acknowledged, maintaining his position near the doorway while his eyes professionally catalogued the room's details. The space resembled a hybrid between the research laboratory and shrine to their shared history—advanced technological components interspersed with artefacts from their academic past. A shelf near the central console held books they had co-authored, scientific journals featuring their publications, and conference badges from symposia they had attended together. Newspaper clippings covered one wall, their headlines chronicling their collaborative achievements and the scandal that terminated their partnership.

"I've prepared refreshments," Price indicated, placing a small table between two monitoring stations. Its surface held an elegant silver tea service that appeared incongruously civilised amid the technological complexity surrounding it. "Earl Grey, if I recall correctly. Your preference during late research sessions."

Hart remained motionless, the particular stillness of a detective assessing potential threats rather than a guest considering refreshments. "The explosives weren't part of our original experiment design," he observed, his gaze moving deliberately across the monitors displaying potential detonation sites.

Price's expression shifted into something adjacent to a smile, though the configuration contained no warmth. "Adaptation is essential to scientific progress, Alan. Our quantum pattern recognition framework required modification for contemporary applications." He moved toward the centre of the room with fluid precision, gesturing toward the surrounding technology with the particular pride of an artist unveiling a masterpiece. "I've enhanced our original design considerably—integration with the founders' surveillance architecture provided unexpected efficiencies."

"And the casualties?" Hart asked, his voice maintaining professional neutrality despite the moral weight behind the question. "Were they also 'adaptations' to the experimental protocol?"

"Calibration requirements," Price corrected, adjusting his glasses with a gesture Hart recognised from countless research presentations. "Precise positioning was necessary to initialise the pattern recognition parameters." He turned toward a specific monitor displaying the university's main administrative building. "But tonight's examination offers the opportunity to minimise further casualties—depending, of course, on your performance."

Hart took three measured steps into the room, reducing the distance between them while maintaining tactical positioning relative to the door. "Explain the parameters," he said, shifting the interaction toward the intellectual framework Price had established, engaging with the puzzle as a means toward potential resolution.

Price's expression registered momentary satisfaction—the configuration of someone whose carefully constructed scenario was proceeding according to design. He moved toward a circular table positioned beneath the primary clock mechanism, its surface occupied by an antique chessboard with pieces arranged in a configuration that immediately registered in Hart's memory with almost physical impact.

"Our final examination consists of five challenges," Price explained, his hand hovering above the chessboard without disturbing the pieces. "Each successfully resolved puzzle temporarily disarms the corresponding explosive device. Completion of all five neutralises the entire system." He gestured toward the synchronised countdowns displayed on each monitor. "Failure at any stage triggers immediate detonation of the remaining devices."

Hart studied the chessboard, his recognition solidifying as he identified the specific arrangement of pieces—a variation of the Sicilian Defence they had explored during their first chess match in the university commons seventeen years earlier. The particular positioning of knights and bishops reflected Price's unconventional approach to securing victory despite Hart's statistical advantage.

"You remember our first game," Price observed, satisfaction evident in his tone. "When you still believed chess was primarily a mathematical exercise rather than psychological warfare." He adjusted a white knight with precise fingers, returning it to exact alignment with the board's grid. "Your opening move, Professor Hart. The clock is ticking."

Hart quickly moved the white bishop, completing the counter-pattern that resolved the chessboard riddle. The pieces now formed a perfect mirror of their first game's concluding arrangement—his adaptation of Price's strategy reflecting memory and analytical understanding. On one of the surrounding monitors, the countdown for the university quad location froze, then reset to display "DIS-ARMED" in steady green letters. Price observed this resolution with the particular stillness of someone whose expectations had been met rather than exceeded, neither impressed nor disappointed by Hart's performance. He stepped from the chessboard toward a second station where an antique music stand held yellowed sheets of hand-written notation, their staves crowded with symbols simultaneously musical and cryptographic.

"One life temporarily preserved," Price noted, his tone suggesting clinical observation rather than moral relief. "Though 'life' might be an overstatement for what most people experience—moving through prescribed patterns without ever recognising the systems that control their movements." His fingers brushed against the musical manuscript with unexpected tenderness as if greeting an old friend. "Your second challenge requires a different cognitive architecture."

Hart approached the music stand, conscious of the steady count-down on the remaining monitors. Clara's voice emerged through static interference in his earpiece: "Leo's tracking the disarmed signal. Confirmation that the university device is neutralised." Her profes-sional calm provided a momentary anchor amid the intellectual tempest Price had engineered.

The manuscript initially appeared as conventional musical nota-tion—five-line staves populated with notes, rests, and dynamic markings—but closer examination revealed subtle abnormalities. Specific notes carried additional symbols, while the time signatures shifted with mathematical rather than musical logic. Hart recognised the fundamental structure with a jolt of memory that manifested as a physical sensation.

"Schoenberg's twelve-tone system," he said, fingers hovering above the manuscript without touching its aged surface. "The composition project you abandoned during our second research collaboration."

Price's eyebrows lifted slightly—the minimal acknowledgement that had always signified Hart had identified something worth pursuing. "Abandoned is an imprecise characterisation," he corrected. He moved to a small control panel where he activated a sequence that caused the overhead lights to dim slightly, emphasising the monitors' glow. "I merely recognised that musical expression required mathematical underpinning beyond conventional harmonic structures."

Hart studied the notation with increasing intensity, recognising how Price had transformed Schoenberg's serial technique into an encryption system. Each twelve-tone row functioned as a cryptographic key, with the dynamic markings providing transformation rules between sequences. The compositional structure created a self-referential system where each musical phrase contained the cypher for decoding the next.

"Your adaptation introduces computational elements Schoenberg never considered," Hart observed, beginning to map the transformation patterns between tone rows. "The dynamic markings function as algorithmic operators rather than expressive indicators."

Price began pacing around the circular room, his movements describing a precise orbit around Hart's stationary position. "Most people mistake technique for meaning," he said, his voice carrying the particular cadence Hart recognised from his university lectures. "They hear musical notes but miss the mathematical relationships. They read news reports but fail to extract the underlying patterns." His circuit brought him to a display panel showing the hospital entrance, its countdown continuing with merciless precision. "They elect officials without recognising the invisible hands guiding their choices."

Hart continued decoding the musical cypher, transforming each twelve-tone row according to the algorithmic rules embedded in the dynamic markings. The solution gradually emerged as a coordinate sequence—latitude and longitude values corresponding to specific locations throughout the city. As he worked, he maintained peripheral awareness of Price's movement, noting how his former colleague's controlled pacing occasionally faltered when passing sure newspaper clippings on the wall.

"The founding families created the original surveillance system to maintain control across generations," Price continued, his lecture taking on the quality of a rehearsed performance. "I merely adapted their infrastructure to expose rather than conceal. Our pattern recognition technology proved remarkably compatible with their architectural design."

Hart aligned the final coordinate sequence, creating a perfect geometric configuration matching the pattern in the music's structure. "The solution forms a pentagram centred on the eastern industrial district," he said, completing the annotation on a pad Price had provided.

The monitor displaying the central library steps immediately shifted to "DISARMED," its countdown freezing with audible electronic acknowledgement. Price observed this second success with a slight tightening around his eyes—the tension Hart had learned to recognise during their academic partnership as frustration temporarily contained behind professional composure.

"Your mathematical aptitude remains impressive," Price conceded, moving to a third station where an ancient stone tablet lay surrounded by reference materials and translation guides. "Though your moral calculus has always been surprisingly flexible."

Hart approached the tablet, recognising its surface as covered with a numerical system that predated Arabic notation. The symbols appeared initially as decorative elements rather than mathematical operators, their arrangement suggesting both calculation and communication. In his earpiece, Clara's voice confirmed the second disarmed explosive, her words partially obscured by increasing signal interference.

"The Babylonian sexagesimal system," Hart identified, studying the tablet's worn surface where sixty distinct symbols combined to form complex numerical expressions. "Base-60 mathematics from approximately 1800 BCE."

Price positioned himself directly opposite Hart, the tablet between them like a stone chessboard where moves would be made not with pieces but with historical interpretation. "The foundation of both our time measurement and angular calculation systems," he confirmed, adjusting his glasses with fingers that displayed a subtle tremor, momentary instability quickly controlled. "Civilisation's first attempt to quantify both temporal and spatial dimensions within a unified mathematical framework."

As Hart began decoding the ancient numerical patterns, Price's professional demeanour subtly shifted—his academic precision giving way to something more personal, rawer. "You remember when the university journal rejected our co-authored paper on pattern recognition in historical encryption systems?" he asked, the question carrying rhetorical weight rather than seeking information. "Three weeks before they published your solo paper on the same subject?"

Hart's fingers paused momentarily above the tablet, the accusation hitting with unexpected force despite the years since that particular academic betrayal. "The editorial board made that decision without consulting me," he said, his voice maintaining professional neutrality despite the uncomfortable heat expanding in his chest— the particular warmth he had recognised as guilt. "I submitted our joint research initially."

"Yet you accepted both the publication and the subsequent grant funding," Price observed, his tone achieving the perfect balance between inquiry and indictment. His circuit around the room brought him to the wall of newspaper clippings, where his fingers brushed against a headline announcing Hart's promotion to department chair—a position Price had been shortlisted for before the scandal. "Just as you accepted the department's decision to distance themselves from me after the research falsification allegations."

Hart continued working through the Babylonian numerical system, translating the sexagesimal values into decimal equivalents while organising them according to positional significance. The pattern gradually became a complex equation whose solution yielded a specific frequency—the transmission parameter for deactivating the third explosive device.

"The falsification evidence was conclusive, Jonathan," Hart said, using Price's first name with deliberate intimacy—a momentary attempt to bridge the professional distance between them. "Three independent reviewers confirmed the experimental data had been manipulated."

.   .   .

"Manipulation implies intent," Price countered, pacing, increasing speed and irregularity. "Statistical anomalies represent pattern emergence rather than fabrication. You understood that distinction better than anyone—yet you remained silent during the ethics investigation." His hand trembled as he adjusted a monitor displaying the eastern industrial district, the movement suggesting emotional intensity barely contained beneath his controlled exterior.

Hart entered the frequency value into the system interface, completing the third challenge with scientific precision despite the emotional undercurrents disturbing his typical analytical calm. The hospital entrance monitor immediately displayed "DISARMED," leaving two active explosive locations counting down with synchronised determination.

Price observed this third success with the particular stillness that had always preceded his most devastating critiques in their academic days. "You're performing admirably, Alan," he said, using Hart's first name with calculated familiarity. "But the actual examination has yet to begin." He moved toward a fourth station positioned directly beneath the tower's clock mechanism, where a complex three-dimensional maze constructed from transparent acrylic contained embedded symbols that glowed with subtle illumination.

"Our greatest shared failure," Price said, gesturing toward the maze with ceremonial precision. "The quantum entanglement experiment that promised breakthrough pattern recognition capabilities but yielded only academic humiliation and professional separation."

Hart approached the maze with growing awareness that Price's elaborate game had never been primarily about intellectual challenge or revenge, but about forcing him to confront the moral compromises and personal betrayals that had preserved his professional standing while contributing to his former colleague's destruction. Each riddle had systematically deconstructed their shared history, each solution revealing not just Hart's analytical capabilities but the ethical boundaries he had crossed in service to career advancement.

"You've recreated our experimental apparatus in physical form," Hart observed, studying the maze whose structure precisely replicated the quantum pattern recognition system they had designed fifteen years earlier. The transparent walls contained embedded formulas etched in microscopic detail. At the same time, light pathways mimicked the quantum state transitions they had attempted to measure and control.

"I've realised its potential," Price corrected, his voice carrying the particular intensity that had always characterised his moments of greatest intellectual conviction. "What you abandoned as failed methodology, I recognised as merely premature implementation." His hands had stopped trembling, replaced by the focused stillness of someone approaching their defining moment. "This fourth challenge requires you to acknowledge what our experiment revealed—and your responsibility for its suppression."

The clock mechanism above them ticked with metronomic precision, each mechanical movement bringing them closer to Price's predetermined moment of revelation or destruction. Hart studied the maze with growing recognition that solving this particular puzzle would require more than analytical intelligence—it demanded a form of moral reckoning he had systematically avoided through years of professional advancement built partially upon Price's academic ruins.

Hart studied the crystalline maze with its embedded formulas and light pathways, recognising not just their quantum experiment's architecture but the particular elegance with which Price had transformed theoretical concepts into physical representations. His fingers hovered above the puzzle's entrance point, tracing potential solution paths with the practised precision that had defined his investigative approach for years. But something shifted within him as the clock mechanism continued its relentless countdown overhead—a recognition that the proper solution lay not in the maze itself but in the human architecture that had constructed it. His hands were numb from the tower's chill. Still, he felt a warmth in his chest, an uncomfortable heat he recognised as guilt transmuted into something adjacent to clarity.

"You've constructed a perfect physical metaphor, Jonathan," Hart said, deliberately stepping back from the maze rather than engaging with its intricate pathways. "But I'm not going to solve this puzzle—at least, not in the way you've anticipated."

Price's expression registered momentary confusion—the particular configuration of features in their academic partnership had always indicated an unexpected variable disrupting his calculations. "The protocol requires completion of all five challenges," he stated, the words carrying the reflexive certainty of someone reciting established parameters. "Deviation results in detonation of remaining devices."

"The protocol is your construction," Hart countered, moving away from the predetermined station toward the central area where their mutual history hung documented on surrounding walls. "Just as the riddles were never primarily tests of my analytical capabilities, but opportunities for you to force a confrontation with our shared past."

In his earpiece, Clara's voice emerged through static: "Minor detonation reported at the eastern perimeter—warning device only. No casualties." The professional detachment in her tone belied the urgency of their situation, and the countdown continued on the remaining monitors with mathematical certainty.

Price adjusted his position to maintain the calculated distance between them, his movements suggesting the particular wariness of someone whose carefully constructed scenario had encountered unexpected deviation. "The quantum maze represents our most significant collaboration," he insisted, gesturing academically toward the abandoned puzzle. "Its solution requires acknowledging the underlying theoretical framework we developed together."

"Which is exactly why I'm choosing a different approach," Hart replied, his voice assuming the quiet certainty that accompanied his most significant investigative breakthroughs. "Because this isn't about quantum theory or pattern recognition algorithms—it's about what happened when the experiment failed and the university launched its ethics investigation."

Hart moved deliberately toward the wall of newspaper clippings, his attention fixed on a specific headline: "PRESTIGIOUS RESEARCH GRANT AWARDED TO QUANTUM THEORY PIONEER." His photograph appeared below the text, looking younger and considerably less burdened. The article did not mention Price's contributions to the theoretical framework that had secured the funding.

"I betrayed you," Hart said, the words emerging with the particular difficulty of truth long suppressed beneath layers of professional rationalisation. "Not in the ways you've implied throughout this elaborate game—not through deliberate sabotage or intentional theft of your research—but through something perhaps more damaging: my silence when it mattered most."

Price remained perfectly still, the particular motionlessness of a predator recalculating approach vectors as prey behaviour deviates from expected patterns. Only his eyes moved, tracking Hart with an analytical intensity that gradually acquired an underlying emotion adjacent to uncertainty.

"When the ethics committee questioned the statistical anomalies in our experimental data," Hart continued, his gaze steady despite the uncomfortable heat expanding in his chest, "I knew they were misinterpreting emergence patterns as manipulation. I understood your methodological approach—that what appeared as data falsification was an early manifestation of the pattern recognition framework we were attempting to establish."

"Yet you said nothing," Price responded, his voice acquiring an unfamiliar ragged quality—his customary precise articulation momentarily fractured by emotional content too powerful to be fully contained by an academic facade. "You allowed them to dismantle my career while preserving your own."

"I was afraid," Hart acknowledged, carrying none of the defensive justification that had characterised his internal narrative for fifteen years. "I'm afraid that defending your approach would compromise my standing with the committee. Afraid that the theoretical framework we'd developed might be fundamentally flawed. Afraid that my academic identity had become so entwined with our collaboration that its failure would destroy me professionally."

Emergency vehicles appeared on one of the surrounding monitors at the eastern industrial district perimeter, their lights creating rhythmic patterns against the gathering darkness. Another minor detonation registered as a warning flare rather than a destructive blast—Price's system implemented preliminary protocols as the main countdown continued its relentless progression toward zero.

. . .

"Fear is an inadequate explanation for systematic betrayal," Price countered. However, his voice had lost some of its earlier certainty—the particular modulation suggesting intellectual position maintained through emotional effort rather than complete conviction. "You continued building your career on our shared theoretical framework while I was excluded from academic circles entirely."

Hart nodded once, acknowledgement rather than defence. "I rationalised my actions through professional necessity," he said, moving slowly along the wall of documented history, each clipping representing another milestone in their diverging trajectories. "Each compromise made the next one easier to justify until I'd constructed an entire professional identity partially built on appropriated collaboration."

Price's carefully maintained composure showed its first significant fracture—a momentary configuration of features suggesting genuine surprise rather than tactical recalculation. His hand moved unconsciously to adjust his glasses, the gesture accompanied by the subtle tremor Hart had observed earlier. "This admission doesn't disarm the devices," he stated, though the declaration carried less certainty than his previous pronouncements.

"No," Hart agreed, continuing his measured circuit of the room, gradually reducing the distance between himself and the central console where the primary detonation controls glowed with ominous promise. "But it addresses the actual purpose behind your elaborate construction. This was never primarily about exposing the founding families' conspiracy, though that provided a convenient framework for your design. It was about forcing me to confront what happened between us."

Clara's voice emerged urgently in his earpiece: "Approaching the main detonator position. Thirty seconds to access window." The professional instruction required no acknowledgement; Hart's trajectory aligned with the tactical opportunity she had identified.

Price moved to intercept, his body positioning suggesting renewed certainty as Hart approached the central control mechanism. "The founding families created a system of surveillance and control that has manipulated this city for generations," he insisted, his academic persona reasserting itself through a theoretical framework. "Our quantum pattern recognition technology integrated with their architectural infrastructure creates the perfect mechanism for exposing centuries of conspiracy."

"Which raises a different riddle entirely," Hart said, stopping at a precise distance that maintained conversational intimacy while positioning himself for potential intervention. "Why would Jonathan Price, whose childhood was shaped by the particular tragedy of losing both parents to a municipal construction accident subsequently covered up by city officials, wait fifteen years to expose the conspiracy he'd identified?"

The question struck with visible impact. Price's expression is momentarily transformed by the vulnerability that emerges when carefully constructed defences encounter an unexpected breach. His hands stilled completely, the tremor replaced by unnatural rigidity that suggested an autonomic response to a psychological shock.

"The accident reports were sealed by judicial order," Price said, his voice barely above a whisper, academic precision temporarily abandoned. "How did you—"

"Because I was there when you received the sealed documents," Hart replied, the memory emerging with painful clarity across fifteen years of intervening history. "Two months before our quantum experiment failed. You showed me the evidence you'd obtained through administrator access credentials—proof that the founding families had authorised substandard materials for the construction project to reduce costs."

Hart took a deliberate step toward the central console, maintaining eye contact with Price, whose customary cold calculation had been replaced by something raw and unprocessed—emotional content breaking through intellectual containment. "You're not exposing the conspiracy to inform the public," Hart continued, his voice gentle despite the room's escalating tension. "You're using our technology to identify specifically which family members were responsible for the decisions that killed your parents."

Price lunged forward with unexpected velocity, his body abandoning academic restraint for physical intervention as Hart reached the detonation controls. They collided with awkward intensity—two men whose intellectual partnership had never included a physical dimension, whose bodies moved with the particular clumsiness of minds prioritising concept over corporeal execution. Price's momentum carried them both against the console's edge, his hands grasping for control mechanisms that Hart deliberately blocked with his body.

"You can't stop it," Price insisted, his voice transformed by emotional urgency rather than intellectual certainty. "The system is already extracting the pattern—identifying every connection, every decision, every individual responsible for maintaining the conspiracy across generations."

Hart maintained position between Price and the controls, one hand finding the emergency shutdown sequence Leo had identified through remote analysis. "I'm not stopping the pattern recognition system," he clarified, fingers executing the disarm protocol deliberately. "Only preventing the detonations that were never necessary to your actual purpose."

The surrounding monitors flickered momentarily, then stabilised with modified displays—the countdown timers frozen, the "ARMED" indicators replaced with neutralised status reports. The pattern recognition analysis continued on separate screens, extracting and organising centuries of concealed information according to Price's established parameters.

"They'll cover it up again," Price said, his resistance diminishing as the immediate threat of detonation receded. His body seemed to contract slightly, academic certainty giving way to something adjacent to despair. "The founding families still control sufficient institutional leverage to suppress evidence, even from our enhanced system."

"Not this time," Hart assured him, nodding toward a specific monitor where data streams indicated active transmission to multiple external servers. "Clara and Leo established mirrored data capture protocols. The pattern your system has extracted is transmitted simultaneously to federal oversight agencies, international transparency organisations, and secure journalistic platforms."

Price's body completed its transition from resistance to recognition, his weight shifting away from Hart as he processed this unexpected development. "You modified my system," he stated, understanding rather than accusation.

"We adapted it," Hart corrected gently. "Just as you adapted our original quantum framework. The pattern will be exposed—but without the accompanying destruction you had planned as an enforcement mechanism."

Beyond the tower's ancient walls, police sirens wailed with increasing proximity—tactical teams coordinating approach now that the immediate explosive threat had been neutralised. Price registered their approach with the stillness of someone calculating remaining options and finding none that aligned with his original intentions.

. . .

"I never falsified that experimental data," he said quietly, the statement emerging not as a defensive justification but as a simple truth offered without expectation of acceptance. "The statistical anomalies represented actual pattern emergence, precisely as our theoretical framework had predicted."

"I know," Hart acknowledged, the admission carrying fifteen years of accumulated professional guilt finally transmuted into recognition. "I've known since reexamining our original data three years after the ethics investigation concluded. By then, your academic reputation had been irreparably damaged, and my silence had evolved from momentary compromise into permanent betrayal."

The sirens converged outside the tower entrance, their wailing harmonics creating a dissonant counterpoint to the steady ticking of the clock mechanism overhead. Price moved toward the wall of newspaper clippings—the documented history of their divergent paths following academic separation—his hand reaching a specific headline announcing his professional disgrace.

"What happens now?" he asked, containing none of the cold calculation or academic certainty that had characterised his persona as The Riddler. The inquiry emerged instead with the particular vulnerability of someone whose elaborate construct of revenge and revelation had been neither entirely thwarted nor completely realised—a man suspended between the identity he had created and the person he had once been.

Hart studied him across the circular room, where their shared history had been transformed into an elaborate game of intellectual and emotional confrontation. The monitors continued displaying their extracted patterns—centuries of conspiracy and control rendered visible through the quantum recognition technology they had conceived together. The dim lighting cast Price's features in shadow, emphasising the isolation that had shaped his transformation from a brilliant colleague to a methodical antagonist.

"Now we complete what our original experiment began," Hart said simply as the first heavy footsteps of tactical officers became audible on the spiral staircase below. "Revealing patterns others have deliberately concealed—including the ones we've hidden from ourselves."

17

UNMASKING TRUTH

The war room at the precinct existed in perpetual twilight, its institutional blinds filtering the morning sun into thin bands that illuminated dust particles and little else. Overhead fluorescents had been dimmed to reduce screen glare, casting the evidence boards and computer monitors in a blue-white glow that emphasized the pallor of three faces that had seen no real sleep in over thirty hours. The room smelled of coffee gone cold, printer toner, and the particular staleness that develops when human bodies remain too long in enclosed spaces, processing information too significant to permit proper rest.

Hart stood before the main whiteboard, where photographs, documents, and handwritten notes formed a complex constellation of corruption. His shoulders carried the subtle tension of someone who had emerged from physical danger only to confront a more insidious threat. The red marker in his hand made a soft tapping sound against his palm as he contemplated the next connection to be drawn, the next name to be added to the growing web of complicity.

Clara moved with the careful precision of someone navigating around the recent injury, her bandaged arm held slightly away from her body as she arranged files on the central table. Each manila folder received her analytical attention before being placed in one of seven piles, their organization reflecting categories of corruption rather than alphabetical or chronological order. Her face betrayed nothing of the pain she must have felt—only the methodical focus that had characterized her professional approach since Hart had known her.

Leo hunched over three keyboards, his typical energetic movements now distilled into economical precision. Cables snaked from his workstation to secured police servers, transferring encrypted data harvested from Price's system into protected digital evidence vaults. The typing created a soft percussive backdrop to their shared concentration, occasionally punctuated by the distinctive sound of authentication protocols being satisfied.

"Price's encryption was sophisticated but ultimately predictable," Leo said without looking up, his voice carrying the particular flatness of someone awake far too long yet must continue functioning. "He wanted this information found on his terms, not ours."

Hart said nothing, his attention fixed on a particular cluster of photographs near the centre of his board. His hand rose, red marker uncapped, and drew a line connecting the image of Judge Raymond Westfield to a document bearing the Parks Department letterhead. The marker made a soft squeaking sound against the whiteboard's surface, the red line appearing vivid and accusatory beneath the room's subdued lighting.

"Third circuit court judge with financial connections to the eastern development project," Clara observed from her position at the table, her uninjured hand reaching for another file without visual guidance. "That makes four judicial appointments directly linked to land acquisition approvals."

Hart stepped back from the board, his eyes narrowing as he assessed the pattern that had emerged through hours of methodical analysis. The red lines formed not just connections but architecture —a structure of corruption that extended from low-level bureaucrats through mid-tier administrators and into the highest levels of city governance. Each line represented money transferred, evidence suppressed, witnesses silenced, and decisions manipulated. Collectively, they revealed a control system operating beneath the city's visible governance for generations.

"Councilman Richter," Hart said quietly, adding another name to the board in his precise handwriting. "Councilwoman Daniels. Judge Westfield." The marker continued its documentation, each name appearing in neat capital letters that belied the moral weight they carried. "Deputy Mayor Calloway."

His hand hesitated before adding the final name, the marker hovering above the blank space as if a physical inscription might make the revelation more real and irrevocable. After a moment's pause, he wrote "COMMISSIONER DAVIS" in letters slightly larger than the others, his jaw tightening as the name took its place at the nexus of multiple red lines.

"It goes deeper than we thought," he said, his voice barely audible above the hum of computer equipment and the distant sounds of the precinct beyond their closed door. The marker remained in his hand, uncapped, forgotten as he absorbed the implications of what they had uncovered.

Clara approached, her movement drawing his attention from the board to her face, which carried none of the shocks he might have expected—only a grim confirmation of suspicions she had apparently harboured longer than he had. She positioned herself beside him, her uninjured arm almost but not quite touching his, providing proximity without demanding a response.

· · ·

"We've known for years that certain cases disappeared into administrative black holes," she said, her voice carrying the particular restraint that characterized her most significant observations. "This just confirms who was operating the trap doors."

Hart's fingers tightened around the marker, the only physical manifestation of the tension building within him. The commissioner had personally recruited him from academia after the scandal with Price, had championed his unorthodox methods when other department heads questioned his approach, and had provided the institutional protection necessary for his analytical work to continue despite procedural objections. The revelation of Davis's corruption represented not just organizational betrayal but personal deception —the particular violation that occurs when trust extended in good faith encounters premeditated exploitation.

"The records indicate systematic financial transfers," Leo announced from his workstation, his voice breaking the momentary silence with a professional detachment that barely concealed his own dismay. "Regular payments to offshore accounts corresponding with key municipal decisions." His fingers executed a command sequence, bringing surveillance photographs onto the main screen—images of handshakes and envelope exchanges in parking garages, restaurant back rooms, and private clubs. "Some transactions date back more than twenty years."

The screen displayed a particular image that caught Hart's attention—Commissioner Davis accepting a thick envelope from a man whose face remained in shadow. The exchange occurred in the parking structure beneath City Hall during what appeared to be early evening hours. The timestamp indicated this transaction had occurred three days before Hart's promotion to lead detective on major crimes, a career advancement Davis had personally championed against departmental scepticism.

. . .

"They knew," Hart said, the realisation crystallising with painful clarity. "They recognised my pattern recognition capabilities as a potential threat and positioned me where they could monitor and control my investigations." His hand finally lowered, the marker capped with deliberate precision that contrasted with the emotional turmoil evident in his eyes. "Every case assignment, every resource allocation, every investigative parameter—all potentially manipulated to protect their architecture of corruption."

Clara's hand finally made contact with his arm, the touch conveying both support and shared purpose. "Which makes Price's exposure all the more significant," she said, her professional assessment cutting through his momentary disillusionment. "He bypassed their control mechanisms completely, using your shared technology to extract patterns they believed were securely concealed."

Leo looked up from his screens, his expression carrying the particular solemnity that occasionally replaced his typical enthusiasm during moments of significant moral weight. "The data extraction is complete," he reported, disconnecting cables with methodical care. "Everything Price's system uncovered is now secured on our isolated servers, with backup copies generating automatically." He hesitated, then added with uncharacteristic gravity, "Including financial records documenting bribes paid to Commissioner Davis every fiscal quarter since before I was born."

Hart turned back to the whiteboard, studying the commissioner's name surrounded by its constellation of red connections. The marker returned to his hand, uncapped with deliberate purpose as he drew a final line connecting Davis directly to the construction project that had killed Price's parents twenty-three years earlier—the accident that had set all subsequent events in motion.

The morning sun had shifted, its filtered light now illuminating the board directly, casting sharp shadows behind each name and document as if providing additional emphasis to their discoveries. Hart stood in this targeted illumination, his silhouette projected onto the floor behind him—elongated and slightly distorted but unmistakably upright despite the weight of what they had uncovered.

Morning light surrendered to afternoon shadows, then to the artificial brightness of overhead fluorescents as day extended into the evening without natural transition or acknowledgement. Time in the war room existed only as digital timestamps on evidence files and the gradual emptying of coffee carafes, immediately replaced by fresh ones delivered by officers whose curious glances met only closed doors and sealed blinds. Inside, the investigation assumed the particular intensity that emerges when professional methodology encounters moral imperative—each document, each data point, each connection representing not just an intellectual puzzle but a human consequence.

Leo hunched over his workstation like a digital archaeologist, excavating through layers of encryption with tools both standardized and improvised. His screens displayed cascading code sequences that reflected blue-white in his tired eyes, which nonetheless maintained the focused intensity of someone translating abstract patterns into concrete evidence. Cables sprouted from his laptop like technological vines, connecting to external drives and processing units that hummed with quiet determination.

"Price used a modified Elliptic Curve algorithm," he explained to no one in particular, his fingers never pausing their percussive dance across the keyboard. "Mathematically sophisticated but philosophically revealing—he built backdoors into his own security system, little mathematical inconsistencies that create access points if you know where to look." A new window opened on his central monitor, displaying financial records organized by date and recipient. "There," he said with quiet satisfaction, "another $50,000 payment to Judge Westfield three days before he dismissed the class action lawsuit against Eastern Chemical."

Hart acknowledged the discovery with a slight nod, his body maintaining the particular restlessness of someone whose analytical process manifested physically. He paced between evidence stations with measured steps, occasionally stopping to add another name, another connection, another date to the whiteboard that now required multiple panels to contain the expanding architecture of corruption. His suit jacket had been discarded hours earlier, his tie loosened but still precisely knotted, and his shirt sleeves rolled with mathematical evenness to expose forearms that bore the tension of sustained concentration.

"The lawsuit dismissal created a precedent for fourteen subsequent environmental cases," he noted, adding this connection to the board with his red marker. "Each dismissal protected municipal liability while concealing evidence of groundwater contamination in the eastern district."

Clara had claimed the conference table as her analytical domain, it's surface disappearing beneath meticulously arranged municipal records—building permits, land acquisitions, zoning variances, environmental impact studies. She moved between documents with the economical precision of someone conserving physical resources while maximizing analytical capacity. Her injured arm remained partially immobilized in its sling, but her uninjured hand compensated with increased efficiency, each movement purposeful and precise.

"The property assessments were systematically manipulated," she observed, arranging three documents in a triangular configuration that revealed their interconnected fabrication. "Landmarked for public development was artificially devalued through falsified environmental concerns, purchased by shell corporations at reduced rates, then rezoned for commercial use once the contamination reports mysteriously disappeared." Her finger traced a pattern of ownership transfers across multiple documents. "The same four shell companies appear in every transaction, all ultimately owned by Westlake Holdings."

Hart stopped his pacing, attention drawn to this new connection. "Westlake Holdings," he repeated, the name triggering recognition in his methodical memory. "That's the parent company that owned the construction firm responsible for the bridge collapse that killed Price's parents."

Leo looked up from his screens, fingers momentarily pausing their relentless typing. "The same Westlake that received the no-bid contract for the hospital expansion project last year," he added, connecting historical crime and contemporary corruption. "I've found board membership documents. Guess who serves as non-executive director?" His screen displayed a corporation registration form where Commissioner Davis's signature appeared on the bottom line, dated five years earlier.

The investigation continued with intensifying precision, each discovery feeding into their collective understanding like tributaries joining a river of revelation. Hart added another panel to the whiteboard, then another, until the corruption's architecture surrounded them on three walls—a visual representation of systems operating beneath the city's legitimate governance for generations.

"Environmental reports falsified to facilitate property acquisition at reduced values," Clara summarised, organising another set of documents into evidence folders. Safety inspections are being manipulated to reduce construction costs on municipal projects. Medical examiner findings altered to conceal liability in workplace deaths." Each category received its folder, colour-coded and precisely labelled in her meticulous handwriting.

"At least seven whistleblowers who attempted to expose aspects of this system have disappeared over the past decade," Hart added, his marker circling names on the third panel. "All cases classified as missing persons rather than potential homicides, all investigations assigned to Detective Weber, who reports directly to Commissioner Davis."

Leo emerged from another layer of encrypted data, his expression tightening with each discovery. "They manipulated crime statistics to create artificial patterns," he said, displaying comparative graphs on his screen. "Redirecting police resources away from neighbourhoods where their business interests operated, manufacturing crime clusters to justify aggressive enforcement in areas they wanted to be cleared for development." His voice carried the particular disillusionment of someone discovering that systems he had trusted were fundamentally corrupted. "The algorithmic patrol assignments I helped optimise last year—they were using my work to enforce their protection scheme."

The digital clock on the wall displayed 8:47 PM when Leo made the discovery that transformed their investigation from comprehensive documentation to irrefutable evidence. His exclamation drew Hart and Clara to his workstation, where his central screen displayed a video file extracted from the most heavily encrypted section of Price's data archive.

"This was triple-encrypted," Leo explained, his voice tight with controlled excitement. "Quantum-resistant algorithms wrapped around military-grade security protocols. Price protected this file more carefully than anything else in the system."

The video began playing—high-quality surveillance footage showing a wood-panelled office that Hart immediately recognised as belonging to the president of the City Council. Commissioner Davis entered the frame, shaking hands with three men whose expensive suits and confident postures suggested significant financial authority. The timestamp indicated this meeting had occurred eighteen months earlier, during the initial planning phase for the Westlake Renewal Project.

"We've ensured the contract specifications will match your bid parameters exactly," Davis said, his voice clear in the high-fidelity audio. "The environmental concerns have been handled, and the historical preservation objections will disappear before the final vote." He accepted an envelope from the tallest of the three men, tucking it into his inner jacket pocket without examining its contents. "The patrol schedules have been adjusted to minimise police presence during the preliminary work. No one will interfere with your timeline."

The man who had handed over the envelope nodded with satisfaction. "The council members understand their role?"

"They've been properly motivated," Davis confirmed, his expression conveying professional assurance rather than moral discomfort. "This project proceeds exactly as planned. No one will ever know what happened at Westlake."

Leo stopped the video, his fingers immediately executing commands that created secured copies on multiple protected servers. "That's direct evidence of bribery, bid-rigging, and conspiracy," he said, the technical terminology failing to obscure the moral significance of what they had witnessed. "And explicit connection to whatever happened at Westlake that they're so determined to keep buried."

Hart stood perfectly still, his body containing the particular tension that precedes significant decision rather than uncertain deliberation. The video transformed abstract patterns into concrete evidence and theoretical corruption into prosecutable crime. His eyes moved from Leo's screen to the sprawling evidence boards surrounding them, then to Clara, whose expression reflected his recognition of the momentous choice that now confronted them.

"Copy everything to secure external drives," he instructed, his voice carrying the quiet authority that emerged during his most significant cases. "Then disconnect from the network entirely. No electronic transmissions of any kind until we determine our next steps." His gaze returned to the frozen image of Commissioner Davis accepting the envelope, the man who had recruited him, mentored him, and, he now understood, monitored him for years. "What we do with this evidence will have consequences beyond any case we've handled before."

The break room existed in a liminal state between occupation and abandonment—institutional coffee maker cooling into bitterness, fluorescent lights humming with the particular emptiness that emerges when spaces designed for social interaction stand temporarily vacant. Through glass walls, Hart could see Clara and Leo still working in the war room, their silhouettes moving with the determined precision of people navigating moral as well as professional obligations. But here, in this momentary isolation, the weight of their discoveries settled across his shoulders with physical insistence, demanding recognition beyond analytical assessment.

A cup of coffee sat untouched before him, its surface forming a perfect black mirror that reflected the overhead lights in the miniature constellation. Hart had poured it twenty minutes earlier, then forgotten its existence as his mind processed the implications of what they had uncovered. The liquid had cooled to room temperature, rendering it doubly unpalatable. Yet, he made no move to consume or discard it—the cup merely occupied space within his visual field while his attention focused elsewhere.

His reflection appeared in the window before him, ghostly and insubstantial against the city lights beyond. The nighttime skyline glittered with electrical precision, each illuminated office and streetlamp representing human activity continuing without awareness of the revelations contained within the precinct's walls. Ordinary citizens moving through their evenings, municipal workers completing their shifts, elected officials returning to comfortable homes—all existed within systems of governance they believed operated according to democratic principles rather than concealed manipulation.

Hart's fingers began an unconscious rhythm against the table's surface, a percussive manifestation of the calculation occurring within his analytical mind. The evidence they had assembled represented not merely criminal conspiracy but foundational corruption —a rot that extended into the city's institutional framework, threatening collapse if suddenly exposed. The commissioner, three judges, multiple council members, department heads, and prominent business leaders were all implicated in decades of coordinated deception.

Exposure meant public panic, collapsed faith in institutions, and destroyed careers and lives. It meant potential violence as citizens confronted the betrayal of their trust, possible economic collapse as municipal bonds lost value, and disruption of essential services as leadership structures disintegrated. It meant chaos, suffering, and uncertainty extending far beyond the corrupt individuals themselves to impact innocent residents who depended on functional governance regardless of its hidden flaws.

Containment, by contrast, offered controlled reform—targeted prosecution of key figures while maintaining institutional stability, gradual correction rather than sudden collapse, and preservation of public confidence during systematic improvement. It meant potentially saving lives that might be lost in the chaos of comprehensive exposure, protecting pensions that might evaporate in municipal bankruptcy, and maintaining services that would suffer during institutional reconstruction.

His jaw muscles tightened as these competing imperatives battled within his consciousness. The analytical framework that had served him through years of detective work offered no clear resolution to this puzzle. Both approaches contained valid ethical considerations, promising certain benefits while guaranteeing specific harms. The equation contained too many variables, potential outcomes, and lives hanging in delicate balance.

His hand reached for the coffee cup with a visible tremor, fingers closing around its ceramic circumference with uncertain pressure. The movement lacked his typical economy and precision, instead displaying the particular hesitation that emerges when physical action becomes a proxy for moral indecision. The cup lifted partially from the table, hovered momentarily, and then returned to its original position without serving any apparent purpose.

"You're thinking about burying it," Clara said from the doorway, her voice carrying neither accusation nor judgment—merely precise observation of a pattern she had recognised through years of partnership.

Hart didn't turn, his gaze fixed on his reflection in the window and the city lights. "People could die in the chaos," he said, the statement emerging with the particular difficulty of someone articulating only one dimension of a complex moral calculation. "Innocent people who depend on these institutions, regardless of the corruption beneath them."

Clara entered the break room with unhurried steps, her movements carrying the careful precision that had characterised her work despite her injury. She positioned herself beside him, her reflection joining his in the window—two figures outlined against the city's nocturnal illumination, their features rendered ghostly by the glass's reflective properties.

"And how many have already died to keep this buried?" she asked, emerging with the particular gentleness she reserved for their most significant conversations. "How many more will suffer if these systems continue operating unchecked?"

Hart's fingers resumed their rhythmic tapping against the table, mathematical precision suggesting computational processing rather than nervous habit. "I've spent my career believing in systems," he said, the admission carrying unexpected vulnerability beneath its analytical framing. "Believing that patterns reveal the truth, that institutions can be trusted if properly understood, that governance functions according to discernible rules rather than concealed manipulation."

"You've spent your career pursuing truth regardless of consequence," Clara corrected, her tone suggesting recalibration rather than contradiction. "Even when that pursuit challenged institutional convenience or professional advancement." Her uninjured hand moved into his peripheral vision, palm upward, offering something that caught the fluorescent light with a subtle gleam. "Even when that pursuit cost you personally."

The lake stone rested in her palm, smooth, dark, and perfectly contoured by years of geological patience followed by Hart's habitual handling. She had retrieved it from his desk in the war room, recognising its significance as both a talisman and a reminder. Its surface reflected nothing, absorbing light rather than returning it, creating the perfect contrast to the city's electrical illumination beyond the window.

"You carried this through our first case together," she reminded him, the stone remaining perfectly centred in her open palm. After we found that child's body in the lake, you said it represented clarity—that sometimes truth feels heavy in your hand but provides solid ground beneath your feet." Her fingers curled slightly, offering the stone without demanding its acceptance. "You weren't thinking about institutional stability then. You were thinking about justice."

Hart turned from the window, his reflection disappearing as he faced his partner directly. Her expression contained neither demand nor expectation—only the particular certainty that had balanced his analytical precision throughout their professional relationship. Where he processed patterns, she assessed their human implications;

where he calculated variables, she recognised consequences; where he established frameworks, she provided purpose.

"Exposure creates vulnerability," he acknowledged, eyes moving between her face and the stone she offered. "But concealment ensures continued corruption."

"Some institutions need to be vulnerable before they can be reformed," she said, the observation carrying the weight of conviction rather than preference. "Some systems must be exposed before they can be rebuilt."

Hart's hand finally moved, accepting the stone from her palm. Its familiar weight and texture provided tactile grounding and a connection to decisions made and truths pursued across years of investigation. His fingers closed around it with the certainty that emerges when physical contact resolves intellectual indecision.

"The truth serves no one if it remains concealed," he said finally, the statement functioning as both a personal reminder and professional commitment. The stone disappeared into his pocket, resuming its habitual position against his leg—a physical anchor connecting analytical framework to moral purpose.

Clara's reflection reappeared in the window as she turned toward the city lights. Her profile carried the subtle satisfaction of someone who had not changed another's mind but merely helped them recognise what they already knew. "What's our next step?" she asked, conveying readiness rather than uncertainty.

Hart left the coffee cup where it sat, forgotten and unnecessary, as he straightened with renewed purpose. "We secure the evidence chain, contact federal authorities, and prepare for controlled disclosure," he said, decisions crystallising into action with the particular clarity that emerges when moral and analytical imperatives finally align. "The system will resist exposure through every available mechanism. We need to ensure the truth emerges regardless of that resistance."

Through the glass walls, Leo remained visible in the war room. His silhouette bent over computer equipment with the focused intensity of someone whose technical expertise had become essential to the moral outcome. Beyond the precinct windows, the city continued its nighttime operations, unaware that its fundamental understanding of municipal governance would be irreversibly transformed by morning.

Dawn arrived with tentative persistence, early light filtering through the blinds in Hart's office with the particular hesitation of a witness unsure whether to come forward. The illumination carried none of the harsh certainty of the afternoon sun or the dramatic contrast of sunset—just the gradual revelation of objects and surfaces as darkness receded into shadow, then shadow into visibility. This transitional light seemed appropriate for the task before them: the careful movement of hidden truth into public awareness, with all the risks and consequences such transition entailed.

Hart's office reflected his analytical mind—precisely arranged furniture, methodically organised case files, and deliberately positioned reference materials created an environment where intellectual efficiency precedes personal comfort. The space usually maintained a particular stillness, but this morning, it hummed with purposeful activity as three people prepared to alter the city's understanding of its governance irrevocably.

Leo sat cross-legged on the floor, surrounded by electronic equipment arranged with the specialised organisation of someone whose technical process required specific spatial relationships. Three external hard drives formed a triangle around his laptop, each connected via cables colour-coded with small tags denoting their purpose and sequence. His fingers moved across the keyboard with practised efficiency, each command executed with the precision of someone who understood that technical procedure had become inseparable from the ethical outcome.

"I've established triple redundancy for all critical files," he explained, his voice carrying the focused calm that had replaced his earlier agitation. "Primary evidence secured on encrypted drives with blockchain verification protocols attached to each document." He looked up from his screen, meeting Hart's gaze with unusual directness. "No one can claim this was fabricated or tampered with. Each file contains embedded authentication markers linked to its source within Price's system."

His hands continued their methodical work while he spoke, connecting a final external drive to his laptop with careful deliberation. "I've created secure transmission packages for federal investigators, automatically executing decryption protocols that activate only when accessed by authorised credentials." The technical terminology carried none of his typical enthusiasm for digital complexity—just the professional precision of someone ensuring that truth, once revealed, could not be technologically undermined.

Clara occupied the visitor's chair near Hart's desk, her phone pressed against her ear as she conducted a conversation in the carefully modulated tones of someone navigating institutional hierarchy and personal trust. Her injured arm remained in its sling, but her posture conveyed none of the physical discomfort that must have accompanied nearly thirty hours of continuous work since leaving the hospital.

· · ·

"Yes, Agent Winters, we have comprehensive documentation," she said, her voice carrying the particular authority that emerged during her most significant professional interactions. "Video evidence, financial records, witness statements, all secured according to federal evidence protocols." She listened briefly, then continued with measured certainty. "Nine AM at City Hall. We're proceeding with public disclosure regardless of jurisdictional questions. This evidence belongs to the public."

She ended the call and immediately began another, her fingers selecting a contact from a carefully curated list she had assembled throughout the night. "Rebecca, it's Detective Morgan," she said, transitioning to a slightly different conversational register—still professional but containing the subtle warmth reserved for trusted journalistic contacts. "We're moving forward with the disclosure we discussed. Nine AM, City Hall press room. Bring your most meticulous fact-checker and someone who understands municipal bond markets."

Hart sat at his desk, fingers moving across his keyboard with deliberate precision as he drafted the statement introducing the public to evidence of generational corruption. Each sentence received his full analytical consideration—words selected not for emotional impact but for factual precision, structures crafted to convey institutional betrayal without triggering panic, and technical terms balanced with accessible explanations. His eyes occasionally lifted from the screen to the photograph on his wall—a young woman with his same analytical gaze but softer features, her expression suggesting intellectual intensity and moral certainty.

The photograph had occupied that position since his first day in this office, a reminder of the sister whose journalism had exposed corporate malfeasance in the pharmaceutical industry, resulting in both significant public health reforms and her subsequent death in a car accident that had never been fully explained. Her work demonstrated that truth served a larger purpose than personal safety, that systems required transparency to function ethically, and that individual courage sometimes necessitated institutional discomfort. The digital document taking shape beneath his fingers continued that legacy, though in different forms and through other methods.

The office contained no chaotic energy that often characterises crisis response—no raised voices, frantic movements, or disorganised urgency. Instead, the three of them worked with the synchronised precision of people who had aligned professional methodology and moral purpose, each contributing specific expertise toward a shared objective. The atmosphere carried a solemnity appropriate to the magnitude of what they prepared to reveal, but beneath that solemnity flowed the particular certainty that emerges when difficult decisions crystallise into necessary action.

Leo closed his laptop with quiet finality, the sound drawing both Hart's and Clara's attention. "Technical preparations complete," he reported, gathering external drives into a specialised carrying case with foam inserts moulded to their dimensions. "Evidence secured, authentication protocols verified, transmission packages ready for distribution." He rose from his cross-legged position with the careful movements of someone whose body had remained too long in one configuration, muscles protesting the sudden change in orientation.

Clara ended her final call by placing her phone on Hart's desk. "Federal agents will meet us at City Hall," she said, her tone suggesting professional satisfaction rather than personal triumph. Key journalists have been notified without specific details—just sufficient information to ensure attendance without enabling premature disclosure."

Hart saved the completed statement to an encrypted drive and then removed it from his computer with the methodical care of someone handling evidence rather than merely digital information. The three converged near the office door, each carrying physical manifestations of their contribution—Hart with his prepared statement, Clara with a portfolio containing key document printouts, and Leo with his case of secured digital evidence.

The dawn light had strengthened during their preparations, and the office was now fully illuminated with the particular clarity that accompanies early morning before the day's complications began to accumulate. They stood in this clean light, three figures united by purpose rather than circumstance, their postures reflecting professional commitment and personal resolve.

"Whatever happens after today, I want you both to know—" Hart began, his voice containing an unusual hesitation, analytical precision momentarily inadequate for the emotional content he attempted to convey.

"We know, Alan," Clara interrupted, a small smile softening her typically composed features. Using his first name carried the intimacy reserved for moments when professional partnership transcended institutional boundaries to become something adjacent to family. "We're with you."

Leo nodded firmly. His typical enthusiasm became more substantial and grounded. "All the way," he added, the simple phrase containing personal loyalty and professional commitment.

They stood together in momentary silence, the significance of their impending action requiring no additional articulation between them. The lake stone pressed against Hart's leg from within his pocket, its familiar weight reminding him of a purpose beyond professional obligation. Clara's injured arm hung in its sling, representing literal blood already shed in pursuit of the truth they now prepared to share. Leo's equipment case contained a technological extension of their collective commitment—evidence preserved beyond individual vulnerability.

The city awaited their revelation, and its governance was about to face its most significant challenge since its founding. Institutions would resist, careers would end, and systems would require reconstruction. But in that moment, in the clear morning light of Hart's office, three people stood in perfect alignment—different methodologies united in service to shared principle, different perspectives focused on common objective, different capabilities directed toward a singular purpose.

Truth, long concealed beneath institutional architecture, prepared for its emergence into public awareness. And they, its temporary custodians, are prepared to facilitate that transition regardless of personal consequences.

The press room at City Hall filled beyond its intended capacity, and journalists were compressed into inadequate space with the particular discomfort they willingly endured when significant news appeared imminent. Television cameras lined the back wall like mechanical sentinels, their red recording lights creating a horizon of electronic vigilance. The air carried the complex scent of too many bodies occupying insufficient ventilation—coffee breath and nervous perspiration mingling with the chemical traces of camera equipment and the lingering mustiness of a municipal building whose maintenance budget had suffered consistent reduction over the past decade.

Murmured speculation created a persistent ambient noise, punctuated occasionally by the mechanical whir of cameras adjusting position or the percussive tapping of laptops being prepared for imminent reporting. The wooden podium stood empty at the front of the room, the city seal affixed to its face gleaming beneath fluorescent lights that seemed explicitly designed to create unflattering shadows beneath human eyes. A clock on the side wall displayed 8:57 in red digital precision, counting down to the scheduled revelation with indifferent electronic accuracy.

The side door opened at precisely 8:59, revealing Hart flanked by Clara and Leo—all three dressed with the formal precision their announcement demanded, their exhaustion concealed beneath professional composure rather than cosmetic intervention. They moved toward the podium with synchronised purpose, each carrying the particular gravity of people who understood they had crossed a threshold between institutional compliance and moral necessity.

Hart's charcoal suit appeared recently pressed despite the night spent without sleep. His tie was knotted with mathematical precision, and his shoes reflected the overhead lights with a subdued gleam. Only his eyes revealed the toll of the past thirty-six hours—their usual analytical focus now layered with the particular weariness accompanying significant moral weight carried too long without respite. He carefully positioned himself behind the podium, placing a thin folder containing his prepared statement directly before him, its edges aligned perfectly with the wooden surface.

Clara stood to his right, her navy blazer concealing the sling that supported her injured arm. Her posture suggested professional alertness despite physical discomfort. Leo took position on Hart's left, the case containing their secured evidence held with both hands before him. His typical animated energy transformed into something more controlled, included, and purposeful.

The room fell silent with uncharacteristic immediacy, the assembled journalists recognising from the team's formal arrangement and solemn expressions that this press conference transcended routine announcement. Cameras adjusted position, focusing lenses with subtle mechanical whirs, their operators ensuring optimal framing for whatever revelation approached.

"Good morning," Hart began, his voice carrying the particular clarity that emerges when technical precision meets moral certainty. "I am Detective Alan Hart. With me are Detective Clara Morgan and Officer Leo Chang of the Major Crimes Division." The introduction contained none of the institutional formalities typically required by department protocol—no mention of the commissioner's authority, no reference to the chain of command, and no acknowledgement of municipal oversight. This absence, while subtle, communicated the independence of their position with more significance than an explicit statement might have achieved.

"Today, we are releasing evidence of a conspiracy that has corrupted the highest levels of this city's government for decades," Hart continued, his tone neither sensational nor apologetic—just the measured delivery of someone presenting factual information whose significance required no emotional amplification. "This conspiracy has involved elected officials, appointed judges, department heads, and business leaders in a coordinated effort to manipulate municipal governance for private financial gain."

The assembled journalists collectively inhaled, followed by the accelerated tapping of laptop keys and the soft clicking of camera shutters. Hart proceeded without acknowledging this reaction, his statement unfolding with the methodical precision that characterised his analytical approach.

"Through systematic examination of evidence obtained during an investigation into multiple homicides, we have documented a pattern of corruption extending across three decades," he explained, each word selected for factual accuracy rather than dramatic impact. "This pattern includes bid rigging on municipal contracts, manipulation of zoning decisions, falsification of environmental safety reports, strategic redirection of police resources, and the deliberate suppression of evidence related to workplace fatalities."

The folder before him remained closed, Hart having committed his statement to memory with the same precise recall he applied to crime scene details and witness statements. His hands rested lightly on the podium's edges, their steady positioning conveying certainty rather than tension despite the magnitude of what he revealed.

"Specific individuals implicated by documented evidence include Police Commissioner Davis, Judge Raymond Westfield, City Council President Simmons, Deputy Mayor Calloway, and executives from Westlake Holdings, Eastern Development Corporation, and Municipal Financing Associates." Each name emerged without emphasis or accusation—simply a factual identification of parties whose actions had been documented beyond reasonable dispute.

Clara maintained perfect stillness beside him, her professional composure unmarred by the significance of names being publicly revealed. Leo shifted his weight almost imperceptibly, the only physical indication of the tension within his carefully maintained exterior.

"The evidence supporting these findings has been secured according to federal evidence protocols," Hart continued, nodding slightly toward the case Leo held. "Complete documentation is being provided simultaneously to the Department of Justice, the State Attorney General's Office, and selected journalistic organisations with demonstrated commitment to factual verification."

Questions erupted from the assembled press corps, voices overlapping with increasing urgency as the scope of Hart's revelation registered in their collective consciousness. Hands raised throughout the room, reporters half-rising from their seats, the professional restraint typically maintained during official announcements fracturing beneath the weight of what they were hearing.

"Commissioner Davis personally involved?"

"How high does this reach in state government?"

"Are there connections to the mayor's office?"

"What specific contracts were compromised?"

"How was this corruption initially discovered?"

Hart raised one hand slightly, the gesture containing none of the panic that often accompanies attempts to control unexpected chaos —just the deliberate signal of someone requesting attention rather than demanding it. The questions subsided with surprising compliance, the journalists' professional instincts recognizing that additional information would emerge more efficiently through an orderly process than continued clamour.

"We will address specific questions in sequence," Hart assured them, his tone maintaining its measured consistency. "Complete documentation packages are being distributed to your organizations as we speak, containing evidence substantiating each allegation along with contextual information necessary for accurate reporting."

As he continued outlining the key findings of their investigation, the lake stone sat on the corner of the podium, visible only to him. It's smooth surface absorbed light rather than reflected it and its solid presence provided a tactile reminder of a purpose beyond the professional obligation. He had placed it there deliberately before beginning his statement, positioning it precisely where his peripheral vision would register its presence without requiring direct observation.

Hart's gaze moved across the assembled crowd with analytical precision, cataloguing individual reactions with the same methodical attention he applied to crime scene evidence. Reporters leaned forward with expressions ranging from shocked disbelief to vindicated suspicion. Technical staff adjusted equipment with renewed urgency, recognising the historical significance of the process. Citizens who had gained access to the press conference displayed emotional responses that were more varied and less restrained than those of their journalistic counterparts—anger, validation, confusion, and grief, all manifesting in physical configurations unique to each individual.

At the back of the room, barely visible beyond the assembled press corps, several city officials moved with careful inconspicuousness toward the exits—their departures neither hurried enough to draw attention nor casual enough to suggest routine movement. Hart registered these retreats without interrupting his statement, his analytical mind simultaneously presenting evidence while observing its immediate impact on those implicated by its content.

As questions resumed with more focused specificity, Hart responded with the particular precision that had characterised his detective work, neither withholding relevant information nor offering speculative extensions beyond documented evidence. His eyes contained not triumph but quiet resolution, the weight of truth finally shared after too long concealed. The uncomfortable heat that had occupied his chest throughout the investigation—that familiar warmth he had recognised as guilt—had transformed into something adjacent to purpose, a different kind of heat that provided sustaining energy rather than consuming discomfort.

The lake stone remained at the podium's edge, connecting this moment of public revelation to personal principles maintained through years of professional challenge. Clara stood beside him, her injured arm a physical reminder of the prices already paid in pursuit of truth. Leo managed their evidence with technical precision, ensuring that documented reality would persist regardless of institutional resistance or individual denial.

Outside the press room windows, the city continued its morning routines—traffic moving through downtown streets, pedestrians navigating sidewalks, municipal employees arriving for work in buildings whose governance was irreversibly transformed even as they entered. The sun had fully risen, illuminating City Hall's limestone facade with the clarity that follows dawn's uncertainty, revealing architectural details, structural features, and superficial imperfections with equal emphasis.

Within this illumination, three figures stood at the podium—different in methodology but united in purpose, distinct in approach but aligned in principle—facing the consequences of choosing truth over convenience, transparency over security, revelation over concealment. Hart's voice continued its measured delivery, presenting evidence without embellishment, revealing corruption without sensationalism, and offering truth without expectation of gratitude or recognition.

The lake stone caught the light from a slightly different angle as Hart shifted position, its surface momentarily gleaming before returning to its characteristic absorption. Like the stone, Hart himself had been shaped by natural and deliberate forces—academic training, professional experience, personal loss, moral challenge—until he emerged as something solid and defined, capable of reflecting light and absorbing impact.

The press conference would continue for another hour, questions would persist for days, investigations would extend for months, and institutional reconstruction might require years. But at this moment, at this podium, Detective Alan Hart had completed the transformation that began when he first recognised patterns of corruption beneath his city's governance—from analytical observer to active participant, from pattern recogniser to truth revealer, from professional detective to moral agent.

Once made, the choice created its certainty. In Hart's eyes, triumph was not a quiet resolution, the particular clarity that emerges when professional obligation aligns perfectly with personal principle.

18

RESETTING THE BOARD

S unlight poured through the freshly adjusted blinds in Hart's office, painting neat stripes across his desk where once chaotic shadows had mirrored his turbulent thoughts. He flipped through case files with calm precision, no longer tapping restless rhythms with his fingers but turning pages with the composed patience of someone who had finally harmonised logic and emotion. The lake stone sat beside his notepad, not as a desperate charm but a quiet companion, a reminder of grief and growth.

Three months had passed since the press conference that shattered city leadership and exposed generations of corruption. The immediate wave of resignations, arrests, and outrage had gradually transitioned to the slower work of rebuilding—fresh appointments, new oversight bodies, and stronger transparency measures. Hart had been pivotal in this shift, earning accolades and inner clarity, though neither had been his goal when he stood on that stage with Clara and Leo.

His office now reflected his inner transformation. Gone were the sprawling webs of evidence that had once swallowed every surface, desperate constellations drawn by a man chasing elusive connections. In their place stood a single, well-maintained board where open cases were analysed with order and focus. Each case had its boundaries, each investigation had its own space, and each mystery was respected, not consumed.

Clara entered with a quiet click of the door, gracefully balancing two mugs in her uninjured hand. Her arm had mostly healed, though it still ached on long days. She set one mug on his desk, its ceramic clinking softly on the wood.

"You cleaned the break room machine," she said, settling into the chair opposite his. "Coffee's almost drinkable now."

Hart took the mug with a nod. "Small system improvements ripple into larger change," he replied, the words academic in structure but lacking the coldness they once carried.

Clara surveyed the tidy office, her trained eye missing nothing. "First time I've seen the floor in over a year," she smirked. "And you filed away the Riddler case." Her tone was light, but the statement carried weight—it marked not just tidying up but healing.

"Not filed. Integrated," Hart corrected gently. He gestured to the single evidence board, where a modest section displayed select remnants of the Riddler case—not as an obsession, but as a point of reference. "Some patterns are worth watching, just not letting them consume you."

Clara nodded, recognising the nuance, her understanding sharpened by shared battles and breakthroughs. "The new chief asked about our report format," she said, sipping her coffee. "I told her we work unconventionally, but we get results."

"Our methods," Hart echoed, catching the plural with quiet appreciation. Where once he might have seen Clara as a junior partner—his logic, her action—he now recognised their methods as collaborative. "The Riddler case changed more than just who runs the department."

"It changed us," Clara agreed plainly. She held his gaze as she always did when it mattered. "Though I'd argue you've changed more. Your tie matches your shirt today."

She teased gently. They were fluent now in emotional shorthand. Hart glanced at his clothes, suddenly aware that his usual mismatched uniform had given way to something more intentional— another outward sign of an inward shift.

"I'm still working through what Jonathan did," he admitted, the words coming easily despite their weight. "Not just his betrayal. But how I contributed to his downfall years ago." His fingers brushed the lake stone, grounding him. "Balance doesn't mean closure. It means knowing when analysis and emotion both belong in the picture."

Clara's face softened. "Balance suits you, Alan," she said, his name feeling natural rather than intimate.

Outside, the precinct had resumed its steady rhythm—officers at desks, civilians waiting, the daily hum of law enforcement carrying on in a post-shock reality. The chaos after Commissioner Davis's arrest had given way to an uneasy but functioning calm.

Hart's eyes drifted to a framed article on his wall—the only visible nod to the Riddler case. The headline read "JUSTICE SERVED," with a photo of him, Clara, and Leo from the press conference. Their expressions were focused, not triumphant. He'd hung it not as a trophy but as a reminder of their shared decision to put truth above comfort.

"Price turned down the deal," Clara said, following his gaze. "Still claims it was all justified."

"They're not mutually exclusive," Hart replied, his voice even.

"His motives held truth. His methods didn't." He paused, considering the man who had been a colleague, an adversary, and something murkier now. "His tech's being retooled for legitimate use."

"Mostly by Leo," Clara added with a smile. "He's adapted Price's theory without inheriting the murder streak."

A vibration from Hart's phone interrupted them. The screen read "Chief Wilson." He answered, listened, and hung up.

"We've been summoned," he said. "Commendation ceremony."

Clara grimaced. "Let me guess. You'll wear the tie that almost matches the jacket?"

Hart gathered files slowly, no longer in a rush. "The award isn't for solving the case. It's for choosing the hard truth over easy silence."

At the door, Clara briefly rested a hand on his arm. The contact spoke of trust, equality, and partnership reshaped by hardship.

"Ready, partner?" she asked, asking simple words with deep meaning.

Hart nodded, and they walked into the hallway side by side.

The digital forensics lab was a blend of old and new—state-of-the-art machines hummed beside tools from investigative eras long past. Holograms projected vivid 3D evidence, while corkboards held traditional, pinned photographs. Hart leaned against a steel table, watching Leo move effortlessly between both worlds. The younger officer's fingers danced across three keyboards, his eyes following patterns on several screens. What had once been a clash between Leo's tech-savvy instincts and Hart's analytical style had become a dynamic collaboration.

Leo wore a wrinkled shirt with sleeves rolled exactly to his forearms. A new analogue watch on his wrist—a quiet nod to old-school methods amid his digital world. His once-erratic energy had cooled into steady precision over the past few months.

"The algorithm pulls behavioural trends from fragmented data," Leo explained, pointing to a shifting graphic on his main screen. "It cross-checks social posts, card transactions, camera footage, and tower pings." The visuals adjusted fluidly with his inputs. "We're seeing 93.7% accuracy in tracking presence, even when someone's trying to stay hidden."

Hart peered at the interface without obligation but with genuine curiosity. His appreciation for tech had grown during the Riddler case, though he remained mindful of its limits.

"It maps presence, not purpose," Hart said, moving closer to a data cluster. He nodded toward a more analogue display—photos from a string of storage unit robberies arranged chronologically. "What does this show you that your software can't?"

Leo stepped to the board thoughtfully. He no longer dismissed physical evidence as outdated—progress he'd made since their first uneasy collaboration.

"The clothes change, but the posture stays the same," Leo said, squinting at the footage. "That shoulder tilt's consistent, even with different outfits." His voice reflected a new attentiveness to detail. "Right hand's used for precise movements, but the heavy lifting's on the left—injury or weakness, maybe."

Hart gave a slight nod. "The body gives away more than the browser history," he noted calmly. "People know to mask their digital trails. Their bodies, not so much."

This case wouldn't grab headlines—it was intentionally low-profile. Hart had chosen it to mentor Leo through foundational work instead of dramatic investigations. Six units, hit over two months, by someone patient and methodical—a rarity in crimes of this kind.

Leo returned to his workstation, adjusting the algorithm with their new insights. "I've factored in posture and hand dominance," he said. The system updated immediately, highlighting new suspect matches. "Now it flags footage where that shoulder tilt shows up, no matter the lighting or clothes."

Hart watched with quiet approval. Leo once resisted the idea of subjective input; now, he has blended digital with human input.

"Cross-check it against transit schedules," Hart said, standing beside Leo, not behind him—a subtle but meaningful change. "Those thirty-minute gaps between hits suggest a structured routine. Not random."

Leo nodded and quickly incorporated the new layer. Almost instantly, correlations emerged—each break-in aligned with departures of a specific express bus nearby.

"The transit station's seven blocks away," Leo confirmed with quiet satisfaction. "96.8% match with the Route 14 northbound line." A 3D map spun into view, showing bus routes, crime scenes, and times all lining up. "He's using the bus as cover and escape."

"And probably lives somewhere on that route," Hart added, scanning the physical map on the wall. "Knows the area, the timing. Likely works in transport or logistics."

They kept refining the profile, shifting seamlessly between software and hard-copy maps. Where there had once been friction, now there was fluency. Their approaches fed into one another rather than clashing.

Leo began backing up files while Hart sorted evidence with similar care as they wrapped up. Their movements were practised and synchronised—not by chance, but from months of learning each other's rhythms.

"There's something I've meant to say," Leo said, unplugging the drives. He slowed his usual quick speech, signalling sincerity. "Back during the Riddler case, when you brought me in. People said I wasn't ready. But you treated my input like it mattered—even when it didn't fit your method."

Hart didn't pause what he was doing. "You cracked the system Price built," he said plainly. "Without your code, we wouldn't have caught the signal in time."

Leo nodded, absorbing the compliment without the wide-eyed pride of his younger self. "But you gave me a room before I'd earned it," he said quietly. "You made space for what I brought to the table."

Hart looked up, serious. Once, he would've deflected with a quote or an academic shrug. Now, he met Leo's eyes.

"Investigations need more than one lens," he said. "Your tools balance mine. One without the other doesn't work."

Leo smiled—not to impress but in shared recognition. He shut his laptop with a soft click.

"Same time tomorrow?" he asked, packing his gear. "I'll check the transit sector for employment records."

"I'll bring the transcripts," Hart replied. "We can run linguistic comparisons."

As they left, Hart noticed Leo adjusting his pace to match his own —not out of deference, but as if their partnership had found its natural stride.

Evelyn Shaw's university office looked more like a scholarly excavation site than a workspace—centuries of accumulated knowledge stacked in precarious towers of yellowed paper and colour-coded tabs. The walls were covered with diagrams linking Renaissance cyphers to quantum computing formulas, all connected by a red thread that charted brilliant yet chaotic relationships across time. Hart navigated the narrow space carefully, sidestepping unstable stacks of books to find the one chair not already occupied by ancient tomes. Outside the window, the university's Gothic buildings served as a reminder of the history surrounding their very modern project.

Evelyn was only marginally more put together than during the Riddler case. Her auburn hair refused to stay in place, and her cardigan—with elbow patches—felt both overly formal and overly casual, fitting her role as the youngest tenured cryptography professor. Her glasses perpetually slid down her nose, adjusted just enough to remain functional.

"I've reworked the section on polyalphabetic cyphers," she said immediately as Hart sat. Her animated hand gestures nearly toppled a nearby pile. "Price's version of the Vigenère system shares traits with fifteenth-century diplomatic codes—especially the Alberti disk systems used by Venetian envoys."

Hart nodded, genuinely interested. Returning to academia had reawakened parts of his mind, which had been long dormant. Still, he now approached theory with the discipline of field experience.

"Context is important," he agreed, pulling a neatly organised folder from his briefcase. "But the paper needs practical grounding. The theory is useful only if it serves the investigation."

Their co-authored work—tentatively titled

Cryptographic Continuity: Historical Cypher Adaptation in Modern Criminal Methodology

—marked Hart's first return to publication since leaving the academic world. Evelyn brought the depth of historical expertise, and Hart got the grounding force of investigative reality.

. . .

"But practical use depends on solid theoretical structure," Evelyn countered, gently handling a centuries-old volume. "Price's system only worked because he understood the math behind those old cyphers."

"And it failed because he ignored human behaviour," Hart replied, not contradicting but building. "We need to address both—the technical history and the psychological factors that twist it."

Her eyes lit up with intellectual excitement. "A hybrid model," she said, voice quickening. "Historical cryptography plus behavioural analysis—so we can not only decode the mechanics but also predict how people manipulate them."

She rummaged through a drawer and pulled out a well-used notebook, full of her dense handwriting and dotted with coffee stains. "I've mapped the tweaks Price made to classical methods," she said, flipping to a diagram. "They show a mindset typical of someone who thinks they're improving the system rather than following it."

Hart leaned in, absorbing the insight. "So a kind of personality fingerprint," he said. "That could help us anticipate how future systems might be modified."

Their process had developed a rhythm over the past two months —Evelyn brought the theoretical leaps, and Hart redirected them toward real-world application without dismissing their value. He no longer saw her detours as distractions but as tools to enhance practical results.

"We'll need more case studies," he added, opening his folder to reveal documents from earlier investigations. "It only matters if it leads somewhere current."

Evelyn nodded, less impulsively than usual. The Riddler case had shown her how valuable her work could be outside lecture halls. Working with Hart, Clara, and Leo had grounded her in a way academic life never had.

. . .

"We should include how Price revived the city's old surveillance grid," she said, pushing up her glasses. "It was built on encryption frameworks from the founding families."

"With carefully worded attribution," Hart cautioned. Parts of the corruption case were still under investigation, and several influential figures remained protected by legal technicalities despite damning evidence.

They kept shaping the manuscript, balancing abstract theory with applied evidence. Hart's structured logic paired neatly with Evelyn's creative insights. Their collaboration wasn't a compromise— it was a merging of minds, a sign of Hart's evolving view that scholarly rigour and fieldwork didn't have to be at odds.

A knock broke their flow. A university courier stood in the doorway, carefully holding a formal envelope.

"Delivery for Detective Hart," he announced. "Signature required."

Hart accepted the envelope, noting its premium quality and wax seal with an unfamiliar crest. He signed without a rush, noting the courier's professionalism and the envelope's clear significance.

After the courier left, Hart read the return address: Municipal Investigations Bureau of Edinburgh, Scotland. The envelope's weight suggested more than just polite correspondence.

"Interesting timing," Evelyn said, eyebrows raised. "An international case file, right as we're discussing cypher history."

Hart opened the envelope with care and scanned the thick, formal pages. "They're asking for consultation," he said. "Series of cases involving elaborate puzzles left at historic sites. Cyphers from medieval Scotland—layered with quantum math."

Evelyn lit up. "That's our entire paper in real life," she said. "Historic methods weaponised with modern tech."

"They're arranging university credentials," Hart added. The invitation was clearly designed to accommodate both his detective and academic identities.

This was more than a consulting job. It was recognition. Acknowledging the dual identity Hart had only recently accepted: part investigator, part scholar. Edinburgh saw it, too—that his strength wasn't choosing between roles but merging them.

"Are you going to take it?" Evelyn asked, her excitement tempered by understanding.

Hart folded the letter with precise hands and slipped it back into its envelope. The lake stone was still in his pocket, its familiar weight grounding him in the past and present.

"Yes," he said quietly. Not eager. Not reluctant. Just certain. "It's not the puzzle. It's how we solve it that matters."

Outside, late sunlight cast a golden glow over students moving between medieval buildings and glass-walled labs. Hart looked out at the seamless blend of past and future and recognised the reflection of his path.

The Riddler case had been a turning point. But this invitation-this new chapter—was a chance to move forward, not as either-or, but as both.

19

NEW GAME

The warehouse stood against the autumn sky like an abandoned cathedral, its corrugated metal walls streaked with rust and industrial grime. Hart paused before entering, his breath forming small clouds in the evening air as he surveyed the building's exterior with the particular attention of someone cataloguing details rather than merely observing them. The crime scene lay within—another puzzle waiting to be decoded—but his approach no longer carried the desperate intensity that had once defined his methodology. Six months after the Riddler case and three since returning from Edinburgh, he had found a different rhythm to his investigations, more measured yet no less effective.

Police lights cast alternating blue and red patterns across the building's façade, their rotation creating a hypnotic sequence that Hart observed with professional detachment. Uniformed officers maintained the perimeter with practised efficiency, their movements suggesting routine rather than urgency despite the circumstances that had brought them to this industrial district on a Tuesday evening in late October.

. . .

"Victim was discovered by a security guard making his rounds at 5:17," Clara said as she joined him outside the entrance, her voice carrying the particular clarity that cut through ambient noise without requiring volume. "Male, approximately forty years old, no identification found at the scene. No obvious cause of death."

Hart nodded once, acknowledgement rather than mere agreement. "And the arrangement?" he asked, already knowing from the dispatch call that this was no ordinary homicide.

"Deliberate," Clara confirmed, her expression suggesting professional assessment rather than emotional reaction. "Precision positioning of both the body and surrounding objects. The responding officers recognised the pattern-based elements immediately and called us directly."

They entered together, ducking beneath the yellow crime scene tape with synchronised movements that reflected years of partnership. The warehouse interior stretched before them like a vast mechanical cavern—exposed pipes traversing the ceiling in complex patterns, metal shelving units standing in ordered rows, and industrial light fixtures casting harsh illumination from above. The space smelled of concrete dust, machine oil, and the emptiness that develops when human activity ceases in places designed for it.

Leo had already established his technical domain near the centre of the warehouse, and portable equipment was deployed around him in concentric circles of increasing complexity. Tablet screens glowed with electronic intensity, casting blue-white illumination across his features as he conducted preliminary digital scans of the area.

"No electronic surveillance inside the building," he reported as Hart and Clara approached, his attention divided between multiple displays with practised efficiency. "The security system is perimeter-only, and the cameras on the northeast corner have been non-functional for at least three weeks." His fingers executed commands across a touchscreen, bringing up architectural schematics of the warehouse. "The building has been mostly vacant for the past four months. Occasional inventory storage but no regular personnel on-site except security."

Hart absorbed this information with analytical precision while his eyes adjusted to the warehouse lighting, which created stark contrasts between illuminated areas and deep shadows. The crime scene occupied the centre of the main floor. This theatrical arrangement immediately registered as intentional rather than circumstantial.

The victim lay supine in the precise centre of a geometric pattern drawn in white chalk across the concrete floor. The design consisted of interconnected shapes—circles, triangles, and squares forming a complex configuration that extended approximately four meters in each direction from the body. Various objects had been arranged at specific points along the pattern's lines and intersections: a mechanical clock with its face removed, exposing its gears and mechanisms; three leather-bound books positioned in a perfect equilateral triangle; a small electronic device resembling a custom-built circuit board; an antique brass compass with its needle pointing northwest rather than north; seven smooth river stones arranged in a precise numerical sequence.

Hart approached the scene with measured steps, his movements economical rather than hesitant. He extracted a small notebook from his inner jacket pocket. Then, he began sketching the pattern with methodical precision, adding numerical annotations that indicated distances and positional relationships. His hand moved across the page with steady purpose, transferring a three-dimensional arrangement into two-dimensional documentation with practised ease.

"The chalk lines were drawn using a straight edge," he observed, kneeling to examine a particular segment without disturbing the scene. "Single application, minimal pressure variation. The person who created this has extensive experience with precise drafting or technical drawing." His fingers hovered above the chalk without touching it, tracing its path through the air as if reconstructing the creator's movements.

Clara circled the pattern's perimeter, her gaze alternating between the crime scene and Hart's methodical examination. "You recognise elements of this arrangement," she stated rather than asked, the observation reflecting her familiarity with Hart's expressions and their associated meanings.

"Components, not the complete configuration," Hart clarified, rising to survey the entire scene from a standing position. His hand moved unconsciously to his jacket pocket, fingers finding the lake stone's familiar smooth surface through the fabric. The stone had evolved from a desperate talisman to a chosen companion, its presence providing a tactile connection to both past cases and present purposes. "The geometric foundation shares structural principles with medieval cryptographic systems, particularly those used by monastic scholars to encode mathematical discoveries they feared might be considered heretical."

Leo looked up from his equipment, his expression registering professional curiosity. "Like the Edinburgh case?" he asked, making the connection that had immediately occurred to Hart as well.

"Similar foundational architecture but different symbolic language," Hart replied, moving toward the arranged objects with focused attention. "The Edinburgh puzzles employed specifically Scottish variations dating from the fourteenth century. This arrangement incorporates elements from multiple historical periods, integrated through a more contemporary mathematical framework."

Hart continued his careful documentation, photographing each component from multiple angles before examining its position relative to the overall pattern. The victim-a middle-aged man with no immediately apparent injuries—occupied the central position with arms arranged precisely at his sides, legs extended straight, and eyes closed as if in peaceful repose rather than death's typical disarray. His clothing suggested a professional occupation—dress shirt, tailored slacks, polished shoes—though all identifying labels had been removed.

"The body is presented as a component of the puzzle rather than its subject," Hart noted, his observation carried by the particular solemnity that acknowledged human tragedy without becoming derailed by an emotional response. "Positioned to form the central node in a communication system rather than the focus of a ritualistic display."

Clara nodded, her understanding of Hart's analytical framework allowing her to follow his reasoning without requiring elaborate explanation. "So the message isn't about the victim specifically," she concluded, "but requires his positioning to complete its structure."

"Precisely," Hart confirmed, returning to examining the arranged objects. He knelt beside the mechanical clock, studying its exposed interior with the particular attention of someone appreciating craftsmanship rather than merely collecting evidence. "The timepiece has been modified," he observed, "its escapement mechanism altered to create a deliberate asymmetry in its operational rhythm."

As Hart continued his methodical analysis, his fingers occasionally returned to the lake stone in his pocket, its smooth surface providing momentary tactile grounding before he proceeded to the next element. The desperate intensity that had characterised his approach during the Riddler case had transformed into something more balanced—analytical precision integrated with emotional awareness and pattern recognition tempered by human understanding.

. . .

"The objects form their subsystem within the larger pattern," he explained, his voice carrying the measured cadence of someone translating complex concepts into accessible observations. "Each positioned to create symbolic and mathematical relationships with the others."

He returned to view the entire scene again, his expression reflecting recognition rather than obsession. The warehouse's industrial features—exposed pipes, metal shelving, concrete floors—starkly contrasted with the meticulously arranged crime scene. The juxtaposition of utilitarian architecture and precise pattern formation suggested a deliberate selection of location rather than convenience.

"Whoever created this wanted it found," Hart said quietly, his observation directed not just to Clara and Leo but to himself. "The puzzle isn't merely evidence—it's an invitation."

Hart moved between the arranged elements with the particular patience of a translator approaching an unfamiliar yet structurally recognisable language. His fingers hovered above each object without touching, maintaining a precise distance that preserved evidence integrity while allowing detailed observation. The mechanical clock's exposed gears reflected the harsh warehouse lighting, creating metallic constellations across its modified interior. He paused longer here than elsewhere, his expression suggesting recognition of something beyond the object's immediate presence—a connection forming in his analytical framework that linked this dismantled timepiece to the broader puzzle surrounding them.

"The escapement mechanism has been modified to create a nonstandard timing sequence," he murmured, his voice carrying the particular timbre of someone thinking aloud rather than consciously communicating. "The gear ratio suggests a numerical pattern rather than chronological function."

Clara stood several feet away, her notebook balanced in her left palm, and she recorded Hart's observations with practised efficiency. Her pen moved across the page in precise shorthand, capturing not just his verbal statements but notations about his movements and attention patterns. Once she might have interjected questions or directed his focus, she allowed his methodical process to unfold without interruption, recognising that his circuitous approach often revealed connections that linear investigation might miss.

"Seven-four-one-seven-four," Hart continued, studying the gear arrangement more closely. "Repeating sequence with deliberate mechanical encoding." He straightened and moved toward the triangle of leather-bound books, kneeling to examine their positioning without disturbing their arrangement. "The books are equidistant from each other, forming a perfect equilateral triangle with sides measuring exactly thirty-seven centimetres."

As Hart continued his methodical examination, Leo focused similarly on the small electronic device at one of the pattern's outer nodes. He connected it to his specialised tablet using a custom interface cable, his expression reflecting the particular concentration of someone navigating unfamiliar digital architecture.

"I've got something," Leo announced, his voice modulating to professional excitement rather than the enthusiastic outbursts that had once characterised his discoveries. This device contains embedded metadata—geographical coordinates and a timestamp." His fingers executed a series of commands across his tablet's screen, extracting the information into a more accessible format. "Coordinates correspond to a location approximately twelve kilometres northeast of our current position. The timestamp indicates 11:47 PM tomorrow."

Hart nodded without looking up from the arrangement of river stones he examined. "Transfer the coordinates to mapping software," he instructed, his tone suggesting collaboration rather than direction. "Check for historical significance or architectural features that might connect to the elements arranged here."

Clara moved closer to Leo, studying the information displayed on his tablet. "The timestamp has the same numerical pattern as the modified clock mechanism," she observed, making a connection that demonstrated her analytical development. "Seven-four-one arrangement in both the minutes and the mechanical modifications."

Hart completed his examination of the stone arrangement, then rose and turned to the warehouse wall nearest the crime scene. What had initially appeared as random marks or industrial damage now revealed itself as deliberate symbols etched into the concrete surface —faint but methodically arranged geometric shapes forming a sequence along the wall at precisely eye level.

His fingers traced these symbols without touching them, his expression displaying recognition rather than the obsessive intensity that had characterised similar moments during the Riddler investigation. "Transitional cypher system," he explained, "combining elements of medieval substitution with binary mathematical principles. The sequence uses architectural references as key markers."

Clara and Leo exchanged glances, their shared observation of Hart's evolved approach requiring no verbal acknowledgement. Where once he might have disappeared into pattern recognition to the exclusion of human connection, he now maintained awareness of both the puzzle and his colleagues, his analysis shared rather than internally contained.

"The coordinate location is a decommissioned water treatment facility," Leo reported, having completed the mapping analysis Hart had requested. "Built in 1974, closed in 2017. City records indicate it's scheduled for demolition next month." His tablet displayed architectural schematics of the facility, highlighting structural features corresponding to some aspects of the crime scene arrangement.

Hart stepped back from the wall and turned to survey the entire scene once more, his body describing a careful circuit around the chalk pattern as he observed it from different angles. This methodical repositioning revealed new perspectives—alignments between objects visible only from specific vantage points, shadows cast by the overhead lighting creating additional geometric patterns across the concrete floor.

"The arrangement must be viewed from multiple perspectives to reveal its complete message," he said, completing his circuit and returning to a position near Clara. "Certain elements align only when observed from specific angles, creating layered informational architecture."

He knelt beside a particular configuration of objects positioned at the pattern's northwestern quadrant—the brass compass, two of the river stones, and a small metallic cube that had initially appeared unremarkable among the more distinctive items. Together, these objects formed a miniature cypher system, their relative positions encoding information through spatial relationships rather than conventional symbols.

Hart said, "This arrangement works as a positional key for understanding the wall markings," as he took out his camera to take pictures of this setup from different angles. He framed each picture perfectly, and his movements showed efficiency because he knew exactly what information needed to be captured and how it would be looked at later.

Before disturbing any element, Hart completed a final documentation sequence—photographs, measurements, and relational diagrams sketched in his notebook. Only then did he extract evidence collection materials from his kit, handling each object with gloved hands and the particular care of someone who recognised that physical evidence contained both factual information and human connection.

After being photographed in place, the metallic cube was sealed in an evidence bag. The brass compass followed its needle, which was still oriented northwest rather than toward magnetic north. Each river stone was collected individually, its smooth surfaces wrapped in protective material before being placed in separate containers.

Throughout this methodical process, Hart maintained awareness of the victim positioned at the pattern's centre—a human being transformed into a puzzle component through another's deliberate action. As the evidence collection neared completion, he paused beside the body, his posture suggesting a moment of acknowledgement rather than a merely professional obligation.

"His placement is precise but not disrespectful," Hart observed quietly, his voice carrying the particular gravity reserved for observations that transcended analytical framework to acknowledge the human dimension. "Whoever arranged this scene viewed him as a necessary component rather than disposable material. The positioning suggests ritualistic purpose rather than trophy presentation."

Clara moved to stand beside him, her presence offering professional support without demanding a verbal response. "You're seeing the person, not just the pattern," she noted, her observation carrying no judgment, only recognition of his evolved perspective.

Hart gave a single nod, a small but meaningful gesture of recognition. He stated that "the puzzle remains incomplete without understanding why this specific individual was selected," incorporating human consideration into his analytical framework instead of ignoring it. "His identity is essential to the pattern's goal—it is not incidental."

After this moment of reflection concluded, Hart returned to professional efficiency, directing the medical examiner's team as they prepared to remove the body. His instructions were precise but not coldly technical, and his approach reflected the particular balance he had developed since the Riddler case—methodical without becoming mechanical, analytical without sacrificing human awareness.

"Document the exact body position before movement," he instructed, "including measurements from all chalk line intersections. The positioning contains informational value beyond symbolic arrangement." His hand moved briefly to his pocket, fingers finding the lake stone's familiar contours through the fabric, its presence providing momentary tactile grounding before he continued coordinating the evidence collection process.

As twilight deepened outside the warehouse, the harsh interior lighting created sharper contrasts between illuminated areas and encroaching shadows. The crime scene gradually transformed from a mysterious tableau to documented evidence, the puzzle's physical components transitioning into collected materials that would continue telling their story in the laboratory rather than in this industrial setting.

The makeshift workspace occupied the warehouse's northwestern corner, a metal sorting table illuminated by portable LED lights that created a perfect circle of clarity amid surrounding industrial shadows. Hart had arranged his notes across the table's surface with methodical precision—sketches of the chalk pattern positioned centrally, photographs of individual elements organised in concentric rings around them, pages of handwritten observations forming the outer boundary. The arrangement mirrored the crime scene's geometric structure, creating a secondary pattern that functioned as a documentation and analytical tool. Clara and Leo joined him at this improvised command centre, forming a tight circle that physically manifested their collaborative approach.

. . .

"The pattern incorporates three distinct informational layers," Hart began, his fingers tracing connections between sketched elements with the particular precision of someone translating complex systems into accessible components. "First, the geometric foundation—a modified hen-decagram with eleven equidistant points along its perimeter and a central node occupied by the victim. Second is the object arrangement—each item is positioned to create specific angular relationships when viewed from designated observation points. Third, the numerical sequences are embedded within physical positioning and the objects themselves."

His explanation lacked the frenetic energy that had characterised similar moments during previous cases, just focused engagement tempered by professional clarity. Once his analytical presentations had accelerated into academic terminology that required translation, he modulated his delivery to incorporate technical precision and practical application.

"The modified clock's gear arrangement creates a repeating numerical sequence," he continued, placing the evidence bag containing this component at a specific position within his documented pattern. "Seven-four-one, recurring through its mechanical structure and positioning relative to the central node. This sequence corresponds with architectural elements at the coordinates Leo extracted from the electronic device."

Leo positioned his tablet beside Hart's sketches, its screen displaying three-dimensional renderings of the water treatment facility identified through the metadata. "The facility's primary filtration tanks are arranged in a seven-four-one configuration," he confirmed, manipulating the image to highlight these structural features. "The sequence also appears in the facility's original building specifications—seven primary chambers, four secondary filtration systems, one central control hub."

The digital rendering rotated on Leo's screen, revealing additional architectural details corresponding to elements from the crime scene arrangement. "The timestamp embedded in the device—11:47 tomorrow night—aligns with the scheduled power grid maintenance for that district," he added, displaying municipal work orders he had accessed through his remote connection to police databases. "The facility will experience a thirty-minute blackout during that exact window."

Hart nodded, acknowledging Leo's contribution with the particular attention of someone integrating new information into an evolving framework rather than merely confirming existing hypotheses. "The temporal element introduces urgency without sacrificing precision," he noted, adding this observation to his handwritten notes with careful script. "The pattern isn't just directing us toward location but specific timing as well."

Clara had been studying the photographs of the wall markings, her expression suggesting analytical consideration rather than confusion. "These symbols incorporate elements from medieval cryptography," she observed, selecting a particular image and positioning it within Hart's documentation array. "But they've been modified to include contemporary mathematical notation—integration symbols alongside traditional substitution cyphers."

Her observation caused Hart to reexamine these photographs with renewed attention. His expression registered the shift that occurs when a significant connection crystallises within an analytical framework. "The integration creates a temporal bridge," he said, recognition evident in his tone. Historical cryptographic methods are applied to contemporary mathematical concepts, connecting past methodology with present applications.

This exchange represented their evolved professional dynamic, each contributing a specialised perspective that enhanced collective understanding rather than competing for investigative primacy. Hart provided analytical architecture, Leo contributed technological expertise, and Clara offered intuitive connections that often bridged conceptual gaps neither man had recognised.

. . .

"The seven smooth stones form their subsystem," Hart continued, arranging their photographs in numerical sequence according to size. "Each positioned at precise intervals along the pattern's perimeter, creating angular relationships that correspond with architectural features at the water treatment facility." His fingers traced imaginary lines between these positions, demonstrating how their arrangement formed secondary geometric patterns within the larger structure.

Leo cross-referenced these positions against his facility schematics, nodding as connections became apparent. "The stone positions correspond exactly with access points in the facility's infrastructure," he confirmed, highlighting these locations on his digital rendering. "Service tunnels, maintenance hatches, emergency exits—seven entry points arranged in descending order of accessibility."

As Hart continued his methodical explanation, his demeanour displayed subtle but significant evolution from previous cases. His intellectual engagement remained evident in his precise terminology and conceptual connections. Still, this focus no longer manifested as obsessive isolation. Instead, his analysis incorporated both Clara's and Leo's contributions. His explanation paused at appropriate intervals to allow questions or observations, and his attention switched between documentation and colleagues with a natural rhythm rather than forced discipline.

"The triangle of leather-bound books initially appeared to function as positional markers," he said, gesturing toward their photographs arranged in equilateral formation. "But closer examination reveals a more specific purpose. Each contains marginalia in distinct handwriting styles, with certain passages marked using a sequential notation system."

Clara leaned closer to examine these details, her analytical attention complementing Hart's approach. "The handwriting samples appear deliberately varied," she noted, "as if demonstrating different individuals' notations rather than stylistic inconsistency from a single author."

. . .

"Precisely," Hart agreed, his tone reflecting professional satisfaction rather than personal validation. "The books function as physical components within the geometric pattern and symbolic representations of multiple perspectives—different observers documenting the same fundamental principles through distinct perceptual frameworks."

Their collaborative analysis continued with increasing synchronisation, each contribution building upon previous observations to create a comprehensive understanding that exceeded what any individual might have achieved independently. Leo's technological expertise provided structural verification for Hart's pattern recognition, while Clara's intuitive connections often identified conceptual relationships that might otherwise have remained obscured by technical detail.

As their preliminary analysis neared completion, Hart gathered his notes with methodical precision, organising them into categorical sequences that would facilitate further investigation once they returned to the precinct. His movements displayed the particular economy of someone who understood exactly what information required immediate attention and what could be temporarily set aside without compromising investigative integrity.

"This arrangement represents more than a simple puzzle or cryptographic challenge," he summarised, his expression reflecting the seriousness appropriate to their investigation despite his evident intellectual engagement. "The multi-layered structure, the precise timing element, the specific location selection—all suggest meticulous planning and significant purpose beyond merely creating an investigative obstacle."

He paused, surveying the documented evidence they had assembled, then continued with measured certainty. "This isn't just about the puzzle—it's about understanding the mind behind it. The arrangement tells us where to look next and why this location was chosen."

Clara nodded, her expression suggesting recognition of the analytical framework Hart was applying—one that integrated puzzle-solving methodology with a traditional investigative approach rather than allowing either to dominate their process. "The water treatment facility provides both symbolic connection and practical functionality," she observed, making the connection Hart had been approaching.

"Someone is using this elaborate system to direct our attention toward a specific location and timing," Hart confirmed, "without revealing their ultimate purpose. The puzzle functions as both a communication method and a filtering mechanism—ensuring that only those who can decode its structure will arrive at the designated location during the precise window of opportunity."

As they prepared to leave, their evidence and documentation were carefully secured for transport. Hart took a final moment to survey the crime scene from the warehouse entrance. The chalk pattern remained visible under the harsh industrial lighting, though now stripped of its arranged components. The victim had been removed with appropriate care, leaving only the geometric structure drawn across the concrete floor. From this distance, the pattern seemed less imposing and more comprehensive—its purpose was partially revealed through their analysis, yet still contained unresolved elements.

Hart's expression reflected neither the obsessive intensity that had characterised similar moments during the Riddler case nor the purely analytical detachment of his earlier career. Instead, his features displayed the particular balance that emerges when intellectual engagement aligns with moral purpose, recognising the puzzle's complexity and awareness of the human consequences embedded within its structure.

. . .

"Tomorrow night at 11:47," he said quietly, his words directed equally to Clara beside him and himself. "Whatever message this arrangement was designed to communicate reaches its intended culmination at that precise moment. Our responsibility extends beyond merely solving the puzzle to understanding why it needed to exist."

With this reflection complete, Hart turned away from the crime scene with deliberate movement, his attention shifting from what they had discovered to what remained understood. The lake stone rested in his pocket, a tactile reminder of past investigations and present purpose—no longer a desperate talisman but a chosen companion to a detective who had learned to integrate analytical precision with human understanding.

www.ingramcontent.com/pod-product-compliance
Lightning Source LLC
Chambersburg PA
CBHW072021020726
47501CB00006B/1899